I0522405

SUMMER'S KEEP

ANNIE M. COLE

Paperback ISBN: 978-1-4958-1229-3
eBook ISBN: 978-1-4958-1230-9

Published January 2017

INFINITY PUBLISHING
1094 New DeHaven Street, Suite 100
West Conshohocken, PA 19428-2713
Toll-free (877) BUY BOOK
Local Phone (610) 941-9999
Fax (610) 941-9959
Info@buybooksontheweb.com
www.buybooksontheweb.com

Dedication

To my Heavenly Father who so graciously gave me my two earthly fathers, Charlie, and step-father, Luke.

CHAPTER 1

There's a place between life and death that no man should ever wander into, and Gage Barrington had set up camp there.

The rattle of palms stirred in the treetops as Gage stuffed his hands in the pockets of his jacket and made his way along the walk on Charleston's East Battery Street. He felt two things the moment he got the news of his father's death: *How is it possible that I'm still breathing and, right after that, why would I want to?*

He stopped in front of an iron gate and turned to face Charleston Harbor. The sea shimmered in a wash of pale morning gold. He took a deep breath, catching the scent of Confederate jasmine, ever present in the balmy January days of the Lowcountry. People on the narrow streets and cobbled walks jogged or strolled casually along. Even with all the warm life surrounding him, the steady blowing sea wind felt cold in his heart. His thoughts turned toward his father.

Breck Barrington had been a single-minded man. The driving force of his life seemed to be the preservation of his blue-blooded ancestry and all the status that kind of life ensured. The successful management of his investments had guaranteed the prominence he craved; as for immortalizing the Barrington name, Breck looked to his son, Gage, to accomplish that end. But Breck's son had a strong will of his own and had resisted the purposeful planning of his life by his father.

The local news reports had simply stated that business tycoon Breck Barrington had died suddenly of a heart attack. Gage knew differently; his father had died from a severed heart. He also knew he had been the one to hold the sword that had swung the fatal blow.

Gage had been away on Terrapin Island when the call came with the news of his father's death. Located off the coast of South Carolina, Terrapin Island was the one place where Gage seemed to keep the black dog of depression at bay. After a brief time on the island, typically he could get back to the family business and carry on as usual—but not this time. This time he had made a decision to tell his father about his plan to leave the family business and branch out on his own, leaving Charleston and his partnership with his father for good. That conversation had taken place three days ago; those were the final words he'd spoken with his father.

Guilt began to seep into him as he stepped through the gate and neared the door to his childhood home. He stopped, his foot poised on the first step of the stone stairs. His mind raced, wondering what would face him beyond the heavily carved door.

The question was answered when the front door suddenly snatched open and a concerned Myra Barrington appeared. Then, with a glad cry, she flew down the stairs and into her son's arms.

"I've been so worried about you!" She turned her face up to meet the azure blue of her son's eyes, more pronounced in a face washed by the South Carolina light. His firm angular jaw was set, and the broad expanse of his shoulders seemed to carry the weight of the world. "You didn't answer your phone. We didn't know what to think. Evan-Cerise is here. She's been beside herself with worry."

A feeling of dread crawled up Gage's spine, but he turned his face to hide the growing trepidation as he held his mother close. With a reassuring squeeze he released her, leading her into the house and into another era. An era without the patriarch, Breck Barrington.

Dusk in the old district of Charleston, with its gas carriage lights warmly shining through the harbor mist, felt peculiar to the two making their way over the cobblestones to Cane Break's, a restaurant down on the waterfront. Even after three months, the presence of Breck Barrington was noticeably absent.

"Your evening plans are really very lovely, son, but I'm not so easily pacified. I'm going to the island with you. The stares and whispers are maddening. There will be more stares and whispers tonight and many interruptions as people come to our table and offer condolences." Myra took the firm arm of her son. "I'm sick of it. I need the island."

"I think you're exaggerating things, Mother," Gage said, pulling Myra in close. "Where are these people? No one has bothered us."

"It's not hard to spot them. They look around, extending and rotating their little necks like periscopes on a submarine. And the men! Don't get me started. It's settled, I'm going to the island with you."

Gage unconsciously rubbed the back of his neck and swore under his breath. He'd seen that determined look in his mother's eyes before and knew he had a fight on his hands. After handling his father's affairs, Gage had stumbled upon more than one skeleton in the old man's closet. He had hoped for a little time alone to figure things out. But one thing was for sure, he was in for a long weekend.

Myra Barrington regarded her son as they drove along the remote island road toward his home, Summer's Keep. The small backwater town of Terrapin Island sat near a tidal creek at the end of a long, dilapidated-looking wooden bridge. Crossing the bridge, the road dipped downward over a marsh as the land flattened out, low and smooth. The town was never truly cut off from the mainland, it only felt that way as you crossed over the tidal estuary with its winding rivulets.

Passing a steady stream of cars leaving the island, Myra remarked, "You seem a little smug now that you have the island to yourself." She glanced out the car window noticing a ramshackle houseboat marooned on a mud flat.

Terrapin Island seemed a world away from Charleston. By contrast, the mostly fishing village with its small shops and scenic views of white sailing masts dotting the horizon boasted of only two restaurants. There, visitors would eat their bodyweight in oysters, then hightail it back across the bridge that linked the small estuary island to the mainland of South Carolina.

Gage flicked her a glance. "They come for the seafood and nautical charm … but every true native of the place knows that when the crowds leave that's when Terrapin becomes home again."

"I guess it's like having company in the house. It's nice to have them for a little while, but even nicer when they leave." She smiled, deepening the lines time and life had etched on her face. "I love it here, the black water and knobby cypress trees, the sounds of island life, all of it. It'll always be home."

Gage cut his eyes to his mother with a smile that belonged more to his eyes than his lips. "The only sound I want to hear is the sound a car makes as it's heading out of town."

"You're becoming a recluse," Myra said, lowering the window and taking in a deep breath. "Just smell that salt air, the mud. It's invigorating. Makes me want to dance and feel alive again."

A jeep loaded down with teenagers passed, their music so loud that the seats in Gage's truck vibrated. "I don't know why people feel the need to blast their music wherever they go … it only drowns out the true music of the island, the wind and the sea."

"You were young once … no, wait, that was me."

He reached over and took Myra's hand, giving it a firm squeeze. "Be nice and I'll buy you ice cream."

"I'm not above an ice cream bribe," she said playfully.

"Let's get settled at the house first, then we'll drive into town for that ice cream … take a look around."

The weatherboard house called Summer's Keep came into view, with its sloping slate roof and twisting vines around the front door. It had belonged to Gage's maternal grandmother, Lilly Rose, and always seemed the kind of place made for a long rainy day with its books and beams and cozy little nooks.

Lilly Rose had inherited the house and land. And no one had been more surprised than Gage to learn that the old home place had been left to him after her passing.

Descended from a long line of fishermen, Myra often seemed to come into her own while visiting the island. Gage could only guess at the reasons his father had objected to his wife Myra's visits here. When Myra turned to face him, he was sure he'd never seen his mother more alive or more beautiful.

That night the winds changed. Howling gusts pressed on the house as Gage looked up from his book. He thought he'd heard the restless roaming of his mother in her room and got up to check on her. Easing the door open, he found her sitting by the window staring out into the night.

"Can't sleep?" he asked.

She answered, without turning around, "We're supposed to be sad and lonely sometimes. It just means we're human."

Gage walked over to the bed and propped against it. "Everything seems worse at night. You've told me that countless times."

"I'm talking about you, son, not me. But that's right. Everything is more depressing at night," she sighed. "That's why I'm a morning person, but not in the way you suppose. My morning isn't a time, it's a place."

Gage searched for some path to break the thread of conversation. From experience he knew his mother's flair for the dramatic and her lecture posture. Rarely did she face the audience when she performed.

"You're stuck in a place, too, you know," she said.

"How's that?"

"You're stuck in evening. You look back on life with a contented sigh, having completed another day's work. You pour a drink and you sit … with a glass of bourbon in one hand and a book in the other."

"What's wrong with that?"

"Nothing … if that's the way you want to finish. You can just slip into eternity with a low pulse and a neatly organized and prearranged life."

"Again, what's wrong with that?" Gage said, somewhat forcefully.

Myra looked over her shoulder. Her smile was like a ray of sun flashing brightly before being covered over again by a passing cloud. "I'm living in the present, but you? You're slowly fading into eternity, day by routine day. I really think you want to die and go be with your father."

The silence was closing, as if being suffocated by having all the oxygen sucked from the room.

Myra was from Scotch-Irish blood whose ancestors fought the British both in the old country and in the Revolutionary War. Her husband, Breck, was from noble English descent. Two more different people had never existed. Myra wore jeans, flat heels, and flowy tunic tops most days, and her auburn hair always seemed to be a bit tousled. Breck was the epitome of refinement, impeccably dressed for every occasion. How their "Cary Grant meets Maureen O'Hara" marriage worked was anybody's guess, but love each other they did — of this, Gage was certain.

At the moment, though, Gage felt very British. "You need to understand this about me, Mother, before you decide the fate of my life. I'm a discontented man. I finally convinced myself to stop pretending I'm not. I don't even try to convince others anymore and I won't lie to you. That's how it is."

Myra faced her son as a hot rush of emotions coursed through her veins. "You may be a Barrington by name, but you're my son, too — with Bain in your blood! You have a soul in there. I see it flickering behind your eyes! Are you really going to spend the rest of your life atoning for that one decision — a decision to be your own *man* and live your own *life*? A life you were gifted for?"

"All my father ever wanted was to honor our family name. A name that dates back to 1273 in the Subsidy Rolls of Cambridgeshire, England. And I threw it back in his face. And not only his name, but his life's blood … my birthright!"

"Your father made his choices. His life was just that, his! And he never asked anybody what they thought about it, either. Now get on with *your* life! You are not the cause of your father's death."

There was a dull ache in Gage's head as he slowly straightened. "You're welcome to stay here, Mother, as long as you like, but I'll be gone most days and won't be back until late at night."

"So, you're going back to Charleston. To Evan-Cerise... another of your father's choices for you." She tossed him a quick glare and turned away, still seeing her son's reflection in the window.

He shook his head. "I bought the old marina down the road, across the marsh bridge. I've decided to rename it—Bainbridge Marina."

Myra turned in surprise. "You named your marina after my family, the Bains?" A lively blush swept into her cheeks and she quickly directed her attention out the window again. "I think that's a fine idea."

The next morning, Gage was in a pensive mood. He tossed his tools in the back of the old work truck, loading it down with what he'd need for the day. He carried around his pain, growing into it like a tree grows around a piece of barbed wire. At the sound of a voice he turned and stared until the form took shape in the early morning fog.

"Uncle Yancey?" he questioned, startled by his disheveled appearance. Yancey Bain was thinner than Gage had ever known him to be, and he looked tired, haggard even. Since the death of his wife, this once robust man seemed defeated somehow. It occurred to Gage that he hadn't seen his uncle for some time. In fact, Yancey had not been present at his brother-in-law's funeral. He cinched a tarp tightly over the bed of the truck then stuck out his hand in greeting.

"Back from the dead." Yancey felt a need to explain his presence. Never one to mince words, he simply blurted out, "My sister called, said you bought Chester's old marina down the road. I want to tag along, if you'll have me."

Gage faced his uncle with a statement. "I'm going to need an overseer for the dock. Since you taught me nearly everything I know about watercraft, you more than qualify." Seeing the spark in his uncle's eyes, he added, "You interested?"

"Let's get to work." With that said, the matter had been settled.

Chapter 2

Meandering toward the sea, Gage, followed by his uncle, traced a route through the rich thirty-acre swath of land known as Summer's Keep. Verdant trees draped with moss and clothed with resurrection fern lined the flat lane from the house to the front gate. A dirt road within the property ran along the fence line to the south where stood the stables and a small garden house. Sassabee Creek defined the southernmost border of Summer's Keep and was by far the most tranquil spot on the land.

Guiding the truck onto the dirt road, Gage rolled to a stop and motioned out the window for his uncle to pull up beside him. He slid his sunglasses to the top of his head. "I'm going over to have a look around, check on Ol' Tar at the stable. Go on down to the marina…I'll meet you there later."

"Right after I run to town for my coffee." With a hand signal, Yancey pulled away.

The backside of the property had yet to be explored thoroughly since the passing of his grandmother, Lilly Rose. Ol' Tar had been well taken care of by Jedidiah, the groundkeeper for Summer's Keep for as long as Gage could remember. But Gage knew some of the horse's legendary spirit had fled and he was anxious to know just how much life could be breathed back into the animal.

Rolling to a stop near the stable, he put it in park and sat back in the seat, taking it all in. In the distance he watched a blue heron rise from the reeds like a phantom, skim the water, and land on a low limb of a cypress. His eyes wandered up a low rise where the wind stirred the branches, allowing a brief glimpse of the garden house behind a shelter of cedars.

Overlooking the marsh, the garden house sat in perfect position to enjoy the tranquil vistas that stretched out before her. Salt marsh grasses and clumps of black needle rush bent low in the breeze as if stroked by a gentle hand. *No wonder Grandmother preferred it here*, he thought.

Summer's Keep had fallen on hard times, but her future looked promising. People around those parts had been taught at their mother's knee to preserve the past. And that was certainly the intention of the present owner, Gage Barrington.

Boots hit the soggy soil as he stepped out of his truck. Narrowing his eyes, he surveyed the barn, relieved to find it in decent enough condition. Encouraged by the neighing sound of excitement coming from inside, he headed in to saddle up and take a look around the property.

The saddle creaked as Gage settled comfortably, leading the steed through sweet grass and arching stems of beautyberry as he nudged the horse along the overgrown trail. Sassabee Creek meandered along the border marking the boundary between Summer's Keep and an old stone parsonage and a church known simply as The Prayer House. According to local property records, the church and its buildings had been deeded to Almighty God in 1944 and were now occupied by the current pastor and overseer, Daniel Muir.

Approaching a bend in the path, the sky darkened abruptly as he entered a sheltering grove of ancient oaks. A damp, earth-smelling scent caught his attention and he turned to see the creek following beside him. Rain-dampened creek dirt had a fragrance altogether different from other dirt. The smell was comforting, familiar somehow, as the water's passage lazed its way along its course toward the sea.

Gage lessened the grip on the reins, comfortable with his surroundings. A small foot bridge came into view behind a willow oak. Years of weather and wear had created a mottled effect on the surface of the bridge. As he crossed over, he spotted the old creek house with its stone façade. To Gage it seemed as rooted in the ground as the headstones that marked the graves in the nearby churchyard. The place was haunting but serene. The overwhelming feeling of loss and the inevitable passage of time confronted him, as it always had, as he scanned the small community. It seemed a forsaken community with its collection of damp structures, and it, as he'd been informed so long ago, belonged to God.

The first sense of being watched came as a crawling sensation on the back of Shanna Muir's neck. She glanced over the area, noticing nothing out of the ordinary among the gravestones but fallen limbs and branches from the recent storm. A thick carpet of moss and a few leaves cushioned her steps as she walked about, not straying too far from the confines of the churchyard.

A limb lay trapped in the filigree of the wrought iron fence outlining the little cemetery and she yanked it out, tossing it aside. Glancing up, her eyes widened at the sight of a man near the creek astride a large black horse. The horse seemed to pick his way, almost delicately, among the fallen branches toward her and then it stopped abruptly near a tree. Shanna stood frozen, feeling a sense of unease as she looked up at the stranger's face. She was not fearful by nature, but the remoteness of the mostly uninhabited community was enough to cause her some concern.

The man stared at her, his face partially masked in the gray drizzling mist. He seemed to scrutinize her with a thoroughness that made her uneasy. She swallowed convulsively, refusing to show fear as she raised her chin in a gesture of defiance and met his eyes. Taking in his appearance with cautious interest, she noticed his face bore the shadow of a close beard. Tawny hair brushed the collar of his jacket, but even at a good distance, she could see the penetrating blue of his eyes.

The stranger relaxed back into the saddle and then abruptly reached into his pocket and pulled out a cell phone. He looked at it and, in an easy manner, turned his mount and disappeared into the trees near the creek.

As she watched the man leave, a decision formed quickly in Shanna's mind. Despite her determination to clean up the grounds, she would wait until someone was with her. For her part, she would limit her wanderings for the sake of safety.

Gage Barrington stood on a palette half submerged in mud. Overlooking his recently purchased business, he kept reminding himself exactly why he'd chosen to buy the broken down marina in the first place. Adding to the bleakness was the incessant rain which began shortly after his purchase a month earlier and hadn't let up since. But now, mercifully, the heavy rain had ceased for the moment and Gage, glad to be out of the stuffy and mildew-saturated office, splashed across the mucky ground to the warehouse.

He stood, examining the outbuildings all hunkered together unpainted and dripping. At the side of a shed, under a tin shelter, a small matted dog sat with his head bowed as if in silent misery at the state of things. For a moment, despair ran through Gage like a sickening dread.

"That you, Mr. Barrington?" a high-pitched voice called out from the direction of the shed. "You sure is a sight for these sore eyes." He let the front legs of the straight-back chair hit the dirt before spreading a smile so wide that the gold cap on his right canine tooth gleamed.

"Jedidiah?" The rain swept in again, causing Gage to hunker deeper into the protection of his jacket.

"Yes, sir." He pointed in the direction of the furthest building. "I done made my rounds and found somethin' … somethin' a-thumpin' in back of that warehouse over there. I been sittin' here waitin' and watchin'. Makin' sure don't nothin' come runnin' out of there."

Gage fought the smile that threatened the corners of his mouth. Jedidiah was hardly the type of man for security detail. But he, along with a preacher named Daniel Muir, had been hired to handle that job along with securing boats and looking after the grounds.

"You wait here while I go check it out."

Rain stung his face as he encountered the wind, walking toward the warehouse. The light was fading and barely detectable, only a faint glow shone through the shroud of gray mist. Pulling open the door, Gage released the latch as he heard a bang echo from somewhere within the building, promptly followed by a muted curse.

Swinging the door open wide, Gage barked sharply as he walked forward, "Who's in here!" The next moment he flipped a switch, illuminating the storeroom.

In a corner of the building, a young boy scrambled to his feet with fists raised, ready to fight.

"You lost, boy?" The little guy shivered, drawing Gage's attention to his ragged appearance and ill-fitting clothes. Looking around, he asked, "Are you alone?"

The boy seemed overwhelmed by the sight of the man and could only nod.

"You can relax. I don't plan on shooting you."

Pale blue eyes narrowed. "I'm just passin' through. Come in here to get outa the rain. No call to get all riled up. I'm leavin'."

Gage casually produced a long cigar, bit the tip off, and spit it to the ground. "You got a name?"

"Quinn Barrington." He wiped his nose on the back of his sleeve.

Gage raised a brow. Striking a match, he puffed the cigar to life, squinting through the smoke. Aware of the boy's full attention.

In the stillness of the warehouse, a low rumble sounded from the direction of Quinn's stomach.

"When's the last time you ate?"

"I ain't hungry." He raised his eyes to the man in front of him. "I guess you're the man that owns this place."

"That I do." He looked around and then looked back at Quinn. "If it's all the same to you, I say we get out of here and go find a place to eat."

"No, thank you. I'll just be going now." He made an attempt to maneuver around the man.

Gage held out his hand, stopping him. "Where's your … mother?"

Quinn's face flushed with irritation. "I ain't got no momma. 'Least not one that matters."

Gage considered the boy a moment. "Well, now, that's interesting. So am I supposed to believe you just happened to float up to my property on the back of a turtle or something?"

"Don't be a durn fool. I ain't never seen nobody do that. That woman, Tinsley, she left me here. Said you was family. But she ain't no momma of mine. I don't care what she says. I ain't got no use for no Barrington neither. Just gonna get myself outa here and head back up to Beaufort. That's what I'm gonna do."

Gage watched the youngster thoughtfully, and his memory flashed back to his father. Breck Barrington had not cared for Tinsley Ingle. She didn't measure up to the standard of a Barrington, according to the patriarch. He thought her selfish and conniving.

But Gage persisted in his relationship with Tinsley, ignoring his father's wishes until one day he'd come home to find his father waiting for him in the study. Breck had closed his checkbook and handed his son a letter from Tinsley, then proceeded to tell Gage that it was all for the best.

Turning his attention back to Quinn, he tried to see his features, but the boy kept his face averted and fidgeted with his ear. Even under a head full of dirty blonde hair, Gage could tell the child couldn't be more than eight years old. That would put him—

"How old are you?"

"Almost eight." Quinn wiped his nose on his sleeve again, uneasy beneath the man's scrutiny.

"Grab your case and come with me."

"Why should I?" The grimy cheeks flexed with irritation.

"Because there's a good chance I'm your father."

The suddenly uncertain boy just stood there, unable to move.

Gage had only taken a few steps when he barked without turning around, "Don't just stand there gawking! Get a move on!"

Quinn snatched up his suitcase with both hands and caught up with the man.

Throwing down his cigar, Gage reached to open the door to his truck. "Hop in."

Quinn eyed him suspiciously, then reluctantly got in, struggling with the case.

"Here, let me have that." Gage lifted the suitcase and placed it behind the seat.

The poor condition of the case did not escape his notice. Missing its handle, it was held together by wide strips of utility tape. He pulled the seat belt around Quinn, securing it tightly.

As he walked around the truck, he looked up to heaven as if asking for divine help. Sliding behind the wheel, he asked, "All set?" At the answering nod, Gage pulled away from the warehouse. "Hope you like shrimp bisque and cheese biscuits."

The boy swallowed hard.

Gage noticed Quinn was careful to avoid looking in his direction. "'Course, you being a Barrington, it's only natural you'd like seafood. Lots of it in Beaufort, too, of course."

Pale blue eyes flew to meet his. "You're from North Carolina, too?" A light gleamed in the depths of his eyes.

Gage felt a pang of sympathy for the ragged boy and regretted bringing up the place. "No, I grew up in a town not far from here, a place between two rivers, Charleston. Now, after we eat, we'll settle in for the night and talk about things in the morning."

Relief flooded Gage as he remembered his mother had gone back to Charleston earlier in the day. He needed some time to sort all of this out before telling Myra Barrington that she could possibly have a grandson.

"I forgot… that's where all them *Barringtons* are from," Quinn said, stressing the name sarcastically. "Tinsley told me all about them people." He turned to stare out the window.

While Quinn was looking away, Gage took the opportunity to study the boy who, in all probability, was his son. That thought — that the small boy sitting in his truck was probably his son — astonished him completely.

He couldn't see Tinsley in Quinn. There were, he supposed, some resemblances. But where Tinsley had dark eyes and almost black hair, Quinn had pale blue eyes and sandy hair. He saw, more than anything, himself in the boy.

"I'm sure you must have been through a lot to have gained such a high opinion of the Barrington family, Quinn, but we're not all that bad once you get to know us. You'll just have to take my word for it."

The reply was barely heard. "That's not what I was told."

CHAPTER 3

S hanna Muir lay still under the bedsheet listening to the rain as it beat a soft tempo on the roof. Her mind lulled as she watched it cascade down the window in slow waves.

Alone in the darkness, in the quiet, she gathered her pillow next to her body. Her thoughts wandered off to the wet grass over the grave of her husband. No words ever came from the grave. James Muir was out of reach for as long as Shanna's life on earth endured.

A sinking despair began to pull her under and she leaped up, gasping for air. Tears coursed down her cheeks. Midnight, solitude, rain, all conspired against her to bring her to the desperate moment.

Then the words of her husband came softly back to her mind. As he lay dying, Shanna gripped his hand and whispered, "What will I do without you?"

He answered, "Take all the love you have for me and give it to the unloved. I have all I need, both now and for eternity."

That moment did one thing for Shanna. It clarified in an instant the need to choose: be someone God could use, or mourn until the day she died. But, somewhere along the way, the line between the two began to dissolve, making her choice … both.

The door to the clinic burst open, and a gust of wind and rain swept in, bringing Shanna Muir with it. "I need to see the doctor," she said, crossing the small lobby to the receptionist's window.

The receptionist slid the glass window open and let out an exhausted sigh. "I told you before, you'll have to wait. You don't have an appointment." She slid the glass back into place, turning her back.

Shanna's pulse began to quicken. "My friend is sick. Please, just tell the doctor I'm here."

Gage moved from the doorway where he and his son had followed the young woman inside, witnessing the exchange. Removing his jacket, he draped it over a chair and motioned for Quinn to take a seat.

Shanna turned away and gave a short, embarrassed nod to the strangers as she took a seat. Perching on the end of the chair, she carefully watched the receptionist, like a cat at a mouse hole.

Stepping up to the window, Gage smiled at the receptionist. "Hi—I'm Gage Barrington and I'm sorry but I don't have an appointment either. I'm new to this clinic and it's my son's first time visiting me on the island. And, wouldn't you know it, he gets sick." He gestured back toward his son. "If his mother finds out, she'll never let me have him on the island again." He winked, flashing a warm smile.

His voice held a slight Tidewater accent, rich and masculine. Each word he spoke seemed to have been carefully chosen, like one would select a fine cigar.

The receptionist practically swooned. Handsome men rarely wandered into their clinic. "Oh, that's quite all right, Mr. Barrington." She smiled and handed him a clipboard. "You just fill this out with all of your information and I'll take care of all the rest."

"Thank you…?"

The receptionist smoothed her hair. "Millie—Millie Givens."

Overhearing the exchange, Shanna shook her head in disbelief. She took a deep breath to calm herself, catching a light scent of aftershave and leather on the air. She watched as he leaned over the counter to fill out the information, noticing his shirt as it stretched tight over the broad expanse of his shoulders.

In the silence of the small room, Dr. Mooreland's booming voice could be heard questioning a patient. "So where did you get that shotgun?"

"I asked my momma for an electric scooter for Christmas and she told me I'd only kill myself. She got me the twelve-gauge instead."

Just then the interior door opened and a rangy teenage boy came out with the doctor following closely on his heels. "You tell your mother to buy you that scooter ... doctor's orders! Put the shotgun away until you're at least twenty-one!" Rubbing the boy's head, he smiled. "You're fortunate it was just buck shot. You might not be so lucky next time."

"You may go back now, Mr. Barrington." Millie extended her hand through the window to receive the clipboard.

Handing over the paperwork, Gage gestured toward Shanna before returning to his seat. "We can wait. This lady was here first."

Millie's reddened face betrayed her embarrassment as the doctor glared at her before turning to Shanna. "Come on back, Shanna. What's bothering you?"

Shanna rushed to explain, "It's not me, Doc, it's Gypsy. She's out in the car."

"Well, bring her in ... let's have a look at her."

Doctors who work in rural communities tend to be general practitioners instead of specialists. Doctor

Les Mooreland was an exception to the rule. He was a capable surgeon who felt making a difference in a remote island town mattered more than making the highest earnings.

A few minutes later, Shanna appeared in the doorway with her arm behind the waist of a pasty white woman. Her eyes were dark and expressionless, and her face gaunt and hollow-looking. Shanna led her through the waiting area, tossing a large canvas tote into a chair before gesturing toward the lobby door. Gage shot up from his seat and opened it for them.

Looking up briefly into the man's eyes, Shanna thought there seemed something familiar about him. She smiled her thanks, then forced her attention on the task at hand.

Gage had taken a seat again and was well into reading a magazine article when the front door opened and in came two emergency medical technicians wheeling a gurney. Without pause they passed through the waiting area and went into the back of the clinic. Moments later they emerged with the sickly woman on a stretcher, wheeling her out to the awaiting ambulance.

Shanna rushed out of the examination room and bumped into Millie in the hallway.

"Payment is due after services are rendered. Dr. Mooreland is, after all, a well-respected doctor and a strong influential man in the community," Millie said.

"Strength is for service, Millie, not status. As for the matter of payment—pro bono, per Dr. Mooreland."

Millie noticed the doctor as he paused in the doorway, a confused look on his face. "Is everything alright, Doctor?"

"I'm not sure, Millie. I'm really not at all sure. Please, if you don't mind, run to the store and get some coffee… we're fresh out and I'm in desperate need of it."

"Of course." Millie stepped back into the front office and snatched up her purse. "I'll only be a minute."

Once Millie had gone, Dr. Mooreland turned around quickly, pulling his cell phone from his coat pocket. Glancing back over his shoulder toward Shanna, he said, "Wait here for me to finish up and I'll go with you. We need to make sure Gypsy is admitted without incident. Her appendix may have ruptured."

Shanna needed no other urging. She took a seat in the lobby to wait for the doctor.

After witnessing the odd events, Gage sat back and ran a hand across his jawline, not sure what to make of it. He studied the young woman seated across from him discreetly, recognizing her as the girl from the cemetery near the old church. Despite her youth, he again perceived an air of seriousness about her. She displayed none of the lightheartedness of many young women. Her tall and willowy form moved with an easy grace, but with an intent directness that was at once both pleasing and disquieting. Mahogany-colored hair fell across her face in a loose wave as she rummaged through her bag. The next minute the doctor casually came to the door and motioned for Gage.

Nodding in reply, he stood and waited for Quinn to join him. "This is just a checkup. Nothing to be concerned about."

"Tell that to the lady that just left outa here on a board." Quinn's eyes filled with fright.

Gage was sure the boy moved toward him a step before giving a short, apprehensive nod.

"I won't leave you," Gage assured him as they followed the doctor to the exam room.

The room was cold and smelled of rubbing alcohol. Quinn eyed the table with the thin sheet of white paper stretched over it. "I done had my shots," he stated nervously, looking around the sterile room. Although distracted by the doctor, he kept a close eye on Gage's reassuring presence. He knew right off that the doctor meant business.

"What is your name, young man?" Dr. Mooreland asked, reading the boy's chart.

"Quinn Barrington."

"Barrington, Barrington… I once had a good friend named Barrington. Well, Quinn, you certainly favor your father," Dr. Mooreland observed. "Have a seat, Mr. Barrington. Quinn, hop up on the table for me and let's have a look at you."

Quinn's jaw squared as he climbed up on the table and sat down facing the doctor. "He ain't my daddy. My daddy's the greatest. Why, if it wasn't for my daddy, there wouldn't be hardly no children in Beaufort."

The doctor cleared his throat, casting a hesitant glance toward the boy's father.

Gage felt the need to explain. "It's a long story, Dr. Mooreland. Quinn and I have only just met. I thought we'd start here today, work our way around the corner to the barber shop and then maybe get some ice cream," he commented goodheartedly. "And doctor… a DNA?"

The doctor nodded, catching the meaning. "Sounds like a good plan. Old Jay Byrd is a fine barber," Dr. Mooreland mumbled, peering into the boy's ears with an otoscope. "Say, you're from Beaufort?"

"Yep," Quinn replied.

"Yes, sir," Gage corrected.

"And your mother still lives there?" he questioned, turning to the boy's other ear as he continued with his examination. "Now, open wide and let me swab your cheek… it may tickle."

"I guess she went back to him. Who knows? She can't never be pleased … that's what Slade says." He wiped his nose on a sleeve then scratched the other ear.

"Slade?"

"My daddy." The words burst out in a rush as he plunged into his statement. "Course, Slade wouldn't marry her on account of her being so selfish. That's why I'm here with him." He stabbed his thumb in the air toward Gage. "She couldn't bring no more money in the house cause some old man up and died."

"Slow down, boy," the doctor admonished with a slight smile. "I'd like to get all this straight in my head. See, I'm confused already; how did you end up here?"

"She told me it was about time for me to meet some more family."

"Ah, I get the picture." Dr. Mooreland peered over his glasses at Gage who had propped his elbows on his knees to rest his head in both hands.

Gage mumbled under his breath.

"Do you understand why it's necessary…?" He let the sentence drop, hoping Gage would fill in the blanks.

Straightening, Gage struggled a moment with his own rising annoyance and embarrassment but managed to continue more calmly. "I'm sure you have your reasons, Doctor."

"That I do. To be such a small island town, you'd be amazed at the goings on here." He shook his head. "But the good news is that this young man seems to be in good shape, other than a plain old cold virus." He turned to address Quinn. "Wait for your father in the lobby, son." The tone of the doctor's voice allowed no argument.

After Quinn left the room, Dr. Mooreland faced Gage. He took a cotton-tipped stick and swabbed his mouth. "If at all possible, see if you can locate his medical records and bring them to me. I want to make sure he's current on his immunizations." He wrote a short note in the file then snapped it shut. "There's a one-day turnaround time on the DNA test. The results can be sent to your cellphone or computer."

"I'll have his records for you. I need the proof of the other for court. These results will be admissible, won't they?"

"Absolutely. It's clear from what I've observed, and I am sure you're aware, that your son has been somewhat neglected. He's underweight and in need of a dentist." The doctor studied the self-possessed man who had taken charge of the child. He saw the warm look of determination and concern in his eyes. "Liquids, Tylenol if he develops a fever and rest. He'll be good as new in no time. If not, bring him back to see me."

"Thank you, Doctor. I'll see to it."

The doctor cleared his throat again. "At the risk of sounding condescending, something tells me you'll do a fine job as a father."

"I wish I had your confidence. I've never been around children very much and I'm more than a little uneasy about it," Gage replied, running a hand through his hair.

"Good. It's the parents that are too lax that cause me concern. This free-range parenting is … well, you see for yourself, don't you?" He calmly folded his hands behind his back. "Should you ever need assistance with your son, say … a sitter perhaps, don't hesitate to call me. I'm a pretty good judge of character and could make a few recommendations."

A slow smile grew on Gage's face as he extended his hand. "Thanks, Doctor, I may just take you up on that."

As they left the clinic and got into the truck, Quinn tossed a bible on the floorboard before pulling himself up into the seat and slamming the door shut.

Gage raised an eyebrow. "A bible is a book, but not just any book."

"Huh?"

"In this world there are holy things and bibles are one of them. They're not holy in and of themselves, but they are holy because God's revelation has been given through them. The way we treat holy things shows how we treat God." He gestured toward the floorboard.

Quinn reached down and lifted the bible from the floorboard, carefully wiping the dirt off before settling it into his lap. "I didn't know."

"So, now you do." Smiling slightly, Gage put the truck in gear and pulled onto the street, wondering the whole time where that sermon had come from. Another thought occurred to him and he hit the brakes. "Where did you get that, anyway?" He pointed to the bible. "You didn't take it from the waiting room, did you?"

"No. That lady in there, she give it to me."

"She *gave* it to me," Gage corrected.

"She give it to you, too?" Quinn looked confused.

"Never mind, we'll take first things first. Let's go lower your ears," he said, pulling up outside the barber shop. Something told Gage he needed to call in the reinforcements with this boy. This child was going to need a village.

CHAPTER 4

The parsonage where Shanna lived had a solid feel about it. The sturdy-beamed ceiling and floors were thick oak or, as in the kitchen and bath, stone. The house was firm and had been built to last several lifetimes. Over the years the old girl had weathered many storms, and Shanna was growing attached to its homey comfort.

The May day was bright and somewhat balmy as she wandered out the back door to pull sheets from the clothesline. A dryer was the one luxury she'd had to make do without since coming to Terrapin Island, but the rewards of fresh-smelling linens far outweighed any disadvantages.

Placing a large sweet-grass basket on the ground, she stepped to the line and began snapping off clothes pins, draping sheets over her arm. Hearing the crunch of slow tires over sand and gravel she glanced up, halting her movements. Lowering the sheets into the basket, she shielded her eyes from the sun and waited for some indication from the driver as to his purpose.

Daniel Muir spent most of his time in a little room in the back of the church, even sleeping there, but he always took his meals with Shanna and would stop in at the parsonage after the work day was complete. But this visitor was not Granddad.

When the black Chevy pickup truck rolled to a stop in front of the house, Shanna quickly grabbed the laundry basket and made her way inside through the back door. With calm deliberation she smoothed her hair and brushed off the front of her shirt as a soft knock came at the door. She hesitated a moment and the persistent knocking came again. Laying a hand on the knob, she took a deep steadying breath and swung it open.

So accustomed to seeing the small stature of Daniel Muir around the house, the doorway seemed filled by the man. Her gaze traveled up from his work boots, over a length of jeans and a lightweight hooded jacket, to the face beneath the brim of a Cooper River Marina cap. She caught her breath at the intensity of his azure blue eyes. Instantly she recognized him. He was the man she'd seen with the boy at the clinic. He had a handsome face, but there was a tense, almost pained look to the chiseled line of his jaw. As he stared at her, his eyes took on grief. The man looked down briefly, as if unsure, then looked up again.

"Miss Muir?"

"Yes." She felt the strength leave her knees.

"I'm Gage Barrington. I own Bainbridge Marina. May I come in?"

Shanna recognized the name but hadn't put the name with the face. "Of course." She stepped aside and allowed him to enter.

He moved past her, taking a deep steadying breath.

"Please." She waved toward the living room. Closing the door, she caught the mixed scents of warm sun, tobacco, and light cologne. "Come in, sit down."

"Thank you."

"Would you care for a drink? Coffee maybe?" she offered, trying to calm her trembling hands.

"Oh, no, thank you." He snatched the cap from his head and ran a quick hand through his hair. "I wouldn't care for any."

He had an unabashed Southern drawl that would have been well at home anywhere in the Lowcountry. His eyes were totally inquisitive, as if searching out something from her.

Shanna's tongue seemed unusually clumsy as she began to worry. Although he didn't seem rushed, and there was no urgency in his voice, still she wondered about the purpose of the man's visit. "I was about to make a pot of coffee. Are you sure you wouldn't care for some? It would be no trouble."

He looked down, shaking his head as he took a seat on the clean but faded sofa.

An invading uneasiness threatened to choke her words as she abruptly sat down on the edge of the chair. "Is everything all right, Mr. Barrington? Granddad?"

Gage held his cap in both hands in front of him, his voice even and sympathetic. "I'm afraid not, Miss Muir. Your grandfather passed away this afternoon."

Shanna drew in a sharp breath. "Passed away? Oh, dear God, no! How?"

"Not sure; we assume a heart attack. Jedidiah found him sitting at his desk, leaning back in his chair with his eyes closed. His glasses were on the desk in front of him. It was as if he'd just carefully set them aside and leaned back to rest."

She stared unblinking at her hands, clinched into fists to steady the trembling. Searing pain gripped her throat as she choked back tears.

"He's off the island at the funeral home. I'll take you there if you'd like."

She swallowed hard. "Yes. Thank you." Standing, she lost her balance, but Gage shot up out of his seat, his arm reaching out to steady her. She swayed and, anticipating it, he grasped her elbow. That was the last thing she remembered.

Then, somewhere in the distance she heard a reassuring voice. "Miss Muir … Miss Muir, it's going to be okay." Her mind barely registered a cool compress and the gentle pressure of a man's hand. Then her eyes opened with a start.

"Did I faint? Please don't tell me I fainted. I don't faint! I've never fainted!" she said, with resistance.

Fleeting humor flitted about the man's features as tiny wrinkles formed at the corners of his eyes. She turned her face away as the room came into focus. Her eyes fixed on Granddad's pipe near his chair. Grasping Gage's forearm, she pulled herself to a sitting position, remembering the purpose of the man's visit.

"I'm driving you to the funeral home, Miss Muir."

The realization was clear, as if the words had been spoken: you are in no condition to handle this on your own. "Shanna … my name is Shanna. And I'd like to shower quickly and change clothes before we go if that's okay."

"Shanna." Gage tested her name on his tongue. "I'm here. I don't care if you need all night to get ready, I'm not going anywhere. You do what you need to do."

Shanna's eyes drifted away toward the chair and pipe again. The moment stretched out. She could smell a fragrance coming from Gage. It was, she realized, peppermint candy. "Why are you doing this? You don't even know me."

"Because Daniel was not only an employee but also a friend. Because I know what it feels like to lose someone close to you. I don't want you to feel alone … to be alone. That's why I'm here for you."

She hadn't thought his answer would affect her, but immediately her eyes welled up and tears spilled down her cheek. Some part of her was relieved that he wanted to stay. She knew she didn't need to be alone. It was a profound agony she felt at being left alive when those she loved so dearly were dead; as if she had been stabbed and left to drain out but never die. She gave him a pained look full of apology. "I'm sorry. Thank you for offering to stay with me. I really think I need someone here right now."

"May I call someone for you while you're getting ready?"

"Yes, please...." She went to the desk and scribbled out a few numbers and handed them to him. "That's my boss, tell her what's happened and let her know that I won't be in for a few days." She tapped the paper. "This is the number for Father Cleo. He's a close personal friend. These other names are deacons from the church; they'll notify the other church members."

"Got it." He took the paper and began punching numbers on his phone, recognizing Dr. Les Mooreland's name and assumed he was a deacon.

Before disappearing into the bedroom, she turned. "Granddad always said he wanted a simple funeral. A pine box and a graveside service, no frills. Only now it just doesn't seem fitting." The slim shoulders fell, dejectedly.

"Honor his wishes — that's what's fitting."

Time always seemed to move on the island just a tick slower than anywhere else; still, it was now the first day of June and summer was full upon them. The tepid wind of the sea island swirled and danced while not a thought was given to the humid air waiting in the wings. Soon everything would be draped in a cloth of heavy moist heat.

Yancey glanced at his watch as he passed the desk of his nephew. "It's 2:00 o'clock. Time for my mandatory coffee break."

Gage looked up from his papers and watched as his uncle pushed through the front door and left it swinging on its hinges as he walked up the sandy road toward his truck.

Despite himself, Gage smiled as he observed the old man amble off like an old cowpoke, heading toward the café where Gage knew he was going. He had never darkened the door of the place himself, but was always surprised to see a gathering of old men on the porch and on the steps out in front of it, their heads nodding as they dozed off throughout the day.

"I'm buying!" Yancey called out over his shoulder, never slowing his pace.

Gage shook his head, taking the hint. Sometimes Yancey could be so exasperating, still there was something about the old man that was likable, too. He had difficulty at the moment figuring out just exactly what that might be. Closing the folder in front of him, he pushed his chair back and caught up with his uncle.

As they pulled the truck near the café, Gage noticed a loose line forming outside. "Did somebody blow a whistle or something? Where did all these people come from?"

"I told you. It's mandatory coffee break. You been on the island all this time and you don't know about mandatory coffee break?" He threw out an arm, gesturing at the crowd of people. "Heck, son, even the tourists know about that."

They walked up wide board steps onto a deep covered porch, giving an otherwise plain shop some appeal. A cowbell clanked against the door as they pushed it open and entered.

Looking around, Gage noticed an artful approach used in the silver spoons suspended above each window sill. Racks displaying everything from local paintings and sweet-grass baskets to an assortment of bakery items hinted of a quaint quirkiness. The layout of mismatched tables with colorful chairs scattered here and there was one of relaxed simplicity. All these things seemed a rebuke to the harsh ugliness of the modern food chain. Despite its humble appearance, the place had charm.

The group ahead of them was taking a lot of time making up their minds about their orders. Impatient, Gage rubbed his hand over his close cut beard as he looked around. He spotted Shanna behind the counter waving them over to the side. He nudged his uncle and pointed in her direction. As they walked up, she handed Yancey his usual coffee — a large black espresso.

Astonished, Yancey didn't think anyone would remember his face, let alone his coffee order. "Thank you, darlin'."

"Now, what for you, Mr. Barrington?" she asked, turning her smoky gray eyes toward him.

"Large coffee — dash of half and half." He glanced at his watch, mindful of the time. It was the last day of school and Quinn would be getting off the bus soon; he had to make it quick.

With a nod, she pushed away from the counter. "Have a seat over there and I'll bring your coffee right out."

"They need that girl back at Magnolias," Gage said, pulling out a high-backed chair and taking a seat. "What's the name of this place, anyway? Something about rain...." He looked around with mild curiosity.

Gage was used to having one-sided conversations with his uncle. Most of the time questions to Yancey were answered with either a grunt or went unanswered altogether. Unless, of course, he was interested in the subject, then you couldn't shut him up.

No sooner had they sat down than Shanna reappeared with Gage's coffee and two pieces of warm pecan pie served with vanilla bean ice cream.

Both men looked up with raised eyebrows at the waitress.

"Thought you might like a little taste of home... Charleston, right?"

"What gave it away?" Gage asked, watching in amusement as the older man looked at Shanna, a slight expression of bafflement on his face.

She pointed to Gage's cap with her finger. "The Cooper River Marina. That's near Charleston, isn't it?"

"You're a skilled observer, Miss...," Yancey waited for her response.

"Muir. Shanna Muir."

"She's Daniel Muir's granddaughter," Gage said, noticing the surprise on his uncle's face. "Don't you remember her from the funeral?"

"Granddaughter-in-law. Now, let me know if you need anything else. By the way...," she turned to Gage, "I appreciate what you did to help me with Granddad's affairs. The pie is on the house." Stepping away, she tossed a dish towel over her shoulder, moving between the tables as she straightened the chairs.

Pausing mid-sip, Gage's eyes went over Yancey's shoulder and took in the young woman with the lithe form and faded blue jeans. He knew the island was small, but it seemed every time he turned around he was bumping into this girl. He tipped his head to one side, and a strong dawning occurred in his eyes as he carefully studied her. "Didn't Daniel say something about his grandson dying as a result of an injury he received in Afghanistan?"

"He did. James was his name. A true hero, to hear Daniel talk about it."

"And didn't James' wife move here from a convent or something in… Mississippi or Alabama?" He gazed at the slim pert nose and delicate features of the girl, his lips pursed in thought.

"Yep, I believe so, come to think of it." Yancey scooped up another forkful of pie. "Wherever she comes from, they sure taught her how to make a mean pecan pie. Probably the best I've ever had … better than Mama's, even."

Shanna knew Gage Barrington was a generous man. He had insisted on paying for Daniel's funeral and would not take no for an answer. She was also aware of something else — the handsome, tawny-haired South Carolinian was staring straight at her. She looked down, giving her full attention to the table she was cleaning. It was hard concentrating on her task with his penetrating eyes boring a hole straight through her.

She was not accustomed to the attention, especially from one so… impressive. But it wasn't only his looks that caused him to stand out from the rest of the population of Terrapin Island. There was something else about the man, a certain intensity he wore as easily as he did the cap that shaded his piercing blue eyes.

She chided herself. Why should she be concerned about him? *He probably just wants a refill on his coffee*, she thought, reaching for the pot.

"How about a warm up," Shanna said as she topped off first one cup then the other.

Tossing down his napkin, Yancey turned toward the girl with a smile. "Best pecan pie I've ever tasted. Your recipe?"

She nodded. "I brought it with me; passed down from a dozen Natchez grandmothers."

"Might've known you're a Mississippi girl," Yancey said, grinning. "Two things Mississippi is famous for: good cooks and beautiful women. With pie like that you could make a fortune in Charleston."

Shanna flushed, twisting her lips to hide a growing smile. "I'll make sure to keep one handy around here just for you."

Yancey threw up his hands. "I'm trying to make you filthy rich, girl. Thank me one day when you're as famous as Paula Dean."

Pushing her hair behind her ear, she smiled at the man. "That's the way of the world, isn't it? We make our pile and then we leave it. Not much purpose in a life like that now, is it?" She smiled to take the edge off her words. Collecting their dishes, she returned to the kitchen.

Gage shifted uncomfortably in his chair; the girl's dart had unintendedly struck a mark.

"Sound like anyone you know?" Yancey asked, swigging down the rest of his coffee.

"Yep. Your mother, Lilly Rose." Gage tossed down a twenty on the table and stood up. "You can take the girl out of the convent, but you can't take the convent out of the girl. We better head back. Quinn will be getting off the bus soon." With one last look at the waitress, he left the café.

Jedidiah ambled through the darkened warehouse and then stopped and straightened as the floor behind him creaked beneath a heavy foot. Wide-eyed he inched around to glimpse the intruder, his foot set for flight. Relief flooded his face as recognition dawned. Wiping his damp forehead with the back of his sleeve, Jedidiah said,

"I sure am glad it's you, Boss. Them no counts down by the river always poking 'round up here, up to no good. I was about ready to lay somebody low."

Gage's eyes flitted through the warehouse, taking stock of its rising content. Stacks of lumber lined the walls with loads ready to be forklifted to nearby docks for replacement and repair. Business was increasing steadily; soon, more workers would be needed to keep up with the demand for more slips.

He passed his hand reflectively over a fresh cut plank. "We're growing, Jedidiah."

"Yes, sir, we surely are. Been meanin' to talk to you 'bout something, Boss. Somethin' that I think you best know 'bout."

Turning away from the timber, his eyes fixed on Jedidiah. "Go ahead, I'm listening."

"That boy's momma? She's here. Here on the island."

"Tinsley? Are you sure?" he questioned, trying to read the man's face.

"Ain't no better offer for a good gossip than to ask what's going on, then, when they tell you somethin', say, 'You don't say.'" He shrugged. "How do you think I know what goes on in this town?" He pulled off his hat and rubbed his head before slapping it on again.

Gage glanced about in frustration. "Where is she?"

"Don't rightly know. Just said she was asking about you and the boy."

"I see. If you happen to hear anything else, let me know, will you?"

"Sure will, Boss. You can count on it."

CHAPTER 5

Almost any group of three is going to form a triangle with two points closer to one another; in the relationship with her parents, Shanna always felt she had been the farthest point.

Early in childhood, Shanna had been caught in a melodrama of her parent's love as they committed, what the family priest called, the sin of unrestraint. So wild had been their love that one reckless night, a bad decision brought an abrupt end to their lives as the couple unintentionally tumbled to their deaths from a Natchez bluff.

The dramatic fashion in which Shanna's parents ended their lives was legendary. From Natchez to Noble, Mississippi, everyone knew of the consuming and uninhibited love of the couple.

Shanna had felt watched, as if the whole town waited for evidence that the crazy gene might resurface again in their only child. It was during those times that she had learned to keep quiet about a lot of things. The things she observed about life she kept to herself. And out of that, an inward life had begun to develop in Shanna.

It had been decided by her paternal grandmother that the best course of action for Shanna was for her to be placed in the care of the church. The grandmother had made a grand gesture, giving up the child to the service of the Lord, much like Hannah had given up Samuel in the biblical story, or so she had stated on numerous occasions. The simple truth of the matter was that Shanna's grandmother had been in poor health and hadn't been able to care for the child.

That's when the priest, Father Cleo, stepped in. Concerned about the wellbeing of both Shanna and the girl's guardian, he took the young girl into the protective care of Holy Trinity Children's home in Natchez, Mississippi.

The years passed and with her education behind her, Shanna moved naturally into a position at the church working with benevolent causes alongside her mentor, Sister Jon-Maureen. The job included room and board at the convent along with a small salary.

But it was Father Cleo who'd saved Shanna's life. He was like a rock in the middle of a swiftly flowing stream, letting the cares of the world rush around and past him. Not only was he a stable and compassionate man, he was a man who drank deeply from the chalice of grace. Not much disturbed him. Only this day, as the bell clanged above the door of the Rainy Day Café, did he seem troubled.

Father Cleo stepped inside the café, gently closing the door behind him. "Shanna," he said, simply. Then, as if a thought suddenly occurred to him, reached back and opened the door to assist an attractive woman outside. He shook his head and grinned.

There was a sheepish cast to his smile which, to Shanna, was his most appealing. "I see you still have a way with the ladies," she said, making her way over to greet him with a hug.

"Call it a curse," he said, giving her a tight squeeze.

She pulled away and locked the door, turning the sign to say, "Closed." "What brings you all this way … checking up on me?"

"I received the news about Daniel late. I'd been away at a retreat. I called … and when I didn't hear from you, I became concerned." He looked puzzled, like he didn't know what to think. He gestured with his hand. "Naturally, I had to come see for myself."

"I'll pour you a cup of coffee." Shanna tapped the top of a table near a window. "Sit here." As she headed toward the kitchen, a frown of worry crossed her brow. She had never seen Father Cleo so troubled, and couldn't help glancing over her shoulder at the priest as she stepped around the counter.

"Nice place," he commented, looking around as he took a seat. He searched in the pocket of his jacket and produced a small flat bag, tossing it on the table.

"I bet you dropped by just to make sure I wasn't talking to myself these days?" she teased. That had been a longstanding joke between them. As a young girl, Shanna had been ever on the lookout for signs in herself of mental illness and was convinced of the fact that talking to yourself was the first red flag you passed on your way to Loonyville.

"Oh, you're a regular window-licking lunatic … but wait … you know that already, don't you?"

Acting as if she hadn't heard, she stepped toward the table with coffee in hand. Noticing the priest's black hair tinged lightly with gray and his dark soulful eyes a full second before her attention was drawn to the tiny white bag on the table. "I hope that's what I think it is."

His voice dropped to a haunted whisper as he responded, "I would never forget such an important thing."

She placed the coffee in front of him and snatched the bag from the table. "Madame Fousteau's pralines! How I have dreamed of these!" She leaned against the wall with her hands working the wrappings.

"You know, there's a good kind of crazy, Shanna," he said, sipping the brew and watching her obvious delight in the candy. He leaned forward, placing his elbows on the table as he held the cup with both hands. "It's the kind of crazy that steps into danger for somebody else, then fights their way back out again."

"I was a handful, wasn't I?" she said, closing her eyes as she savored the taste of home in the creamy praline.

"Always the righter of wrongs. I'm beginning to regret ever putting you and Sister Jon-Maureen together. A formidable force if there ever was one. More than a few of these gray hairs are there because of you," he said, cocking his head as he gave her a rueful smile.

Shanna watched him narrowly as she finished off the praline, wondering about the purpose behind his sudden appearance.

Father Cleo fixed his eyes on her. Though only moments ago Shanna had seemed so happy and childlike, now her face hinted of regret. The gray of her eyes deepened as she apprehensively swept her hair behind her ears, a habit she'd had all her life. The young woman before him was splendid, quite a change from the ragged little girl of so long ago. This woman had a peculiar nobleness about her. One that exuded a kind of sadness. "Yes," Father Cleo remarked, "a formidable force indeed."

"So, you traveled all this way to bring me a few pralines? Or do you have something else on your mind?" Shanna asked and waited expectantly until he nodded.

"Yes." He put down the coffee cup and slid it away from him. "How would you like to leave here and come back to Natchez? We could use the help."

For a moment she felt stunned. Almost hesitantly she asked, "You mean move away from Terrapin Island? From … James?"

"I know this seems rather sudden, but I've been thinking about it for a while. When your grandmother passed away, she left in my care a modest sum of money for you along with the deed to Noble Hill. It was to be given to you when you turned twenty-three. I've been holding on to it for you." Father Cleo went on. "Oh, and happy birthday, by the way."

She felt her throat tighten a little. "I can't believe you remembered my birthday."

"You know, you really ought to learn when to shut up, Shanna. That's very insulting."

She looked out the window and shrugged. "I guess I've grown used to not being important to anyone around here anymore. You're the only person who even knows it's my birthday."

Father Cleo turned to stare at her. "I just told you that you have some money and you own your own house and all you seem to be concerned about is that I remembered your birthday! As if I would ever forget."

"I'm just surprised a little, that's all." She smiled and pulled out a chair and sank into it, hearing the hum of the ceiling fan in the suddenly quiet room.

"You may need this money when you move back home. It will help you get established. There's not much left for you here."

Shanna looked at him wonderingly. Some part of her was pleased that he wanted her home, to get back to the life they'd known before James. Glancing out the window again, she noticed the light had dissolved a little over the tree line in the distance near where James lay buried. She couldn't think of leaving … not with her husband here on the island.

As if reading Shanna's thoughts, Father Cleo steepled his fingers at chest level and stared at them. "Of course, I got to know James while you two dated. Nothing pleased that boy more than spending his furlough with you in Natchez. Even put up with my restrictions with a good attitude. But moving you here was the only thing we ever collaborated on. Even though it must've seemed we were opposed in our views, we had very much in common." He clasped his fingers together in a posture of prayer. "He texted me often, checking on you. The day you married him was the happiest day of his life. Neither of us ever wanted you to regret that decision. Your happiness and wellbeing was our first concern. Your husband loved you, Shanna, and he was truly a Godly man."

She stared reflectively down at the toe of her small grey shoe as memories flooded her mind. "Yes, he was a Godly man … and so are you. But I think I'll stay here for a while. I'd like to make sure the church gets settled with a new pastor. Granddad would've wanted that."

Father Cleo nodded, reached into the inside pocket of his jacket, and pulled out an envelope and handed it to her. "Here. I trust you'll use it wisely. Now, come on. I made reservations for us in Charleston for your birthday. I'll catch you up on all the news from home."

CHAPTER 6

S hanna stared out as the rain pelted the windowpanes before sliding down the glass in a long runnel. Finding the office to the marina had not been difficult, but waiting for Gage Barrington had tried her patience to no end. She was beginning to wonder if inquiring about a job had been a bad idea. But she had to realize the owner was a busy man. Bainbridge Marina was fast becoming the largest business on Terrapin Island.

She had been directed to the office by a friendly man named Jedidiah. The room, clean and well-ordered, held a faint scent of tobacco. A large metal desk occupied most of the space and faced a window that overlooked the marina. Positioned behind the desk sat a massive bookcase with neatly organized volumes displaying titles that ranged from the American Revolutionary War to the Civil War, which Shanna assumed held some importance to the man.

In the hallway outside the office, quick footsteps stopped abruptly at the door, followed by a comment in a deep voice to someone passing. She turned from the window and faced Mr. Barrington as he entered. Seeing the seriousness on his face, she became suddenly aware of just how foolish it was for her to be here. Whatever her circumstances, they hardly compared to what this man dealt with in running a booming operation such as this.

Recognizing the young woman, Gage contained his aggravation at being pulled from his duties and crossed the room, pulling off his rain jacket and hanging it on a hook near his desk.

"Shanna. What brings you out this way? Please." He indicated a chair as he picked up the application on his desk and began scanning it.

She smoothed her skirt under her as she sat down, feeling suddenly shaky.

The chair creaked under his weight as he sat at his desk. He looked up, meeting the woman's eyes.

"I'm here about a job. Dr. Mooreland said I should talk with you."

His brows rose in surprise. "Dr. Mooreland?"

"Yes."

The blue eyes narrowed. "What sort of a job are you looking for?"

"I'm only working part-time at the café. Rainy has hired her daughter, so now I'll have even less hours. I work for Three Course Catering on the weekends, but I need a full-time position during the week," she said, then added in a rush of words, "My weekend job will not interfere with a full-time position." She folded her hands in her lap and sat up straight.

Gage gave the application his undivided attention. "Twenty-three's pretty young to work so many hours. Not much time left for a social life."

She leaned back, ignoring the remark. "I understand from Doc that you're in need of someone to do light cleaning and run errands. I'm certainly qualified for that."

The corner of his mouth lifted slightly as he realized she was good at deflecting personal questions. "I think you've been misinformed."

Her fingers bit painfully into her wrist. She glanced around. "You're probably right. It doesn't appear to me that you need it. Thank you for your time." She stood to leave and then stared in mute surprise as Gage came to his feet.

"No, I mean this place will require more that *light* cleaning. It's filthy. My office is the only sanitized spot in the whole place." He grabbed a set of keys from his desk. "Come on, I'll show you what needs to be done."

"You mean you're hiring me?" she asked, wide-eyed.

"If Dr. Mooreland recommends you, that's good enough for me."

"What's the wage? You haven't mentioned it," Shanna pointed out.

"Just what you asked for." He nodded toward her application on his desk. "Although you may regret it after you see what's in store for you."

He led Shanna through the building, pausing at each room to give a brief description of what would be expected. She noticed the dust and what appeared to be motor oil on the floor right away, along with discarded paper and trash collecting beneath the desks and furnishings. The small kitchen, break room, and two restrooms stood in greatest need of her services.

"Where is the supply closet?" she asked, showing none of the disgust she felt at the condition of the restrooms.

"Up front in the lobby. When the guys come in from the docks and warehouses, the front lobby is where they land—and it shows. Diesel, oil, and mud get tracked in. There's a box of latex gloves on the top shelve. I recommend using them."

"You can count on it."

"When can you start?"

"Now. I brought a change of clothes in my bag out in the car, just in case."

He liked her confidence and that she came ready to work. "Good. You can get started."

When Gage left her, she grabbed her bag from the car and headed to the bathroom to change into her jeans and a tee-shirt. She set to work, dragging out a heavy broom, mops, cleaning supplies, and a bucket. With an angular broom, she swept beneath desks, chairs and furniture, raking out piles of dust and trash before collecting it and tossing it into the garbage. She preferred to work alone, humming to herself as she concentrated on the job at hand. The occupants of the building were busy working on boats at the docks and in the warehouses. Occasionally someone would come in, but no one disturbed her. Her activities were ignored for the most part as employees went about their duties.

As Shanna approached the restroom, the words of Father Cleo sprang to her mind. *Life, it's not always pretty, but it's always beautiful.* "Not sure I can find the beauty in here, Father … but I'm trying." She sat on her heels and lifted a stack of greasy magazines off the floor, startling a mouse that went scurrying between her legs. Surprised, she sprawled backward and yelped as she hit the floor.

Immediately a slick-haired young man, who had been watching Shanna from the doorway, slung the apron he'd been holding and rushed to help. When he saw Shanna's face as she pushed off the floor to stand, he stopped clumsily in mid-stride, unable to say a word. His mouth slackened and he stared dumbfounded.

"This is Dupe Dodd," Gage said, having just witnessed the scene. "He's a good hand with boats and usually yaks all the time," he dropped a hand on Dupe's shoulder as he continued, "at least when he's not busy gawking."

Dupe's cheeks splotched red. "Sorry … I mean … uh.…"

"Shanna," Gage informed him bluntly. He had never seen the teen so affected by a pretty face before. "Now give her the apron you brought her."

"Oh, yeah … I, uh, got this apron for you. We use these when we clean fish … so the guts, I mean … here." Dupe turned around and snatched up the canvas apron, dusted it good with his hand, smiled, and presented it to her and then stood there as if waiting for her approval. "It'll keep all the oil and dirt off you," he said with pride in his voice.

"Thank you, Dupe." Shanna gave the boy a bright smile, trying to put him at ease.

Dupe was suddenly fumble-footed in confusion. After a moment of hesitancy, he mumbled a few words about work and help and then slipped out the door and was gone.

Gage shoved a case of motor oil out of the way with his foot. "Sorry about that. He's a good guy and he'll help you in any way he can. It's just his imagination has a tendency to run away with him at times. He struts around some, but he's harmless."

Her gaze flicked up as she tied the apron strings behind her back. "I've been around teenage boys before. It's fine, they don't bother me."

"Good. Something tells me you'll see a lot of him. Well, I'll let you get back to work then."

Shanna responded with a nod of her head and turned back to her work.

With the work day complete, Shanna collected her things and began making her way out the door. Under the darkening sky were a scattering of men covering their heads with their arms as they ran through the rain toward their cars.

She stood under the shelter of the overhang, waiting for a break in the rain. Men pushed past her without notice as they craned their necks looking up the road. A long, exaggerated wolf whistle trilled out from among them. Following their eyes, Shanna saw a woman walking toward them down the shell-crushed road. Boots thumped and umbrellas popped as men hurried to offer the attractive brunette cover from the rain.

Gage noticed the scene from the dock where he'd been working to secure a shrimp boat to the moorings. He'd seen the commotion and was stopped by it. Angered, it moved him from the arena of the spectator to personal involvement. His eyes did not waver nor did he speak as he brushed past the men, snatching an umbrella from one of them as he made his way to the overhang where Shanna stood.

Propping his boot on the lower step, he said, "It might be some time before this rain slacks up. Let me walk you to your car."

In a startled voice Shanna replied, "Thank you."

Leading Shanna through the rain under the cover of an umbrella, he waited as she got inside the car and cranked the engine. "Drive safely, now … see you tomorrow." With that, he tapped the hood of the car and turned his attention back to the unexpected guest.

Shanna pulled away feeling a wave of warmth flow down her spine. The man certainly had manners, she'd give him that. She'd never admit it to a soul in this world, but she secretly adored the attentive treatment, especially in front of all those hard-ankle men who had so easily dismissed her.

A little crowd had gathered near the office door. Gage narrowed his eyes. The woman responsible for all the disturbance looked up as if sensing being watched. He knew her instantly. With a deep breath, he pushed down his feelings. He knew in his gut that this meeting was inevitable.

Chapter 7

Fog began to creep in, lightly veiling a crescent moon that hung from a sky of weathered tin. The sound of a distant ship's horn bellowed, then faded as its passage filled the quiet night. Every word the couple spoke held a note of familiarity as Gage and Tinsley walked the dock.

He stopped and faced her. "Why didn't you tell me you were pregnant?"

"Two words—your father." Tinsley worried the ring on her finger. "He convinced me that I was no good for you … and I believed him."

Running a hand through his hair in frustration, he paused. "He bought you off, didn't he?"

"He … arranged support—but I knew if I didn't take the money we would starve. It was the only thing I could do."

"No." Gage said. "It wasn't."

"I know that now, but at the time I was just a frightened girl. That was over eight years ago. I was only twenty-three!" she said, pleading. "You have to understand, Gage. Your father was so intimidating. And—I had to think of the baby."

As they continued walking, Tinsley waited for some evidence of Gage's acceptance of her excuse, but he gave no sign of belief.

"I'm sorry I just showed up here unannounced. I didn't want to upset Quinn by coming to your home, but I had to see you ... *and* I had to make sure Quinn was doing okay," Tinsley said, in a voice that was oddly broken.

A long silence ensued. Finally, he spoke of what worried him. "Tinsley, Quinn says you've never been around much. Said a man named Slade has been taking care of him. Is that true?"

Her lips quivered with her words. "He made me do it—Slade. He forced me to work, to provide for all of them. When your father passed away, he knew the money would stop and I was sent out to make a living anyway I could. Waitressing, cleaning up after people. I couldn't do it anymore. So I ran away. That's why I brought Quinn to you, don't you see? I couldn't drag the poor boy to who knows where. I don't have anywhere to go. Slade doesn't know where I am, but if he finds me...."

"What?"

"He'll beat me. I swear, Gage, I'm terrified of him," she said, her voice growing louder. "You don't know how evil he is."

Reaching the car, Gage took Tinsley's hand. Her words about Slade didn't match up with what Quinn had said about the man. Still, Quinn was a boy and maybe he didn't know the full story. "Look. You said yourself that Slade has no idea where to find you. And if what you say is true, he probably doesn't have the money to search for you either. I want you to take this." He pressed some money into her hand. "It's not much, but it's all I have with me. Take it."

"Thank you. I'll stretch it as far as I can." Tinsley's chin quivered when she spoke as all the emotion she could gather perked to the surface.

Opening the car door, he waited while Tinsley stood undecided. She looked around, hesitantly. "This fog is getting thick. I hope I can make it back to the mainland." She brushed her hair behind her ear. "I've never been very good at driving in fog. It scares me."

Gage rubbed a hand across his jawline as he considered the girl. She looked the same — prettier, even. But where he had known her to be carefree and somewhat playful before, now there was a hardness about her. Maybe the hardships of life had stripped all humor from her.

He pulled a cell phone from his front pocket. "Hold on. I may be able to find a place for you tonight."

Tinsley inched over to lean against the car, eyeing him speculatively as he scrolled through his numbers before tapping the screen. "Why can't I stay with you?"

His brow raised before he turned his attention to the call he'd placed. "Shanna? This is Gage. Sorry to bother you, but I was wondering if I could ask a favor. I have a visitor. Her name is Tinsley — she's my son's mother. The fog has her locked in on the island. She needs a place to stay tonight."

The attractive woman from the marina with fine dark hair and fox sharp features stood at Shanna's door. "You must be Tinsley. I'm Shanna Muir," she stuck out her hand in greeting. "Please, come in."

Tinsley paused at the door, ignored the hand, and looked back over her shoulder as Gage pulled away. If she had hoped to see him hesitate about leaving her with a stranger, she was disappointed.

"I was just about to have a bite to eat. Will you join me?" At the answering nod, Shanna led Tinsley into the kitchen.

Sensing the tension and aware of the woman's exacting scrutiny, Shanna didn't pepper her guest with a lot of questions; instead, she allowed her to eat her meal in silence.

Tinsley looked up from her plate of chicken casserole. "So, you're a nun?"

Caught off guard by the question, Shanna cleared her throat. "No." She held the glass to her lips and took a sip of tea. "What made you think that?"

Watching her for several seconds, Tinsley added skeptically, "Gage told me that you came from a convent in Mississippi."

Shanna pressed her lips together and nodded. "I did. But I moved here to the parsonage when I got married. My husband passed away recently."

"And now you take in complete strangers and pray to God that I'm not some psycho axe murderer who preys on helpless do-gooders." Perceiving that her taunt had hit its mark, Tinsley smiled. "It's just like Gage to have his very own saint to take care of his…messes. How many of his castoffs have you taken in over the years?"

Shoving down the feeling of irritation at being made fun of, Shanna reasoned that hauling off and smacking the woman in the face would probably not advance the cause of Christ. "Only you."

"Relax. I'm not that bad, really. I mean, I've never murdered anyone—yet." She laughed, and an evil glint appeared in her dark eyes.

The chair scraped across the floor as Shanna stood and began gathering the dishes. "God knows that you and I are a thousand times worse than we think we are, still he stands ready to forgive us and clean us up…if we ask him." She crossed to the soapstone sink and began washing dishes. "The towels are in the second drawer…I wash, you dry."

Tinsley smiled, half amused by the cool directness of the girl. "I'm not really the domestic type."

Shanna shrugged. She wasn't about to coddle a grown woman. "Consider it payment for room and board." She raised the kitchen window a few inches, filling the room with sweet air and the swelling hum of summer insects. Snatching a dish towel from the drawer, she tossed it to her.

Time deepened. Methodically Tinsley wiped a dish. Her gaze cut to Shanna. "So why did you take me in tonight? Do you think I'm worthy of help, or are you and Gage...."

"He's my employer—nothing else," Shanna stated. "I don't judge whether a person is worthy of help, I just help and leave all that other stuff to God."

"Have you met my son, Quinn?" she asked, setting the plate to the side before picking up another one.

"Yes. He's a sweet boy. I met him briefly at the doctor's office the other day."

"Oh."

Shanna's irritation was apparent. "Nothing was wrong with him—he just had a checkup. In case you were wondering."

Tinsley dismissed the comment with a shrug. "Quinn has always been able to take care of himself. I never worry about him too much."

Shanna shook the suds from her hands before wiping them on a towel. She found little that she liked about the woman. A long silence followed.

Tinsley tossed the dishtowel on the counter. "Got a place where I can smoke?"

Bottles clanked as Shanna yanked open the refrigerator door. "Out back. Want a Coke?"

"No... just a cigarette."

The mist began its retreat, moving slowly around the cedars, caressing every textured part of them as it drifted westward. Then, the night shone like silver dust tossed into a purple sky. Shanna covered a yawn as soothing night sounds from the creek floated around them.

Tinsley tossed a pack of Newports on the patio table between them as she plopped into her seat. "Smoking relaxes me."

"Here." Shanna slid an empty candle container toward her. "A makeshift ashtray."

She lit her cigarette. "So, how long have you worked for Gage?" She took a long drag, sucking it in and holding it before tilting her head up and blowing out a stream of smoke. Pretending to be mildly interested, she picked a piece of tobacco off her tongue.

"First day."

Tinsley sat up straight. "What! You mean Gage sent me to stay with a complete stranger?"

"It appears that way, yes." Despite herself, Shanna couldn't resist commenting. "But don't worry, I haven't murdered anyone … yet."

Chapter 8

It had not been difficult for Shanna to avoid seeing Gage the next day—he'd been busy on the docks most of the morning. Questions about Tinsley were sure to come up, she had no doubt about that. Still, she wondered briefly what she would say. While it was true that a certain animosity had developed between Shanna and Tinsley, all in all her houseguest had been treated kindly.

It was shortly after noon when Shanna was told by one of the dock workers that Gage wanted to see her in his office. Putting down her mop, she wiped her hands on a towel before heading down the hall. She knocked once on the door frame and then in a soft voice inquired, "You wanted to see me?"

Gage pushed back from his desk and fastened his eyes on her. "Please, have a seat. I just wanted to say thank you for dealing with my drama last night."

Shanna smoothed her hair behind her ear and sat down, giving a small shrug. "It was fine."

He nodded, taking on a tone of understanding. "Shanna, I've heard from practically everyone around here that you go out of your way to help people. I value that. You seem to be honest, so, I'll ask you," he raised one eye brow, "what's your take on Tinsley?"

She shifted uncomfortably. "A few hours with someone is not enough time to form a good judgment about a person. I hardly know her." She felt awkward discussing a woman that obviously shared a past and maybe even a present with the man in front of her.

Gage tapped his fingers stiffly on the desk. He waited, watching her lips move silently, mouthing a few words.

"I think she's selfish and conniving and doesn't give a rip about her son," Shanna blurted out, shocking herself with the admission.

"Thank you," he said. Gage felt the same stab of hopelessness he felt that night so long ago. "Selfish, conniving—I've heard her described by those very words once before."

Somewhat stunned by his response, Shanna didn't know what to say next. Finding no words, she got up from the chair, nodded once, and left the room.

That evening, lights from the dock gave off a dim wavy glow over the oil-black surface of the water. The boat engine whined as it puffed out white smoke, growing louder through the fog.

Gage lay beside the motor working a wrench with a tight hand. "You've been watching those horror movies again, haven't you, Jedidiah?" Gage teased, talking over the noise of the engine before finally shutting it off.

"I'm tellin' you the truth, Boss. There's somethin' up at that old fish house, marsh house, or whatever you call it." Jedidiah pointed to where a tributary dead-ended and a shack stood on the bank near a wall of tall grass. "I see a spooky light in that place. That's how them haints do it…float around from room to room." He shuddered. "It ain't every night, but it's been three nights this week. That ain't no good sign."

Gage worked the tool with a firm grip then tossed it into his toolbox with a clang. "I'm sure it's nothing. Probably a beam from a lighthouse reflecting off the windows."

Jedidiah shook his head. "No, sir … that ain't no lighthouse beam."

Adjusting the cap on his head, he sat up. "I'll check it out on my way home." There was a laugh in his voice. "Go stay with Quinn until I finish up here. He's in the office. But don't fill his head with all that ghost business. It's hard enough to get that boy to sleep at night as it is."

"Want me to come with you?" Jedidiah asked, reluctantly.

"No, that won't be necessary. I'll look the place over. I'm sure it's nothing."

Shanna was mid-sentence when she heard the floorboard on the porch creaking as a shadow drifted past the window. She froze, put her finger to her lips to silence Gypsy, and turned off the flashlight. A moment hardly passed before the squeaking came back again. Then, after a long pause, a light rap of knuckles came against the wood before the front door eased open.

Shanna held her breath as the door gently closed. In the dead silence that followed, she eased down to lift a slender post from the floor and raised the column into striking position. Just as she was about to swing, her wrist was seized. She fought, wildly twisting, scratching as she struggled to gain her freedom. "Run, Gypsy, run! Get away!"

"Will you be still!" Gage yelled, and when she would not, increased the pressure on her delicate wrist. Stubbornly Shanna resisted the pain and would not give up until Gypsy tried to make her escape. Gage released

Shanna's wrist and hooked the fleeing girl with his outstretched arm.

"Let me go!" Gypsy demanded, beating his arm with her fists.

Gage turned around, not willing to turn his back on the she-cat that was trying to claw him away from Gypsy. "Will you two stop it! I'm Gage Barrington and I own this place!"

All struggling ceased with the statement.

"Where is the flashlight?" Gage demanded, as provoked with himself as he was with them. He felt around the table until he located it, then turned it on, directing the beam at the two women. His brows gathered with concern as he studied them, and with a gruff calmness asked, "Shanna … are you okay? Gypsy?"

Shanna could think of nothing that she had either done or said to give away their secret. Franticly she searched her mind trying to recall what she could have let slip. From the look on Gage's face, he seemed to imagine the worst.

"I'm perfectly fine," Shanna murmured.

He continued to study her, making no move to leave. As his gaze swept over her, it seemed to heat where it touched, making her look away.

"If you're sure you're okay."

Despite an overwhelming sense of shame and a desire to explain everything to him, she could not. She had to think of Gypsy and couldn't risk being found out. "I'm sure."

Gage neither smiled nor frowned but nodded, and handed Shanna the flashlight as he walked past her to the door. A moment later his truck lights flashed across the wall and before Shanna could think again, he was gone.

A sign reading THREE COURSE CATERING swung high on its hinges above the doorway of an old Victorian home, squeaking in the stiff breeze. Shanna glanced up the steps as the door came open and Gage Barrington came out. The corners of his mouth threatened to give way to amusement as he observed her closely. She hesitated, finding the bright eyes fastened on her. Annoyed with herself, she asked, "Out to manhandle more women this morning, Mr. Barrington?"

"Actually, that isn't my first priority," he answered smoothly. "But the day *is* young."

She didn't miss the slow spread of his smile. Pointedly ignoring him, she turned and stumbled as her foot missed the step. Immediately she felt his hand beneath her elbow, helping her along.

"I'm perfectly capable of climbing steps, Mr. Barrington."

"Let's just not take a chance, how about it." He flashed a smile, aware he was annoying her, but helpless to do anything about it.

Shanna had to admit, if only to herself, the Charlestonian had the charm and manners to handle himself well in anyone's presence. He carried himself as one born to wealth and position, yet Shanna knew firsthand that he was equally at home with a crew of roughneck laborers and more comfortable around a smoky bar room than a yacht club.

"Thank you, but I believe I can find my way from here without tripping or fainting...."

"Or attacking," he said, finishing her sentence. He held up his arm displaying bright red scratch marks of varying sizes up and down his arm.

Shanna stepped back, unconsciously clasping a hand over her mouth. "Did I do that?" she mumbled from behind her hand.

Gage nodded. "Imagine how much fun it was explaining these to my girlfriend. I trust you've had your shots."

Shanna looked away, but that didn't keep Gage from seeing her raised profile as she tried to respond with dignity. "I'm sorry. We were hiding from Gypsy's handler and you scared us."

Then a realization dawned. "Is that why you were at the marsh house ... hiding?"

Her first instinct was to deny it, but she knew she couldn't lie to the man. "Yes, and I'm sorry I trespassed. Gypsy and I were having a little discussion. I had some money for her to help her start over. I didn't think anyone would find us there. It won't happen again."

Gage nodded. "Good. You're welcome to have your discussions in the office at the marina. At least there you'll have air conditioning and Jedidiah around for protection. Although after last night, I'm considering making a lateral move and have you and Jedidiah swap positions." He twisted his lips to cover his smirk.

"Funny."

"I'm surprised I didn't find you melted in a puddle from the heat. That marsh house is stifling."

"Mississippi girls are too used to the heat to melt that easily." Before Shanna could comment further, the door behind them opened and a striking woman stepped out.

"It's all settled. Molly will have everything ready for the party. See, I told you it would be easy." The beautiful woman reached for Gage's arm and squeezed it affectionately.

Gage cleared his throat and half turned to Shanna. "Evan-Cerise, this is Shanna Muir. She works for me at the marina."

Shanna had already taken in the raven hair and dark eyes of the woman. The pale peach summer dress she wore fit her curved form well. She understood now why Gage had seemed in such good spirits. "Hello," she said, more than a little in awe of the attractive woman.

Evan-Cerise smiled. "I can't say I've ever met any of Gage's employees, but you're certainly not what I would have expected," she stated brightly. "Are you a dock worker?"

"Shanna is in maintenance, Evan-Cerise," Gage corrected. "She keeps things straight and organized. As you well know, I can't handle disorder."

Shanna's white teeth gleamed in a reckless smile. "I do my best." She hesitated for an awkward moment. "Well, I better get going. It was nice to have met you, Evan-Cerise."

"Same here." Evan-Cerise regarded the girl as she went inside the shop, her thoughts running rampant. "Do you have any other women working for you at your marina?"

Surprised by the question, Gage was slow to reply. "No, just Shanna." Usually it was only the women of Charleston's society circles that concerned Evan-Cerise. He looked at her in puzzlement and had to hold back a grin.

"Where did you happen to find her?"

"Her husband's grandfather worked for me before he passed away. I imagine she needed the job to help make ends meet with the loss of his income. She and her husband lived with him."

"Oh, so she's married?" She couldn't keep the relief out of her voice.

"No, her husband died as well, about a year ago; from injuries sustained in Afghanistan, I believe. She hasn't told me, but that's what I hear." He narrowed his eyes. "Why the interest?"

She shrugged. "Just wondering." Smiling, she hooked her hand through his arm and walked with him toward the truck. "I want to know more about what you do down here on this godforsaken island, that's all."

CHAPTER 9

Shanna swung open the kitchen door of Three Course Catering and found owner Molly Mudford busy preparing a large tray of assorted meats and cheeses. Molly was a broad woman, large-boned and somewhat fat.

Molly paused in folding a piece of roast beef and looked over her shoulder toward Shanna. "Is it time for you, already?" she questioned, tucking the meat into place on the tray. She pushed back from the counter and wiped her hands on the large white apron.

"I'm early. I wanted to get a head start on those pie orders." She gestured toward the front of the shop. "What was Gage Barrington doing here? You know he's my boss, right?"

"He's your boss Monday through Friday. I'm your boss on Saturday. And, to answer your first question, he's having a dinner party at his house tonight. And, guess who's gonna be serving?"

"You? I hope."

Laughing out loud at the girl's audacity, Molly had already come to the conclusion that Shanna was as blunt honest as any person she'd ever known. "No; as a matter of fact, that's what I pay you for. Can you see me making a fool of myself trying to tiptoe around all those high-class folks?" She pranced over to the refrigerator with her hands in the air, mockingly.

Shanna bristled at the thought of going, but knew she had no choice in the matter if she wanted to keep her job. She enjoyed working for Molly and needed the extra money. She pulled out a coffee grinder and began preparing a pot. While the coffee brewed, she stood at the kitchen sink tying on her apron and looking out at the sea.

"You might as well know: you'll be wearing a dress. That's my policy." Molly's eyes scanned the girl. "Wouldn't hurt for you to fix your hair, either. I can't even tell what you look like with all that swooping mess across your face."

"I'm not wearing heels—period."

"I don't have one thing against wearing flats."

"Good, 'cause I'm not wearing heels."

"You said that already."

"Just making sure we have an understanding."

Shanna crossed the room and lifted a bowl from a stack placed neatly on a shelf. In her opinion, you could tell a lot about a person by their kitchen. Molly's was both rigorously clean and well equipped. Peering at the counter, she read the order.

"It's not a large order, is it… what, maybe seven people?"

"Nine, and Mr. Barrington specifically asked for pecan pie. Said it was his favorite."

Shanna twisted her lips to contain her smile. "Well, I believe we can handle that."

Myra Barrington's presence in her son's home brought with it a lightness and charm not seen in the house in a long time. The atmosphere improved considerably as soft music and sea breezes blew in off the porch. Even

Gage relaxed a little, even though he had sworn off liquor since Quinn had come to live with him. Tonight, he seemed comfortable without it.

When Myra first met Quinn, she held his curious stare for a long moment. Knowing instinctively not to rush the encounter, she had not showered him with questions, expecting him to answer. Instead, she slid a piece of chocolate cake in front of him. With that simple gesture he smiled, leaving her feeling wonderfully light-headed as she stepped away to pour a glass of milk. It would take time for Quinn to come around, but she was a patient woman. Her grandson was well on his way to owning her heart.

She was in the process of ironing out table linens when the kitchen door opened and her son and Evan-Cerise came in.

"Any luck finding someone to cater on the island?" Myra asked, inspecting a napkin for stains before handing it over to Quinn for folding.

"Yep, Three Course Catering will be handling everything." Gage lifted a napkin from a stack that was folded in a French Pleat. Inspecting it, he eyed his son, "Nice job. Where'd you learn how to fold like that?"

"Mimi," Quinn answered. Sliding off the chair, he grabbed the entire stack from the table and gave them to his dad for inspection. "All but that last one."

Glancing over the work, Gage nodded. "Looks good." He mouthed to his mother over the top of Quinn's head, "Mimi?"

Myra beamed. No words were necessary to express her delight.

The moment Gage had received the results from the DNA paternity test, he went with his gut and called his mother. By the time he had hung up the phone, he felt lighter. Things were changing for all of them, and changing fast.

Just as the sun dipped and the island cooled down for the evening, Shanna walked up the flagstone path to Summer's Keep. Passing a buzzing Virginia rose shrub, she glanced around the house. Vines covered the front entry, draping partially over a window as if the bashful house were peeking at you. Sea air mixed with laughter blew from around the house and, from the sound of things, the party was well underway.

Pausing at the door, she looked back at the assortment of expensive cars parked irregularly in the yard. It was clearly a wealth-dominated gathering. For the first time in a long time, Shanna felt a little out-of-her-element.

A voice called from across the yard, startling her. "Well, if it isn't my favorite pie maker."

She turned to find Yancey walking up behind her, relieved to see his familiar face. "I'm glad to see you here."

Coming to stand beside her, Yancey held a tactful silence, smiling down at her.

"What?" she questioned, sensing mischief. Everything about Yancey seemed vibrant, except his eyes — they always seemed sad.

"I was just thinking how much my sister is going to enjoy meeting you. She likes a woman who knows her own mind and is not afraid to speak it. Birds of a feather … come on, I'll introduce you." Opening the door, Yancey led her inside.

Hearing the back door open, Myra looked up from where she'd been mixing lemonade and noticed a young woman on the arm of her brother.

"Well, hello," she said, with some surprise.

Quinn pointed over the counter. "That's Shanna. She works for my dad." He waved. "I still got my bible," he said, wide-eyed and smiling.

"Good," Shanna said, "You know, some people call it their sword."

Quinn's face brightened, obviously pleased. "I got my sword."

Yancey made the introductions. "Myra, this is Shanna Muir. Shanna, this is my sister, Myra Barrington." He knew instinctively that his sister would respect the girl. Shanna's unapologetic belief in Jesus required boldness. Too few people had that kind of nerve in the world today and Myra Barrington admired courage, especially courage that ran counter to culture.

Myra extended her hand. "I'm so glad you could join us. Tell me, Shanna, are you from the island originally? I know of a family of Muirs from here. Perhaps you're related."

"Shanna is from Mississippi," Yancey supplied.

Myra raised her brow, noticing a wash of color cover the girl's face. "Mississippi? Well, I want to hear all about your home. I've never been to Mississippi, but I've had a secret love affair with the Mississippi River since reading the works of Mark Twain." She took Shanna by the hand, attempting to lead her into the next room. "Come on out with the other guests. Gage will be thrilled to know you're here."

Shanna hesitated and turned slightly toward Yancey, as if asking for help. "I, uh … I'm here with Three Course Catering—working. The owner, Molly, is on her way with the food."

In the awkward silence, Myra felt it necessary to dissolve a little kindness and let it seep into the air. "Well, you just look so pretty I thought you were here for the party." She patted Shanna's hand before letting it go. "That's a lovely dress … the creamy color looks beautiful with your skin."

"Thank you, Mrs. Barrington. You're very kind."

"Myra … and please, make yourself at home. Gage has this *rarely* used kitchen all out of sync. Feel free to prowl around; that's the only way I can find anything, and the best way I've found to snoop."

Shanna laughed at that and it loosened some of the tightness she felt in her throat.

Myra regarded the girl, then smiled softly. "My son hasn't mentioned you. I had no idea he has a woman working for him … interesting."

"Oh, well, that's because I'm just the cleaning lady. He wouldn't have any need to mention me."

Yancey piped in, "I can say this for her: she makes the best pecan pie I've ever put in my mouth." A thought struck him. "Say, you didn't happen to bring one along, did you?"

"I just happen to have one or two. Molly's bringing them. Now," she glanced around, "I better get to work. She'll have my hide if I'm not prepared."

The evening was progressing nicely as Shanna pushed the kitchen door open with her hip and stepped into the dining room, carrying a large soup tureen. She arranged the first course of the meal, placing the rich velvety soup in the center of the table with baskets of dark crusted bread on either side.

The French doors to the porch were set wide, allowing a slight breeze to stir, flickering the candle flames. Crystal goblets sparkled in the light as soft music floated above the buzz of voices coming from outside. The adjoining living area was masculine in atmosphere and furnished by a large fireplace on one wall, sea chests for tables, and a comfortable-looking leather sofa flanked by a pair of mismatched chairs. The wooden floor looked to have been chosen to cope with outdoor life near the sea, while a large sisal rug centered the furnishings. Simple, robust ornaments like a navigational instrument, barometer, and glass floats gave the entire room a maritime feel.

In the low light of the porch, Gage watched Shanna as she went about her work, busily arranging the table.

After putting the finishing touches on the table, Shanna glanced up and saw that Gage's eyes were locked on her. In that brief look she felt her breath catch before she stepped away from the table and walked toward him. "Dinner is served." She turned, thankful to escape once more to the kitchen. But before she could get away, Gage addressed her.

"Shanna!" He got to his feet to meet her in the doorway. "This is Shanna Muir," Gage commented to his guests, as if someone had asked. As he looked at her, his words seemed only for her. "A woman of many talents. She works for me at the marina and, apparently, she's made our dinner tonight."

From his seated position on the porch, a man with deep creases in bronzed skin asked, "So, what does this Shanna Muir do for you at your marina?"

"I clean," Shanna said, unapologetically.

The man rose from his seat, laughing. "You mean the same hands that scrub your toilets, Gage, made my dinner?"

"The very same," Shanna answered promptly, not giving Gage a chance to respond.

Gage turned and looked at his friend, grounding out a warning. "Renault, be respectful. Don't abuse the privileges of a guest."

Renault slapped his host on the back. "Just having a little fun, Gage, meant no harm. Lighten-up, friend. I knew you'd get all stiff not drinking tonight."

Shanna made no attempt to move, determined to stand and face the guests, smiling as each person filed by. Evan-Cerise passed by first and smiled. Then a woman, the feminine version of Renault, along with a younger couple with fixed faces of monotony, moved toward the table. They all seemed cool and aloof, as if they were nobility, keeping themselves from the common people. Notably absent from the little soiree were Yancey, Myra, and Quinn.

Suddenly realizing that Gage had spoken to her, she glanced around. He held his eyes on her and was apparently waiting for her answer.

"I said we can start without the others. They took Quinn for a walk to the stables. If you don't mind, just keep their plates warm for them. They can have their meal when they get in."

Shanna nodded, moving toward the door of the kitchen. "I'll take care of it. You just enjoy your meal."

Renault tapped the table with his fingertips and eyed Gage. "Well, now that your *cleaning lady* has given you permission to enjoy your meal, how about telling me what's all this nonsense I hear about you leaving Charleston for good?" He looked around the table, waiting for the others to join in. "We're still business partners, after all. I'd like for you to make an appearance at the office once in a while … keep up the image. Don't forget, you're the Barrington in Barrington and Porcher."

Evan-Cerise had a weapon in her arsenal, and she was about to employ it. It certainly couldn't hurt to throw some vintage Charleston out, get the conversation back on familiar territory. "I miss our dinners at Cane Break's." Evan-Cerise adjusted the napkin in her lap. "And the guys at the Yacht Club miss you, too, Gage. They send their greetings from the Holy City."

"Ah, yes, the Charleston Harbor Rat Pack. Still holding down the fort—keeping all those outsiders out," Gage commented as he sipped his drink. "It wouldn't do to have the unaccepted slip in among the accepted."

In some exasperation, Evan-Cerise responded, "You say that as if it's a bad thing. After all, the town belongs to you, and your people and has for a few centuries now."

"We all come from somewhere, Evan-Cerise." Gage stretched his shoulders back as if something annoyed him.

Renault's wife, a small mousey woman with faded blue eyes shot through with spidery red veins, chimed into the conversation. "Be careful living here, Gage. You mustn't let yourself go all native and fall to the level of these island people."

The dinner conversation filtered through the door to the kitchen. Shanna was not used to this sort of snobbery, but had certainly heard of it. She listened to the woman with mild curiosity before turning away to fill the tea carafe. Thankful that in her circle of friends, haughtiness was practically nonexistent.

Shanna pushed through the door and glanced at the glasses of the guests and began refilling as needed.

Seeing an opportunity to draw a comparison, Evan-Cerise spoke to Shanna as she filled her glass. "Tell me, Shanna, what are your thoughts about the dangers of a person 'going native' as they say, by living around these island people."

Moving to the next glass, Shanna calmly remarked, "One of the most dehumanizing things I see in people is the way they put a price on nearly everybody. They try to determine a person's value by what that person possesses … their wealth or family name. Jesus says we're valuable simply because we are."

Gage gave her an odd quirk of a grin. "I've always admired your directness, Shanna. Especially this time."

"Truer words might not ever have been spoken," Myra declared as she came through the French doors. "What's all this nonsense about Charleston…can't you see how the island has worked its magic on my son? Why, I've never seen him more content."

"Don't get your back up, Myra. We're just concerned that Gage might forget who he is out here amongst these backward island people, that's all." Renault winked at Myra. "Your own husband had the same concern for you, if I remember correctly."

"Breck didn't want me here for the simple reason he couldn't handle me once the island had me again. He was afraid of this place. Just like you are for some reason. You may have been my husband's business partner, but you don't control me or my son any more than Breck did." Her blow had been powerful enough to make Renault stiffen. She paused at the table, trying to decide whether she would join them.

The dining room was silent, except for the sound of light laughter drifting through the still swinging kitchen door. Shanna had disappeared from the room.

Molly looked over her shoulder as Shanna entered the kitchen. "You say something?"

Shanna rubbed the end of her nose. "I'm just laughing to myself."

The plump woman chuckled and her chest bounced. "You do surprise me, girl. And who would've ever known there was a girl hiding behind those ratty jeans and tee-shirts? You should wear your hair up more often. What do they call that, that…," she made a circular motion with her finger in the direction of Shanna's hair.

"A messy bun."

As Molly studied the girl, the change seemed to have more substance than just clothing and hairstyle. She began to realize that this was a woman many of them had not really known. Her laid-back manner made her easy to be around, but something told Molly there was a lot yet to learn about Shanna Muir. "Well, I like it … just be careful not to let your looks go to your head."

After a quick head shake, Shanna said, "You have nothing to worry about there, I assure you."

"Good, now get these plates of brisket out there before they cool. I'm coming with the veggies."

CHAPTER 10

The Barrington house gradually began to settle into the quiet routines of late evening. With the guests gone, the only sounds that could be heard were of Shanna and Molly as they quietly cleaned up the dining room.

Myra had taken Quinn to bed, leaving Gage alone on the wide porch to wind down from the tension and excitement of the evening. The rhythmic sounds of the distant sea soon eased the stiffness of his body and Gage began to relax. He pulled out a cigar and bit off the tip, tilting his head as he caught the sound of a phone ringing. A few minutes later, Molly stood in the doorway.

"Mr. Barrington? Dr. Mooreland called. He's on his way over to speak with you. He asked that Shanna wait for him." Molly shrugged in response to the question in Gage's eyes.

"That's fine, Molly." He stared at the cigar in his hand. "Do you mind having Shanna make some more coffee?"

"Not at all. I'll tell her on my way out. Good night."

"Thank you, again. Everything was delicious. Oh, and Molly … there's an envelope for you on the table."

"Thank you."

Molly's eyes grew wide as she opened the envelope, bumping the swinging door with her hip as she stepped into the kitchen. "We did good tonight, little girl," Molly said, waving a few bills in the air. "Mr. Barrington is a generous man. Now, put on some coffee. Dr. Mooreland is on his way over here and wants you to wait for him." Without another word, Molly gathered her things and pulled the door closed behind her, leaving Shanna alone in the kitchen.

She pulled two cups from the cupboard and placed them near the Keurig, straightening the counter as she waited, wondering what on earth Dr. Mooreland could want with them.

Soon a flash of lights came through the window and Shanna went to the door, waiting as the doctor walked up the flagstones.

Dr. Mooreland looked up, seeing Shanna. "Where's Gage?"

"He's on the porch. What is it?" Shanna questioned, trying to keep the stress out of her voice.

"I want to talk with both of you."

Shanna directed him to the porch. "I'm right behind you, just let me get the coffee."

By the time Shanna got the tray of coffee to the porch, the men stopped talking and both turned to stare at her.

"What?" she asked, setting the tray down before casting an apprehensive look in their direction?

Dr. Mooreland spoke up. "I think Gypsy's 'handler,' for lack of a better word, came into the office today and questioned Millie. He wanted to know where Gypsy was and who brought her in for treatment. Millie unwittingly gave him your name."

Shanna's shoulders fell, and the strain of the long day and night showed in her face.

"Now, I have taken the liberty of telling Gage about our ministry and how we try and help some of the homeless locals. But this is a particularly dangerous man we're dealing with here. I think he's one of the ring leaders of human trafficking along our coast. To this man's way of thinking, we're interfering with his business. I came here to get you. I think you need to stay with my wife and me for a few days, just until things settle down."

Shanna raised her eyes and managed a smile. "That won't be necessary."

Gage reached for his cup, took a slow pull of coffee, and eased back in his chair. "You should really think about reconsidering." He saw the defiance flash into her eyes. "You're taking a risk."

"I decided a long time ago that what we do is worth the risk. It does require a fair amount of lunacy, I admit. But the Gospel doesn't rise and fall on the temperament of a human trafficker. I'll be fine." His easy manner and strong opinion was beginning to annoy her.

Unfazed by Shanna's determination, Gage asked Dr. Mooreland, "Did Millie say what the guy looked like?"

The doctor mimicked Gage's posture and sat back in the chair. "She described him as having medium height, a lean build, and a scraggly beard. And, I'm sorry to say, that's about all she noticed."

Myra stepped out to the porch. "Was this a male or a female, Les?"

"Unless the Circus is in town, Mother, I'm going with a male," Gage responded, annoyed with his mother's eavesdropping. "So I take it you and Dr. Mooreland know each other?"

"Have for many years," Myra added. "Good to see you, Les."

Deep in thought, Gage took another pull of his coffee, then said, "She needs to stay here."

Shanna snapped her head in his direction. "What?"

Dr. Mooreland looked surprised. "Here?"

Leaning forward, Gage rested his elbows on his thighs as he held up his hands. "It makes perfect sense. We're far enough off the main road that our comings and goings won't be noticed. She can blend in."

"Thank you both for your concern and your offers, but I'd rather not draw your families into my trouble. I'll take extra precaution and won't do anything foolish. Besides, I have a gun."

Quick to respond, Dr. Mooreland added, "Your judgment of the situation is lacking, Shanna. Think of Gypsy. If this man gets to you, he may well try to take you the way he took Gypsy and those other girls. The horror those girls have faced is unimaginable."

A shudder ran through Shanna as she slid into a chair, a little stunned. "I won't stay with either of you. I won't bring my troubles to your doorstep." She ran a hand over her forehead. "I'll leave the island … go back to Natchez before I'll do that. This may go away on its own. I mean, right now the guy just asked a question. Could be we're overreacting."

"No, you stay and we fight," Myra said, her Irish blood beginning to simmer just beneath the surface.

Dr. Mooreland paused. "*We* fight, Myra?"

Gage sat back in his chair. "Looks like we've just joined the cause," he stated, flatly. "If Shanna wants to go home, then I'll have some of my men posted outside her house for a while."

"I can't let you do that." Shanna got up and started for the door. "Look, guys, thanks for your concern. It really means a lot, but I'm fine … promise. If I need help, you'll be the first people I call. Just pray."

Gage's tone became sharp. "This is not the time for a little prayer, Shanna, it's time for action."

"Any time is the right time to pray, Gage. I hope you remember that," Shanna said, her voice full of conviction. She left the porch without another word, feeling his eyes on her back until she left the house.

The moon swamped the land with a toss from her silver bucket and night was well underway. The sound of tree frogs and crickets resonated on the hot night air.

Shanna yanked the damp sheet away from her body and sat up in bed, frustrated. With so much on her mind, sleep was not coming near her. She pulled at the nightgown that stuck to her skin, seeking relief from the heat. Hoping for a stray breeze, she got up and went to the window. Branches of the huge oaks swayed, sweeping the sweet night air into the bedroom. With a tightened throat she glanced around the room, seeing it with the eyes of a stranger. The small bed, dark wooden floors, and windows that had offered a pleasant view of the grounds near the stream all seemed different now. The recent threats had robbed her peace.

Before turning away from the window, her eyes caught a movement of a shadow along the edge of the woods. She pressed close to the wall, watching as the figure moved through the trees.

Cautiously she stepped back to lift the gun from the bedside table and eased to the window, lifting the curtain to get a better view. Her fingers fell, dropping the drape. "Gage Barrington," she said out loud. "What is he doing here?"

When she opened the front door wide, she found him leaning on his truck, smoking a cigar.

"You might as well come inside," she said in a low voice.

"What are you going to do with that?" he nodded toward the gun.

"Shoot somebody if I have to…but I'm glad I don't have to. Now, are you coming inside?"

"I'm not leaving until morning," he explained. "Does the invitation still stand?"

She found it difficult to think. Did he think she needed to be looked after? "It's not necessary for you stay here, but if you won't leave, you can sleep on the couch."

Gage pushed off the truck, masking a grin with his hand. "That's fine, but what will all those good church folks think when they see my truck parked here early in the morning?"

Shanna hunched her shoulders indifferently. "That you're the first one to church."

Deep laughter echoed in the night. "The day *I* go to church with you is the day *you* agree to go gator hunting with me."

"Agreed." Shanna smiled at the astonished look on his face.

He rubbed his chin, wondering why he'd been so worried about this woman in the first place. Oh, he knew someone might try to get her, but if they did, they'd bring her back—with an apology note.

He had to admit she had an engaging way about her. Or maybe the word was *aggravating,* so that women usually and men almost always accepted whatever she said without question. He had no doubt she'd march him right into church and plant him on the front row without a second thought.

"Let's call it even and go our separate ways in the morning, how about it?" he said.

"A deal is a deal."

He raised a brow. "Am I to understand that you'd be willing to go into snake-infested waters to search for alligators if it meant that I would go to church with you?"

"That's the idea. Now, come on inside and I'll fix us something to drink."

Gage paused just inside the door. "Make it strong. As crazy as this sounds, I might just have to drink my way through this." As he closed the door behind him he looked around, surveying the simple but tidy house. He remembered the faint smell of lemon oil and old wood from his previous visit.

Amusement softened Shanna's eyes. "I won't make you sit on the front row, if that's what you're worried about." She strode to the little kitchen and got out two glasses.

He dismissed her comment with a sweep of his hand before taking a seat on the couch. Pressing down, he tested the comfort of the cushions as he spoke over his shoulder into the other room. "I hear the music coming from your church sometimes. Especially this past winter. Voices carry strong through the cold air."

She came through the door and handed Gage a cool slick glass of lemonade. "I have a—"

"Pecan pie?" he finished, looking hopeful.

She shook her head. "A few petite fours … small cakes. They were left over from a little girl's birthday party," she clarified, seeing his incredulous expression.

"I'll pass on the sissy cake." He toasted with his glass. "To keeping my manhood."

She leaned against the wall, trying to hide her smirk. "So tell me, Mr. Barrington…."

Shaking his head, he interrupted as he held the drink away from his lips. "Look, now that I'm spending the night with you and everything, we really should be on a first-name basis. I know I'm older than you, but I'm not so old that I'm stiff about formality." He drained the glass, not sure why he was feeling uncomfortable all of a sudden.

"I didn't mean to imply you're old. I respect you, that's all." A worried frown crossed her face as a brisk wind rose up, moaning around the house and pressing against the door. "I believe this island wind tries to blow life into everyone, no matter how stiff they are."

He chose to ignore the "stiff" comment, as some part of him knew it to be true. And, she was right about the island. It was the home of half his blood, as Charleston was the home of the other half... the ambitious, fast-moving half. He'd come back to the island time and again for the fresh wind to stir his soul back to life.

The door creaked and popped from the push of the wind. She glanced at it as if expecting to see someone burst through at any moment. "How long have you been watching my house?"

Rubbing the rough night's beard on his face as if thinking, he answered, "This is *my* first night. Jedidiah, Dupe, and Yancey ... the last two weeks. Switching up, of course." He placed his glass on the coffee table and stretched his feet out in front of him, amused to see a temper darken her face.

"Dupe! He can't even drive yet, can he? What is he, fifteen?"

"Eighteen."

"I can take care of myself."

"So you said."

A little line of annoyance formed between her eyes.

Anxious to change the subject, he asked, "So, tell me about the creek out there. I hear it has quite a history."

She tried to ignore the awkwardness of having her boss in her home and the aggravation of having him meddle in her life like some sort of self-imposed guardian. She needed no other encouragement to relate the story.

"People from miles around come to Sassabee Creek hoping for a miracle and swearing by the water's ability to restore."

He hesitated, wondering if she might add more to the story. When she showed no intention of saying anything further, he asked, "You mean—Holy Water?"

Shanna pushed away from the wall and sauntered toward the window, tapping the cord of the blind and setting it into motion. "It appears so, yes. The story goes that a young woman found three gravely wounded British soldiers left to die. Another soldier had been left behind to bury them. The woman took the soldiers to the healing creek and they recovered, leaving the men to astonish the garrison in Charleston that had left them for dead. Since then, people have been coming to the creek hoping for supernatural help."

It was a full moment before Gage released his breath. "What a fascinating story. Tell me, do you believe in the power of the creek water to heal?"

Shanna tilted her glass in her hand and smiled. "There's a lot that's mysterious about our faith, but there's nothing magic about it. Magic breeds superstition. Some people believe that the creek waters provide them with a supernatural advantage, a source to extract power from the divine. But God can't be managed or used like that. He is a personal God, not an impersonal power."

His eyes burned into hers and it seemed an eternity before he turned away. He patted his pockets as if he'd forgotten something.

Shanna's curiosity was stirred. "What?"

"Oh, here it is. I've been meaning to give this to you." He pulled from his pocket a small plastic bag and handed it to her. "I found this in the creek when I was looking over the land. The sun came out for a split second that day and the metal gleamed, otherwise I wouldn't have noticed it."

Shanna lifted a kite-shaped metal tag from the bag, turning it reverently in her hand. The name *Charleston* was stamped beneath a small hole and under that, the number 333 followed by the word *Servant* 1844. Wonder colored her voice. "What is it?"

"A slave tag."

A hush fell over the room. After a long moment of studying the object, she returned it to Gage. "There's a sad and powerful story here. This person must've gone to the creek looking for hope. I'd like to believe he or she found it."

His voice changed perceptibly, dropping so low that she had to strain to hear it. "You can keep it if you'd like. That's actually the second slave tag I've found in my life."

Intrigued, her voice lowered to match his, sounding as soft and quiet as the touch of a feather. "Where did you find the other?" She crossed to the chair and sat, pulling her feet under her as she waited expectantly for the story to unfold.

Gage leaned back, resting an arm across the back of the couch. "My ancestors on my father's side were sea merchants. They came to this country in 1765, 100 years before the Civil War. They bought and sold Carolina Gold rice, indigo, tobacco and cotton. They also bought and sold —

"Slaves?"

He was quiet a moment, then a head-nod was his answer. "Both before and after the American Revolution. It was profitable and my family was considered the merchant elite in the early days of the American Republic. They had many slaves of their own. Those slaves maintained the house and property, worked in the fields, but the skilled laborers were hired out. Everything *they* did their master got the credit for. All the glory and wealth went to the master." His eyes trailed off, wandering to a spot on the floor.

Shanna shuddered, rubbing her arms with her hands. "That's a bondservant."

The words broke his trance and he looked up at her. "Yes, that's right," he said, a little surprised at her knowledge of the word. He began to rub his thumb over the metal for a long time, perhaps a minute, as if remembering.

"So, you found it on your property?"

"I was digging in the backyard and unearthed part of the slave tag. My father insisted I donate it to one of our museums in Charleston, but I kept it hidden until he had forgotten about it. I showed the tag to LuBelle, our housekeeper. I'll never forget the look on her face."

His words caused a conflict of emotions in Shanna as she imagined what LuBelle must've felt seeing the tag. She swallowed hard, not at all sure she wanted him to continue.

"The emotions I saw on her face that day were the same ones I just saw on yours."

There was an unspoken intention in his words rousing Shanna from her daze. "My husband called himself a bondservant. A bondservant of Christ. Everything he did he wanted God to get glory from it in some way."

The woman's answer caused Gage to sit up and tilt his head. "Tell me about him."

She took a sip of her drink, feeling the silence grow tense. "James Muir. He was a soldier and a man full of faith in God." The roof creaked against the strain of the wind and the lights flickered.

He had a fleeting impulse to ask her about her love for the man, but dismissed it. He shifted his position on the couch, leaning forward slightly. "So tell me, how long were you two married?"

Shanna ran a hand through her hair. "It never stops feeling unnatural; in one day I was both a bride and a widow. We married in the morning and by afternoon he was gone." She gripped the arm of the chair, her knuckles turning white. "I knew we'd have our challenges ahead of us, but I had no idea our marriage wouldn't last through the day."

"Had you known each other long?"

Her answer came surprisingly easy. "We met through a 'Support the Troops' program I joined at church. At first we corresponded through social media and emails, mostly. Then he came to Natchez and we dated while he was on furlough. I had never met anyone like him." Flashing a grin, she shook her head. "We connected … understood each other. I never had to explain myself to James; he somehow always knew what I was thinking."

He looked away from her, as if something pained him. "That's rare in relationships."

"Now James and his grandfather lay side-by-side in the cemetery out there. I can't bear the thought of ever leaving him." She shrugged. "I love him and I guess that's all there is to know."

His eyes dropped and he stared at the floor in thoughtful concentration for a long moment. Shanna was different from the other women he'd known. No doubt about that. Not that she wasn't pretty — she was, in a natural kind of way. But there was something else about her that he couldn't quite comprehend.

The locals understood that Shanna was the kind of person who wouldn't ignore the pain of others. Courageously acting on their behalf time and time again. He'd suspected the young woman had scars, not on the surface, but hidden deep inside. When he looked at her again, his gaze direct and unflinching, he said, "I'm sorry. I know it's painful. I won't bring it up again."

His warm, masculine voice was like a soothing balm and she relaxed a little. "Will not speaking of it ease the hurt?" she said.

"No. But when you've lost someone, it doesn't help to keep opening the wound. That only delays the healing."

"I disagree. I think you need to open the wound and get some air to it. Grief is the price you pay for loving someone … well worth the cost if you ask me. Maybe *you* should try it."

Gage pulled his head back slightly and asked, "What makes you think *I* grieve?"

"What I see in your eyes … makes me think you grieve." She paid attention to people, got involved in their trouble if they so much as cracked the door. That was something she understood about herself. But something else was telling her this particular door wasn't going to budge without a little prodding.

He swallowed hard. "Yeah, well, that's why they make bourbon," he said, hoping she would let the subject drop.

She understood him well enough, she believed, to know that he wouldn't have said it if some part of him hadn't meant it. "You must be a closet drinker. I've never seen you drink. Do you drink often?"

"I used to. Before my son came to live with me. By evening … my desire to do right and be a useful human being just leaves me. Then I tell myself the lie that it relaxes me."

"The truth?"

"I need it to seal me in when I have very little left inside to give."

She recognized the pain and felt connected to it. "Everything seems worse at night. I'm not sure why, but it's easier to bear things during the day. By nightfall, it's as if we become more vulnerable somehow."

"You sound like my mother."

"I like your mother. I'll take that as a compliment."

They seemed enclosed in their own world, as if all the trouble and conflict of their lives were outside the walls of the stone house. The wind changed. Wailing gusts blew against the house and through the open window. The curtains billowed out, making a flapping sound. Shanna went to close the window as a deafening crash of thunder boomed, rattling the panes and jarring the house down to the foundation. Rain spattered the glass in fat drops before the lights flickered, then went out.

She felt her way to a large basket near the couch and pulled out a comforter and a pillow, placing them on the end of the couch. "I guess that's our signal to hush up and go to bed."

As his eyes adjusted to the darkness, Gage pulled off his shoes, preparing himself for another sleepless night. How he functioned on so little sleep was anybody's guess. "I hope the storm won't keep you awake."

"Oh, I get my best sleep during a storm. Wild wind and rain raging outside while you're tucked safely away in your bed? For me, contentment enters the room with a wild storm outside. Let it rain. People make too much fuss about sunshine."

The lights came on and Shanna reached for her book of poetry on the small table beside her chair.

His voice cracked and he cleared his throat, pointing to her book. "You're fond of reading?"

She closed her hand tightly over the book. "Yes. This is a book of poetry, but I read most anything, especially novels. They're so much more imaginative than movies to me."

The smile in his extraordinary eyes seemed like a gift to her. She offered him the book and it fell open to a well-worn page.

"May I?" he asked, smoothing his hand over the hardcover.

"Of course. Henry Van Dyke wrote this one and, as you can see, it's one of my favorites."

Gage surprised her by reading the poem out loud. His warm tidewater accent sent shivers down her spine as he brought the piece to life.

> "I am standing upon the seashore.
> A ship at my side spreads her white
> sails to the morning breeze and starts
> for the blue ocean.
> She is an object of beauty and strength.
> I stand and watch her until at length
> she hangs like a speck of white cloud
> just where the sea and sky come
> to mingle with each other.
> Then, someone at my side says,
> "There, she is gone!"
> "Gone where?"
> Gone from my sight. That is all.
> She is just as large in mast and hull
> And spar as she was when she left my side
> And she is just as able to bear her
> Load of living freight to her destined port.
> Her diminished size is in me, not in her.
> And just at the moment when someone
> At my side says, "There, she is gone!"
> There are other eyes watching her coming,
> And other voices ready to take up the glad
> Shout,
> "Here she comes!"
> "And that is dying."

Gage gently closed the book and handed it to her.

"Thank you," Shanna whispered, then quietly left the room.

He pulled the pillow across his lap, punched a hole in the center of it, and stuffed it under his head. Listening to the steady patter of rain against the windows, his eyes grew heavy and his breathing rhythmic as he drifted off to sleep.

CHAPTER 11

There was no shame, no sense of having strayed, not the slightest feeling of regret that she'd done what she'd done. Allowing another man into her home to "keep watch" was not in her plan. There was no harm done. In fact, she'd had the best sleep of her life and she hated to admit it.

Unbidden, the words of her husband came drifting back, *till death do us part.* But for some strange reason, those words never had an effect on Shanna. Whether in life or death, parting with James had never been an option.

Dressed and ready for church, Shanna crossed the room and slid her feet into her flats. "There's fresh coffee and cinnamon rolls in the kitchen. Compliments of Three Coarse Catering—help yourself."

Gage tucked his shirt into his jeans and adjusted his belt, avoiding her eyes. "No, thanks. I need to get back."

Speechless, she just stood there for a moment before she finally blurted out, "I thought we made a deal."

"What?" He gave a half laugh. "You're still welcome to come alligator-hunting with us. We're heading out this afternoon." He noticed a flash in her eyes. "You mad?"

"I didn't say anything."

"You don't have to; your eyes do the talking."

His eyes took in the sight before him. Dressed in a yellow cotton dress with her hair pulled away from her face and held behind her neck by a crooked tortoiseshell clasp, a strange sense of rightness came over him. Something inside of him said, *This is where you should be*. And it was that particular feeling that disturbed his mind more than guilt ever could.

He willed his thoughts on a different subject, avoiding her eyes. "Go with us this afternoon and I'll go with you—another time."

"Deal."

Heat rose in intense waves above the metal roofs of Bainbridge Marina. And when the fickle breeze quieted, the tall saw grass seemed to wilt under the sun's furious beating. Boats crowded near the dock where Gage and his friend, Lynch Droke, stood squinting in the glaring sun as they inspected the sleek fiberglass watercraft.

"I'll lay it open for you," Gage said, as he peeled back the engine hatch. He swiped his forehead with the back of his arm and started to explain all the features of the new motor when he noticed his friend's attention was directed elsewhere. Glancing over his shoulder, he saw Shanna and Quinn digging in a patch of dirt near the warehouse.

Turning his attention back to the boat, Gage continued, "The gel coat on the hull, deck, and interior has been redone. I replaced the rub rail, boot-strip and CF numbers. Everything's good."

Gage had known his friend for more than half his life. Before Lynch had joined the Navy, they'd spent a lot of time together. He'd realized early on the man's weakness for women, always more of a touch-and-feel kind of sailor, a habit that had stuck with him even after leaving the service. And that, thought Gage, had been the trouble all along.

"Take her out...see how she performs," Gage said, wiping his hands on a grease rag.

"Well now, that's mighty generous of you, old friend," Lynch said, slapping Gage on the back and looking toward Shanna.

"I'm talking about the boat," he shot back, flinging his friend's hand off his back.

"Of course." He grinned, then motioned with his head toward the warehouse. "She anything to you?"

"A valued employee." Adjusting his cap, Gage narrowed his eyes.

Lynch was the guy you wanted along when things got ugly. The unexpected storm at sea, the challenge in a bar room, all of which needed experience as well as a willingness to meet the test. They'd found that in each other right along with their shared love of all things nautical. But, where women were concerned, they were polar opposites. Gage idled into those treacherous waters, Lynch met them at full throttle.

"I can say this for you, Gage: you've always had good taste in women. Seems a little young, though. Even for you."

Gage stepped back and nodded toward the boat. "When you've finished gawking at the hired help, I'd like for you to get in and check her out."

Lynch stepped aboard, steadying himself in the rocking vessel, but his smiling eyes never left his friend. "Evan-Cerise just doesn't do it for you, does she? You don't love her. You should let her go."

"What?" The critical part of his brain had told him the same thing, but hearing it from his closest friend annoyed him. "Evan-Cerise is a gorgeous woman. As if I have to explain that to you."

"Being beautiful is beside the point." Lynch threw his dart with complete accuracy so Gage could not dodge the question. "Do you love her?"

"Is there some law that states a man shouldn't value affection, a common upbringing? What does love, whatever that is, have to do with anything?"

"Well, you tried … now I guess you're going to settle." Lynch toasted with his beer bottle. "Here's to Gage Barrington, the man who settled for feeling nothing more for his future wife than the affection one has for a house pet."

Tossing the bowline across the hull, Gage clinched his jaw. "Feeling affection is better than feeling up everything with a pulse, you Jack—"

Lynch revved the engine, drowning out the reply. He threw his head back and laughed like a pirate as he eased the boat from the slip and headed for the open sea.

The lapping of water against the dock was all that was left of the vessel's passage as it shimmered in the cruel heat of the day. A few pelicans remained perched on the pilings and a long-legged crane stepped its way carefully through the shallow water, but not much else stirred.

Gage picked up his wrench and tossed it in the toolbox as he thought about Evan-Cerise. Lately, even a casual conversation with her had been strained. Had she always been so self-absorbed? So materialistic? Or a more frightening question to ask: had he? He'd begun to notice little things. Like the way she spent her time talking about frivolous things like shoes and purses. Or how she seemed to always work her praise of herself for her purchases tirelessly into the discussion. Had she changed?

He spotted his son jumping on the end of a shovel, working it back and forth in the dirt. "Need a little help with that?" he called, glad for the distraction from his trail of thoughts.

Gage was still several feet away from his son when he glanced around and saw Shanna standing by an unfamiliar car talking to a man. The man wore the black of a priest and, when he turned, he could see his white collar. In some puzzlement, he watched her tenderly place a kiss on the priest's cheek.

Quinn, seeing the direction of his father's eyes, tugged on his sleeve to hurry the digging along. "You wanna dig for worms or stare at folks?"

"Who's that Shanna's talking to?" Gage snatched the shovel from Quinn's hand and pressed his foot on the metal, turning up the soil.

"That's Father Cleo. She said he's her daddy."

Gage raised an eyebrow at about the same time Yancey walked up from behind.

Looking over Gage's shoulder, Yancey squinted. "Well, would you look at that? She's got a regulation dock worker outfit on. Rolled up sleeves, boots and everything. 'Course, she fills hers out better than most." He looked down at the dirt, then back to Gage. "You plantin' a garden?"

"No, we're diggin' for worms," Quinn piped in.

Yancey rubbed the boy's head. "Don't be forgetting your old uncle when you catch all those fish. I'd like to drop a few in Crisco Lake about sundown."

"I won't forget you. I'm gonna go get my pole," the boy said, before running off to the shed.

Yancey smirked. "I heard about your little sleepover the other night." He motioned over his shoulder with his thumb. "Had to call a priest now, did she?"

Gage halted near the end of a row and, narrowing his eyes, watched the old man closely. "You don't have anything to worry about there. That woman is only interested in my salvation."

Yancey arched a brow. "Well, now ... how do you like that? A woman interested in more than your name, your money, or your handsome Bain looks. A woman who's interested in your very soul. Sister has to hear about this!"

"Leave Mother out of it." Gage ran a frustrated hand through his hair. "Your sister needs a hobby besides my life." He stabbed the dirt with the shovel. Lately it seemed whenever he tried to rejoin his well-ordered life, a certain holier-than-thou female intruded into his thoughts, giving him more than he wanted to think about.

As if summoned by his thoughts, Shanna and the priest walked up to them. "Hey, guys, I'd like for you to meet Father Cleo. He's here visiting from Natchez."

Gage took notice of Shanna's calm and serene face as she looked at the priest. *A face concealing the heart of a warrior*, he thought. She wasn't fooling him. "Father Cleo," he said, extending his hand. "Will you be staying a while on the island?"

"No, I'm afraid not. I'll have to make other arrangements back on the mainland. But I do plan to drop by when I have an opportunity. I have a few speaking engagements in Charleston. A convention. In fact, I'm on my way there now."

Not even trying to hide her disappointment, Shanna said, "I don't see why you can't stay with me and drive over from here. It's not all that far."

Gage tugged off his work gloves. "Actually, Father, I would consider it a favor if you would reconsider and stay with Shanna for a few days." He paused, wondering if he should continue. He saw that he had the undivided attention of the priest, so he added, "You see, Shanna has… entangled herself, for lack of a better word, into the affairs of a local man thought to be involved with sex trafficking. We've been taking turns keeping watch around her place until things settle down. So far, nothing out of the ordinary has happened, but you can't be too careful."

Father Cleo turned to stare at Shanna as if stunned for a moment, then slowly shook his head. He was quick to assure Gage. "She's not as imprudent as she sometimes seems… only zealous. I'll stay a few days. In the meantime," he looked pointedly at Shanna, "you can fill me in on what you've been up to."

Shanna tilted her head, trying to hold back an incredulous grin. "Oh, you know me, Father. A little of this, a little of that."

The priest contemplated her, turned and completely ignored her to shake Yancey's hand. "And you must be the man who knows how to appreciate a good Mississippi pecan pie. Shanna's told me all about you."

Yancey clasped the man's hand and gripped his shoulder. "That's right, Father. I keep tellin' the girl she can make a fortune around here with that recipe. You come by my house, we'll have a good Lowcountry boil. And, if these boys have any luck, we'll have a few fish to go along with it. What do you say, Father?"

Gage spoke up. "My mother is visiting and she'll get to tell all her friends back in Charleston that she entertained a priest for the weekend. It will be scandalous and she'll love every minute of it."

"I'm due for a good scandal!" Father Cleo said, slipping his hand into his pocket, jiggling change. "But I'll have to take a rain check. I'll be spending much of my time in Charleston."

There was something about the drowsy little fishing island that was not too different from the way it must've been a hundred years ago. It was timeless and simple and maybe even a little haunted. Shanna rubbed her arms as she waited to board the johnboat, not at all sure what she had gotten herself into.

A white egret posed motionless on a piling as the johnboat bobbed in the wake of a passing shrimper. Further out, a craft with billowing white sails rose and fell with the waves, capturing Shanna's attention.

"Pretty, isn't it?" Gage said, seeing the direction of her attention. Then taking Shanna's hand, he helped her step into the boat, directing her to the center seat facing the rear of the boat. He could smell soap on her sun-warmed skin, lavender mingled with some sultry spice.

After handing Quinn the fishing gear and an ice chest, Gage got in and, once the boat became stable, started the small outboard motor. The water swirled and churned from the boat as he eased them to the middle of the creek.

"This is going to be tedious for the next little while but trust me, once we get out of this bay and start up the creek, the rewards are worth it," Gage said.

After a while he noticed a landmark and killed the motor, sliding out a paddle.

The intensity in which Gage viewed life, the sheer focus on his surroundings, was unsettling. He didn't talk a lot but he looked at everything, noticed everything in his line of vision and to a deeper level than most.

Passing through the soft sway of cordgrass, they ventured farther away from the sea as the johnboat entered Sassabee Creek. The mouth of the creek opened into a wider stretch of water where bald cypresses towered overhead. An osprey took off from a low-lying limb, skimming the dark water as he passed underneath its weathered branches.

Just beneath the glittering surface of the water, a long, dark, ghostly shape of an alligator appeared. The gator never surfaced but glided lazily beside the boat. Gage kept up his steady, leisurely paddling, not looking to the right or left but smiling at Shanna's widened eyes as she focused on the reptile.

She trailed a hand through the water, though somewhat cautiously, avoiding his amused stare. But the deep chuckle coming from his chest was the final straw. Feeling an urge to interrupt his musing, she reached over and smacked the water, sending a spray across his face.

He was startled slightly as water splattered on his face. Opening one eye he peered at her beneath his cap.

Quinn covered his mouth with his hand, holding in the laugh as he watched water trickle down his dad's face.

Gage made no move to wipe it away, but continued to stare at Shanna as if he considered what to do to her.

"You asked for it, Dad," Quinn said, serious now in defense of Shanna. "You was laughing at her for being scared of gators."

"Were," he corrected.

A small snide smile twisted Shanna's lips as she looked him in the eye. "I don't handle being laughed at too well. Call it a character flaw."

"Glad to know you have a flaw. I never would have imagined."

No matter how calm the voice, his eyes held a strange confidence that unnerved her. *He's not going to be simple to handle,* she thought. Although he was well mannered, not just on the surface but shot all the way through, he also had an infuriatingly controlled response to most things.

"Hold still—both of you. Don't—move—a muscle." The deadly calm of Gage's voice caused immediate obedience.

The boat drifted as Gage gradually lifted the paddle, easing it into striking position, then smack! He struck the surface of the water with enough force to ricochet the sound through the air, startling birds into flight. A heavy spray of water fell across Shanna, soaking her shirt. Sheened with creek water, she pulled her damp shirt away from her body and stared at him incredulously.

"Water moccasin. We're good," he said, before adjusting his cap and sliding his hand down the paddle as he casually pulled it through the water. He averted his eyes a minute before taking a quick glance back at her.

The two sitting in front of him sat frozen. Shanna, half turned, as if to flee, while Quinn held on to the sides of the boat. The wide-eyed stares and open mouths were too much for Gage's composure and his roguish grin gave way. "Just kidding."

Shanna clamped her mouth shut and faced him. The sun had darkened his skin to a deep tan and his eyes seemed to shine all the more as the lines around his eyes crinkled. He looked handsome and manly—alive. The pleasure on his face astonished her and she couldn't hold on to her anger in the face of such expressive joy.

"You scared at least a year off my life," she said, matter-of-factly.

He threw his head back and laughed. "That just means you'll get to heaven quicker, doesn't it? Thought you'd be glad about that."

Shanna looked different, he thought. Little changes that somehow made her seem more real, less saintly.

It was good to see this side of her and know that some things in life were still capable of surprising him.

Quinn's lips pursed. "I ain't never seen you do that."

"What? Tease?" Gage asked, skeptically.

"No, laugh and have fun."

"Well, we're all still getting to know each another, aren't we?" he said, jolted by his son's observation.

To discover he had a son had been a shock to Gage. To learn of his father's cover-up, even more of a shock. The whole affair had been tidily cleaned up like an unwanted mess. Tough to swallow for a man who, at the core of his being, believed strongly in his family. Now, he realized, he'd been given another chance. Maybe now he could shake the restless unhappiness that had trailed him like the hounds of hades most of his adult life.

The boat glided along the passage where the trees hung over the water, leaving only a shaft of light at the top of their lacy branches.

Gage pointed up to where the limbs came together, almost joining. "You can navigate down the middle of this creek by following the light and staying under that line — or, for a more memorable experience, by moonlight."

Shanna could feel the redness wash up her neck into her cheeks. She was certain the comment had been nothing but casual conversation. Still, he was looking at her intently and she was sure he'd noticed her embarrassment, so of course he knew she was reading something into his words.

"You'd have to be crazy to do a foolish thing like that," Quinn said, scratching a mosquito bite on the back of his neck. "You'd never catch me out here on the water at night... too many things can happen to a person in the dark."

Shanna sat there trying to make herself seem very comfortable. She glanced around, not knowing where to look or what to say, but Gage was kind, and he tried to ease the situation.

"I suppose that's true, son, but one sailor a long time ago had a very different experience on Sassabee Creek. He navigated up this creek one night in his canoe and as he rounded the bend for the first time, he said, 'If a man can see this wonder in the moonlight without losing a heartbeat or two, that man has no romance in his soul.'"

"What kinda sissy sailor said that?" Quinn asked.

"Well, it certainly wasn't Blackbeard," Gage stated, noticing Quinn's eyes round as moons. Ah, now he had the little man's attention. "Blackbeard's real name was Edward Teach, and he was one fearsome English pirate captain."

"You knew Blackbeard?!"

Shanna twisted her lips to contain her smile, then looked over her shoulder.

The lines on Gage's forehead deepened. "No, I was always too busy working to ever meet the man." He continued, "Blackbeard used to weave these slow-burning fuses in his dark beard and hair and light them. They would smoke and burn and scare the daylights out of people. He flew a black flag on his ship with a skeleton on it to intimidate opposing ship crews into surrendering without a fight. And, most of the time, it worked. It's been said that Blackbeard chose little out-of-the-way places like Sassabee Creek to hide his treasures."

Now, totally enthralled with the story, Quinn looked around then let out a rush of words, "What happened to him—Blackbeard, where did he go?"

"Well, he captured a French merchant vessel and renamed her Queen Anne's Revenge. She had forty powerful guns on her. He ran the Queen Anne aground on a sandbar near Beaufort, North Carolina. He hopped off and settled down for a while … even married a young local girl."

"Naww," the boy said in disbelief.

Gage saw Quinn straighten in his seat. "As a matter of fact they've discovered the remains of the Queen Anne's Revenge recently and have recovered all sorts of treasures from her. They're all now at the North Carolina Maritime Museum in Beaufort."

"That's where I'm from! Oh, man, do I wish I could go there."

"Come to think of it, I've been meaning to check that place out myself. Maybe we should go. That's just what we should do." A sense of pride filled him as he watched a smile spread across his son's face.

"Can Shanna go, too?"

"Of course!" He let his eyes drift over and settle on her. "If she wants."

"I wouldn't miss seeing Blackbeard's treasure for anything in the world," she replied.

CHAPTER 12

The early morning sunrise was cool through the mist as the dock swayed gently beneath Shanna's feet. An old fisherman, deeply lined from years in the sun, set a crab pot at the end on the pier. He worked thick calloused fingers through a weighted net, squinting as he eyed the rosy sky as Shanna quietly passed, making her way to the marina office.

Terrapin Island was like a place she'd had in her mind all along. A shadowy vision of sea and inlets, gentle winds and easy rhythms that had lingered in her thoughts since early childhood dreams and imaginations. But this morning, she was not so sure the island was the safe haven she'd always thought it to be.

It was six o'clock in the morning and Bainbridge Marina was slowly stirring to life. Pushing through the moisture-warped door to the office, Shanna was met with the slight scent of Bay Rum cologne. Glancing up she saw Gage, shirtless and standing in front of the sink in the bathroom splashing cologne into his hands. He slapped it on the sides of his neck and the green, spicy clove scent permeated the air.

"Oh, hey," Gage said, looking over his shoulder before snatching his shirt from the towel rack, "I didn't hear you come in."

"Bay Rum?" Shanna asked. The spicy notes were strong, but they played well together. She'd learned from other days that when it dried down it mellowed nicely.

He faced the mirror, rubbed a nick with his finger. "My grandfather, Broder Bain, used to wear it. Guess I wear it to keep the old man around, sort of feels like a natural part of the landscape."

"I bet they used to haul that in from the Caribbean when the rum, sugar and spices arrived on these shores. Three hundred years ago."

He cocked an eye at her through the mirror. "It does kind of evoke the historic trade days of the Carolinas... glad you noticed." He studied her, catching the slight Mississippi drawl that sometimes appeared when she was upset. "What's wrong?"

"What makes you think something's wrong?"

"Because your chin sticks out when you're bothered by something."

"I'm fine." After a brief scan of the room, she went to the closet and began pulling out her supplies.

Gage shrugged, snatched up his hat, and headed for the dock.

An old rope fender nudged the dock as Shanna reached the boat where Gage was working. He'd been pumping out water from the boat since the break of dawn. Recent rains had flooded the craft, but the owner paid extra to see to it that his vessel was in tiptop shape for his excursion later in the day.

As she watched the play of muscles roll along his arms and across his back, she sensed an annoyance. He was mannerly to the core, but he wasn't nearly as tame as he pretended to be. There was something raw and determined about Gage Barrington. She warned herself to respect it. He wasn't what she had been used to, as men go, but Shanna was finding herself admiring the man, even if she wasn't quite sure about him. Oh, she knew that Southern men from Virginia to Texas could be wild and unpredictable, but most of their mamas raised them to be polite.

Gage stopped the pump and glanced around, noticing Shanna. She looked fresh and young in denim capris and a crisp white blouse. Her appearance caught him off-guard; he couldn't remember ever seeing her so, so … did she change clothes? Seeing the distress on her face, he questioned, "Is everything alright?"

She nodded her head, but didn't speak.

He tossed the pump aside and maneuvered toward her, extending his hand until she clasped it. He felt the trembling in her fingers as he pulled her up into the boat.

Hesitantly she looked at him, seeing concern in his eyes. Her own began to take on fear. Brushing a hand across her cheek, she spoke. "Father Cleo found a note last night."

He took a deep breath and looked at her. "A note? What did it say?"

She swallowed hard, then stared up at him with uncertainty. "It fluttered down from the ceiling at my house. It says, 'Make your home in me, as I make mine in you. John' and then there are some faded numbers after that."

"May I see it?" he asked, tapping the paper she gripped in her hand.

Handing him the note, she sat down on a cushioned boat seat and watched his face for his reaction.

He examined the paper in a shaft of soft light, then questioned, "You say this came from the ceiling?"

She nodded. "And it's signed—John. Who is that?" she asked, realizing she had spoken with desperation in her voice. "Do you think it's the man that's looking for me…Gypsy's handler?"

He smiled and showed her the note. "It's a scripture reference. John 15:4. My grandmother, Lilly Rose, wrote this. It's her handwriting. She tended to put things down in plain language. I think you'll recognize it best as 'Abide in me, and I'll abide in you'. I know that one because she made me memorize it one summer before I could take out the canoe."

"You mean she put that sticky note on the ceiling beam in the parsonage—on purpose?" she asked, in astonishment.

He shrugged his shoulders. "Don't expect me to explain Lilly Rose. But the best explanation would be that it probably blew in somehow and landed on the beam, sticking there."

"So, did your grandmother go around writing random scripture verses on paper, tossing them to the wind?"

"Probably," he said, without smiling.

"Well, in that case I'm relieved. I don't know why I got so worked up about it. I'm probably going to be leaving soon, anyway." She blew the hair out of her eyes.

He cocked his head at her. "What? Why?"

"We're getting a new pastor at The Prayer House. He'll need the parsonage."

"I see." Gage's thoughts tumbled over each other. "Well, speaking of Lilly Rose, would you like to see her old home? It's not far from the parsonage, just across the creek and up a small rise. It's near the stable. You're welcome to it. It's just sitting there on the backside of Summer's Keep going to waste."

"What? You mean you're offering me a place to stay?"

"Yeah, that's just what I'm offering. After work we can drive over, let you look around. But don't get too excited. It's been sitting there empty for a while now. The last time I checked on the place, the garden had almost claimed it."

When they got to the garden house later that day, the sun was disappearing behind a gnarled oak. The soft light shimmered on the moss which hung like a gray shawl draped over knobby shoulders.

A plethora of scents and colors began reviving Shanna's senses as she stepped out of the truck. *An hour spent here would wake up even the weariest of souls,* she thought as she brushed her hand against the soft petals of wild primrose.

The low iron gate separated the order of the lawn from the riotous profusion of climbing vines and greenery of the garden. She moved through the gate, her fingers trailing lightly over the cool curve of iron. She felt the need to touch everything around her. Glancing over her shoulder, she noticed Gage who had stopped near the gate, his arms crossed over his chest, grinning.

"Where is the house?" she asked, in some confusion.

He pointed, directing her attention toward the garden.

Turning, she scanned the area twice before she glimpsed it. It was almost hidden behind a dense patch of wild grass and flowering vines. The blue frame of a large mullioned window first came into focus, and then the lines and curves of the house began to appear, as if the shy little cottage had come out of hiding. Flanking the door were tall shutters that had lost several teeth and hung crookedly from their hinges.

"Oh, my goodness!" She took a deep, steadying breath while she took in the sights around her.

The garden house occupied the prettiest and quietest part of Summer's Keep with a nice view of the slow-moving creek beyond. Feeling her curiosity grow, she asked, "Did your family use this house?"

"At one time, yes. We put up guests here. That is, until Lilly Rose decided she wanted to make it her permanent residence after my grandfather passed away." He brushed away a cobweb as he worked his way down the path to the door.

Shanna toyed with the charm on her necklace as she studied the house. It didn't seem dead, only abandoned, neglected, as if waiting for someone to step in and take on the job of bringing order out of the chaos. "Tell me about your grandmother."

"Some say she was a saint, others, a mystic." He shrugged. "Whatever she was, she was all of that here." He gestured toward the shady side of the garden house. "That was my favorite spot as a boy. Lilly Rose used to pretend not to notice me so she wouldn't have to tell my father where I was. She'd look up from her gardening once in a while and her green eyes would do this weird kind of thing … sort of wrinkle into kindness." Reluctantly, he added, "She died here … is that going to bother you?"

"If death bothered me, why would I choose to live near a cemetery?"

He caught his remark before it escaped. "That's not what I meant. Would you be afraid to stay here? Would the idea of living in a place where someone had passed away frighten you? A place where ghosts or memories, or whatever you'd call it, are thought to be."

"Why are you telling me this?" It was as if the once-solid ground under her feet had suddenly turned to water. Her hopes began to sink.

"You'll hear it in town sooner or later. You might as well know what people are saying."

"Really?" She turned back to look at the house. "People don't have anything better to do than make up stories about somebody's grandmother?" she said, her voice raising an octave. "What could they possibly say?"

"Well, the latest story circulating is from two teenagers who were up the road parking one night. They said they'd been there about ten minutes or so when they saw Lilly Rose and another figure walking up the sandy road before disappearing into the woods. Said he knew it was Lilly Rose because of the easy swing of her stride. My grandmother had a unique way of walking; everyone who knew her would recognize it."

Eying him skeptically, she said, "I'm not afraid of a story some teenage boy tells his girlfriend. Just let me know the price."

He looked at her keenly. "Don't let me upset your moral balance, but I really just want to help out a friend. Is that so hard to believe?"

Shanna nodded her head and made a sort of humming sound. "Humm.... Mmm...."

"Well... that's just sad."

Why did this infuriating man constantly throw her off balance, and so effortlessly? "It's just... well, I'm not used to *friends* offering me anything without something in exchange."

"Sounds like you need to pick better friends." He reached past her and cleared the overgrown Jackson vine from around the doorframe. Turning the knob, he kicked the door loose from its tightly held frame and pushed it open. "But if you insist on paying... you can feed my horse, Ole Tar. He's over there in the stable. You can clean up this place, make it livable again."

"Deal. I'll clean out the stable, too. I'm good at it."

"Look at my face. Do you think I'd let you do that?"

Shanna pressed her lips into a firm line. "Look at my face—do *you* think I'd stay in a house without paying my way?"

Frustrated, Gage said, "We'll talk about it later."

She came in after him, the overpowering scent of dried herbs and old roses hung thick and heady in the small space. A lovely square table sat near the blue window. *Why am I trembling?* Running a hand over the smooth surface of the wood, she glanced out the window. The view was charming, yet more than that. It felt familiar somehow. "Did your grandmother know James?" She had no idea why she'd asked that question.

"She did." He diverted his eyes. "You think this may work out for you?"

Off limits, she decided. She wouldn't push it, and dropped the subject for the time being. "I'll certainly give it some thought." Her gaze fixed on the creek in the distance, tapping her fingernail against her teeth, thinking about the possibilities. "The bridge down there, is it safe?"

"It's solid. I take Ol' Tar across it on our rides. Why?"

"I like the idea of being near James." Thinking about her words, she added, "I don't mean I think he's actually there, of course." She looked at her hands, speaking without looking up. "I just like the idea of knowing I have family ... close by."

Though he had suspected Shanna's interest in the garden house by the way she'd responded to his offer to see it, the real possibility that she may choose to live in it danced a chill up his spine. Still, something seemed to be pushing Gage, driving him. He felt it. He tossed his keys in his hand, wondering about it. Then, with a final catch of his keys, said, "Well, the offer stands … whatever you decide is good with me."

"I've decided. I want it."

"Great! We'll see about getting you moved."

CHAPTER 13

Terrapin Island dozed beneath a white hot sky. During the course of a day, the weather could change from 102 degrees in the shade to 20 degrees cooler after a downpour. The town was peppered with tourists, scurrying up and down the tree-lined sidewalks, hurrying to eat their lunches and make their purchases before the next storm rolled in.

Shanna wandered down Main Street, sipping an iced blackberry tea as she peeked into the shop windows. Rounding the corner, she spied a turquoise door wearing a yellow wreath of dried flowers. A woman smiled at her from the display window where she was arranging fancy soaps in a silver bowl.

Finishing off the rest of her tea, she tossed the cup in the trash before pulling open the turquoise door. She heard the tiny sound of a tinkling bell as the fresh scent of a citrus candle wafted past her. Her eyes flitted around the shop, taking in the colorful boxes and bottles that held fragrant oils, lotions, and bath gels.

"Well hello, Shanna!" a woman called from behind a rack of thick towels.

Looking around for the owner of the voice, she discovered Evan-Cerise, her cool demeanor even more pronounced in her white linen suit. Evan-Cerise's eyes dip slightly as they took in Shanna's faded jeans and cotton shirt. For the first time in a while Shanna didn't feel self-conscious of her appearance around the gorgeous Charlestonian. She knew she looked and felt like an ordinary small-town woman; someone who had a couple of jobs and a house to keep. A woman with a life. And that was just fine with her.

"Hi, Evan-Cerise. This place smells wonderful. I've never been in here," she said, taking in all of the many toiletries. "Do you come here often?"

"Whenever I come to the island, this is my first stop … it's my favorite bath shop. Gage is waiting for me at the bookstore. He wouldn't be caught dead in here," she said, and then her look turned serious. "Uh, Shanna." Her voice dropped to a whisper. "I've been meaning to ask you something: does Tinsley show up at the marina often?"

Stalling for a moment to collect her thoughts, she replied, "I've seen her a few times, but not all that often."

Evan-Cerise's eyes shifted at the thought. "Sorry, I didn't mean to put you on the spot. I know as an employee you're not at liberty to discuss your boss's business with just anybody. I care about him, that's all, and want what's best for him. Tinsley has never been good for him." She shrugged. "He just doesn't see how she really is."

"I understand," Shanna said, sensing the love the woman had for Gage.

"Well, I came in here for something that smells like lavender and verbena. Gage asked for it specifically. They just so happen to carry a full line of products with that scent."

"Good choice. Those have always been favorites of mine." She stepped away. "It was good talking to you and seeing you again, Evan-Cerise."

"Same here."

After the woman left, Shanna browsed around the small shop, sampling lotions and fragrances from bars of soap. Picking up a square of lavender and lemongrass soap, she waved it under her nose. "Oh, this is definitely it." Reaching the counter, she placed two bars down to be checked out. "Can you please place these in separate bags?"

"Would you like them wrapped?" the woman behind the counter asked. "We have a nice little mesh wrap that's pretty."

"That would be nice, thank you."

"I couldn't help overhearing; you must work for Gage Barrington." The woman glanced up from the package she was wrapping to smile at Shanna. "You must be good at whatever it is you do for him down at the marina. Patience with women isn't Gage's strong suit," she said, in a tone of familiarity with the man. "I've known him for quite a while."

Shanna took the backhanded compliment in stride. "I can clean with the best of them. As for any other skills, I leave that sort of thing to the professionals." She glanced down at the soap, noticing the meticulous way the bar was being wrapped.

Not to be so easily dismissed, the young woman added one final stab. "I knew your husband, James. We went to school together. In fact, we were once … oh, well, that doesn't matter now, does it. Let's just say we were about as close as two people can get."

The bell on the door tinkled softly, but Shanna remained stock still.

"We all thought it must've been a powerful blast from that roadside bomb to have left James in that pitiful condition. You can imagine our surprise to hear he was getting married — I mean — in the shape he was in … hardly able — "

"You can still thrust the dagger with the best of them, can't you, Jill," said the unmistakable voice of Gage Barrington from behind them. "Gossip is still the breath of life to you, it seems."

Shanna's chin began to tremble as it jutted out defiantly, making words impossible. Her shoulders tipped in a shrug as she inhaled, fighting to stop the mistiness that was beginning to affect her vision.

Overhearing the harsh words hurled at Shanna, anger swept Gage with torrential suddenness. "I'm surprised you're still in business with that serpent's tongue of yours." His eyes never wavered as they rested coldly on her. "What do you know about love—nothing. Trying to understand it will only frustrate you."

Gage was defending her! Shanna straightened her back and did her best to smile. "I changed my mind about the soap," she said, her voice trembling with emotion. She hurriedly moved past Gage toward the door.

Stopping her with a light touch of his hand, he asked, "Are you okay?"

She nodded once, then the bell on the door tinkled softly as she left the shop.

Once outside, she took in a deep breath of sea air and made her way down the brick sidewalk to the familiar Victorian house belonging to Molly Mudford.

The sun was streaming down in bright rays from an azure blue sky as American flags popped and snapped in the breeze all along Main Street. Shanna stepped around the corner and onto the cobblestone side street where Molly's house came into view. Once a ship captain's house, it was situated grandly on a small rise in front of the boat harbor.

To the agony of conservationists, the town's ramshackle waterfront had gotten a much needed makeover recently with the restoration of several shops, cafés, and the newly renovated Bainbridge Marina. But the old world style of the tiny fishing island remained intact. Terrapin Island was seldom thought of as a tourist destination, but no one could argue that to sea-loving people, the secret of her charm was getting out.

Under the cry of seagulls, Shanna felt rather than heard the creaking wooden boards under her feet as she stepped across the porch. With her hand on the doorknob, she hesitated and turned to look down the street. She spotted Gage talking to Evan-Cerise. *Why did he come to my defense?*

Gage seemed to take an unusual pride and interest in most everything associated with the marina — make that everyone. He knew how many boats were in the slips and which ones were missing. He watched weather reports and would navigate out to warn unsuspecting boaters to keep alert. In the heat of summer when the temperatures would soar, sudden thunderstorms, black and savage, could pop up to wreak havoc on unprepared boaters. More than once Gage had had to head out for coves, creeks, and inlets to help stranded boaters or offer escorts back to safe harbor.

She considered the man as he stood talking to Evan-Cerise. He wore jeans, faded to white around the knees, and a denim shirt with sleeves rolled to his elbows. His shoulders were broad, and his arms were the color of butternut stain. From the picture she'd seen of Breck Barrington, Gage had inherited his father's good looks — the firm mouth, strong face with manly creases, and blue eyes that could go broken-ice cold in a matter of seconds. A fact she had just witnessed firsthand. She watched as he kissed Evan-Cerise on the cheek before stepping toward his truck.

Pushing open the door to Three Course Catering, Shanna stopped abruptly. Molly stood in the foyer, her massive arms set on her hips while a sharp frown distorted her face.

"What? I'm not late. It's not even noon yet," she said in the tone of a petulant teenager.

The woman's foot began tapping out a tempo. "I hear tell you're gonna move into Lilly Rose's garden house up at Summer's Keep. Is that right? You know it's haunted, don't you?"

"Good gracious! How did you know about that? I just decided yesterday!" Shanna informed her, throwing her hands in the air. "This place beats all. Who told you? I'm curious. *Who* could possibly know *that*?"

"I do," answered a distinctly masculine voice coming from the direction of the front room.

Shanna shot a quick glanced over her shoulder. Leaning against the doorway was a solidly built man wearing jeans and a t-shirt with a cap pulled down low over his eyes. In a rough way, he was rather handsome. Thick chested and tall, the man had a distinctive dark mole below his lip. Beneath the brim of his cap, short wisps of dark brown hair curled upward.

"And you are?" Shanna asked, mimicking Molly's stance. He looked vaguely familiar.

"Lynch Droke," he bowed forward, "at your service." He gave a wide devilish grin.

His roguish smile unsettled Shanna as she exchanged a confused look with Molly.

"I'm here to help you move," Lynch said, answering the question neither woman had asked.

A thought suddenly struck Shanna. "Oh, Gage must've sent you!" Visibly relaxing, she goes on to explain to Molly. "The new pastor will be moving into the parsonage soon and Gage has offered me the use of the garden house. That is, until I decide if I'll be staying on the island."

Molly shook her head slowly. "Don't start that again. Lordy mercy—I already told you once! You're *staying!*"

Sliding his hands into the pockets of his jeans, Lynch gave a brief nod. "When you two ladies finish arguing, just point me in the direction of the parsonage. I want to get started before it gets too late."

Embarrassed, Shanna was quick to respond. "I'm sorry, Mr. Droke, but...."

"Lynch."

"Lynch. You see, I wasn't expecting you and I haven't had time to pack my things." She pushed her hair behind her ear and smiled. "If you wouldn't mind, can you give me until tomorrow? I know tomorrow is Sunday—I don't want to pull you away from church services or anything. In fact, I'll be going to church in the morning...."

He straightened, interrupting her. "Well then, I'll just go to church with you. We'll move afterwards."

Shanna stopped, looked up, and arched a brow toward the man. "Excuse me?"

"If you don't mind ... that is. I'll need lunch afterward if I'm going to work."

"Oh! Don't worry about that; I'll fix a lunch for you," she rushed to assure him.

Lynch shook his head. "No, ma'am. That'll be just that much more to clean up. We can drop by The Iron Gate Café after church. I'm partial to their chicken." He winked at Shanna as he pushed off the wall. "They have a pretty good strawberry pretzel salad from what I hear. I bet you'll like it." And with that said, he turned and left the house.

Yancey fished a hand in his front pocket and, drawing out a business card, handed it to Gage. "There's a man here to see you. Says he's the Norwegian and he's come to build the seawall. Said Lynch sent him."

Gage studied the card, flipping it over in his hand to read a brief note scrawled on the back. He made no comment, much to his uncle's disappointment, and pushed up from his chair.

"Where you going?"

"To see this Norwegian."

Yancey reached back into his pocket and pulled out a stick of gum. Folding it in half, he slid it into his mouth. "Don't make the mistake of shaking the beast's hand." He chewed contemplatively. "He nearly cracked my knuckles!"

As Gage approached the Norwegian, he noted the man's appearance from a distance, thinking he looked like one of those wooden figures of a seaman you could buy at any souvenir stand along the coast. "Let's see what the old seadog has to say," he said to himself.

The Norwegian stared at Gage as he walked toward him, unblinking. He removed the pipe from his mouth, stuck out his hand to meet Gage's ready handshake.

"I'd like to know right off if you can guarantee the new wall will withstand the fiercest storms and last another hundred years," Gage said, smiling at the face as rough and worn as leather. It seemed to him as if he could see the wild Atlantic toss about in the old man's pewter eyes.

There was a gruff pride to his voice as he answered, "I've been battling that old woman out there for forty-three years. Haven't won a battle yet. She always gets her way."

"That may be true," Gage murmured, pausing beside the crumbling wall. "But I hear from Lynch you're used to giving her something to think about."

The old man chuckled deep as he puffed on his pipe. "That I do, sir. That I do."

"When can you start and what shall I call you?" He tapped the business card against his palm, looking around. "Have you seen Lynch?"

"Next Monday, Nor, and no. I haven't seen Lynch since church let out this morning."

Gage's head shot around and he squinted at the man. "Church?" He'd never heard the words "Lynch" and "church" in the same sentence.

Nor pointed with his pipe. "The Prayer House." He struck a thoughtful pose. "You know; it always strikes me at how so many of our hymns have a nautical theme. The pastor called out the name of the first song and nobody even needed the hymnal in front of them."

What was Lynch up to, Gage wondered, as he half listened to the Norwegian recite the lines, *In every high and stormy gale my anchor holds within the veil.*

"Do you know what those words mean—within the veil?" Nor asked.

"Um…no." Gage scratched under his cap, looking around for any sign of Lynch. He knew his friend well enough to suspect he was up to something.

"It's where the very presence of God is. I don't know much about that temple they talk about in the bible, but I do know that the curtain of the temple was torn in two, top to bottom, when Christ died. That veil used to separate us from God. Christ changed all that." The Norwegian smiled ponderingly. "And to think we get to live *with* God every day. Us. Common everyday folks." He briefly cast his eyes upward as if sending up a silent prayer before ambling off to his truck.

Has everybody on this blasted island sipped the Kool-Aid? Gage thought.

As a boy he remembered listening to his grandmother, Lilly Rose, talk about the sermons from The Prayer House. But it was his father who had refused to allow his son anywhere near the church. "They're a peculiar people with strange ways and customs. They practice Gullah black magic," Breck had said. All his father's objections seemed only to stir Gage's own boyish curiosity.

Once, when Gage was visiting his grandmother, he had wandered down the rutted road to take a look around; see for himself what all the fuss was about. The visit had been something of a disappointment to him. Totally unmarked by a sign of any kind, the church's loose and peeling boards threatened to expose the skin and bones of the place. He'd found the doors wide open and a single soul of what he assumed to be the pastor inside, standing behind the pulpit and practicing his sermon. Gage had quietly slipped into a pew unnoticed.

"Whatsoever you do to the least of my brothers — you do to *me!*" The preacher shouted, mopping his glistening forehead with the back of his hand. "That aint' hard for nobody to understand now, is it? What you do to others is what you do to *The One* who saved you from an eternity of separation from God. And through the finished work on the cross of Calvary, *His* blood ran red and *your* sins washed white! Hallelujah!"

There had been a vase of wildflowers on a small table in front of the pulpit. A low humming ceiling fan had scattered dried petals across the wooden floor, and the pages of an opened hymnal rustled under the draft. Gage's presence in the church had gone unnoticed by the preacher, as if the old man had been whisked up into some ecstasy, unmindful of the fallen world.

With a shake of his head, Gage turned his mind back to Lynch. He imagined his friend's dour face as he halfheartedly sang out the old hymns like a funeral dirge. Smiling, he said to himself, "I hope it was worth it to him." He was still thinking of his friend and laughing to himself when Evan-Cerise pulled up.

"I came by so you can take me to lunch," Evan-Cerise said, flashing a bright smile as she slid her sunglasses to the top of her head.

"Best idea I've heard all day. Scoot over, I'll drive."

Moments later Gage and Evan-Cerise walked through the sea-air rusted entrance of The Iron Gate Café. They were led to a small table on the quiet side of the patio, overlooking the water where colorful boats bobbed lazily in the current.

Taking the menu offered by the hostess, Evan-Cerise playfully teased, "You must love this place. It's becoming a habit on my visits." She looked over the menu with a certain amount of boredom before snapping it shut. "With all the new restaurants popping up, why do we always end up here?"

"Because nothing is more tranquil than the reassuring sound of the sea lapping at the sides of these old boards. Close your eyes," he said. "Now, listen. Can you get *that* just any ole place? Sit back, unwind, and let the peaceful mood take you."

"Well, well, would you look at that!" Lynch said as he sat his glass down on the table and leaned back, grinning. "A couple of reprobates out trying to beat the good church folks to dinner."

The peace of the moment was suddenly shattered by the comment coming from the deep gravelly voice he'd know anywhere. Gage turned and saw Lynch and Shanna seated in the far corner of the patio.

Shanna smiled, reached over, and grabbed an envelope from her purse. Placing her napkin on the table, she slid from her chair and crossed the patio to her boss' table. "I just want to say thanks. Lynch is going to be a tremendous help with the move." She looked at Evan-Cerise who seemed distracted, digging around in her oversized purse before pulling out a small bag.

"This is for you," Evan- Cerise said, handing Shanna a small white embossed bag. With elbows on the table and her hands sliding together, she smiled. "Gage told me what happened in the soap shop the other day. I will *not* go back there again. That was rude and tasteless. These soaps are from a little place near my home in Charleston. I hope you enjoy them."

"Oh, thank you! What a kind gesture." She lifted one from the bag and took a deep sniff. "Lavender and verbena… my favorite!"

"I thought I remembered you saying that," she said, a smile of satisfaction on her lips.

Shanna extended the envelope toward Gage. "Let me know if this is not enough to cover it." She winced slightly as she put pressure on her foot.

Gage waved off the envelope. "What happened to you?" He stared down at her slender sandaled foot, noticing a dark red blotch veining up from the heel.

"I caught my shoe in the crack of a board down by the bridge. My foot twisted and came out of my sandal. Must've picked up a splinter."

Gage could feel his temper rise, covering over his easy mood. "It looks infected!"

Shanna shrugged. "I'll have Dr. Mooreland look at it."

"You're lucky you just picked up a splinter," Gage growled.

"What's that supposed to mean?"

"It means you've got a real talent for drawing the dregs of society." He got up from the table and brushed past her, heading toward Lynch.

"That's because the same God who flung the universe from his fingertips is the very same God who cares about the dregs of society!" she called to his back.

Stopping in mid stride, he gave himself a minute, then turned around slowly and walked back to her. "You know, maybe God has that job all lined out for somebody else. Somebody," he scanned her willowy frame, "a little more intimidating." He saw the temper flash into her eyes — hotter than he'd expected.

"Let me clear something up for you," Shanna said, pointing her finger at him. "I do what I do because I care what happens to people and I want to make a difference in their lives. It's as simple as that. And, just so you'll know, I don't see a *blasted* thing wrong with that either!"

He hadn't meant to insult her, but he saw quite clearly he had. "No need to get all upset. I didn't mean to offend you. I just don't understand you."

She swept her hair behind her ear, kept her eyes focused on his. "Is it so hard for you to understand that I could care about someone else and try to do whatever I can to give them a little hope?"

"Yes, I guess it is."

"Well, that's just sad," she said, using the very same words he'd once used on her. Her tone was flat, final. She slapped the envelope out in front of him again.

"What's this?"

"I'm paying for Lynch."

"Oh — for the love of ... I don't want your money. And I sure as heck didn't give him to you." Anger was simmering on low just beneath the surface. "Take what you think you owe me and give it to your bridge people." His scowl deepened as he returned to his table, yanked back his chair, and took a seat.

"Ah ... you finally get it," she muttered as she tapped the envelope against her palm. "There's hope for you yet." She maneuvered toward Lynch, leaving Gage to stare after her.

Evan-Cerise folded her hands sedately in her lap and looked up to find Lynch escorting Shanna from the patio, a somewhat devilish expression on his face as he paused by their table.

Lynch covertly winked at Evan-Cerise, then whispered to Gage. "I think they're having a Civil War reenactment in the harbor Saturday night. Better make sure the horn works on your boat so you can run alongside and cheer. I hear there's even going to be cannon fire this time." He turned to Evan-Cerise. "It's been known to bring tears of appreciation to the old man's eyes."

A tick of annoyance developed in his cheek. Gage leaned toward his friend and began to lecture as if to a bad-mannered child. "The person who can sail into Charleston Harbor without feeling overwhelmed by the history has no sense of history at all! I would even question his patriotism. Good thing you got out of the Navy before they discovered that about you. You'd have been court-martialed!"

Lynch threw his head back and laughed. His reverberating laughter echoing across the patio. Slapping Gage's back, he headed toward the door.

The comment came shyly, hesitantly from Evan-Cerise. "That was nice of you to hire Lynch to help Shanna move to Summer's Keep."

"I did no such thing," Gage replied, glaring at the back of his friend's head. He watched him walk out of the café with his hand resting lightly on the small of Shanna's back.

After their meal, Gage and Evan-Cerise drove back to the marina. As if to add insult to injury, Gage spotted Tinsley hovering near the doorway of the office. He didn't want to deal with her today, or any day for that matter.

Getting out of the car, he turned back and leaned in to give Evan-Cerise directions. "Go on to the house. I'll see what she wants."

"Do you think you ought to…?" Evan-Cerise began.

"Yancey's bringing Quinn by in a minute. I'll finish up here and come on home." He leaned over and kissed her.

Tinsley smiled as Evan-Cerise drove off, pleased as she stood aside to allow Gage to enter the office. She leaned into him, just the faintest touch of her body against his, then followed him inside.

"We're all together at long last," Tinsley said, her heels tapping on the floor behind him with each step.

Gage looked around the room, spotting Quinn behind Yancey's desk. "Where's Uncle Yancey?"

"In back." Quinn motioned with his thumb toward the breakroom. "Bathroom. Said his coffee kicked in."

Tinsley sat on the corner of the desk near her son. "You've done well for yourself, Gage. It's obvious you're where you need to be. I'm happy for you." She slid her hand across the desk, fingering a pen. "I wish I were as sure about where *we'll* end up." She glanced at Quinn, giving him a sympathetic smile. "Hopefully someplace nice like this."

Gage caught the intent of her words, and it stiffened his back. He glanced at Quinn and watched as his son's eyes went to slits.

"Leave me out of your plans," Quinn said, then raised his arm to shield his face as Tinsley flung the pen across the desk toward him. It bounced off his arm and landed on the floor.

Gage jumped forward. "You better rethink it, Tinsley."

Quick tears sprang to Tinsley's eyes as she widened them. She dabbed at her tears and sniffed. "He gets me so upset and I just lose it. I know he doesn't understand, Gage. I was hoping maybe you could help him understand. He's just a boy and doesn't know why I've had to live like I do. Whatever troubles we've had in the past, we can put them aside and support each other now. That's what I want more than anything…another chance to be a family. You've just got to see that I need help from you."

Something in the way she said it, so desperate, so self-seeking, made him stop. A chill ran up his spine.

The tears were streaming down her face now. "If you can't do that, I'll just take Quinn and go. We won't bother you anymore." She slid off the desk and made an attempt to leave. As she started for the door, she motioned for Quinn to follow.

Gage's legs were weak as water, but he stood on them. Seeing the panicked-stricken face of his son brought everything into sharp focus. A steadiness he did not feel overcame him and he walked to the desk, pulled open a drawer, and took out a pad. Scrawled a number on it. "That's my number. Call me in a few days and we'll talk. Give me some time, Tinsley." He took her arm and walked her to the door. "Leave Quinn with me while I think on this. I'll come up with something…promise."

"Okay, Gage." She ran a slow hand down the front of his shirt. "I'll call you…later," she said, shutting the door with a soft click.

He had to sit down. Running a hand through his hair, he leaned back in the chair and let out a steady breath. He relaxed a little as Tinsley's car sent a reflected flash across the windows as she pulled away.

Once his mother was out of sight, Quinn moved to the door. "I'll wait for you in the truck." When his dad didn't respond, he questioned in a low tone, "Are you okay, Dad?"

"Yeah…just thinking." Something gripped in his gut. Gage felt physically ill.

The boy nodded. "I hope you can think real good." Quinn looked at his dad intently. He wasn't sure what he was seeing in the man's blue eyes, but whatever it was, it was scaring him. "Don't you worry none about me—I can take care of myself. She ain't never around no way. If she takes me, heck, I'll just get away again. Done it before."

Gage rose, crossed the room, and went to the compact refrigerator where he took out a bottled water. He gulped it down before speaking. "No, son, that won't be necessary. You aren't going anywhere."

Chapter 14

Far out to sea, a squall line gathered like an ever growing mountain range, roiling and collecting darkness against the eastern sky. The low rumblings were all but ignored in the Monday busyness as each person at the marina went about their duties. Soon, the light would be swallowed up, hampering the daily routine.

Gage rolled the truck to a stop outside the office of the marina. He got out and walked to the passenger side to open the door for Evan-Cerise. He helped her from the vehicle as if knowing the protocol involved in escorting someone of royal blood.

Everything about Evan-Cerise spoke of a privileged life: the cut of her hair, the understated clothes, the minimal but expensive jewelry. And, most of all, the dignified way she carried herself.

Shanna found herself drawn to the woman, and for some odd reason that God only knew, she liked her. Stopping mid-swipe down the front of the vending machine glass, she watched the pair through the reflection. A small laugh slipped from her mouth, drawing the attention of the couple. She cleared her throat, gaining control of herself as she continued tidying up the outdoor refreshment area.

"Did I miss something?" Gage noticed Quinn who was sitting Indian style on the ground organizing his tackle box. His attention shifted to Shanna.

Shanna faced him, imagining the eyes behind his dark lenses were studying her. She knew them to be intense, direct, and at the moment, probably irritated.

As if on cue, Quinn piped up. "Yeah, Dad. Everybody knows Evan-Cerise don't like your truck none. She's just being nice riding in it."

Gage's attention shifted to Evan-Cerise. "Is that true?"

Evan-Cerise licked her lips before speaking. "It's not that I don't *like* your truck…it's just awkward getting in and out of it."

Squinting from the sun, Quinn looked up at Evan-Cerise. "I heard you tell Lynch that you hated that truck 'cause it smelled like gas and fish and dirty rope. You said I prolly got bugs in my hair, too, and I ride in that truck." He wiped his nose with the back of his hand. "I remembered that 'cause it was funny."

Evan-Cerise turned several shades of red before Lynch walked up and changed the subject. "Did you call the restaurant about tonight?" Lynch asked, looking pointedly at Gage as he wiped his hands on a rag.

Primed by the jolt of what he had just heard from his son, Gage responded, "It's all been arranged. Except your date, of course. And that, as usual, might take some persuading or involve an exchange of money somewhere along the line."

"Oh, I have a date," he said, grinning.

Gage looked surprised. "Good. What time is she due back at the massage parlor?"

Shanna crossed her arms in front of her and shot Gage a look of annoyance. "That's one job I *don't* have on this island."

Gage's mouth gaped open: that was the last thing he'd expected to hear. "You—and—Lynch?" he stammered.

Lynch winked at Shanna. "It took some convincing, but like I told her, life is too short to miss out on Harbor Grill's blackened amberjack."

Feeling suddenly uncomfortable, Gage looked at his wristwatch. "Well, then, guess we'll see y'all tonight. Come on you two—Quinn," he placed his hands on the boy's shoulders and squeezed. "Try and keep your bugs to yourself, will you, son?"

The boy shrugged under the pressure of his Father's grip. "Awe, Dad, what's the fun in that."

A century's worth of wood soap rubbed into the grain of the floors of the Harbor Grill Restaurant gave the place a sense of permanence. The Temptations crooned the words, *it was just my imagination,* and the soft and rhythmic sound floated on the air. The room felt suspended over the sea as the rippling surface of Charleston Harbor cast quivering reflections through the dimly lit room.

With Shanna at his side, Lynch led her by the elbow as they walked across the dining room. They spotted Gage at a corner table near the window. In the low candlelight he could see that his friend had shucked his tie and suit coat and rolled up the sleeves of his white shirt. Except for the narrowed eyes, Lynch thought he looked as cool and confident as he'd ever seen him.

Gage stood up, reaching for his friend's hand. "I see you bathed for the occasion." They were like two war buddies, linked by their past.

"I think the occasion warrants it," Lynch said, sliding a chair out for Shanna and grinning wickedly at his friend.

Gage winked a hello to Shanna and scanned her lavender dress, noticing how the color made her complexion glow. "You're lovely," he said. She wore a single teardrop pearl necklace that rested against her golden skin. It was as if he were seeing her for the first time and he marveled at how often he'd felt that way around her.

She gave a brief nod of thanks and smiled.

Lynch glanced over the room. "Your date cut out on you already?" Loosening his tie, he looked over his shoulder and spotted Evan-Cerise, sighing his relief. "I was beginning to worry we'd have to put up with all of your ancient war stories again. Looks like now we'll at least have a shot at a decent conversation."

Shanna glanced up, admiring Evan-Cerise as she strolled to the table. You could almost imagine her twirling a parasol and batting her lashes when she flashed her coy smile. She was a true Southern beauty.

"Sorry I'm late," Evan-Cerise said, leaning down to kiss Gage's cheek. "Renault caught me just as I was leaving the office ... loaded me down with papers for you to look over and sign. He said you ran out on him too fast. They're about some big takeover he's working on."

Gage stood, pulling out her chair. "Sounds ... hostile."

Evan-Cerise saw the muscle tighten in his jaw and dropped the subject.

The evening progressed nicely as light-hearted banter was exchanged between the three friends. Lynch was boasting about his navigational skills in all forms and bodies of water.

"So how do you know where the rocks are?" Evan-Cerise asked, a slight v appeared on her forehead between her eyes.

"I don't," he bragged. "I know where they're not."

"What about Lynch Rock?" Gage leaned forward and whispered across the table to Shanna. "If you're a sailor, it's not a good thing to have a rock named after you."

Shanna smiled, noticing Gage's bright eyes. *Why can't blue eyes just be blue. Why do they have to practically sparkle?*

They'd covered topics ranging from business to boats and now the conversation seemed to be leading into literature.

Smiling occasionally, Shanna listened as they discussed their passions. She missed James. And the longer she sat there, the more she missed him. She had a sense of being away from her tribe. A misplaced feeling that made her want to slip out without being noticed. She calmed herself by lightly swaying to the honey-smooth voices of the Chi Lites singing, *Oh Girl, I'd be in trouble if you left me now.*

As the plates arrived and the table grew quiet, Gage noticed Shanna's distance. Her eyes hazed over like the blue smoke of memory. She wore tiny pearl earrings, he noted, when she tucked her hair behind her ear and studied her plate. "So, Shanna. Did you know that Evan-Cerise is an avid reader of poetry … like you?" he said, cutting into his blackened fish.

Startled to be drawn into the conversation, she responded, "Oh?" She took a sip of tea, her throat feeling suddenly dry.

Evan-Cerise flipped her hair over her shoulder. "I worked hard for my degree in literature, even though I don't really use it. But yes, I love poetry. Some of my favorites are well known, but I like just as many of our local poets right here in the Carolinas. We're known for our creatives in our part of the world. None compare, really. Even the music we're listening to now is called Carolina beach music." Evan-Cerise straightened herself proudly in her seat. "Tell me, who do you consider to be good: someone from … Mississippi?"

Shanna was pricked by the woman's rather haughty attitude. To her way of thinking, Evan-Cerise stood in need of a good yank off her high horse. "Oh, well of course we have Elvis, William Faulkner, Tennessee Williams and such, but one of my *favorite* poets is from right here in the Carolinas."

"Well, I'm not surprised," Evan-Cerise said. "Who? Or, better yet, recite a line or two for us if you can and I'll see if I can guess." She smiled, rubbing her hands together in obvious delight.

"Well, okay, I'll try." She looked up to the ceiling, mouthing the words as she collected the poem in her thoughts. "'If Id'a seed you was coming, Id'a knowed what to do, Id'a rizzed both arms, and Id'a wove at you'."

The sweet tone of her voice and the soft smile on her lips were such that a long moment passed before the full impact of her words sank in. Lynch choked and gave up all thought of containing his laughter as he threw his head back and roared. Evan-Cerise sat confused, missing the joke.

Gage considered the young girl over the rim of his tea glass, then raised it to her in a toast. His voice was rich and, with his tidewater accent, drawled, "Well spoken. Personally, I've *always* been a fan of Earnest T. Bass." He flashed a wide, charming smile.

Evan-Cerise's eyes showed confusion as she tried to make sense of the poem. She glanced at Shanna where her attention was drawn to her braided bracelet. "Is that a Gullah bracelet?" she asked, deciding to change the subject.

"I don't know. Jedidiah gave it to me. He said it was made of sweet grass."

Lynch pointed with his fork, chewing his amberjack. "That's a Gullah magic bracelet. Meant to protect you from evil."

"Oh? I didn't know," Shanna said, casually and unconcerned.

"It doesn't seem to be working," Gage muttered in his glass. At Shanna's questioning stare, he gestured with it toward Lynch.

A smile broke across Shanna's face. "There's not an evil bone in this man's body." She tapped Lynch's arm. "In fact, I've found him to be a perfect gentleman."

"Here now," Lynch interrupted. "You'll ruin my reputation as a blackguard."

"Tell me, Shanna," Evan-Cerise said, dabbing the corners of her mouth with her napkin. "What is a typical service like at The Prayer House? I've heard a lot of different things about the church over the years. It will be interesting to hear your perspective."

"It's different from the churches you're probably familiar with, where you have this one-way lecture from a pastor to the congregation. At The Prayer House it's more relaxed and the pastor gets more of a response from the people of the church."

She lifted her brows and nodded, scooping up a fork full of shrimp and grits. "My father would always forbid me to go to places like that on the islands… I guess that's why I'm so curious about it."

"There are still plenty of superstitions around the islands from what I see. All that haint blue painted on ceilings and doors, that's just folklore. Only God can protect you from evil spirits." She lifted up her wrist, displaying the bracelet. "He made the grass and also the hands that formed this bracelet."

Evan-Cerise knit her brow. "So, Gage tells me that you help a lot of those bridge people. How do you think you make a difference in their lives?"

"I love them, pray for them, help them however I can. That's how it works. It's the same for anybody. But it's easier to help people who have difficulties. They have a better chance of receiving it."

"Why is that?" she asked.

"They recognize their need. They know they need help." Shanna's expression was regretful as she sipped her tea. "Usually someone from a privileged life doesn't recognize a need at all. They have more money to throw at their problems ... to try and fill the emptiness with things that never satisfy."

Gage gave her a curious look, like she had spoken to him in Cajun or something.

"I want to visit your church sometime," Evan-Cerise said.

"Oh, you'll like it," Lynch said. "They sing out — raise the roof with their voices!"

"Will you take me, Gage?" she asked.

Gage started to shift uncomfortably in his chair so Shanna answered instead. "You can be my guest, anytime."

Quinn Barrington was nothing like his mother from what Shanna could see. She paused with her broom to observe the child as he sat at a high table sorting boat keys by number.

It was hard to ignore those eyes; they were as intense and unsettling as his father's. There were secrets in them too, she recognized that. The pain and wounds of childhood she knew all too well. As Quinn looked up she saw it, a quick glint of fear in his baby blues before he lowered them again.

She pushed the broom into the corner, sweeping out a tiny pile of dust. "Why don't you ask your dad if you can go home with me for a while? I need some help with a little weeding."

"Depends."

"On?" Shanna asked, waiting for a response from the boy.

"On if you got ice cream."

"Is that the price you're asking?" She planned on getting to the heart of the matter with the boy and if ice cream would do the trick, ice cream it would be.

"Yep—that's my price."

"Well, don't just sit there, go ask your father."

An hour later Quinn was knee-deep in weeds and underbrush. He crawled his way beneath a thick butterfly bush and began yanking out weeds, tossing them behind him.

A door slammed and a pleasant humming drifted through the air as Shanna made her way down the garden path. She saw two spindly legs sticking out from under a bush.

"Looks good," she said, noticing a scattering of dead grass and weeds behind him. She held firmly to a slick glass of lemonade.

The slim boy backed out from underneath the shrub, stood and hitched up his pants. He sucked his cut finger and then shook it. "That lemonade for me?"

"None other." She handed Quinn the glass. "Well, it's obvious you've done this kind of work before. I bet your mother made you work in her garden, too."

The boy took a big gulp of lemonade, swallowed hard, and wiped his mouth with his sleeve. "That woman ain't never even been to no garden. All she's been to is a bar." He handed the glass back to her.

Shanna felt a pang of pity for the young boy but did her best not to let it show. Lowering herself onto a bench, she pointed to a patch of dandelions near an old crepe myrtle.

"I ain't goin' nowhere with her neither. Don't care what she says." He snatched up a handful of dandelion leaves and threw them down with force before moving to the next one. "We ain't no stinkin' family." A hint of tears shone from his eyes as he spoke. "Never been around for no more'n a day—don't even care that I got first place in pull-ups on the monkey bars at school."

Shanna controlled her emotions only slightly. She knew Quinn needed to get it out. Tucking her hands under her legs, she sat still and listened as he talked on for several more minutes.

Abruptly the uncertain boy stopped, as if searching for something to say to hide his embarrassment. "If this is good enough, I'll take that ice cream now. I better be gettin' on home."

"You've earned it," Shanna said, getting up and walking over to the boy. "Quinn," she pushed the hair from his forehead, "you're going to grow up and be as good a man as your father...maybe even better." She rubbed his head.

Quinn stared at her, then turned his face away to hide a grin. He was devoted to Shanna, and so wanted her attention that he seemed to find a way to spend every waking moment that he could around her.

Even if all the troubles hadn't been worked out, Shanna felt good that Quinn had been able to voice his fear and frustration to her. It seemed with every handful of weeds torn from the ground, another misery spewed from the little guy's mouth.

Then a dread dropped in Shanna's stomach. Deep down she knew it was only a matter of time before demands would be made and threats imposed for a financial settlement. Quinn would be used as a means to get what she wanted. Something had to be done before that happened. Gage had to be warned.

Gage thought of Tinsley's threat as he stepped out of the shower, giving his damp hair a rub with a towel. He ran a hand over the stubble on his face, choosing to ignore it as he jerked on loose cotton pants and grabbed a shirt off the bed, pulling it on as he headed toward the kitchen.

A knock on the door startled him and he turned, hurriedly buttoning his shirt. "What the...." He looked through the glass seeing Shanna as he pulled the door open. "Hey, come in. You're back early. Is everything all right?" He looked around. "Where's Quinn?"

"He's coming. Everything's fine." She stood in front of him and smiled softly. "We need to talk."

He swept an arm toward the kitchen table. "Look, if it's about the other day...."

"No. It's not." She slid into a chair and waited until Gage sat down across from her.

He gestured toward the refrigerator. "Can I get you something to drink? Eat?"

"Oh, no thank you," she responded, annoyed that his good manners were taking away some of her steam and getting in the way of her purpose for being there.

"I make a pretty mean grilled cheese sandwich if you're interested." However casual his tone, there was a keen awareness in his eyes.

"I'm here to talk about Quinn."

"Quinn?" He looked toward the door as if expecting him to come through it at any minute. "Do I need to occupy him so we can talk?"

"That might be a good idea."

"I'll get him. He's probably checking on that dog … the nameless one," he said, then smirked.

Ten minutes later Gage walked back into the kitchen, shaking his head. "Bonanza reruns. It's marathon night," he said. "He's good for at least an hour." He dropped into the chair and faced her.

Gage's eyes caught hers and held her in a grip as firm as any tight hold. She sat fixed to the spot. Swallowing hard, she said, "It's probably out of your scope of experiences, but it's not out of mine, so I'll say what I think, if that's okay."

"You have the floor."

Shanna rubbed the cool surface of the table with her hands. "I believe Tinsley is using Quinn to blackmail you into giving her money; a great deal of money. Once she gets it, she'll disappear again until the money runs out. For Quinn's sake, you may need to take legal action. He's afraid. Afraid of being forced to leave you … afraid mostly of having to go away with her."

As he started to speak, a cold dread swept in. He knew she was telling the truth. The thought of Quinn being afraid; his security and peace threatened, choked his words.

Shanna pressed on, "The boy is a pawn in her game. A way to extort money from you. And, since you seem to have an unlimited supply of it, she'll clamp down on you until there is nothing left. She'll leave when that happens and take Quinn with her."

Gage felt tired, as though he had a slow leak of blood. "You've got the idea that since I come from what you consider a privileged life, I'm incapable of seeing the vile side of people. But you're wrong." Unconsciously, he placed his elbows on the table and rubbed his forehead with his fingertips. "I've seen greed up close. I've seen how the love of money can corrupt a good person. I'm not blind, Shanna, nor stupid. I have to admit it's hard to believe Tinsley has changed so much. One look at Quinn when she's around convinces me she's not the same person I remember. I appreciate the warning *and* your concern. Quinn thinks a lot of you. Thank you for being there for him."

The moan of a saxophone lamenting on the air filled in the silence. "Coltrane?" Shanna asked, keeping her eyes on him. She was beginning to regret causing the man more grief. It was becoming clear to her that Gage Barrington was nobody's fool and the pain he felt was bone-deep.

"Grover Washington, Jr.… You like the sax?" It was then he noticed she wore a cotton blouse the color of faded indigo. Two silver bracelets jingled at her wrist as she pushed back her hair. She smelled of lavender and everything about her at that moment relaxed him.

She sat back in a slow, deliberate motion and lightly rubbed her arms. "I like that… it's soothing."

"Would you like to add anything more to your warning, or have you said your peace?"

"That's all." She made a move to get up.

"Don't go." He waved her back down. "Would you like that drink now?" Noticing her reluctance, he added, "Tea or lemonade… or both mixed together. I think they call that an Arnold Palmer."

"That sounds nice, but I need to go. Father Cleo will be coming back from Charleston soon. If I'm not home when he gets in, he'll call out the National Guard."

Gage took out his phone and handed it to her. "Give him a call, see where he is. Tell him where you are."

She tucked her hair behind her ears as she reached for the phone. "Are you always this bossy?"

"Only when I'm desperate. It's been too long since I've had a decent conversation."

Shanna tapped her finger on his phone. "You should use one of these more often. I'm sure there are plenty of women back in Charleston just waiting for a call from you. I know of one in particular." She punched a number, waited for an answer, and began chatting for a few moments.

Gage watched her face, the way her eyebrows lifted, the way her lips curved to the side as if suppressing a grin. When she handed the phone back to him, he shook his head. "Sorry, I'm lousy at eavesdropping. What did he say?"

"They must have a few smooth talkers over in that Holy City of yours. I can't believe it, but they've convinced him to dine out with a group from the conference. He'll be awhile." She leaned back and hooked an arm over the back of her chair. "So, I'm all yours. What do you consider a decent conversation? Books? Boats? Battles? Or boys?"

"All of the above." For a brief moment he let his gaze wander over her in a curious fashion. Though she had worked for him for months now, he'd hardly noticed her. As he considered her, he pursed his lips. There was little he could do about that now, still it didn't sit well with him. He should've paid more attention to someone like Shanna.

She gave a wry smile. "I'm familiar with the battle of Vicksburg. Want to start there?"

He leaned toward her slightly and whispered, "Why don't we go out on the porch? A storm is brewing. It's a slow mover … that usually means a good soaking rain and a lot of thunder. Then you can enlighten me."

"I'm sure you'll be enthralled." The chair scraped against the floor as she stood up.

Working with Gage she'd learned a few things about the man: his love for books, boats, and a good ominous storm. There seemed to be nothing he liked better than to watch a thunderhead gather and move over the island. He could smell a squall coming from miles away. He knew storms, knew the island; the fickle moods of the flatland rivers and tidal creeks, but there was one thing he didn't seem to have a clue about—his need for God.

"Need some help…," Shanna's words were drowned out by a jarring clap of thunder and she jumped.

He handed her a glass. "I can spike this if you need something to soothe your fears." He grinned, seeing her lips twist.

Ignoring his comment, she approached the porch.

The promised scent of rain wafted through the open French doors. No matter the activity at the Barrington house, all were done in style and comfort. She hovered near the doors and her eyes swept the outdoor room. Shining black cast-iron benches with large cushioned pillows surrounded an oversized antique table. Tall shutters flanked the doors, giving the space an elegant, refined feel as soft jazz floated above the low rumble of reverberating thunder.

Coming to stand beside her, Gage directed her to the far corner of the porch nearest the house. "That spot will keep you dry the longest, unless the winds pick up, then we'll just get sprayed. I believe it was Bob Marley who said, 'Some people feel the rain, others just get wet.' Which are you?"

"Hanging around you, I'm learning to feel it," she quipped.

As they sat down a wind rose up, bowing the limbs of the trees, tossing them to and fro in gusts of salty air. It was a coming together of warm and cool, dark and light, dry and wet. Flashes of lightning illuminated the trees, silhouetting their thrashing forms.

He inhaled. "Is there anything more exhilarating than this?"

Shanna paused a moment. "Oh, yes...."

He turned to her, and in a low voice barely heard over the rain, he said, "Then I want to know it."

The air was charged and Shanna's heart seemed to slam into her chest. "I was thinking of my husband," she said, over the rise of the wind.

Gage was silent, and then it was as if he were coming back from a long way off. "You must have really loved him."

She rubbed her arms, feeling the dampness sink into her skin. A gust of air pushed across the porch, banging a shutter against the house. "I did and I do."

His strong voice echoed around her. "Losing your husband on your wedding day...well, there are no words for a tragedy such as that."

She sampled the tea he'd made for her and it was then he noticed she wore no rings. He wondered why. She had exquisite hands. Working hands, but lovely and useful. The silver bracelets rested against the smooth skin of her wrist. Her fingers were delicate and her nails bare, free of polish and clean, short, functional. He tried to image that hand with a professional manicure, red or blue polish and fake tips, her fingers dripping with diamonds. He shook his head, dismissing the image. He liked her hands bare, he realized, and wondered if more women might not be more alluring taking their cue from Shanna.

Her head angled. "You haven't really lost a person when you know where they are. I know where James is; I just miss him. But thank you."

"I admire your faith, your courage. You have the kind of courage it takes to cause one person to stand up for another. That's rare."

"Don't get the impression I'm not afraid sometimes." She set her jaw. "It's just that some things are more important than my fear."

"And, of course, you're right…well spoken." He raised his glass to her.

"I get all courageous whenever someone tries to intimidate me or someone else. I'm stubborn that way, or stupid that way. Whatever else it is, I own it. Just don't confuse stubbornness or stupidity with bravery. My husband was a brave man." She ran a finger around the lip of the glass.

Gage leaned in to follow the conversation over the sound of pelting rain. "How so?"

"For a soldier to follow a course of action to a known end, that takes courage. What I do is nothing beside that. James was not without fear, but he was noble in his trembling."

He thought about her words, admiring a man he'd never known. Then, changing the subject, he asked, "Are you from Natchez originally?"

"Noble. It's a small river town about 30 miles north of Natchez. The town was named after our home place, Noble Hill; it kind of grew around it. My ancestor, Glen Noble, was the first one there. He was a Scotsman. He was also a cotton farmer, but before that, he fought the British with Major General Andrew Jackson."

He shifted toward her with keen interest. "In the battle of New Orleans?"

"Yep, that's the one. After the war he visited Natchez with Jackson. That's where he met his wife, Shanna Solene." She felt the corners of her mouth tug upward. "I was named after her."

"So, how did he acquire lands to the north of Natchez? How did Noble Hill come about?" he asked, shifting his body so he faced her.

The genuine interest Gage seemed to have in her family's history startled her, so she told him. "Shanna Solene's family had the connections. They knew about the land opportunity from an advisor and used it as a means to keep their daughter close by. At one time," she said slowly, thinking of it, "Noble was a bustling river port. In fact, an old dirt carriage road leads from the house down to the river where there's a loading dock. There's an abandoned brick building on the property that sits just under the hill. It used to be an inn for riverboat travelers."

"So, is Noble Hill still standing?"

"It's still standing. Needs work, but it's home to me. I feel I belong to it … at least I used to."

For some reason he thought of Shanna's husband, buried not too far from the garden house's doorstep.

"These days there's not much in Noble to go back to. The town dried up once the riverboats stopped hauling and the railroads took over. The river still has a lot of traffic, though. Mostly from barges. There's a lumberyard up river near Port St. Joe that keeps the barges busy, but for some reason it bypasses Noble. That wasn't always the case."

He stared out at the night, the rain coming down in a liquid curtain of gray as his mind wandered. "I'm familiar with the lumberyard, on paper anyway." He thought about how not too long ago there had been a time when he would have laughed in the face of anyone who would have dared to suggest that a dirt road country girl from Noble Mississippi would hold his interest so completely. "Do you still have family living there?"

"A few cousins live around the area. My parents died young. I was raised by my grandmother. We never really had much, but we did our best to keep the place up after

Granddad died, until she became ill. That's when I went to live with Father Cleo in Natchez."

"Do you miss your home?"

She shrugged. "I guess when your family has lived and worked on a piece of land for as long as mine have, it just kind of seeps into your blood."

"So, Father Cleo…he took you away from all that poverty and sickness."

Shanna's back straightened. "Poverty and sickness aren't the worst things that can happen to a person. The worst thing is to live without meaning, without love, purpose, hope—without God. I was never w-ithout any of that."

For a moment Gage stared at her as if convinced she had taken leave of her senses. "I can see the priest instilled quite a lot of religion into you during your formative years."

Shanna inclined her head slightly. "I'm not religious; far from it. Besides, I came to Father Cleo with my faith intact. We're both Christ followers, but I'm not even Catholic."

Quirking a brow, he left no doubt that he considered her words untrue. "And you two seem to get along so well."

"We get along because we found out early that we both drink from the same well of grace." Tucking her tongue thoughtfully in her cheek, she met the skeptical blue eyes. "We've had our differences. It's just that love has always prevailed."

The turn of the conversation made him want to squirm. Feeling the need to change the subject, he asked, "So, with pretty hands like yours, why don't you wear rings on your fingers?"

Now it was Shanna's turn to squirm. "Because I did once, and that was enough for me."

CHAPTER 15

T he heat of the night lifted from the ground like a released spirit and was replaced by a damp coolness, thin and easy to breathe. The garden house lay dark with the moon outlining her soft curves as Father Cleo made his way to the door.

"Beautiful night, Father," he said in whispered prayer, fishing for a key to open the small blue door.

Entering the house, it took a moment for his eyes to adjust to the darkness. Then he noticed Shanna through the doorway of her bedroom sitting up in bed. "What are you still doing up?"

"It takes me a long time to go to sleep."

He didn't say anything, but moved toward the coffee table where he emptied his pockets and removed his watch in what seemed like a nightly ritual.

"Did you have a nice time in Charleston?" she asked.

"Um-hmm." He sat down in the chair next to the window and began taking off his shoes.

A moment later the bathroom light came on, followed by a gradual darkness and a click as the door shut. Then came the all-too-familiar whooshing and knocking pipe sound that always accompanied a shower.

She rolled onto her side and waited until the light from the door grew wider then went out. Next came the squeak of springs as he settled on the couch.

"The moon is so bright tonight. Just look how it falls across the floor in angles," she whispered in the dark.

Father Cleo shifted and the clean scent of soap wafted into Shanna's room. A long moment passed in silence.

"Ever wonder if it's true what they say about full moons…how they make people do crazy things?" She flipped her pillow, pressing the cool pillowcase against her cheek. "Do you think this house is haunted? Have you seen a ghost in here? Sister Jon Maureen said that you can see things normal people can't see because you were born with a veil over your eyes. Said you once saw an old monk in the sanctuary kneeling at his prayers before he just vanished into thin air. Is that true?"

A low throaty growl sounded from the direction of the couch.

"You sound hoarse. Can I get you something? A glass of water?"

Merciful heavens. "Do you have earplugs?"

Incensed, Shanna remarked. "I don't snore."

"Snoring I could handle. I've never heard you prattle on so much. What do you do, empty out all of your words before you can sleep at night?"

"Like I told you, it takes me a long time to go to sleep. Don't you remember buying that little thing for me that played the sounds of rain and thunderstorms? Whatever happened to that, anyway?"

He raised up on an elbow and looked straight at Shanna. "Might I suggest something?"

"What?"

"Prayer. *Silent* prayer." He gave her one of those looks that, even in the dark, made it clear the conversation was over.

Father Cleo rose early in the morning and puttered about the kitchen, happy he'd found the coffee. He closed Shanna's bedroom door so the sound of coffee brewing wouldn't carry to the bedroom. While the coffee brewed he stood at the kitchen window and watched the humming birds give chase around the lantana. His mind turned to Shanna.

The first time Shanna mentioned leaving Holy Cross, Father Cleo had not taken her seriously. "Some birds are not meant to be caged," she had said. "Some of us feel imprisoned by the structure… not secured by it."

"Tell me about him," Father Cleo had simply said. And he'd had to conceal a grin at the complete surprise on her face. A young girl's infatuation, he had mistakenly thought. He knew they had met through a "support the troops with prayer" social media site, and that they had clicked, instantly.

"His name is James Muir and I love him."

It didn't matter one bit to Father Cleo whose DNA mixed to make Shanna Muir. She had been his child since the first day he had laid eyes on her. And nothing was ever going to change that. He'd stubbornly held to his beliefs that they were family, in spite of the attempts of others to discourage their familial bond.

He was torn from his trance as the door behind him creaked and Shanna turned her questioning eyes toward him. She wore a white chenille robe and her eyes were swollen with sleep, her hair falling in a tangled wave across her shoulder.

She had seen the priest engrossed in his musings before, but she couldn't help watching him. "I hope you're praying for me."

"Something like that… did I wake you? I tried to be quiet."

"I didn't hear you, but I smelled the coffee. Is it ready?"

"Should be…sit down and I'll pour us a cup." He fetched the pot as she sat down, pouring the black liquid into bone china cups. "Still take it black?"

"Just like a longshoreman," she said with a wink, sipping the steaming brew.

Father Cleo broached a subject Shanna would have preferred avoiding. "Why do you feel the need to stay here?"

She inhaled deeply to get her breath. "Because James is here."

"No, he's not."

The gray eyes avoided the priest and her shoulders slumped slightly. A sick feeling developed in her gut as she braced for the rebuke she was dead sure would come.

"Sometimes, as a person goes along, he meets up with another on the path. You begin to walk together and experience much along the way." He stared into his coffee and was still for several moments. "Then the day comes when you must part. And it's the most painful thing you'll ever have to do. But what you've shared on the way is yours together and no one will ever be able to take that from you. The time will come when you'll be reunited again. And on that day you'll realize that nothing created, no man, nor woman, nor any earthly thing will ever begin to compare to the love you'll have in Christ Jesus."

Shanna sat, drawing herself up into a small form as tears coursed down her cheeks.

"God doesn't want you to live with that dragging weight of death around your ankles, Shanna. He wants you to live light and free." His eyes probed her features: there seemed to be an ember in the ashes, a spark of life still in her, unwilling to die. *That*, he thought, *takes no small amount of courage.*

In the same way a flame burns through the darkest night, one thought spoke clearly in Shanna's mind. *Take all the love that you have for me and give it to the unloved. I have all I need, both now and forever.*

She raised her gray eyes to his. "James always told me that our life was our ministry ... and we should try to make a difference, wherever we find ourselves. Love the unloved ... that's what he wanted from me." The admission made her throat tighten to a degree that made further words difficult.

Father Cleo chewed his lip in concentration with an almost undetectable nod of his head. "I agree. Not long ago I started seeing the work I was doing outside of the church to be just as important as the work I was doing inside, maybe more so. So, I agree with your James — our lives are our ministries. And every person that crosses our path is important. Now, that brings me to another question." He leaned closer. "Tell me about this man, Gage Barrington."

"Gage?" Shanna's eyebrows rose sharply, but Father Cleo had already stepped over to get more coffee.

"Go on, I'm listening," he said, refilling his cup.

She paused to reform her thoughts, surprised at the priest's obvious interest in the subject. "Gage is a very capable man. He's mannerly, loves his family, and seems to really care about his employees." She spread her hand. "I mean, he offered me this garden house. Who would do that for their cleaning lady?"

"I cannot imagine." Father Cleo let the dismay sound in his voice, then chuckled.

Her face fell into annoyance. "It's not like that, I assure you. He has a drop-dead gorgeous girlfriend." She shrugged. "Anyway, he can be distant. He never really opens up, so...."

The priest gave a light shrug and sat down with his coffee. "So … he's remote."

"Oh, he's more than remote—try quarantined."

"It sounds as if you're lamenting a relationship. How can you feel loss for something you've never had?"

"What?" She sat back, folding her arms over her chest.

"I'm merely pointing out the fact that you've never really gotten to know him. But more importantly, does he know God? You must find out. He's come across your path for a reason, don't you think?" He took a slow pull of his coffee.

She struggled to contain her laughter at the ridiculous idea. "And just how am I supposed to do that? He's my boss, for heaven's sake. Besides, he looks at me sometimes like I'm part of some cult."

He steepled his hands and began as if to lecture a student. "By love, of course. Most people respond to it. One word of encouragement, one kindness, one show of respect … it can all have a major impact. You wouldn't hesitate if he were disadvantaged. You mustn't avoid the rich, Shanna. They need Jesus, too. They're harder to reach sometimes because they don't recognize their need as quickly as the less fortunate. But they suffer just as much." He tapped his chest near his heart. "In here."

She opened her mouth to reply, but Father Cleo was already getting up from the table as if the matter had already been settled.

CHAPTER 16

Gage arrived at the Port St. Joe Lumberyard under a clear sky. The rains had moved out, leaving behind slick streets and the scent of wet sawdust on the air. The site of the lumberyard appeared to have been carefully chosen. It was far enough from town so that the noise from the mill would not disturb the residents nestled in a protected spot beneath a hill. The Mississippi River ran close by, where wood would be loaded and hauled by barge up and down the river.

He glanced around then stood for a moment collecting his thoughts. "I own a lumberyard," he said to himself. Scanning stacks of fresh cut wood, he savored the pungent scent. There was a feeling of excitement; everything was new to him and ready to be explored.

At the entrance, he encountered a man mopping a wooden boardwalk that led to a building identified as the sawmill. Bright red splatters were smeared then diluted as the mop swished back and forth inches from Gage's feet. He heard the shrill sound of a saw in the distance followed by a crash, then a curse.

"Blood?" Gage asked the man with the mop, half joking.

"Yes, sir," the man said casually. "It was Terrance this time. Must've fallen asleep … same as the others. Different man, different day is all."

Gage stepped by the man, carefully noticing the stained boards that led all the way to the sawmill door. He had learned from the previous owner that the mill currently operated continuously. And, according to his sources, knew that the only way for an employee to earn a decent wage was to work two shifts.

While sifting through some of his father's documents, he'd stumbled upon the opportunity to purchase the lumberyard. Deciding the deal was just too good to pass up: he immediately began to set in motion plans for the acquisition.

Before him was a challenge. Barrington men tended to thrive on the thrill of a new challenge with a sense of expectancy. Like his father before him, Gage had a head for business, but that's where the similarities ended. They had been polar opposite in the way they viewed people. The son had the desire to understand the deeper truths about a person, whereas the father had seen them only as a means to an end and treated them as such.

After his arrival in Port St. Joe Gage had tried to secure a room, only to be informed that a Civil War convention was in town and there were no vacancies. So after spending the majority of the day getting acquainted with the workings of his new business, he decided to try his luck for accommodations a little farther south.

The first glimpse of Noble, Mississippi, was anything but impressive. The sight of the ancient, crumbling town with its damaged roofs and decaying boards might've caused a less determined soul to run the other way.

The windows of several businesses were boarded, their front doors crisscrossed with two-by-fours. In the middle of town was a hole-in-the-wall joint with a line three-deep.

Gage parked his truck on the far side of the street. A bluesy tune wailed from somewhere close by. Curious about the line of people, he stepped closer to read the words "Solly's Hot Tamales" on a rusted and dented sign.

One look at the crowd and Gage felt out of place. Barely a handful of people had given any notice to the man who held himself apart with a certain composure. As his turn came to order, he realized there was only one item on the menu.

"Uh, I guess I'll have a tamale?"

"You need more than one hot tamale, baby … why don't you order a half dozen," said a plump brown woman, wiping her hands on the white apron stretched taunt across her belly. She gave a hoot of laughter before she added, "If you don't get enough, that'll just make you mad. And we can't have that. No, we can't have that."

"If you say so," Gage said, uncertainly.

She set a plate of hot, steamy corn shucks and crackers on the counter along with a bottle of Tabasco Sauce and a bottled Coke.

"Crackers?" he questioned, lifting an eyebrow as he peeled off a twenty from his money clip.

"Well, baby," the waitress drawled, handing him a plastic fork and knife, "you cut off a little of the hot tamale, spread it on the cracker, douse it with some hot sauce, and *that's* how you eat a delta hot tamale."

"Delta pâté?" Gage asked, grinning at the confused look on the woman's face. He winked, picked up his plate, and headed to the nearest picnic table.

"Call it what you want to, baby … most folks 'round here eat it straight out of tha shuck and just call it plain ole' good."

After gorging himself on the delta food, Gage stood and popped a cream-filled chocolate mint into his mouth. It had been taped to the last pack of crackers, as if to punctuate the end of the meal.

"Delicious," he called to the waitress, who waved as she shut the window and flipped over a sign that read, "All Gone. Come Back Tomorrow."

The afternoon heat had risen, and the hot moist air began to work its suffocating presence into Gage. He walked a space, then paused to knead the back of his neck as he looked around. He spotted an old man under the hood of a late model Ford and decided to ask for directions.

"Excuse me, sir, but can you tell me where I might find Noble Hill?" He waited, but the man made no effort to answer his question. He tried again, thinking the old man may not have heard him. "Noble Hill. Can you tell me where it is?" he asked, a good bit louder this time.

The old man straightened, took out a faded red rag from his back pocket, and began wiping his grease-stained hands as he eyed Gage. "You got business with the Nobles?"

Not caring for the man's attitude, a tic began in his cheek as he clenched his jaw. "My business is just that — my business."

The old man sized Gage up then nodded toward a fork in the road. "Take the left fork toward the river. You can't miss it. It's the only place you'll find down that road." He met his eyes directly. "Good people, the Nobles. Folks around here think a lot them. Wouldn't want nothing to happen to their place."

"That's good to know." The firm look he gave the old man warned him away from any further questions. "Thank you."

Getting back in his truck, Gage pulled out in the direction he'd been given. Glancing briefly in the rearview mirror, he saw the man step away from the

Ford and watch him as he turned onto the road that led to the house. A cry of blues notes wheedled its way through the air behind him.

Noble Hill was both sad and beautiful. Tall brick chimneys rose above the tree line, giving the overall structure a sense of stability. Brick steps covered in lichen climbed gracefully from what appeared to have been a carriage road in front of the house. An iron hitching post where horses had once been tethered leaned near a massive cedar.

At the top of the steps, a rusted gate stood ajar in front of a wide brick walk edged with centuries-old boxwoods. Their sharp, pungent scent settled around Gage as he got out of the truck and looked around.

The lawn was cut but nothing was trimmed. Making his way up the steps to the door he paused, noticing an antique windup doorbell that looked like it had been married to the door for a hundred years. Charm, timeless character—all the descriptive words that flashed through his mind before it came to rest on one: *enduring*. The place was shabby, but in an old Southern genteel way.

Trying the door, he was surprised to find it unlocked. He twisted the stiff knob, pushed open the door, and stepped inside as the squeak of rusted hinges echoed through the empty foyer.

The house became silent and only the low rumble of an approaching storm intruded upon the calm. Boards creaked under Gage's feet, marking his passage through the front entry that ran the full depth of the house. Doorways leading off to other rooms flanked the main hall. A simple stairway with a curved banister led up to a landing with doors visible off the narrow hallway.

With his purpose in mind, he mounted the stairs, peering into several rooms only to discover bits and pieces of furniture, an odd chair, sheets and blankets stacked in piles on beds.

At the end of the corridor was a dark and strangely shadowed alcove. Finding a door, he eased it open. His eyes were drawn up to a rough-hewn wooden crucifix suspended behind an iron bed, dark and ominous. The contrast of the painted iron bed, smooth white eyelet linens and a dark coarse cross was oddly striking. The room was decorated simply, keeping the focus on two adjacent windows, and not much else. He sensed this was the room he had been searching for.

Even with a storm brewing, the understated beauty of the delta could be seen from double windows facing the river. Fields white and green with new cotton flanked the house for as far as the eye could see. An alley of trees formed a dappled path where light, subtly shifting from deep blue to smoky violet, stretched toward the Mississippi River. "The Mighty Mississippi," Gage whispered, feeling the pull of the current in his soul.

There in the silence, a gust of wind whistled down the chimney and something like a feeling of intimacy seemed to awaken within him. As if that which was being felt within his soul was also being absorbed, listened to and taken to heart.

Surprised by the encounter, Gage stood motionless, not wanting to move for fear of losing the holy hush. He'd come to the house on the chance that something good might come from it. It had been less than a twenty-minute drive from Port St. Joe, and the opportunity to check in on Shanna's home place had been too good to pass up. Besides, maybe he would find a piece or two to bring back to her, some remembrance or keepsake from her old home.

But as he stood there, with the light slowly fading and the river unhurriedly moving toward the gulf, an awareness began to penetrate. God seemed present with him. Emanating from the very plaster of the walls. Struck by the thought, he had to admit, if only to himself, that it had never really occurred to him that the presence of God was something that might be sensed. Chills ran up his arms and he brushed them away. God seemed to be examining him, or so Gage thought.

Gaining a grasp of the situation, he realized in an instant how much of his life had been spent disregarding God. Truth be told, he'd pretty much ignored him altogether his whole life. Growing up, the only time Gage ever remembered hearing the name of Jesus Christ in his father's house was on Sunday morning when their housekeeper, LuBelle, listened to her preacher, the Reverend Slack, on the radio. Or when somebody fell down the stairs. Gage choked out a simple but heartfelt prayer. *God, help me.*

Soon, the failing light brightened as flashes of lightning lit the room and the rain came. Overcome with a sudden fatigue, he stretched out across the bed and closed his eyes. Resting his body on the mattress, he became still, listening to the pouring rain as it piped through the gutters.

The cleansing rain continued, beating a soft tempo on the roof, cooling it down from the heat of the day. Thunder resonated through the room. Gage lay there thinking of his failings, his sorrows, his sins — his life before God. Spent, he drifted off in a deep sleep.

The heat of the morning sun bore through a small east window and into the room where Gage lay. Moment by moment the temperature began to rise by sweltering degrees until the occupant of the bed stirred uncomfortably.

"Good Lord," Gage said, pushing up from the bed as sudden realization set in. He blinked red-rimmed eyes at the light flooding the room and looked around, more than a little stunned. It was a full moment before everything began to dawn. *Was I drugged? What was in that tamale?*

Muttering a curse, he shot up out of bed. The wooden crucifix caught his eye and his thoughts began to ease. He had no time to find a logical explanation, settling for now on the excuse he had simply been dog-tired from the strain. Buying and learning the ropes of a new business, who wouldn't be exhausted. He remembered praying, but that was the last thing he remembered.

Seizing the piece with both hands, he lifted the cross from the nail. He didn't have any idea how he ended up staying the night in the old house, but one thing he knew: he wasn't going home empty-handed. Surely the cross holds some memory for Shanna. And, if he got caught stealing in the Bible Belt, a cross was probably the best thing to be found in your possession.

Rounding the corner toward his truck, he spotted a woman, silver hair bright in the sun. She was leaning delicately on a smooth walking stick. Her face gleamed as she struggled to catch her breath. Suddenly and with certainty Gage knew he liked the woman. A wide smile broke across his face. "You caught me—red-handed." He lifted his arms and the cross high above his head in a mock show of surrender.

"That's a start, young man, that's a start." Her faded blue eyes danced with suspicion. "Tell me, what are you planning to do with that cross? Not burn it in somebody's yard like a fool, are you?"

"What? Me?" he choked out in astonishment.

"I could see a sheet on you."

Feeling appalled at the insult, he said sternly, "I plan to give it to Shanna Muir. Shanna *Noble* Muir!"

With a ragged sigh, the old woman shook her head. "Nothing has grieved me as much as that child's physical absence. I hold her history in my very own heart. I love that girl, and she loves me, too. We never have to say it over and over like some folks do … we just know it. Sometimes it's the knowing, not just the saying that counts." She lifted her chin. "Folks around here call me Miss Lynn. I've been the caretaker for the Nobles for forty-three years."

"Gage Barrington. Shanna works for me back on Terrapin Island."

It seemed odd to Gage to think of Miss Lynn as beautiful, but, he did. She practically shimmered with joy and life. In fact, he was having trouble not laughing at the absurdity of the situation. If she was not seventy, then she was pushing it hard.

"Shanna will be comforted having her cross back. It was always something of her signature in my mind. She never slept without it hanging over her bed … until she moved to Holy Cross. I knew she would leave that place one day." Her blue eyes held his in an unwavering look. "Living in the cages of conformity never did suit her well. That girl's meant to be let loose on the world."

His face betrayed a doubtful belief of her statement. "You're telling me Shanna Muir doesn't like being tied down to a place?"

"Not at all. I'm saying she's shaken by what she believes. Dispensing hope to the hopeless and sticking up for the defenseless. It consumes her."

"You don't need to convince me. I get that about her," he said, wanting to get off the subject.

Miss Lynn continued on, as if she hadn't heard. "She used to ask me to help her make sandwiches for the poor folks down by the river. Peanut butter and honey.

Funny," she said, her voice hitting a low note, "what you remember."

"People lived down there?" He glanced over his shoulder down the old carriage road.

"Those poor souls lived in shacks and a few shotgun houses. Some even stayed in the old abandoned inn. A few were pretty rough characters, but that didn't bother Shanna. 'Course, back then my husband, Pete, would follow along behind her and that little red wagon she pulled all loaded up with food. She was never allowed to go further than the end of the gravel, but she could stand under a tree near the road and pass out sandwiches. Nothing wrong with passing out sandwiches for a temporary fix, mind you, but that girl was never satisfied to leave it at that. That Shanna—she goes in for the save, my Pete always said, God rest his soul."

"I don't doubt that in the least, Miss Lynn," he said. "Can you think of anything else she may want from her home? Some remembrance of her childhood?"

Miss Lynn shrugged, smiling sweetly, "I don't rightly know. What you have is all I remember she cherished." She tapped her finger against her lips. "But, if you'd like, I can show you around the house. I'm still caretaking. Father Cleo sends a check each month for upkeep of the house—the grass and such. I look after the place. Now that Shanna's reached age, it all belongs to her. She may decide to sell it—if she doesn't move back home, that is." She straightened and, in a small voice, continued, "There's not much left for her in South Carolina, or so Father Cleo tells me."

A frown grew and his mouth opened to respond, but he quickly decided to change the subject. He waved toward the house. "Why was the door unlocked? Aren't you afraid of thieves and vandals?"

The elder smiled mischievously as they walked toward the house. "Why, Mr. Barrington, everyone around these parts knows the house is haunted." She winked. "No one in their right mind would do what you just did and actually spend the night. The whole town is probably buzzing about you over their coffee this very morning."

Gage grunted sarcastically.

"Mr. Barrington?" Miss Lynn stopped and looked at him closely. "You seem overly interested in the girl. Is she a little more to you than an employee? A girlfriend perhaps?"

"Hardly!" he denied. "I have a girlfriend, Miss Lynn. I just like to look out for my … employees."

"I see." Miss Lynn stated resolutely. Then, with the privilege of old age, she added, "You must love her then, very much."

Gage struggled to contain his laughter at the ridiculous idea. "I assure you, Miss Lynn, I only have Shanna's best interests at heart. I feel a certain … responsibility toward her. She is a widow and had been living with her husband's grandfather until he passed away recently. He also worked for me. Now, if there is some crime in trying to do a kind thing for a person who has suffered so much loss in their life — then guilty as charged."

"Mr. Barrington?"

"Gage."

"Gage. Where is she living now?" Her voice was restrained and innocent.

He stared down into those cornflower blue eyes and had the distinct impression he was being lampooned. He slapped his cap on his head and adjusted it down over his eyes, forcing a smile. "It was a pleasure meeting you, Miss Lynn. I'll be sure to tell Shanna that you are doing well and taking good care of the place."

"Kiss her for me, will you?"

Gage opened his mouth to reply, but Miss Lynn was already tapping her stick on the bricks as she walked up the steps toward the house.

Later that same morning Gage arrived at the lumberyard as the shift changed. He raised a hand and halted the men as they neared the gate. A frown crossed his brow as he observed an old man moving through the crowd toward him. The man had a disjointed gait and looked shopworn from overuse as he elbowed his way to the front.

"What's all this about?" the man asked, staring up at Gage.

"And you are?"

"My name's Dayne and I'm foreman of this crew." He squinted in the misty light, his lips drawn back from uneven teeth.

A curious crowd had gathered and as they pressed in, a low grumbling could be heard. Gage gave little attention to the banter. He accepted the men's talk as just that. As he looked over the crew, they seemed like outcasts trapped in some backward way of life with little hope beyond a meager existence. Many bore the vacant stares of hopelessness.

"My name is Gage Barrington. I'm the new owner of the lumberyard. Changes will be made across the board—starting today. I want all foremen to meet at the front office for a briefing. The rest of you will be off until Monday."

Dayne's voice deepened to a rasping snarl. "What do you expect these men to live on while you decide their fate?"

"Bonus pay, of course."

The foreman spit tobacco from his mouth, his eyes glaring at Gage. "Bonus pay. You mean you're gonna *pay* my men for not being here?" Low laughter broke out among the men as Dayne wiped his mouth with his sleeve.

"*My* men — and that's the general idea." Gage was oddly calm, but there was an air of seriousness about him. "I want the mill shut down while we reorganize. Get word to all the foremen about the meeting. Once my men arrive, we'll get started."

"You bringing in more men? Why?" Dayne asked, suspiciously.

Being questioned by an employee never set well with Gage, but he held himself in tight rein, reasoning the man was mostly looking after his crew. "I see a need for more workers, shorter shifts, and better wages. No one needs to fear losing their job if they're not a slacker. Do you see things differently?"

The foreman hitched up his pants, puffed out his chest and backing away a few steps, barked an order. "You heard the man. Go home, get some rest, and report back here first thing Monday morning!"

CHAPTER 17

A week later, Gage rolled into Summer's Keep and was met on the dirt road by the familiar slim form of his son, Quinn. He had spied the boy running along the bushes until he slipped through a break in the shrubs and reached the road.

"Hop in," Gage said, mussing the head of the boy as he ran up to the truck window. "Where's Mimi?"

"Down at the garden house. She was sayin' goodbye to Shanna's daddy the priest," Quinn said, out-of-breath.

"Father Cleo's leaving?"

"Yep. He already left. Can I ride in the back?"

"Sure, hang on. Let's go find Mimi."

The boy slapped a cap on his head and grinned as he scrambled up the tailgate, turned around, and hung his legs off the back. They drove across the property, carefully navigating between trees and shrubs. Spotting Myra in the garden, Gage parked and then saw Quinn through the rearview mirror hop off the back of the truck and run toward the stable.

"Not much has changed here, has it?" Gage said, smiling hesitantly as he pulled open the squeaky gate. He knew his mother had avoided the garden house since her mother's passing.

"Summertime has always had a way of drawing me to the garden house. Mother and I used to have some long conversations sitting right here on this bench." Myra swallowed hard against the rising emotion as cicadas droned their familiar tune in the summer air.

"I miss her, too," Gage whispered, sensing his mother's grief.

"Lilly Rose broke all the rules when gardening." She half-laughed. "The same way she did with most confining things. She started this garden the day she was given a rosebush by her love. She named it Summer's Keep. After that the land became known as Summer's Keep." Myra gently fingered a delicate pink bud. "That must've been *some* summer."

Gage raised a wondering brow at his mother. "Summer's Keep—a rosebush? Why did I not know that?"

Myra looked at her son and calmly pointed out, "Don't feel so bad, son. I didn't know it until Mother was well on in years and started reminiscing. My father must've been quite the romantic. In fact, she said she always took the first and the last rose to bloom on this bush every year. The garden house was built for her around it. The big house came later, after Yancey was born." She looked thoughtfully at her son. "This place was entwined with my mother's heart."

He examined the rosebush, rubbing his thumb across a thorn. "Funny…what you remember," he said, thinking back to his grandmother. "She used to gaze out over the land, a million miles away. Become so mesmerized at the way the wind swept through a field of marsh grass or how a hummingbird would zigzag around a shrub. Always stared off toward Sassabee Creek, lost in a daze."

Myra dipped her head under a tumble of trellised blooms. "You know, Summer's Keep is a *wild* rose bush. It escapes the weakening effects of modern rose breeding. In fact, it seems to defy the pampered stereotype of a beautiful rose. It's a strong, time-tested survivor. Wild roses are also more fragrant. Yes, there's nothing quite like the charm of a beautiful wild rose."

Gage knew his mother well enough to know that it had always been her style to speak her insights in the form of riddles. She was subtle that way. "I take it you're drawing some sort of comparison?"

"Who, me? What on earth are you talking about?" She ran a light hand over a deep purple clematis as a light breeze fluttered the fragile blooms. "I'm merely pointing out the obvious. A less…cultivated rose can be…Eden."

Two young women sat on the pier near the waterfront under the white moon. A child stretched out beside them, swatting at willow flies. It was a peaceful scene, but profoundly sad. They huddled together like bewildered children, unable to think past the moment.

Shanna knew them, their stories, and the fierce pride that prevented them from getting the help they so desperately needed. Her crying wasn't out-of-control, but she was obviously moved by the scene. Swiping her cheek, she waited a bit, then turned back to put the finishing touches on the cruiser she was cleaning.

Earlier in the day, a small fleet of horn-tooting cruisers had arrived at the marina. Unloading a party of well-heeled mainlanders, they were intent on taking in the sights and possibly a meal at one of the restaurants. Thanks to her boss's highbrow Charleston friends, the picturesque port was fast becoming a favorite of the international yachting fraternity. A fact that was beginning to annoy Shanna.

Threatening to tell the self-important yachtsman to find some other lackey to clean his boat, she had clamped down hard on her tongue when the man began peeling off a one-hundred-dollar bill. Easy money for a few short hours — well worth the time. Besides, now that Father Cleo was on his way back home to Mississippi, what else did she have to do?

As it was, she'd tried to dodge Gage for pride's sake. He had returned from his business trip that afternoon and it hadn't been hard to avoid him, up to this point. Now, with all of the dockworkers gone, her presence could hardly be ignored. No doubt he'd wonder why she was still here.

The quiet stillness of the inlet was broken by the whine of a boat engine as a single lighted watercraft came around the bend. It left in its wake a luminous path beneath the silver moon. Gage stretched his hand against the frame, observing Shanna from the window of his office. He hadn't realized the girl was still around until he'd heard her all-too-familiar humming floating up from Conner Black's cruiser.

He watched through the shadows, noting a look of determination on her face. Even in the darkness he could see the firm set of her jaw. Then, the yellow dock light lit a wet path down her cheek. The emotion seemed at odds with the rest of her. Mad? Sad? He couldn't tell.

It seemed Shanna's nature to do whatever it took to accomplish her mission in life, and for that Gage was envious. He confessed to himself that he'd spent the majority of his life unhappy, restless, and bored. With work, money, and even his friends. What he wouldn't give to have an ounce of Shanna Muir's passion for a cause bigger than himself.

She came in from the dock and, after putting away her cleaning supplies, paused at the window and stared out. Thinking back, it now seemed strange to Shanna that on the day of James' funeral all she had wanted was to have her father's arms around her. Strange because her father had never really had the chance to have been a part of her life; still, she longed for him. She wanted her father to put his arms around her and tell her that everything was going to be okay — something he'd never once done. But, on that tragic day, Shanna had longed to be someone's much loved child. As she looked out over the little huddle of humanity, she imagined those two girls wanted that, too.

"More outcasts in your line of vision?" Gage asked, getting up from his desk. He tossed a stack of papers aside and reached for his cell phone, scrolling his messages.

She answered without turning around. "Not those two."

Something in her voice caused him to look up. She turned away from the window, a defeated look on her face.

Intrigued, he stepped around the desk and went into the room where Shanna stood. He moved beside her at the window, crossing his arms over his chest as he planted his feet wide. "Couldn't get anywhere with them, huh?"

Inwardly, Shanna groaned as she turned away. "No. They shut me down every time."

"What do you know about them?" Gage reached into his shirt for a cigar, then searched his jeans pocket for a lighter.

"They're sisters. Both have been molested by their mother's live-in boyfriend. One has a child by him, or so I've been told. They're homeless because *they* left. They come here to the docks at night because it's safe and cool. I can't help them; they refuse help of any kind."

"They must receive some kind of help." His teeth clamped firmly on the cigar.

She looked a little reluctant, but added, "I throw out milk, bread, cheese, fruit… sometimes even whole boxes of granola bars. I put a few other necessities in the outdoor restroom." The cigar drooped from Gage's mouth and she twisted her lips to cover a smile at the incredulous expression on his face. "But I have to be sneaky about it. Make it look like we're just wasteful around here. I'm afraid if they get too desperate, they'll fall prey to the human traffickers."

A dawning occurred in Gage's eyes and he snatched the cigar from his mouth. "So is *that* why you scour the garbage bins?" He gave a half laugh. "And all this time I thought you were just OCD." He ran a hand across his close cut beard in thought. "They can't hang out on the docks, though."

She shot him a look that could have stopped a stampeding buffalo in a dead run. "Look, I understand having them here is not good for the kind of business you're wanting to attract. But…."

Holding up a hand, he cut her off mid-sentence. A thought hit him and began to grow as he stared out at the prideful pair and the child. "Stay here," he ordered.

She jumped as the door slammed behind him. Rushing to the window, her eyes widened as she witnessed the scene. The women looked shocked, then caught as Gage stormed up and began what could only be described as a good chewing out. Slashing his hands through the air, he pointed to first one girl and then the other, as if giving a reprimand. *What on earth is he doing?* Then, startling her, he began walking toward the old abandoned houseboat they'd named Hettie Sue, the little displaced group following close on his heels.

The old boat had her best days behind her but was still quite tight, seaworthy, and clean… albeit not much to look at on the outside. Gage stepped aboard and ran a hand over the top of the door frame, pulling off a magnetic box containing the key to the door. He held the key in his fist and seemed to bark more orders. He threw the cigar into the water, then pointed at the oldest woman.

To Shanna's surprise, the woman stepped onto the boat and took the key. She closed her fingers around the plastic float on the ring and dropped her head, staring at the key in her small hand. Gage hopped off the boat, leaving the women and the child to see after themselves.

Stunned, Shanna could only stare as Gage came back inside. He walked right by her, then continued on to his office, tossing his keys in the air as he caught them. *Was he whistling?* She followed him, stopping at his office door.

"What'd you do?"

Gage peered at her questioningly. "You mean with the vagrants?" He pointed with his thumb. "I put them to work… gave them jobs in exchange for room and board on Hettie Sue. I told them firmly that freeloaders would not be tolerated. I expect them to pull their weight around here. I want those decks hosed down every morning and the trash picked up. I won't pay them a penny over dockworkers' pay, either."

Shanna stepped closer, a soft smile curving her lips as she leaned over the desk. "Thank you," she whispered, then turned to leave.

It had been two weeks since Gage had returned from Barrington Lumber, but no one had seen much of the man. He spent his days with the Norwegian and several handpicked employees working on some project nobody talked about.

But today, as Gage worked on a warehouse door near the dock he heard a yell, followed by a loud splash. He looked up from the rusted hinge he was filing to see Shanna, with the houseboat sister's child astride her hip and her finger pointed at Dupe who was busy slapping water to keep afloat. Shanna heaved the little girl higher on her hip as she walked past the suddenly repentant Dupe who yelled out his apology for whatever stupid thing the boy had said or done to Shanna. Gage grinned, turning back to his work.

At the end of the day, Shanna headed home, intent to walk over and pay a visit to the cemetery before the night closed in. It had become her habit to visit the grave of her husband, then go home for a long, languid bath each evening, soaking her sore muscles in mind numbing fragrant heat.

As the sun began to sink behind the cedars, washing the backs of headstones in a golden light, there arose a chirp of a cricket somewhere in the graveyard. A sound so faint and lonely that Shanna had to swallow hard against the rising tightness in her throat. She bent down to brush her hand over the engraved name of her husband, the coolness of the stone sending a chill through her arm as she wiped away a single leaf caught by a web.

"I'll have to say you're the tidiest person I've ever met. Not that I'm complaining," a low, unquestionably masculine voice stated. "I've just never given much thought to cleaning a headstone."

Startled, Shanna twisted her head to see Gage leaning against the wrought iron post, holding a package under his arm. She wiped the hair out of her eyes and straightened. "I didn't hear you come up. Have you been here long?" Whenever Gage had sought her out before, she had been met with bad news. She wondered what dreadful event had happened this time.

"Long enough to see that you have this fatal capacity for absorbing all the hardships and sadness you can find in the world. In fact, you seem to seek it out on a regular basis."

"It's called compassion. You need to try it sometime." She rounded the headstone and faced him, brushing the spider web from her hand.

"Yeah, well, there comes a point when you just need to let go and have some fun. Unless of course you enjoy the melancholy. Some people do, you know." Humor was heavy in his words. "But I have to give it to you, nobody I know takes on the difficulties of this world so remarkably well."

"The result of long practice," she said, glaring at him with her hands on her hips. Her patience was running out, then her curiosity was stirred as her eyes fell on the package. She couldn't fathom why he'd come to the cemetery and he didn't seem in a hurry to tell her. In fact, he seemed to be enjoying himself. She found him regarding her with a tolerantly amused smile, as one would a child in a snit.

Gage considered the girl who stood erect facing him, doing her best to try to contain her aggravation. "I have something for you," he said.

Shanna dropped her arms, completely unprepared to deal with his statement. She could find no words to say.

Ah, now I have her attention. A smirk crossed his lips as he watched her, waiting for a response. When none came he moved forward and handed her the parchment-covered package. The scent of lavender, warmed and diffused by her heated blood, blended in the air with the sharp smell of evergreen.

She stood there a moment, holding the package. "What is it?"

"There's only one way to find out … open it."

Curious about the oddly shaped form in her hands, she began to gently tear off the paper, peeling back the thin tissue sheets. There was a sharp intake of breath and her voice quavered as she tore through the remaining parchment. "My cross! Oh, my goodness! How in the world did you get it!"

"I had business in Port St. Joe. Since I was in the neighborhood, I decided to check out Noble Hill." He looked at her a moment. "I see why you have such fond memories of the place. It's really very beautiful, even in … less than perfect condition."

Shanna lifted the cross to her nose and breathed deeply. The sandalwood fragrance of the wood washed over her and seemed to smooth away the jagged edges of her troubled mind. "This scent transports me back home. Thank you for this … it's a crucial part of me."

She had often walked the beaches, hoping to find something by which she might construct a cross. The tide hauled in all manner of things: shells, sea glass, an occasional twisted piece of driftwood. But secretly, her heart had longed for the familiar form she now held in her hands.

"I'm glad you like it. Stealing a cross has always been on my bucket list."

She laughed. "Well, I guess you can check that one off. I…." She caught sight of a dark blue SUV pulling up beside the gate, interrupting her comment. The next moment, the occupant got out of the vehicle and began walking toward them.

On instinct, Gage moved to stand in front of Shanna as he faced the man. "Hello," Gage said, giving the stranger an opportunity to identify himself.

"Hello there. I'm looking for Shanna Muir," the man called. "I was told I might find her here."

Shanna glanced around Gage and froze, jolted to see her dead husband's eyes looking curiously back at her. She felt as if she were standing on a rock that had abruptly given way, plunging her downward in a free fall.

"Shanna?" the man inquired.

"Yes," she answered, fixated on the stranger's face that so resembled her dead husband's. He was larger than James, but with the same gorgeous head of dark hair, only this man's was silvered at the temples. His warm brown eyes looked first at the grave, paused a long moment, took in the cross she held, and then looked at her with concern in his tear-rimmed eyes.

"I'm Gabriel Muir, your father-in-law."

Gage heard Shanna's sharp intake of breath for the second time that day. He reached for the man's hand. "I'm Gage Barrington."

"Breck's son?" Gabriel responded, almost cheerfully. He took Gage's hand, pumping it enthusiastically. "I was a friend of your dad's many years ago. How is he?"

A shadow fell over his face. "He passed away last January."

Gabriel turned aside, tightened his lips in visible pain. Not able to find any worthy comment, he asked, "And, your mother?"

A grin creased the lines around his mouth. "Sassy as ever. I'll tell her you asked about her."

"Please do." Caught off guard by the news and the emotion it aroused, Gabriel felt a need to explain. "I've known your mother for many years. Be sure to tell her how very sorry I am for her loss."

"I will, thank you."

"I thought a lot of your grandmother. In fact," he nodded toward the headstone, "my son and Lilly Rose were quite close. He would have wanted to be buried next to her."

Gage stuffed his hands in his pockets. "So I've heard."

"Before she died, I watched her grip James' hand and tell him, 'Take all the love you have for me and give it to those without it.' He held on to that…she was very influential in his life."

Shanna lowered her eyes briefly and toyed with her silver bracelets. James had said similar words to her before he died, but she didn't feel the need to share it. It felt too private, too personal to be discussed in the open air.

Gabriel turned his attention to Shanna. "I came here hoping to find you. Dr. Mooreland said you sometimes come here." He nodded toward the parsonage. "I heard you moved your things out of the house. Why?"

She looked confused. "Because the new pastor needs it. He's been on the mission field in some remote part of India. It's not the lap of luxury, as you well know, but it's a comfortable home. I'm sure he'll appreciate it."

Gabriel tugged on his ear before speaking. "I'm the man, Shanna. I didn't move here to uproot you from your home. When Dr. Mooreland contacted me about my father, he also told me about you. And," he cleared his throat, "he asked me to pray about stepping in as pastor of The Prayer House."

Shanna swallowed hard in nervous reaction to his words. "*You* are our new pastor? Why hasn't anyone told me? I don't understand," she said, more hurt and confused than she cared to admit.

"I asked them not to. I wanted to meet you first. Explain my absence from my family."

Shanna's lips trembled, but she still formed the questions that had bothered her. "But your son—he needed you. Your father, he needed you, too! Why didn't you come?"

Gabriel's brows came together in a worried frown. "I hope to have a chance to explain these things to you. You're the only family I have left. I came here to meet you. Get to know you. I have a room in town. I have no intention of moving you out of your home," he assured her. "You belonged to my son and as far as I'm concerned, that makes us family."

Gage glanced at Shanna, trying to read her reaction to her father-in-law's words.

"May I buy you both dinner?" Gabriel asked, rubbing his hands together as he looked first to Shanna, then to Gage.

Hesitant to leave Shanna with a man they'd met only five minutes ago, Gage waited for some signal from her. When none came, he said, "Thanks, but I really need to be going."

"Shanna?" Gabriel asked, raising his eyes expectantly.

"I'd like that."

Chapter 18

Autumn had taken a firm hold, and the moody clouds looked faded and worn, like a puckered quilt that had seen too many washings. Gage smelled the coming storm; his eyes squinted toward the wall of gunmetal gray as he worked to finish up the boat repair. When the wind picked up, he stopped what he was doing to help an old fisherman named Boutros secure his boat.

"She's gonna be a nasty one," Boutros observed, tossing out a line to Gage. The wind caught a bucket and rattled it across the pier.

"Good day fishing?" Gage asked. He liked Boutros well enough, though the man had an almost sacred devotion to his fishing spot. He'd even been known to blindfold his fishing buddies on their way to and from his honey hole.

The old man smiled. "Good enough."

"Want to let me in on your secret hole?" Gage let his smile widen, his eyes pirate sharp as the wind swept through his sandy hair.

Boutros pushed his cap back, scratched his forehead. "I kissed a girl when I was around thirteen years old and told my buddy about it. The next time I went to see her, his bike was parked out on her lawn. Never again."

"Fair enough," Gage said, laughing.

"I believe you have a visitor."

Glancing around, Gage noticed his mother's car pulling up to the office. "Good talking to you, Boutros."

Myra had taken her grandson to Dr. Mooreland for his last immunization. A job Gage had been only too happy to relinquish to his mother. Quinn Barrington had a mind of his own and expressed it often, except where his grandmother was concerned. Quinn's relationship with Myra seemed on a whole other level and he was yet to understand it.

Stepping into the front office, Gage spied Quinn sitting at Yancey's desk, doodling. "Well, what did the doctor say? You all fixed up?"

Myra spoke from across the room where she had been talking to Shanna, watching her mop. "Yes, but Quinn says he's probably going to be sore so he wants to skip school for the rest of the day."

"Eight-year-olds don't get to make those kind of decisions. This is not a case of the tail wagging the dog, I assure you."

"I made an important decision at eight…a vow actually, to God," Shanna added, making herself part of the conversation, her eyes on the swishing movement of the mop.

Gage looked at her. "A vow? Well, even God himself wouldn't hold you to a vow you made at such a young age."

"That makes it all the more important, don't you think?" She looked up from her work, a bit of rebellion showing in her gray eyes.

"Depends on the vow, I guess," Gage said gruffly, as he observed his mother trying her best to contain her laughter. He shushed her with a point of his finger. "You're not helping matters, Mother."

"I pledged to God to take up for the stupid and the weak," Shanna said, decisively.

"Well, you certainly seem to be holding up your end of the bargain." Gage cast a look in Quinn's direction. "You're going to school!"

The boy looked dejected, then perked up and asked, "Can Shanna make my lunch?"

Eyeing his son, looking for the tactic, he asked, "Why? Don't you like the meals they serve at school?"

"Yeah, but I've always wanted somebody to do that for me. Like those other kids with good mommas."

Quinn's statement had created a new atmosphere in the room. Gage took a deep breath, held it, and then let it out slowly.

Propping her mop against the wall, Shanna moved toward the breakroom. "I'm on it," she said, her voice cracking oddly.

Quinn slid out of the desk chair and trailed behind Shanna, unaware of the impact of his words. He rubbed a finger across the bridge of his nose as he caught up to her. "You got any of those Little Debbie Cakes left? Hey, did you know Dupe can stuff five oatmeal pies in his mouth at one time?" he said, disappearing into the break room.

Myra followed Gage into his office and moved to the bookshelves. She began scanning the titles as her son took a seat at the desk. She ran a slow finger over a silver framed picture of Evan-Cerise. "There will always be women who will steal your breath, son, but the one who causes you to breathe deeply? That's the one you should keep."

With a heavy sign, Gage turned his attention to his mother with a look of impatience. "Who are you talking about, Mother?" He began sorting through a stack of papers on his desk again.

"I'm talking about that lovely girl in there fixing lunch for your son."

"What?" He looked up, squinting in confusion, as if he hadn't heard her correctly. "That girl is *in* the world but not *of* it, like some sort of — I don't know — saint," he said, impatiently. "Her feet never touch the dirt like the rest of us." Then, as if to prove his point he added, "Who have you ever known to make a vow to God at the age of eight? Nobody! End of discussion."

Myra pulled out a thick volume and thumbed through it like someone looking for pictures. "And that's a bad thing?" She slapped the book shut, looking directly in her son's eyes.

"I don't think of her that way. And, trust me, she doesn't care either. I mean, let's be honest, she certainly doesn't try to get noticed."

"Oh, for heaven's sake, Gage, beautiful things don't ask for attention."

"Well, you're way off on this one. I have a girlfriend, remember? One I understand. And besides, Shanna Muir is still married. Married to a dead man."

Turning his attention back to his work, he shuffled papers around, trying to pretend he wasn't distracted. Why wouldn't Shanna let the man die in peace instead of carrying on like he was over in the churchyard taking a nap under the cedars? Was it because she never really had a permanent family? Was she just going to linger forever in her eternal world of the undead?

He'd always thought some people needed to be pushed into acceptance over a loss. But with Shanna, he wasn't sure about that. The shock might be too much for her. "It's like she wants to hang around that grave until what she loves misses her and calls her in. You should've seen her face yesterday when she met her father-in-law for the first time. It was like she'd seen a ghost."

"Gabriel?" Myra's pulse quickened a beat or two. With weak knees trembling beneath her, she rested her back against the wooden bookcase. "He's here?"

Gage shot to his feet. "Mother! Are you alright?"

"Fine, fine, son … just a little light-headed. Please — get some water for me."

With Gage out of the room, Myra sat down to collect herself. *So, he's here.* With the full weight of emotions bearing down on her, she thought calmly, *He has every right to be, after all. It doesn't matter to me one way or the other,* she told herself. How easy it was to think those words, and how impossible it was to believe them.

Myra glanced up as her son came through the door handing her a glass of water, his concern rampant on his face. "I'm calling Dr. Mooreland."

"That's not necessary, son. I'm fine, really."

"I've asked too much of you. You're exhausted."

She pulled back in surprise. "Since when can't I handle a little boy? I'm just dehydrated, that's all. Don't make too much of this."

Gage's eyes searched hers — she wasn't the color of ash anymore. He dropped a light kiss on her head and said, "You're staying with us for a while. I want to keep an eye on you." He grabbed his cell phone off the desk and left the room.

Myra nodded and resolved herself to the fact that there would be no talking him out of it. She could tell that her son had not been satisfied with her explanations. She sat tense and silent in her chair, all too aware that Gabriel Muir was on the same island she'd just been sentenced to. From the front room she'd heard a few words being exchanged before the door opened and shut. Now, all was quiet except the swishing sound of a broom. The sound grew closer and closer until Shanna stood in the doorway.

"Would you like a cup of tea? I have a few petit fours—the guys won't touch sissy cakes, that's why I still have them," Shanna said, and winked.

"That would be so nice. Will you join me?" Myra asked, hopefully.

Shanna looked over her shoulder toward the front door. She felt a strange desire all of a sudden to be treated as a lady and enjoy a cup of tea with this fine woman. In some ways she felt her job at times required that she curb her softer side, and that was evident in her work-reddened hands. She rubbed her callouses with a thumb. "I believe I will."

Moments later Shanna came into the room carrying a makeshift tray made from a cardboard box lid, two cups of tea, and a plate of small frosted cakes. She placed it on the corner of the desk.

"I can't believe I'm doing this. If the guys see me in here having a tea party with you, I'll never hear the end of it."

"Oh, don't pay any attention to them." Myra waved her hand in the air. "I'll tell Gage you didn't want me to sit in here all by my lonesome and that I insisted you join me, which I did."

Reaching for a cup, Shanna smiled. "Good. Now I can relax and enjoy my tea." She took a sip and closed her eyes, savoring the warmth of the mellow brew. "Sister Jon-Maureen and I used to have tea together every afternoon at four-o-clock. I enjoyed it so much—looked forward to it."

"Speaking of enjoyment, do you enjoy working for my son?" Myra asked, and with a wistful smile she picked up her tea and took a sip.

"I do. He's been very good to me and I'm grateful for my job. He's a good man."

"I suppose there's not a man in all of Charleston who does a better job with his investments than Gage. My husband was good, but my son has a remarkable degree of interest in his projects. He takes great pride in making his business undertakings profitable, as this one is. But, now ... I think he's ready for a new challenge. There's a certain look he gets when he's ready to do something else. I think he has his eye on Mississippi." She paused, as if she had wanted to see a flicker of emotion pass across the girl's face, but if she did, she was disappointed.

"He has certainly turned this place around," Shanna said, then carefully sipped her tea.

"His father described a new business venture as something 'waiting to be tickled.'" Myra laughed lightly. "Nobody knows how to tickle a response out of something quite like Gage. In fact, if I were a betting woman, I'd say that that boy of mine is planning to sell marine ready lumber to the whole East Coast! He purchased the lumber company in Mississippi from Barrington and Porcher ... he hasn't said why, but I know my son. He's up to something."

"May I ask you something, Myra?" Shanna said, hesitantly.

"Well of course. It's just us girls here now. What's on your mind?"

Shanna tugged on her hair and rubbed a hand over her tee shirt. "I need some advice. Molly has been after me to make myself more presentable. In the catering business, we go into some really nice places and serve. And, well, I don't want to be an embarrassment. My life with the nuns was a little lacking when it came to fashion."

Myra perked up. "You mean you'd like some fashion advice?"

"If it will not be too much trouble. I mean, I love the way you and Evan-Cerise dress. Evan-Cerise dresses like she has a serious bank account and I certainly don't. That girl is a walking billboard for style." Her clear gray eyes looked away, wistfully.

Fanning her hand, Myra dismissed Shanna's statement. "You don't have to have a lot of money to look good. Listen, it's better to have a few simple pieces of good clothing that fit you well than one blingy bag that will break the bank. Upscale consignment stores are plentiful."

"Where do I start?"

"Choose clothes made from either cotton, cashmere, silk, linen…anything natural, no synthetic blend. Old money crowds love the understated. If you can't afford the real thing, do what the wealthy do: get the cheapest, simplest watch you can find with a basic black or brown leather band, small and discreet. Go for simple, unbranded designs like a plain leather purse. Expensive clothes don't feature brands prominently. Trust me on this one."

Biting the tip of her fingernail, Shanna thought about what she'd heard. "So basically less is more."

"Exactly. Shoes make the outfit. Put your money there and let your clothes be items of mysterious origin." Myra considered the girl. "Get yourself a good haircut and keep it up every month. Keep your natural look with only a minimal amount of makeup. The lavender fragrance you wear is delightful and doesn't have that 'bought at the mall' smell. Never talk about money. No gum chewing and I don't need to tell you not to swear. You already have the heart of a lady; this will only help you look like one."

"Thank you, Myra." Just then they heard the front door open followed by a shuffling sound across the linoleum floor. Shanna placed her cup on the tray. "That's Jedidiah," she said, getting up from her chair. "Let me see what he needs."

Jedidiah gauged the weather by the aches in his rheumatoid elbows and knees. From the sound of his dragging feet, Shanna could almost predict meteorological conditions.

"Miss Shanna, you got any BC powder back there in that medicine box? My old knees are tellin' me we're in for a mother of a storm!" He shook out a few M&Ms in the palm of his hand and began sorting them by color.

Shanna nodded her answer then turned her attention to the window at the sound of wheels moving over crushed oyster shells. Gage had moved his truck so it faced the horizon and sat behind the wheel just staring out. He seemed to be in a sort of settlement with the sea, as if he'd been communicating, reading signs, listening.

Dupe waved until he gained his boss' attention and communicated something to him. Raising his head, Gage acknowledged the gesture and almost immediately his gaze shifted to the office window and fixed on Shanna. She waited for some reaction, some gesture to break the spell, but he gave none before he returned his attention to the sea.

The ocean swells came high and very slowly. And, to the casual observer, the languid pace might have seemed reassuring, but not to Gage. In fact, the quietness seemed far more ominous. He would never again underestimate the fickle nature of Atlantic storms.

With the prolonged autumn heat, the waters had warmed to the temperature of a bath. Gage prayed softly to himself as he watched the sky. Instantly he was propelled back in time to one of the deadliest storms ever to target South Carolina. Within twenty-four hours twelve people, including his grandfather, Broder Bain, had lost their lives on the island, and all because the storm had taken an unexpected turn.

"Gage!" Yancey's gravelly voice called out as he ambled closer to the truck window. "Dupe says he's securing everything — at your order. If you're thinking what I'm thinking, we best get these people off the island."

He nodded and, as he got out of the truck, again scanned the horizon to the east. "Yeah, looks like we're in for it. My gut tells me the meteorologists missed this one."

"My elbow's been tellin' me the same thing," Jedidiah supplied as he ambled up to the truck. "Might be late tomorrow, even the next day, but it sure is comin'."

A steady breeze shoved clouds across a gray sky. No sign of a storm on the horizon, but the ocean rose in great blue-green swells. "Most likely the advance guard of the storm," Gage said. The noise he felt more than heard was the pounding caused by high breakers falling upon the beach.

Most days the waters around the marina were as placid as a big lake, with waves that gently lapped the shore. But the immense swells were gathering slowly, silently toward the island.

Gage had at least two good reasons for what he did next: first, he wanted to protect his family and employees. Second, he never again wanted to suffer through another senseless and tragic loss of life. The victims had been family, friends, neighbors, people who were part of the island. He knew the seas were both seductive and deadly. Only this time, he was going to be prepared for it.

The door squeaked open as Gage, followed by Jedidiah and Yancey, came into the office. Silently Shanna followed them with her eyes, sensing some kind of trouble brewing. When Gage spoke, his voice had a tone of authority, his manner confident. As she observed him, it came to her that he had always been a man who gave orders quietly and people obeyed, but never had she seen him so intent. After he'd instructed the men, he ushered his mother out the door. Her curiosity began to grow.

She listened closely, going about her duties as preparations were being made for some big event. They spoke of transporting the houseboat sisters and their child, Ol' Tar, and even the nameless dog to higher ground. Though she couldn't exactly follow all that was going on, only that foul weather seemed imminent, a strange excitement began to build inside her. The thing Shanna loved about severe weather was the way it forced things to the surface; important things like life and God and family. How it brought into sharp focus the only things that really matter.

It was early afternoon before Shanna became the object of her boss's attention. She was replacing a trash bag in his office when she noticed Gage's occasional glance. He smoothed out a set of drawings on his desk, anchoring the corners down with weighted objects. Deliberately she continued working, not looking up until he called her name.

"Shanna," Gage said, regarding her closely, "I think it's wise that we move to the mainland for a few days. We're going to encourage as many as we can to seek higher ground. Charleston is further north and more protected by the barrier islands. Most will stay in a hotel we've arranged for them. As you know, we have a home there and I'd like for you to stay with us until this storm passes through."

Shanna nodded, blowing away a strand of auburn hair from her forehead. It certainly didn't help her attitude to know that she'd been considered only after the nameless mutt. "Thanks, but I'll be fine," she said, turning away to collect the trash. "I've always loved a bracing wind. Kinda makes me feel alive." A second later she started in surprise as a hand came upon her shoulder, turning her around.

"This is serious, Shanna. I want you to listen."

She hesitated, finding it difficult to respond as his eyes fixed on her with a steady gaze. "I'll leave if I see it's coming this way. The weather report says it may hit further south."

Gage was silent and thoughtful, then mentioned a subject he would have preferred avoiding. "By then it'll be too late. You'll be stuck in traffic and in a worse predicament. Flooding is the danger. It can sweep you away without a trace... the way it did my grandfather and eleven more people on this island once before. They wouldn't listen — either."

The words hit her with a crashing impact that almost staggered her.

Seeing her abrupt change, he watched her face closely as he rolled one of the drawings, sliding it into a cardboard cylinder. "Take my advice. Leave with us in the morning."

The next morning Gage casually raised his eyes and squinted through the smoke as it curled from his cigar. "Looks like Shanna and Gabriel have decided to leave with us."

Myra turned at the mention of the names to see the two getting out of a dark blue SUV. "You invited Gabriel Muir — to our house?"

"Why? Is that a problem?" Gage paused a long moment to consider his mother. Then, he leisurely examined his cigar. "Gabriel didn't want Shanna driving alone. He offered to help transport anyone else who might need assistance. I thought since he was a man of the cloth he'd be safe enough to have in our home. But, obviously … I'm mistaken."

Myra missed the mild sarcasm and turned square-jawed to her son. "Of course he's safe — he's the kindest most decent man I have ever known!" With that, she turned on her heel and left Gage to stare after her.

In the busyness of the morning, Gage had not even spoken to Shanna. But now as he faced her, his eyes softened. She'd worked hard helping with the relocation, but now she held herself apart with a stately grace that was at once both lovely and a little disconcerting. Stepping over to the SUV, he held open the passenger door and helped her up. He spoke to Gabriel who was behind the wheel, set and ready to go. "We're about ready to pull out." At the man's nod, Gage glanced at Shanna briefly, perceiving an air of seriousness about her. She displayed none of the reluctance he'd met with before. Still, he was hardly flattered that she seemed willing to go with him only after considering all the other alternatives. He gently shut the door.

There was an unhurried determination about Gage as he prepared the group to leave. A brief smile crossed his face and for an instant Shanna saw the man he must've been before so much sorrow had happened in his life. When she thought back on her own life, she worried at times that she probably hadn't laughed enough and she was dead sure Gage Barrington never found the pleasure in a good fall-on-the-floor uncontrollable kind of silliness either.

For an instant she felt sorry for Quinn. But, on the other side of it, Gage was solid. And she liked his shoulders, she decided, as she watched him walk away. They weren't overly bulked up like some mirror-gazing bodybuilder, but they were broad and strong. Strong enough to handle the pressures of life. She ran a finger down the glass of the car window. A person could do without laughing, but not without joy. She knew bone deep that there was only one source of joy, and Gage Barrington needed to find that source.

CHAPTER 19

T he sound of a shutter slamming somewhere on the Charleston house startled Shanna from a sound sleep. She stirred beneath the covers, listening to the rising wind wail around the house as the clock on the mantle chimed out the first hour. Easing from the warmth of the bed, she turned on the lamp, slid into her robe, and tied it around her waist. Wandering over to a small bookcase, she selected Tolstoy's *What Men Live By* and moved to the chair by the window, pulling a lightweight quilt from the bed to cover her legs.

Moments later, she looked up from he r book with a start. Becoming still she listened, wondering what had made the light tapping sound. She tucked the quilt underneath her legs, pulling them closer in the chair. *The wind*, she surmised, until she heard it again. Staring across the dim room toward the door, she thought she saw the doorknob twist, then slowly ease back into place.

Her heart seemed to slam against her chest. She bit the end of her fingernail, her eyes fixed on the door. A trembling came to her hand. Realizing she would not rest until her curiosity was satisfied, she squashed her fears, went to the door, and carefully eased it open.

Glancing about the darkened hallway, nothing seemed unusual. As she was closing the door, a flickering shadow reflecting on the wall caught her attention. Determined to investigate, she tiptoed down the corridor and made her way noiselessly down the stairs.

In the predawn darkness of the morning, Gage stood before a low burning fire. Sleep had eluded him. The same old pattern was occurring, common on his visits to his father's home. Forced to look within himself, his thoughts would not allow him peace. Only persistent stubbornness had dismissed all notions that Breck Barrington still had a hold on Gage.

He had come to the house seeking safety for his family, escaping the gathering threat of the storm. He had gotten to the point where he couldn't bear the thought of another assault on their lives, making up his mind to flee the island and bring as many with him as he could. But he would never have guessed the squall that had awaited his arrival earlier that night.

His thoughts tumbled around in his head, thinking of Evan-Cerise and her black shiny hair, warm smile, and sultry brown eyes. Slowly and without effort, a vision of clear gray eyes crept into his mind. The soft humming that even now made him think of her. His faint pulse began to pick up as he stood before the hearth, unaware that the subject of his thoughts had entered the room behind him. In a reflective mood, he stared into the flames before briefly turning aside to the end table to pour a generous drink.

As Shanna watched, it seemed to her as if a torment had been poured into his glass; he seized it, swallowing it down to the last dregs. Gage had a poise that came from a good life and a steady flow of money. It was the first time she had seen him in any other environment but that of the island, and it was like coming into a room with a stranger. It concerned her, especially as she'd witnessed the angry, almost reckless way he'd tossed back his drink. It was all she could do to stand there and not run to the safety of her bedroom.

The change, she sensed, had more to do with his surroundings. The realization dawned that it had been, after all, his father's home. He appeared to be able to hold himself apart from the world of Breck Barrington, and yet, a small part of him fit stiffly within it. More than anything, the man seemed as if he could use a friend.

"You seem to be deep in thought," Shanna murmured.

Gage looked around in surprise. His eyes found hers and widened, staring at her with intensity as if unsure if he was seeing flesh and blood.

"Did I startle you?" Her face split into a wide, white grin.

Even the misery Gage felt could not stop the sudden trip-hammer pounding in his chest. Rubbing a hand across his face he said, "No, it's just that *you're* the last person I expected to see at this hour."

Hugging her arms over her chest with a hint of the same grin on her lips, she said, "Sorry to disappoint you."

"I'm not disappointed, Shanna," he said, her name smooth on his tongue. "Please, sit. Couldn't sleep? Did the storm wake you?"

She smiled in embarrassment. "I heard something at my door ... or at least I thought I did."

"This place has all the usual sounds sleeping houses make — the squeaking joists, popping beams — but it's so much worse in high wind. It sometimes sounds like a creaking ship at sea." He waved toward the windows, empty glass in his hand. "I believe the eye of the storm has come ashore a little south of us. Terrapin took the brunt of it."

"Have you heard of any damage reports?" she asked, smoothing her robe as she took a seat in a leather wingback. She spotted the amber bottle of what looked like bourbon on the side table.

"So far only minor damage has been reported. We won't know the truth of the matter until after sunrise."

She glanced around the room noticing the large mahogany bookcase, Georgian sofa, and wing chairs. She imagined the furnishings sailed right up to their front door directly from Old England a few centuries ago. Gas porch lights glimmered through the tall rain-splattered windows, creating a tawny glow on the library table. It was obviously an English gentleman's study.

While the wind and rain played havoc outside, Shanna felt snug and safe within the walls of the sturdy home. The fire was comforting, warming the air which held a slightly spicy note of Bay Rum. This part of Charleston had always intrigued her. It was a life she could only dream about, far removed from the way she had grown up. But she also knew that wealth and privilege were no guarantee of happiness and fulfillment. As if to prove her point, she looked into the tense face of her host.

"The power is out on the island and some of the roads are closed. It may be several days before we can get back. That's all I know at this point." He rubbed his face in thought. "I wish now I'd thought to grab the blueprints for Barrington Lumber."

She heard the ache of loneliness and sorrow in his voice, realizing he was still grieving the loss of his father. *How hard it must be for him to come back to his father's house,* she thought. It had not quite been a year since his passing. The words of Father Cleo came back to her. *You win him by love.*

Her expression softened as she looked up at him. "If it weren't for you, I'd be stuck on the island by myself—and in the dark!" She shook her head. "Now it looks like you're going to have to put up with us for a few more days."

From his position he saw the gleam in her eyes. "I wouldn't mind that," he drawled. Glancing at her briefly, he held up his glass to her. "I would offer...."

She declined with a shake of her head.

"I may be able to get my hands on some cocoa?" he said, regarding her closely.

Her eyes lit-up as they found his, and he laughed when he saw his answer. "I'll just be a minute."

While Gage was out of the room, she sank back into her chair and gazed at the fire, a soft smile of contentment touching her lips.

The cup of cocoa rattled on a saucer as Gage placed it on a table near Shanna. He sat down in the wingback next to her. "Have you enjoyed getting to know your father-in-law? My mother speaks very highly of him. It seems they were friends when they were younger."

She responded without hesitation. "He's a wonderful man. I only wish he'd been able to spend some time with James before...."

"Why couldn't he?"

"He was in a remote part of India. He and his wife lived among an unreached people group for ten years. She died there several years ago and Gabriel wanted to complete her work before coming home. His wife had a special love for the people of that region, especially the children. He said it had been her lifelong dream to work among them. It was a week before the news reached Gabriel of his son's death. After Gabriel had spoken with his father, he decided to stay on a little longer. That all changed when he got word of his father's death."

"An unreached people group?" Gage shifted in his chair, waiting for an answer.

"People without knowledge of the Gospel message concerning Christ, the Kingdom of God, and salvation. James' parents were missionaries."

"Oh, I see." The warm amber liquid began working its way through Gage's bloodstream, loosening his tongue. "Is that what you are? A missionary?"

"I certainly hope so."

"Oh, you definitely are. You're proof that you don't have to go across the world to endanger your health, your peace, and your life. You can do it all right here!" His thoroughly blue eyes locked on her with concentration.

"Well, I was partially raised by nuns," she quipped.

"When are you going to remove the veil and see that girl for what she really is?"

Feeling somewhat mocked, Shanna questioned, "Who are you talking about?"

"Gypsy. You can't save everyone, you know. Some people are going to ignore your message and go their own way. What *you* want for her doesn't make *her* want it for herself. You can only help a person who genuinely wants it."

"How do you know she doesn't want it?" Shanna felt a strong desire to defend Gypsy.

"I know because she's come to me—many times—for … well, you know the answer to that." Gage unconsciously twirled his empty glass. "Even showed me a list of options once … for other girls."

Shanna's jaw fell slack. "Well, I hope you got your money's worth," she snapped, getting to her feet.

"What! Let me assure you, I don't have to…." He let the statement drop as if sudden reasoning came to his mind. "I mean, if you think for one minute that I would stoop to picking up a prostitute, you are sadly mistaken. I only meant to say that Gypsy is fooling you. She's using you."

"Using me? For what—bible studies! Look, you don't understand. Girls like Gypsy are usually without family, taken from other cities, and forced to engage in this activity. There *is* no one to call, nowhere to turn. They're stuck. We offer them a way out. Sometimes that can take a while, but we wait." She rubbed her forehead with the tips of her fingers. "You're right about one thing, though. We can't save them all."

"Why do you do it? Really? What do you get out of it—points to take with you to the other side?"

Shanna's breath left her in a sudden gasp. "Look, I'm not stupid enough to try and reason with a drunk. Ask me that question again when you're sober." She plopped down into the chair.

"You think I'm drunk? I am not—yet!"

"I thought you gave up drinking?" Gage was about to turn away when Shanna laid a restraining hand on his arm. "I'm sorry. What you do in your own home is none of my business."

"I had a visitor…earlier," he muttered beneath his breath, not at all sure why he felt a need to confide in her.

Her gaze flicked to his, revealing her confusion. "Tinsley?"

He shook his head. "Lynch. He's in love with Evan-Cerise."

Shanna waited until he settled down. His deep sigh telling her all she needed to know. She'd learned from Father Cleo that it was far more valuable to be quiet and attentive when someone was troubled than spew a gush of words. He taught her to focus on the individual with the skill of a poised harpoon thrower to insure the greatest result from the dart. "I'm sorry," she said, and meant it.

"Don't be." The words seemed to get lodged in his throat and he cleared it. "I'm going to confess something: I haven't been fair to Evan-Cerise. She's a beautiful woman and a sweet person and she deserves better than what she's gotten from me." He reached over and poured another drink, studying the liquid in the glass as he held it in his hand. The fire sparkled through the crystal as prisms danced in the light. Without warning, he tossed the contents into the fire, causing a combustion of flames.

Drumming her fingers on the arm of the chair, she said calmly, "Well, that was dramatic. Why didn't you throw in the whole glass for more effect—like they do in the movies?"

He did his best to look annoyed, and nearly succeeded, but then a smile crept across his face.

Her lips curved as she sat up in the chair. "So Lynch loves her. How does she feel about him?"

"Apparently the same. Although he says I was her first choice." He laughed, scoffing. "Said she realized that to have the love of a man and not merely the affection of a man was a thrilling thing. Lynch said he knew that I didn't love Evan-Cerise and he got tired of waiting for me to let her go, so he took matters into his own hands." He gave a half-laugh. "And all this time I thought Lynch was a player. Turns out he's a one-woman man. I just so happened to have had *his* woman."

She kept her eyes on him for a moment longer, then eased back into the chair and stared into the fire. "You don't seem overly upset. Are you incapable of loving someone? Or are you just not good at picking women?"

"Yes, to both questions."

The room was dark and eerily shadowed from the fire light. Only the mournful wail of the rising wind and the crackle of the fire intruded upon the stillness. Against the wall, leather-bound volumes filled the shelves, glowing from the brightly flickering yellow and orange flames.

Sparks flew upward through the chimney after a log slipped in the fireplace. Shanna glanced at Gage. "You read the Bible?"

"No. I'm an avid reader, though." The bourbon did its work, relaxing his body. He was aware of her attention on him.

"There's your problem."

"I have a problem?"

"I'm afraid you do. We all do. You know, the Bible isn't so much God telling us things about life; it's him speaking life into us. A life can fade quickly without it."

Gage tried to ignore her overstated religiousness, not wanting to cause an argument, but he couldn't seem to control his tongue. "I bet you're one of those Christians that boasts to everyone that alcohol has never touched your lips, all the while stammering around trying to explain why Jesus' first miracle was turning water into wine." He didn't look at her so he didn't see the briefest smile play about her lips.

"Let me guess: Grandmother Lilly Rose made you memorize the miracles of Jesus before you could use the canoe?"

"Who else?"

A warmness flushed her cheeks and it was not from the heat of the fire. Her voice was tiny. "Once, when I was about sixteen-years-old, Archbishop Lancer came to our church in Natchez to hold Midnight Mass. Earlier that evening I had been given a gift by a young monk, Brother John. It was a little crystal decanter with a pump, spigot, and six tiny crystal glasses."

"A wine decanter?" Gage said, leaning back in the chair, folding his hands behind his head as he stared into the flames, listening intently.

"Brother John had been invited to a Christmas party at the church. He had gifts for everyone, except me, whom he didn't realize would be there. He seemed embarrassed not to have a gift for me. I saw him whisper to Sister Jon Maureen and then a moment later, he presented me the gift.

"Well, I was so taken with the gift and felt so grown up all of a sudden that when the party was over, I went directly to the closet where the communion wine was stored and filled up my little decanter."

"I can only imagine what happened next."

"Yep, I got plastered. The pump fascinated me. I kept trying it out. But that's not the worst of it. Before Mass I was introduced to Archbishop Lancer by Father Cleo. He said, 'Shanna Muir, His Excellency, Archbishop Lancer.' I took the bishop's hand, kissed his ring, and slurred, '*And I* am a Humble Recipient of God's Divine Grace.'"

Gage laughed in amazement. "Did they know you were drunk?"

"Everyone knew I was drunk. I was also sick as a dog. Even missed Midnight Mass. Didn't have a free minute without work for the next six months. Father Cleo is old school when it comes to punishment. I was told later that the archbishop said that I had my theology correct, but my speech needed work; I sounded a bit slurred." She shook her head, still embarrassed by the incident.

Gage reached out a hand and with a single tug pulled on her arm. "It's good to know you're made out of flesh and blood. I was beginning to wonder."

"Well, then, now you know." She got up and patted his arm in a kind of silent gesture of understanding.

"Someday you will find what you're looking for. Or maybe you won't. Or maybe you'll find something much better. Trust God with it. Good night, Gage."

"Good night, Shanna. By the way, should I ever decide to crack open a bible, where do you suggest I start?"

"Ephesians 5:18. I have it carved into my mind. 'Do not get drunk on wine, which leads to debauchery. Instead, be filled with the Spirit.' See, you're not the only one forced to memorize scripture." Shanna winked, then left the room.

Chapter 20

After a restless night, Myra Barrington settled back with her morning coffee in the courtyard at a small iron table. Along with the splashing gurgle of a wall fountain, the sound of chainsaws mingled in the Sunday morning air as the bells of St. Michael's tolled in the distance. In the aftermath of the storm, a certain tranquility had settled around the city. Faint sounds of beeping utility trucks could be heard as first responders continued their work to remove the debris from the streets and set about to restore order to the city.

The storm of high wind and slashing rain had struck with such ferocity that rows of Palmettos lining the street had swirled like cheap pinwheels. When the winds lessened in the wee hours of the morning, every man in the house left to assist in the cleanup and rescue effort, leaving the others to await their return.

The wrought-iron gate to the courtyard squeaked as Gabriel entered from the back alleyway. "I've always heard that there's no tired like the weariness of a preacher in a coastal town," he said to Myra, a sheepish grin on his face. "I just found out it's true."

"Rough night?" Myra asked, wrapping her silk robe around her waist tightly. She looked over her shoulder and caught the attention of her housekeeper, LuBelle, who had been threading Jackson vine through the trellis it had escaped from in the storm. She raised two fingers. LuBelle nodded and headed for the kitchen. The aroma of hot biscuits and strong savory coffee floated out as the housekeeper bumped the door closed with her hip.

Inhaling the deeply appreciated smell, Gabriel let out a sigh. "Yes. In fact, we spent most of the night pulling people from flooded cars and flooded houses. Cleared a few roads." He broke off a mint leaf from a plant in a terracotta pot and crushed it between his fingers before tapping it on his tongue. "Things went much better once the Utility Department joined us. Their chainsaws mean business."

"I know you're all exhausted."

Gabriel had the look of an overused paper cup, crumpled from too much use. "I'm beat. And so are the others. But it feels good to have been able to help."

"Please sit down, Gabriel. LuBelle is getting our breakfast." Nervous and unable to think of anything to say, she picked up her spoon and dipped it into her coffee like a paddle going against the flow of the creek. It was a full moment before she released her breath. It was a rare day that Myra Barrington ran out of words.

"Was that LuBelle?" Gabriel asked. "Imagine that, she's still with you after all of these years. You two have been friends for a long time." He pulled out a chair and joined Myra at the table.

"We're not as energetic as we once were, but we're still doing our best trying to take care of each other. She's been with me through it all, and Lord knows we've had our share of ups and downs." Her eyes lingered on him a moment, taking in his warmth and honest scents of leather and sweat that clung to him, arousing feelings she could not even explain to herself. "She's raising two of her grandchildren. Took them in when her daughter ran off with the butcher from the Winn Dixie. Oh, but she has a strong faith...more than I've ever thought to have."

The love Myra had for LuBelle was evident, causing Gabriel to smile. He remembered LuBelle vowing never to leave Myra, and as far as Gabriel could see, she'd made good on her promise. They seemed connected somehow, like they were linked together by an invisible chain. He leaned toward Myra and whispered, "Any chance you can talk her into making some of that old fashion peanut butter fudge she used to make for us?"

Amused, Myra leaned forward and mimicked his posture. "I'll see what I can do. LuBelle is not above a bribe."

Yancey's gruff voice called from behind as he came through the gate. "First the priest, now the old boyfriend, and a preacher at that!"

"I know. I'm quite the scandal," Myra said, straightening in her seat, mildly annoyed at being interrupted.

"Boyfriend?" Gage questioned, following close on Yancey's heels. He looked first to his mother, then to Gabriel. "You two dated?"

"Yes, but that was long before your father," Myra said, hoping the subject would drop.

Seeing his sister's obvious discomfort and deriving pleasure from it, Yancey continued to tease. "And just look at you now, entertaining a preacher in your nightgown—and on The Lord's Day to boot! I remember a time when you cared about what people thought of you."

"Yes, and that was the longest five minutes of my life. Now, would you like breakfast or would you prefer to take your meal in front of the television so you won't miss the Holier than Thou Hour?"

Yancey grinned. "Now don't get your back up, Sis, I'm just kidding. Need my rest. I'll grab something to eat on my way to bed." He threw up his hand and took himself to the door, giving his sister cause to shake her head as her eyes followed him into the house. Her brother lifted his heavy shoulders to convey his indifference. "Makes no difference to me if you want to flirt with a preacher in your pajamas," he mumbled, before disappearing into the shadows of the house.

Gage glanced around. "Where's the rest of the crew?"

"Quinn is having breakfast in the kitchen so he can watch cartoons. I haven't seen Shanna. She's probably sleeping in." It occurred to Myra that she should probably check on the girl. "I'll just go knock on her door; make sure she's alright. I tried to look in on her last night when I noticed her light on. It was such an ungodly hour but her door was locked."

"No need for that," LuBelle said, coming out the back door carrying two plates of ham and biscuits. "She left about an hour ago. Some woman named Molly picked her up. Said to tell you she'd be back after a while."

Gage rubbed his chin, heard the scratch of the stubble. "You don't think they're foolish enough to head to the island?"

LuBelle shrugged. "She looked mighty antsy. I ain't no mind reader, but I'd say that's exactly where they're going."

Panic hit Gage right between the eyes. He pulled out his cell phone — what a single man with no current prospects of a girlfriend was doing worrying about a grown woman was a question he didn't want to ask himself. Still wondering about his state of mental health, he put a call into Shanna.

"Who is he calling?" Myra asked, carefully watching her anxious son as he rushed into the house, leaving the door open behind him.

"My guess would be Shanna—sweet merciful heavens!" Gabriel swore to the sky.

Myra glanced back in surprise.

Grabbing a biscuit, Gabriel stuffed it with ham and pushed up from the table. "We'll be on the island."

The island lay quiet in the aftermath of the storm. The squall had hit Terrapin Island without warning, sudden and violent. The gales and breaking waves capsized small boats and washed larger ones onto the shore, littering the beaches with their remains. Molly and Shanna drove over barely detectable roads piled high with sand and strewn with debris. A stilted home sat squat in the dunes with overturned outbuildings, assorted deck chairs and limbs scattered about.

"Don't look so worried, girl. I've seen it a lot worse. The town was built where it is, hidden from the ocean side, on purpose. It's nestled in the marshes for a reason—to lessen the brunt of the storm." Molly popped a Bit-o-Honey in her mouth and began to chew. "This part of the island always gets the worst of it."

Shanna stared through the mud-splattered windshield and was not encouraged by her friend's words. Most of the island seemed to have been rearranged overnight. Familiar landmarks had all but disappeared. Missing were the vine-smothered chimney stacks of an old planter's house and the rusted roof of Doo Lottie's store, a sight every visitor to the island would first see when coming off the bridge from the mainland.

"Just a warning: when we get to town, there are some people you don't need to make contact with—looters! It could get bad. The best and the worst in people come out in a tragedy. I'm afraid we may have beaten the good folks here."

Shanna turned to Molly, an incredulous look on her face. "You don't think anybody from the island would steal, do you?"

Lifting an eyebrow, Molly stopped chewing and swallowed hard. "Stealing is the least of our worries. There are some on the island who exist only to inflict pain on others." She looked back at the road. "There's a dangerous element here, Shanna. Flooding tends to wash the rats out of hiding."

Absently, Shanna pushed her hair away from her forehead. "I just want to find Gypsy. That's why I came. And to help the people that stayed behind. A few provisions can go a long way at a time like this."

Molly squawked, "A few provisions! You nearly bought out the store, girl! That's all well and good, but avoid looking anyone you see in the eye. A random glance is enough to draw too much attention to yourself." Molly patted Shanna's leg. "I know you mean well. Just be cautious. We're in this together."

"You make it sound like we're going into war," Shanna quipped, with a hint of sarcasm. "I've worked around these people for a while now. They're harmless."

Molly shifted in the seat, almost afraid to venture a question and yet could not resist. "And that brings up another question I've been meaning to ask you. Why? Why do you do it?" She saw the bewilderment in Shanna's face and smiled.

"What? Help people?"

"Yeah. I mean, most people just write a check and let someone else deal with it. You gotta get all down and dirty with it."

She blew the hair out of her eyes. "I don't want to stand before God one day all clean and untouched. I want to stand there with dirt on my clothes and rough hands and sore muscles from helping someone. I want him to know that I lived, really lived, and cared about what he cares about—people. Father Cleo taught me that there are two eternal things—the Word of God and people. People matter to God and they better matter to us."

"Well!" Molly slapped her hands on the steering wheel after a brief pause of silence. "Let's hope you're right and all these harmless people are just waiting to be helped." She scanned the storm-damaged landscape. "I sure hope you're right."

It was nearly an hour later when they rolled up to the marina. Three Course Catering had weathered the storm fairly well and besides losing a few shingles, nothing of significance had blown off the house. The front gate at the entrance to Summer's Keep was locked. Visible from the road were a few downed trees, toppled from the rain-saturated ground and pushed over in the high wind. Located on the highest point on the island, the position of the house probably saved her from damage.

"You need me to go in with you?" Molly asked.

"No, I got it. I just want to pick up a set of drawings. Gage mentioned he needed them last night and I think I know where they are."

"Here." Molly handed over a pistol. "You know how to use a gun?"

Shanna's eyes took on a flinty shade of gray as she slid the piece into the pocket of her rain jacket. "I'm from Mississippi—what do you think."

She got out of the car with key in hand, headed for the office door. As she fumbled with the lock, a movement beside her drew her attention. Recognizing Gypsy, she pushed the door open with relief. "I've been looking everywhere for you," Shanna said. "Are you okay? I have some supplies with me. Just—"

A thin man with a patchy beard pushed his way around Gypsy, surprising Shanna as he forced himself inside the office, pushing Shanna in front of him. His bulbous nose was shot through with broken veins, and the gleam that burned in his eyes made Shanna slide her hand in her pocket until she felt the cool metal against her palm.

Shanna watched as Gypsy casually entered the room and shut the door behind her. Her stone-cold eyes, black with Kohl liner, looked vacant. "Are you okay? Has this man hurt you? You seem … different?"

The man reached behind Gypsy's neck and, with a sick smile, gently kneaded her muscles. "Let's just say she's way off her meds."

"*Let's* just get this over with," Gypsy snapped, flinging the hand from her neck. "Do as I say. Get what we're after and let's go."

Assessing the situation in a hurry, Shanna stepped back a few paces and stated firmly, "You need to leave—now!"

Harsh laughter rang out from the woman. "What? And I thought we were so close. Is that any way to treat an old friend?"

Shanna spoke into her malevolent eyes. "The woman I remember has always been welcome here." She found it difficult to merge the person in front of her with the Gypsy she knew, or thought she knew. They had done everything in their power to help Gypsy escape the harsh life of a prostitute. Now, as she looked at the loathing in the woman's eyes, it became apparent they had all been fooled.

"Guess you didn't figure Gypsy might not want your help," the man said, sneering. "She doesn't need you or anything you're offering. She's doing just fine with her little business operation."

Shanna tried to brace herself for what would happen next. One way or the other, she knew it wouldn't be good for one of them.

The man laughed as he added, "Not that we didn't appreciate the free health care when Gypsy was so sick. We especially enjoyed the pain meds from the hospital. Oh, and the money you and the good doctor kept sending to the girls through Gypsy. *New life money*, I believe is what you called it. So what if she had to sit through a bible study or two." He winked at Gypsy. "That didn't hurt you any now, did it? Plus, it kept you people from interfering with our little operation."

At very close range Shanna saw the burning, spitting rage that set fire to Gypsy's eyes. It was a true test of Shanna's resolve to remain poised and not cave in to the emotions running rampant through her bloodstream. She glanced away from Gypsy who began prowling around the room like some animal of prey.

"Where do you keep the cash? In here?" Gypsy pulled open a desk drawer and drummed her fingers on a metal strongbox.

"I have no idea," Shanna said, pulling the gun from her pocket and pointing it at her. She gave the startled pair the same close attention one might give a poisonous snake. "But you're not taking a blessed thing from this marina."

The man's tone was almost pleasant as the sound of heavy and quick footsteps sounded on the deck outside. "We've done nothing swrong? You're the one with the gun pointed at us." He shrugged. "There's no law against visiting an old friend."

The door behind Shanna burst open and there stood Sheriff McCrae, his bald head glistening with sweat and one hand on his holster. "You got uninvited visitors, Shanna?" he asked in his odd tenor voice.

"Yes, sir. They wanted to know where we keep the cash." Shanna glanced at Gypsy, the hurt she felt causing her throat to tighten. By the look of desperation on the woman's face, Shanna knew the game was over for her.

"Look, Sheriff," the man said, showing his palms, "we're empty-handed. As far as I know, there's no law saying you can't ask a question, is there?"

Sheriff McCrae shifted his eyes toward Shanna. "More going on here than a potential robbery?"

"Human trafficking," Shanna said, standing erect. The battle line had been drawn. Hearing the gun slide out of the sheriff's holster, she tucked hers back into her pocket. Instinctively she braced for this new storm, sinking her roots around the rock of the truth. "I'll tell you all I know."

The gruff man pointed his finger at Gypsy. "I work for her."

"I want a lawyer," Gypsy stated firmly.

By the time Gage and Gabriel pulled up at the sheriff's office, they'd learned that Leon Smith, thirty-seven, of South Carolina, and Gina "Gypsy" Douglas, twenty-eight, of Georgia, were arrested and charged with two counts of first degree human trafficking. Five of the six victims were found in a hotel room in the 500 block of Eastern Shore Drive. The evidence in the room suggested six girls were being sexually exploited.

Gage drew off his rain jacket and tossed it across the truck seat. He frowned, realizing that if it hadn't been for the call he'd received from Molly, he might have spent the entire day chasing Shanna all over the island. Molly had been the one to call the sheriff when she had seen two people follow Shanna into the marina office.

Gabriel snatched his phone from the console. "I'll go talk to Sheriff McCrae. We went to school together. He'll level with me about all of this."

Walking up to the red brick building, they pushed through the glass door and noticed Shanna seated near the wall. She sat stiff and rigid on the seat, her jaw set and her eyes betraying no emotion. A call came from the hallway, and recognizing the voice, Gabriel turned and walked toward the sheriff.

Before Gage moved toward Shanna, he studied the girl and couldn't help but wonder at the grit it had taken to point a gun at someone you'd spent a year trying to rescue. He'd never met anyone quite like Shanna, and she seemed so oblivious to the fact that she disturbed his peace of mind like no other. Walking near her, he braced a hand against the wall and asked in a low, hushed tone, "You okay?"

Eyeing him uncertainly, Shanna pushed her fingers through her hair and asked the question that had been troubling her all afternoon. "I know you don't owe it to me, and I'll understand if you say no, but I was wondering if you might consider hiring me again if I ever come back to the island."

He rubbed his chin as he thought about her question. "You going somewhere?"

She gave a quick nod. "Natchez. Sheriff McCrae asked me to leave the area for a while. The minute they identified the crime as human trafficking, they reached out to their Federal and State partners. They want some time to investigate and make sure no one else is involved. They think it's a good idea for me to leave the area for a while, until they have some answers."

Gage looked away as if thinking, then turned back and said, "Stay with us. You'll be safe at Summer's Keep."

She shook her head. "No, but thank you. I have some business to take care of in Noble and I plan to visit Father Cleo in Natchez for a while." She hesitated. "I'll leave in a few days. My job?"

"Will be here when you get back."

There appeared to be no other option for Shanna but to return to Mississippi for a short while. She hated to admit it and felt a coward for it, but after learning the horrific details about Gypsy and the human trafficking ring, she wanted to put some distance between her and the kind of people who enslaved others for profit.

After packing her things and loading them into the car, she took one last look around the garden house. She'd been careful to scrub the place clean and put things in order, not wanting Gage to think she didn't appreciate his generosity in allowing her to stay there.

Distractedly Shanna rubbed a rag sprayed with furniture polish over the kitchen table, trying to sort out her own feelings. She felt a start of tears in her eyes at the thought of leaving James. She sniffed them away, clutched the bouquet of late autumn wildflowers from the vase on the table, and headed out the door toward the cemetery.

At the gravesite, the deep depression Shanna had fought so hard to keep buried and hidden started to slowly perk to the surface. She had to rummage deep to find a shred of hope to hold on to; deeper still not to lose all sense of what it meant to be a Christ follower in an insanely evil world. *Does anything we do make a difference?*

Shanna held her head in her hands, wanting to scream out her grief and frustration. The sound of a fish splashing in the water filled her head and in that instant she remembered. "The creek!" She shot up from the ground and ran toward Sassabee Creek, wading feet first into the water until she was waist deep. In one sudden plunge, she went backward into the current, holding herself under until the breath left her lungs.

Gage led Ol' Tar from the stable on the day Shanna was to leave Terrapin Island. He clutched an envelope that had been placed in his hand for safekeeping by Quinn, marked with the words, "To Shanna, from Quinn." He had hoped to see her one last time before she left. After repeated knocks on the garden house door, he realized she wasn't around, though her car was still there. Gage folded the note in half and, with slow movements, tugged Ol' Tar toward Shanna's car and stuffed the letter in the crack of the door before mounting his horse.

Riding along the bank of the creek, Gage jerked the reins back, halting the steed as his anxious eyes locked where a motionless figure lay partially submerged in the water of Sassabee Creek. Jumping off his horse, he slid down the embankment and splashed through the water. He trudged through mud that sucked at his boots until her reached the girl, lifting her from the murky water in one smooth swoop.

Abruptly, Shanna felt the intense feeling of desperation give way as hands reached down and snatched her from the stream. Before she could react, she was pressed close to a hard chest and cradled there like a ragdoll. Tightly held, her mind searched for reason as she coughed and blinked through the wetness. When her eyes focused, she stared up into the face of Gage Barrington. He was so close she had no problem discerning every detail of his face. She watched the tightening of his jaw as he clenched his teeth. The warm spicy scent of him moved around her and she breathed it in. His gaze settled on her, the same absorbing stare she'd come to know.

He sat her down on the creek bank, brushing wet hair from her face. A thought came to his mind and tugged his memory. He pulled back and looked at her, then dismissed the thought and wouldn't let his mind go in that direction. But Gage failed to find reassurance in the expressionless face, the lifeless gray eyes.

Releasing his breath, he attempted to gather his words into some form of thought. "You sure picked a cold day to take a swim, Shanna Muir." He pulled off his jacket and tucked it around her shoulders, plopping down on the bank next to her. She tipped into him, seeking his warmth, and his arm naturally came around her. Not a word was spoken for a long time until the shivering subsided. "I'm taking a wild guess here," Gage said, "but are you looking for some sort of healing?"

A head nod was her answer. She sat there with mud and sand caked and drying on her skin, staring at the clouds reflected in the water. Gathering all of the dignity she could muster, she said, "I ... I guess the water doesn't work for me. I'm not — sick, just depressed ... I suppose."

Gage stared across the creek, thinking about her words for a long time, then said, "That reminds me of a story."

"Of course it does?" she returned, with mild sarcasm.

Gage peered at her, wondering just what to think about the stringy-haired, soaking wet, little smart-mouthed girl. "*Listen*," he said, emphasizing the word. "It was a one-act play by Thornton Wilder called, 'The Angel That Troubled the Waters.' It told of the power of the pool of Bethesda to heal whenever an angel stirred its waters. It's about a physician who came to the pool hoping to be the first one in so he could be healed of his depression or melancholy, one of those mental ailments. Well, one day the angel finally appeared at the pool to trouble the waters but he blocks the physician just as he is ready to step into the pool. The angel tells the physician to draw back, for this moment is not for him. The man begs for help, but the angel insists that healing is not intended for him. After much pleading from the physician, a prophetic word comes from the angel: 'Without your wounds where would your power be? It is your melancholy that makes your low voice tremble into the hearts of men and women. The very angels themselves cannot persuade the wretched and blundering children on earth as can one human being broken on the wheels of living. In love's service, only wounded soldiers can serve. Physician, draw back.'"

Shanna dropped her head, thinking about his words for a long time. Glancing up, she looked Gage dead in the eye. "I'm sure gonna miss you *and* your stories."

CHAPTER 21

The days slowly passed since Shanna went away and Gage Barrington wasn't getting any nicer. Everyone around the man had started to see small signs that told them Gage was living dangerously on edge. He was working more and sleeping less. Minor arguments broke out regularly among the crew, coming with more and more frequency as the days went by. It had been six weeks since Shanna had left and no one had heard a word from her.

Gage walked along the narrow beach near the marina as the waves crashed onto the shore, their sound filling the air but not his empty heart. Sand shifted beneath his bare feet but it was the wind that reminded him of her. "I love a bracing wind. It makes me feel alive!" Shanna had once said to him. But as he watched the rhythmical movement of the tide as it rearranged shells and rolled seaweed, he knew a homesickness he had never experienced.

The haunting tones of the bell buoy clanged on the air joining the cry of seagulls, and his heart ached. *She comes and goes, surges and retreats. She's high and low and I can no more control her than I can the tide.* Some part of Gage knew that one day she would go. One day when she had the strength to release her husband. He ran a frustrated hand through his hair. "Get back to work,

Gage," he said, forcefully. "That's the only way you're gonna keep that girl off your mind."

Gage jerked open the office door, his intense stare circling the room where the dockworkers usually gathered. It was here where they took their breaks and blew off steam, picking at each other and telling tall tales. His eyes paused and snapped fire when he noticed the door to the supply closet open and Jedidiah fumbling around with a mop and bucket.

"Leave that for Shanna! You're not qualified to clean up around here!" Gage bellowed, before tossing a set of keys across a desk where Dupe sat. "Go lock up the warehouses!" He snatched up a cup and walked toward the coffee pot.

Sliding out of the chair, Dupe cast a worried look in the direction of Jedidiah. Jedidiah motioned with his head toward the door and Dupe grabbed the keys and left the room.

Jedidiah calmly walked across the room, propped the mop against the wall, and placed the bucket down on the floor beside him. "We miss her, too, Boss. But no amount of missing somebody is ever gonna bring them back. Now, we stickin' to this here floor. Pretty soon we all gonna be trapped in here like bugs on flypaper. We got to go on livin' and doin'. If you can't, you best go get that Mississippi girl."

Gage's coffee cup clanked loudly as he banged it down on the counter. He rubbed his forehead as if to get relief from a persistent ache. "We get along just fine here. True, we might be getting a little dirty, but that's nothing we can't fix." He signaled with his hand. "Carry on with your cleaning." Brushing past the men, he went into his office and slammed the door.

Crossing his arms over his chest, Gage glared out the window, his thoughts far away. He knew he had to get a hold of himself. Not just for his sake, but for everyone's. When he finally emerged from his office, he found the others gone and Jedidiah close by. The dark brown eyes questioned, and it was a long thoughtful moment before Gage replied, "We're going to Mississippi. This cleanup from the storm has taken too much time. We need to get back to the lumberyard."

"And Shanna?" Jedidiah asked, hopeful. "We gonna check on her, too, ain't we Boss?"

A hint of a smile crossed his face. "We just might."

Gage saw a quick flash of white teeth before the man turned and snatched up his mop bucket. "Who you want to go and who you want to stay?"

"You, Uncle Yancey, and Nor, go with me. The rest will stay. I'll put Lynch in charge of the marina. Dupe can handle your job."

Jedidiah, along with nearly everybody else on Terrapin Island, had heard the rumors that Lynch Droke had taken Gage's girlfriend. "Lynch? But I thought—"

"You thought wrong. Lynch and I are partners now. I know of none better to oversee the marina."

"You're a better man than me, Boss. Ain't no way I'm gonna partner up with no woman-stealin' dog like that."

"You can't steal something from someone if they never had it in the first place. Evan-Cerise belongs with Lynch. He loves her more than I ever could."

"When do we leave?" Jedidiah unconsciously rubbed the ache in his leg. "Before this rain moves in, I hope."

"By noon tomorrow."

A chilly breeze blew against Gage's cheek and set the flags flapping above his head. The clang of hardware against the pole banged as if sounding out a warning. Yancey muttered low behind his nephew as he began to feel the tenseness. Gage stopped and stared toward the

Mississippi River, stroking his chin thoughtfully as he frowned. "Seems not much has changed since I've been away. Business as usual."

Yancey threw up his hands. "Want me to clear them all out for you? We'll hire all new people—get rid of that bunch of riffraff, starting with the site manager, Gunner."

"Hold up," Gage said abruptly, signaling to Nor. "It may come to that but, in the meantime, take Nor to the warehouse and show him around. I'm going to the sawmill."

Gage tucked himself out of the way in a corner of the mill and began counting heads. He could make out the familiar crew belonging to the foreman, Dayne. He looked at his watch, noticing the time; two hours into the second shift and no new workers. *Where were the other employees he had hired?* The mill was stifling and there was no movement of air. Sawdust hung like thick gauze over everything.

He slipped out into the cool dark of an early winter evening. As he walked across the boards toward his truck, he thought about the men, their families, and the decisions he would have to make. Those decisions would impact so many lives…still, insubordination could not go unpunished.

Later that evening Gage was alone, and then it began to rain as he walked headed down toward the church. All his life he had done things his way, making decisions based on his gut, but not today. He hadn't a clue where it would lead him…somewhere within the will of God, he hoped.

Gage had picked out the church based entirely upon the look of it. It was in the heart of the city of Port St. Joe and appeared to have shaped the very landscape of the town to a great extent. The century-old stone and stained glass structure told a powerful story of devotion and faithfulness to Gage's way of thinking. As he crossed the street, the rain grew worse. Taking the wide front steps two at a time, he yanked on the massive wooden door, relieved to find it unlocked.

As he stepped inside, the door closed behind him with a loud click, echoing through the cool and cavernous vestibule. Small candles burned near the wall, the smell of incense wafting around him as he brushed off the wetness from his hair. Gage wasn't Catholic, but somewhere along the way he'd heard that the doors to a Catholic church remained open and people were encouraged to stop by and pray.

Pushing through the interior doors to the sanctuary, he stopped and gazed upward, admiring the painted cherubim circling overhead. He slipped into a pew and debated a moment whether to kneel or sit. He figured God could hear his prayers just as well from a sitting position. Others in the church came and went quietly, never making eye contact with Gage or seeming to notice him sitting there. Once he relaxed a little, he tuned out all the distractions and got down to business. He closed his eyes and prayed, clumsily at first and then after a while it got easier.

I've ignored you for a long time. Whatever you decide about me is fair. You've seen it all … I know how bad I've been. My sins are staring me down. I'm asking for forgiveness and a fresh start. I'm asking for mercy. Yes, mercy. Use me, don't throw me out. Show me mercy and I'll look for ways to show it to others. Others as undeserving as I.

He could sense movement, phantomlike around him as he assumed people passed by his pew. He sat for what seemed like a long time, listening to the gentle patter of rain on the roof, not really thinking; just being.

Then, unbidden, he heard these clear words in his head. *Having done all, stand!*

Instantly Gage felt the words had some meaning for him. What that was, he didn't have a clue. Getting up, he whispered a quiet thank you. "This won't be the last time we meet like this." He walked out of the church, satisfied that he'd heard from God and determined to carve out time to meet with him regularly.

The next morning, the same wary-faced kid stood inside the doorway blocking the light into Gage's office. Gage snapped his laptop shut and looked up at the boy. "Well? What does the site manager want to say through you now?"

"Gunner sends his report. Wants you to know that in his opinion it would not be wise to cut hours from the workers. They might rebel."

Gage turned to the messenger. "You tell Gunner...." Then he thought, *Gunner wants a frontal assault. I'll give him one.* "Tell Gunner to do as ordered or turn in his notice."

Before the hour was out, Gunner was pushing his way through the door, red-faced and ready for a fight.

Gage calmly pulled a cigar from his desk drawer, bit off the tip, struck a match, and puffed it to life.

Gunner started in, his voice taking on a superior tone. "Look around you. Most of these men can barely read! All they know is work and now you want to take that away from them. We don't need more crews, we need to be left alone to do our job!" Gunner banged his fist on the desk for emphasis.

Through the thin veil of smoke, Gunner could see something in Gage's eyes. He'd heard a few of the South Carolina men talk about a deathly calmness that came over Gage's face when he was angry, but he had not witnessed it before now. His eyes seemed to flash with the heat of it.

Gage said nothing, pushed his chair back, and stood up facing the man. "Gunner, you have failed to implement my plan. We've discussed the same issue not once, but twice. Despite my repeated warnings, you haven't followed through. Because of this, your services are no longer needed. You may pick up your check at the front desk."

Shocked, Gunner could only stammer. "You're letting me go!" Once the idea began to sink in, he turned furious and stabbed his finger in front of Gage's face. "Mark my words. Before this is over, you'll regret ever laying eyes on me."

"Leave the premises," Gage stated boldly, sliding open the top desk drawer. "Or do I need to escort you out the door?" Gage's half-drawn pistol was visible to the man, helping him make the decision to leave.

"You haven't heard the last from me," Gunner threatened before he stormed out, slamming the door behind him.

Gage's frown faded to be replaced by a troubled introspection. He stepped to the window and stood gazing out. Just then, a knock sounded on the door frame. Turning, he saw Dayne standing in the doorway.

"Sorry to interrupt, Boss, but did I just see Gunner leave out of here?"

"You did and, not of his own volition."

Dayne was still considering what his reply should be when Yancey, followed by Nor, stepped around the corner.

"If that man ever puts his foot down on this property again, he'll have to sip Jell-O through a straw for the rest of his life!" Yancey declared, his Irish blood coming to a rolling boil.

"Dayne—do you have anything to add?" Gage asked, noticing the beads of sweat popping up on the man's forehead.

The foreman rubbed his hands together anxiously. His voice was pleading in the dead silence of the room. "Times are hard, Boss. Most of my men are just trying to keep body and soul together, provide for their families, and keep a roof over their heads."

Gage tapped out his cigar in the ashtray. "And how have I made that harder for them with less hours and better pay?"

Dayne rubbed his nose with the back of his hand. "Guess now that Gunner and his men have gone, it's safe to tell you."

Gage narrowed his eyes. "*His* men?"

"Yes, sir. About six of them. They flew out of here like cinders in a high wind."

"I see. Tell me what?"

"Gunner and his men, they threatened my crew. Told them that things were to go on as before until he told them different. And, if they didn't do it, they'd wash up down river in New Orleans."

"And they believed him?"

"Yes, sir."

"What else do you know about them?"

"I know they were stealing from you. Stealing one out of every five loads of lumber hauled out of here—using their own transport trucks."

Gage's face stiffened with suppressed rage. "Round up all the foremen. We'll meet in the warehouse—immediately."

"Yes, sir," Dayne replied, then turned to carry out the orders.

Gage tossed the pistol back into the drawer and pushed it closed. "Well, I guess we're all learning this lumber business the hard way."

Almost a whole year had passed since the death of Gage's father and the voice of Breck Barrington was no longer dominant in the head of his son. A new, quiet voice now seemed to beckon him. Gage's self-seeking approach to life was dissolving by tiny degrees. The desire to achieve in order to prove his worth was losing its hold. God, it seemed, was nudging him toward a new life. One in which it was not based on status or position.

Gage had kept his word to God and now met with him at the church on a regular basis. He'd even downloaded a bible on his phone and was little by little making his way through the books of the New Testament. At first he went easy, opening the door to this new life gradually, taking a long look inside. And then he began to seek out that which was hidden there. Over the course of time he began to recognize the voice of the Author of life.

Father Dominic stood on the portico of Saint Stephen's Cathedral, his attention on the man walking toward the corner café on Bluff Street. He studied the figure with hawk eyes, trying to discern what he saw. The stranger was certainly a man's man, a lean six-footer with wide shoulders and sandy hair. Sharp blue eyes and a close-cut beard over his jawline ruled his face. A cautious concern crept into the priest's eyes. *What could be troubling this man who so frequently visits my church?*

"Do you know that man, Father?"

Father Dominic turned to the soft voice behind him. "Mercy! Well now, isn't this a surprise. What brings you across the river?"

Mercy shivered and adjusted her lightweight sweater more securely around her regal shoulders. "I came to pick up the clothing Mrs. Doone collected for the girls." She nodded toward the café. "Is that man a member of your church?" She stepped out of the shadow of the portico to find warmth from the sun.

"No, no. I don't believe he's catholic. I've never seen him at mass and he doesn't genuflect or make the sign of the cross … he just sits and, I assume, prays and reads the bible." A throaty laugh escaped him. "At first when I saw he was staring into his phone, I thought he was texting. But my view over his shoulder from the balcony told me that he was actually reading scripture."

"Father!" she admonished. "You couldn't see from that distance without a pair of binoculars."

"Exactly. We just so happen to have a pair up there. They're quite good."

Mercy stared at the café the man had disappeared into. "Any idea where he comes from?"

Father Dominic paused, looked embarrassed. "According to Mrs. Doone, he's the new owner of the lumberyard. Changed the name to Barrington Lumber."

"Well, it must be true then. Mrs. Doone seldom gets her facts wrong." The priest's eyes rose sharply, but Mercy had already rushed on to another topic. "I have a situation at the home, Father. As you know, once our mothers have their babies we try and help them get jobs so that they can get on their feet. Well, Sugar Land is just not big enough to handle the demand anymore. I'm having to broaden my search and expand into new territory." She thoughtfully chewed on the corner of her lip. Her eyes slowly narrowed as she stared at the café. The determined gleam that shone from them caused Father Dominic some concern.

"Mercy — ?" he began in an anxious tone. "What are you thinking?"

"I'm thinking of meeting Mr. Barrington."

As the waitress slipped the check on the table, Gage glanced at it and reached for his wallet. At the same time, he looked up to find an attractive middle-aged woman standing beside his table. She was tall and stately with dark eyes and light olive skin coloring. She stuck out her hand, smiling warmly.

"Mr. Barrington?" she said.

Surprised anyone in the café knew his name, he answered with a startled, "Yes." The woman's eyes lit up and Gage could almost see the wheels begin to turn behind their dark depths.

"My name is Mercy and I'd like to talk to you about how you can be used of God to make a difference in a few desperate lives."

Gage's face went ridged. He met Mercy's gaze and held it as he silently recalled his prayer. *I'm asking for mercy. Yes, mercy. Use me, don't throw me out. Show me mercy and I'll look for ways to show it to others. Others as undeserving as I.* He cleared his throat. "You have my attention. Please," he indicated the chair across from him, "tell me what's on your mind."

CHAPTER 22

It was nearing Christmas and the warmth of the home known as Noble Hill enveloped Shanna as she walked through the door. She sat down her luggage. All was quiet. Looking around, she rolled her shoulders, stiff from lifting the heavy suitcase.

She felt tired, worn-out from living out of a bag. Although Father Cleo had made every effort to make Shanna feel at home in Natchez, she couldn't shake the feeling of being displaced.

Glancing through the door to the sitting room, Shanna felt her throat tighten. The room had been a gathering place for the Noble family for many generations. The mantel, stripped of its embellishments years ago, held firm. The old fireplace hadn't seen the home fires burning in what seemed an eternity.

Beside the hearth was an empty space near the large window where by now would have stood a tall fresh Christmas tree all decked out in colored lights and tinsel. She imagined hearing the sound of rolling wheels on the wooden boards from her baby doll carriage from years gone by. Shanna's grandmother had lived with them and, in fact, had told her the story of her father staying up all night one Christmas Eve to put together every intricate piece of that complicated carriage. Funny, but Shanna had forgotten that story until just that moment.

Images of Shanna's parents flashed through her mind as the spirit of Christmases past began to slowly reveal themselves. There had been laughter, and hugs and … for a brief cherished moment, Shanna felt she had been loved.

The old relic of a house seemed at that moment alive with love and warmth by the long departed souls that had once called it home. Through her exhaustion, a new desire began to kindle a small flame in Shanna's heart. A desire to make and keep a home.

With his day at the lumberyard done, Gage came to a crossroads: call his mother and have her fly to the airport in Jackson with his son, or travel back to Charleston for Christmas and risk a complete shut-down of the lumberyard? He debated a moment, knowing the hotel where he and the others were staying was no fit place to spend Christmas. A delay in operations would cost him and leave the company vulnerable should Gunner and his men ever decide to make good on their threats.

Yet the thought of spending Christmas without his son, their very first Christmas together, was almost too much to bear.

He pulled out his cell phone, hesitating. He hadn't heard from Shanna in months—and he was a man of pride. But thoughts of his son pushed him to make the call. "Shanna? This is Gage Barrington. I have a favor to ask."

Noble Hill could be seen through the trees from a good distance away and seemed to be waiting, like a hopeful mother watching for her children to come home. The amber glow from the porch windows shone into the night, reflecting in the haze and hovering above the house like a halo.

Questions began popping into Gage's mind one after the other. Too many for his peace. He wished he had not come. Pulling up to the front of the house, he reluctantly got out.

Gage helped his mother out of the truck first, then hooked Quinn's belt loop with his finger as the overly anxious boy scrambled out. "Slow down, son—here," he said, grabbing a bag off the backseat and giving it to him. "I'll come back and get the rest of the luggage later."

As Gage approached the porch, two steps ahead of Quinn, he saw a crack in the door. There in the light was Shanna. She stepped out onto the porch and came forward, smiling. Quinn pushed past his dad, dropped the bag, and wrapped his arms tightly around Shanna's waist. When the boy let go, Gage put out his hand and said, "It's good to see you, Shanna. Thanks for having us."

Shanna clasped his hand. There was not much strength in her grip. The extraordinary life that had always sparkled from her eyes had dimmed somehow. Concern showed on Gage's face. The next second, he glanced beside Shanna and noticed Mrs. Lynn standing at her elbow.

"Mr. Barrington! How good it is to see you again." Mrs. Lynn waved to the rest of the family. "Welcome, welcome and come on in. We've been so excited all day!"

A look passed between Gage and Mrs. Lynn, a question. As she answered with her eyes, confirming to Gage what he had suspected, something was wrong.

Shanna reached for Quinn's hand and motioned for Myra. "We'll get you settled in first, then you can come down to the kitchen and have a little snack. Mrs. Lynn and I made cookies." She smiled down at the boy as they entered the foyer and mounted the stairs.

Gage stood in the doorway and winked at Shanna as she turned to glance at him. He made it his purpose to catch Mrs. Lynn alone and question her about Shanna. Something was wrong and he intended to get to the bottom of it.

"Mrs. Lynn?" he said, following her into the kitchen. He was somewhat wary of being heard by the others in the house.

The woman turned around with a look of understanding on her face. "You noticed. Well, I'm not surprised."

"What's wrong? Is she sick?"

"Not sick in the way you imagine, but sick, in a sense."

"I don't understand." He tilted his head and narrowed his eyes, waiting for an explanation.

"The poor child feels useless and alone. The longer she stays away from people, the worse she gets. It's not really depression, but something similar. She went through this once before, as a child."

"You mean she's isolated herself? Here?"

"To put it plainly, yes. Although I don't think it's intentional." She moved toward the counter. As Gage sat down at the kitchen table, Mrs. Lynn hurried to pour him a cup of coffee.

Glancing around, he took in his surroundings. The setting evoked the effortless simplicity of a rural kitchen, yet the heart and soul of the house was unmistakably Southern. Wooden ladder-back chairs were tucked under a softly worn floral tablecloth. Time-worn chipped plates, in a variety of designs, gave a nod to the past as if purposefully displaying the surviving pieces of wedding patterns from generations of Nobles.

Sliding a cup of coffee in front of Gage, Mrs. Lynn sat down across from him. She brushed a wayward strand away from her forehead with the back of her hand "Her heart pumps God's Word like blood through veins. But without an outlet, she gets what I call 'put out of action.' The only cure I know is service. That's why I was so thrilled to hear that you and your lovely family were coming here for a visit."

"I had my doubts about coming. I didn't want to be an intrusion."

"Intrusion? She was so excited—called me right away and we've been working on this house ever since, getting it ready. I thought once she started dating again, it might help pull her out of her doldrums. There had been a series of days when nothing stirred her, not even the half-dead homeless man living down by the river. Oh, she helped him, but something was missing."

He lifted his voice. "Dating? Shanna?"

"Oh, yes, a very nice man. He's a State Trooper. Trooper Sky Norris. But as I was saying, when that girl stumbles and falls, she's not down for long. God has a firm grip on her hand. I knew something would happen like this to spark life back into her before too long. I was just about ready to call Father Cleo when Shanna told me about your call. You being here is the shot in the arm that girl needs. She thinks a lot of your family."

Gage was clearly bothered by her words; pulling a slow hand across his whiskered face, he made a quick decision. "I, uh, found a place across the river in Sugar Land … Briarleigh Inn. They have cottages and I'm renting four of them for myself and my South Carolina crew. I met a lady in town recently who told me about them. That was after I had contacted Shanna. We'll stay a night or two here first, since Shanna is expecting us."

Mrs. Lynn folded her arms sedately. "Hopefully by then she will have gotten some of her spirit back."

"We'll see what can be done about that," he reassured her, anxious to leave the now suffocating room and put some sky above his head. "I better go out and finish bringing in the suitcases."

Myra and Quinn were shown to a room that connected to a smaller room. It was there that Shanna turned down the bed for Quinn.

"This room used to be an old sleeping porch," Shanna said, smoothing out the faded quilt. "In fact, way back before air conditioning, this was the room everyone fought over in the summer, the low purring motor of the ceiling fan lulling our senses."

Myra was the type of person who made a throaty hum when a particular truth resonated with her. "I slept on a sleeping porch many a night … at Summer's Keep." Her attention was caught momentarily on Quinn as she watched him shed his jacket, shoes, and then scramble into bed, pulling off his jeans once he was hidden under the covers. "LuBelle and I would stay up half the night talking until one of us would just fall out from fatigue. I've never had a better sleep than on that porch."

Shanna looked surprised. "How long have you and LuBelle known each other?"

"She's been with me through it all, and Lord knows we've had our share of ups and downs. She's crazy to have put up with me all these years, but we get each other." She smiled down at Quinn whose eyes were now droopy with sleep. "Oh, she has way more faith than I ever did; still, she always sees the best in me and not the worst."

A sigh came from someplace deep inside of Shanna. "I wish I had a friend like that. You're a blessed woman."

Myra was silent a moment. "People turn up in their own time, in their own way."

She was still thinking about Myra's words when Gage entered the room, placing their suitcases on a bench at the foot of the larger bed. Myra's gaze traveled over the simple white quilt covering, and though unspoken, her meaning was clear. She was anxious to slip beneath the fresh-smelling coverings of the four-poster bed for some much needed rest.

Gage pushed a hand on the bed and looked at his mother. "Looks comfortable. If you'd like to turn in, I can take Quinn downstairs with me. Give you some privacy."

Myra moved past him and opened a door, revealing a small gray-painted bathroom trimmed in glossy white. A window with fresh white shutters dominated the far wall. The air held a hint of paint and patchouli. A claw-foot porcelain tub, a pedestal sink and a toilet, were all present. Beneath the window sat an oversized wicker basket full of thick towels and an assortment of toiletries. She turned to her son, her eyes dancing with her unspoken request.

Gage smiled, seeing his answer. "Then you'll have it." He winked at his mother before turning to find Quinn.

Shanna stepped through the narrow doorway separating the rooms. "No need to bother. Your son is out like a light," she whispered. "He fell asleep while your mother and I were talking." Shanna ran her fingers through her tousled hair, feeling the need to smooth down her unruly tresses.

"I think he likes being here," Gage added, seeing the little mound under the covers. Smiling to himself, he took in the scene a long moment before turning away and leaving the room.

Strange how often in the weeks Shanna had been gone that she had been thrust to his mind. He felt again that certain contentment he had once felt, that strange sense of rightness which came over him at odd times in her presence. But now, it was all very clear to Gage and all very bitter to swallow. His prayer had been answered and Shanna had at last released her husband and was free to love again.

He let himself out the front door and wandered along the porch, pacing methodically, glancing up at the steady stars and watching the path of moonlight on the river. He found a seat in an old wicker rocker and pulled out a cigar, savoring the aroma as he rolled it beneath his nose. Car lights came down the lane in front of the old house and stopped just behind his truck. It was a Highway Patrol car. The front door opened and Shanna came out, bounding down the steps toward the car. As she disappeared inside the vehicle, a cold, tight feeling began to form in the pit of Gage's stomach. He sat in the darkness, wanting to leave but unable to do so. He struck a match and puffed his cigar to life, the red embers glowing in the night.

A car door opened and shut and the patrol car eased away and then turned around, leaving behind only a slight wind that rustled a few fallen leaves on the street. Shanna slowly came up the walk, grazing the tops of the pungent boxwoods with her hand reflectively.

He took a deep full-chest breath. "I hope we're not the cause of your boyfriend leaving so quickly."

Startled, Shanna turned to the voice and stopped. "No—he's working, and he's just a friend." A thought hit her. "I'm sorry, Gage. I got so excited about seeing Quinn and your mother I forgot all about showing you to your room. Did Mrs. Lynn take you up before she left?"

He was looking at her as if he'd never seen a woman before. A sudden stab of jealousy hit him square between the eyes, making him half angry with himself. What right had he to be jealous? "No—I'll find it."

Shanna appeared to be laughing at herself as she walked up the steps. "I'm sure you're tired like the rest of them. Come on, I'll show you."

"I know where it is," Gage stated, a little more harshly than he intended.

Shanna raised her eyebrow.

"I've stayed the night here before."

"Here? At Noble Hill? But—" Her voice trailed off.

It seemed to him that she wanted to ask more, but she stopped and just looked at him. For some reason he became evasive. "It was … by accident."

"Is there some secret about it?"

"None worth mentioning."

"Mention it anyway," she said, getting annoyed with his elusiveness. She turned her body and planted her feet firmly so that she was completely facing him.

"I had stopped by to see if I might find something to bring back to you. Some keepsake. When I found the door unlocked, I decide to have a look around. I went directly upstairs, hoping to find your bedroom. As I remember, a storm was brewing and I decided to wait it out. Once I found the cross hanging on the wall in what I assumed to be your bedroom, I fell across the bed and went to sleep. I didn't move 'til morning."

"Why didn't you tell me? Good manners would call for it, don't you think?"

"If you're interested in that sort of thing, which I am not."

"Since when?" she said under her breath as she brushed off a piece of imaginary dust from her jeans.

She was determined not to pick a fight with him. Grandmother Noble would roll over in her grave if she were to insult a guest of Noble Hill.

He considered her for a moment. She folded a piece of paper she had in her hand and stuck it in the pocket of her jeans. A deepening curiosity began to take root. Her sleeves were rolled up past her elbows, as if she'd spent the day laboring on the river bank. The low, velvet soft voice stirred something in Gage's memory. But it was her eyes that caused him concern. "Are you going to church here? By the way you're behaving, I think not."

"What! *You're* asking me?" Oh, he was pushing it. She didn't know how much longer she could hold off. Her body began to twitch so she plopped down in the chair next to him and pulled a blanket off the back of the chair, tucking it around her legs. "When was the last time *you* darkened the doorway of a church?"

He leaned forward, his cigar resting between long, tanned fingers. He ran a hand beneath his nose and she could have sworn he was grinning. "Just this morning, actually."

She rolled her eyes and looked away. "Stopping to ask for directions from the preacher doesn't count."

"I wasn't asking for directions from the preacher," he said, taking a slow pull from his cigar. "I was asking directions from the Creator."

She jerked her head around and stared at him in disbelief. "This is Friday, not Sunday."

"You once told me that any time is the right time to begin to pray, did you not?"

"I did."

"So I figured any *place* would do as well. My first initial impulse to pray started from a place of … call it — self-pity. I found a church, after normal business hours, of course," he smiled, seeing her look of shock. "There, my pity met up with something stronger. After that I began meeting with God on a regular basis and somewhere along the way all that self-pity got transformed into a type of … I don't know, call it compassion. It's still pity, but I've been removed from it." He remained focused on his cigar, thinking that explained it pretty well.

She clamped down on her tongue, not at all sure about the sincerity of his words, but afraid to question them just in case he was telling the truth.

He looked up, turning his intense blue eyes on her. "What has happened to you?"

Dropping her eyes to her hands, she said in a voice low as a whisper, "When I was asked to leave Terrapin Island, I felt like a failure." She pushed her foot on the porch boards to set the rocker in motion. "I had poured so much into Gypsy, sacrificed for her … and she betrayed me so casually." She looked up at him, her eyes shimmering in pools of gray. "I can't even say what's bothering me. I go over all the years, wondering if anything I've ever done has made a difference to anyone."

He turned pensive. "Compassion is probably one of the noblest emotions human beings can express. Self-pity, the most despicable. Compassion lets you see into another person's circumstances and it gives you the desire to do something about it. It moves you to action. Self-pity extinguishes the light within you." He had her attention now. He could see it all over her face. "Don't let your light go out, Shanna. Many of us have been directed by it. *You* can't save anybody. That's not your job. All you can do is love them enough to tell them the truth and point the way. The rest is up to God."

Shanna was silent as she thought about the absurdity of the situation. Gage … preaching to *her*? She folded down the sleeves of her shirt and began to button them against the chill in the air. She realized in that instant how much she needed to be reminded of his words. She also realized how very much she'd missed Gage Barrington and his "bombs" of occasional wisdom.

Leisurely, Gage took the cigar from his mouth and blew a long ribbon of smoke above his head. "A cold front is moving in tonight. We better get inside." As he tapped out his cigar, he slipped his lighter into his pocket and felt something. "Oh, I almost forgot. Give me your hand."

She opened her fist in front of him and he tucked a little stone heart in the palm of her hand, squeezed it and said, "This is to remember your husband by. I found it resting on top of his grave, just under the soil. Thought you might like to have it … as a remembrance. You know I'm big on those."

Shanna slowly unfurled her hand and blinked twice at the small stone. "You visited James' grave?" she asked, with an incredulous look on her face. At his nod, she struck a motherlode of bottled-up tears. The blanket fell to her feet as she stood and deliberately turned her back to him, her body racked with sobs.

Gage jumped to his feet and stood behind her, encircling his arms around her shoulders. He held her close while the awful ache of sorrow found its release. "Hey, it's okay," he murmured huskily into her ear. His cheek twitched. *Of all the stupid things I've ever done, this one takes the cake.*

Shanna turned around in the strong arms that held her and faced Gage. "I had no idea I would react like this," she apologized, wiping her cheeks with the back of her hand. "That was the sweetest gesture. Thank you for this."

Taken completely off guard by her comment, he raised his eyebrows in a question. As he gazed down into her face, he wondered if he'd ever understand the girl.

Closing her eyes, she raised her face to his, clutching the stone tightly to her chest. The next moment she felt warm lips over hers. Gage deepened the kiss and it felt to her like the incoming tide of the island, rushing in to fill all the cracks and dry places with fresh, living water. Before she could respond, he pulled her closer and kissed her so thoroughly and extensively that she almost expected to feel a tremor from the ground beneath her feet.

He pulled back slightly, his eyes searching her face. "Well, if it's all the same to you," he said in a low tone, "I'm going to keep my eye out for more rocks."

Shanna nodded, not able to find breath enough to speak. *Did I kiss him, or did he kiss me?* She hesitated a moment before she said, "Sorry … guess I got caught up in the moment."

He rubbed his cheek, a boyish grin on his face.

There was no way Shanna was going to admit to him how powerful that knee-weakening kiss had been. She played it off as nothing, shrugging slightly. "It happens. It was just a kiss. Don't worry about it."

CHAPTER 23

Gage felt as if he had momentarily lost consciousness. With a sense of stabbing pain at her flippant words, he returned to awareness. He tried to put on an air of indifference, block the memory of her soft lips from his mind, and pretend he hadn't felt as if he'd drawn life from them. Who was he kidding—Shanna Muir had allowed him to kiss her in response to the thought of her husband, James. Besides, no woman who is up close and personal with God is easily disturbed by something as fleshly as a kiss.

Turning aside to take a deep breath of the cool night air, he gathered his thoughts. The moments passed like ages. "We better get inside," he said, then spoke as he opened the door for her. "I appreciate you letting us barge in on you tonight. Quinn was anxious to see you."

Shanna rubbed the small pebble with her thumb. Without word or explanation, she stepped through the door in front of him and motioned for him to follow.

Gage stood in the doorway of the room Shanna had entered and glanced around. He had missed this room on his earlier visit. Compared to the sitting room, it was rather small. Mellow walls and comfortable furnishings expressed a sense of calm. The fireplace was dark and clear of ashes, and there was a stack of cut logs and a tin bucket of kindling sitting on the hearth. "Nice room," he said. "How about I build a fire?"

Putting on a brighter smile, Shanna turned and said, "That would be nice."

His eyes lingered on her a moment, taking full note of her smile before he nodded toward the window. "Bet you have a nice view to go with the room." He turned his attention to search for a lighter along the mantel, or anything that he might use to start a fire. His fingers touched a small box of stick matches.

"I love this room." She stepped to the window and looked out. "The river out there is the focal point and center of the turning world of the Delta. I've always thought this window captures the heart of it, like a painting."

The brick fireplace was in some disrepair but was still usable. After wrestling with the damper, it opened and soon a brightly lit orange fire was flickering on the grates. He eased back to sit on the sofa, watching the progress of the fire as the flames licked and heaped over the dry wood.

"Comfortable couch," he said, patting the fabric.

"Yeah, well, I splurged on the sofa and armchair for this room." She moved to the chair and sank into it. "I gravitate here. It puts me in a semicomatose state on nights like this. Almost anything can be handled when I'm in this room, or so it seems."

"I'm envious." He got up, reached over, and placed another log on the fire.

Shanna passed Gage a doubtful glance. "I've seen your Charleston home, remember? This place doesn't begin to compare with what you're used to."

Settling back down on the couch, he said, "Like a lot of East Coast homes, ours is too tense … formal. All those antiques can look more like a historic furniture museum than a living room where you're supposed to relax." He let out a breath. "No, I prefer this. And, Summer's Keep, of course. I try to strike a balance with the low-key style of my island home. Kinda counteracts the city home."

"I for one can't wait to plan for Christmas in this house. Having a child here… well, it just doesn't get better than that. Who was it that said, 'The soul is healed by being with children.' I think whoever it was might be on to something."

"Dostoyevsky. But… we're not staying for Christmas, Shanna. Just a couple of days. I've rented a few cottages at Briarleigh Inn—across the river in Sugar Land. Uncle Yancey, Jedidiah, and Nor are on their way over there now. We didn't come here to interrupt your plans."

"Oh," she said, trying hard to keep the disappointment out of her voice.

"I met a woman in Port St. Joe who told me about the cottages. Then, oddly enough, I get a phone call right after that from my cousin, Samuel Warren. He tells me that he's friends with Mack Blackwell who owns Briarleigh Inn. Samuel's wife, Madeline, makes bath products for the inn."

"Is your cousin from Louisiana?" Thoughtfully Shanna lifted a small throw from the corner of the couch and placed it across her lap, tucking her legs beside her.

"No, he's from Moss Bay, Alabama, near Mobile. But he worked with me for many years in South Carolina. He's a developer. His mother and my mother are first cousins. His mother passed away a while back, but she was originally from South Carolina." Gage stretched his shoulders back as if something pained him. "I picked up my cigar habit from Samuel. We spent a lot of time together working business deals in Charleston. Every time we cinched a deal, he'd drag out this ornately carved wooden box, open the lid, and pull out a fine cigar. I got to where I expected it, like a reward. And I've been rewarding myself with them ever since."

Shanna wanted the image of Gage and the mystery woman who'd suggested the inn wiped from her mind. "Is he still in South Carolina?" she asked, pretending her interest.

He shifted his position on the couch. "He moved back home to Alabama right after his father died to help raise his younger brother, Jude. And to take care of the family home, Beauchene."

She glanced at her hands, tracing the back of the smooth skin absentmindedly with a finger. A log dropped deeper into the fire. "Why did you leave the business world in Charleston?"

He took a deep breath, and then exhaled slowly. "I got sick of going to work and having to put on a certain suit and a certain face to go with it. Sick of feeling like I was living someone else's dream. I don't put that face on anymore. Or, any other face for that matter." Gage was suddenly apprehensive. "But I'm entrenched here now. And, Lord help me, I've just made about the dumbest decision a man can make all because I think it's what God wants me to do."

Shanna's attention perked. "What decision?"

"I hired six women from a home for unwed mothers to run part of my lumberyard operation." He shook his head in thought. If someone had told Gage Barrington that they had done such a stupid thing, he would have regarded that person as a lunatic. The full comprehension of what he had committed himself to undertake was enough to make a man question his sanity. Risking a sideways glance at Shanna, he wasn't surprised by the interest he saw on her face. It sounded more like something *she* would do. "The woman I met in Port St. Joe runs the place. Mercy is her name."

"Bon Secour?" she asked, the hope rising in her voice.

"Yes, why? Do you know about the place?"

"I know Mercy. We've sent a few girls from Holy Trinity to her. So … what will they do for you?"

"They'll be responsible for building loads for deliveries mostly, and overseeing the loading and unloading of lumber. All of that will require supervising the forklift operators and keeping track of inventory." Gage winced. "That should be interesting," he said under his breath. "They'll keep management aware of any delays or discrepancies."

"Do you load onto barges or trucks?" she asked. Everything began to rearrange itself in her mind.

"Both," he answered, somewhat surprised at her interest.

"The lumber you sell, what is it used for, mainly?"

"Marine pilings, dock hardware, seawalls, bulkheads—it's treated lumber for outside use in the ground or in saltwater." He leaned forward until the wide gray eyes came to meet his. "South Carolina's coast and the Gulf Coast need my lumber, especially now. I fully intend to deliver it to them, no matter who walks off the job."

Arching a brow, she looked at him meaningfully. "You lost some employees?"

"Six, to be exact. But as you know … they've been replaced." Gage could see her interest and he wondered about it.

Abruptly, she got up from the chair and smiled at him, slightly embarrassed by her unchecked inquisitiveness. "Well, I guess I better get to bed. Just lock up for me if you don't mind." She looked back before leaving the room. "Are you sure you can find your way to your room?"

"Right at the top of the stairs, second door on the left."

Half smiling, Shanna considered him for a moment, nodded, and left the room.

Gage followed her with his eyes through the partially closed door as she climbed the stairs. He'd thought back to Noble Hill more times than he cared to remember. In his mind it was always Shanna's room where he'd find himself. The room where the crucifix hung above the white bed and the windows looked out over the curve of the Mississippi River.

The attachment Gage felt to Shanna was stronger than he understood. He thought about their last meeting at Sassabee Creek and wondered if somehow something had been transferred to them from that mysterious water. He admired the woman. In fact, he considered her the finest person he'd ever known.

As Shanna entered her bedroom, she picked through her pocket and pulled out the note from Sky Norris and read it. *There is a rumor of a plan to burn Barrington Lumber to the ground on Christmas Day.* The words hit her with such force she backed on to her bed and sat, staring blankly at the wall. With all the determination she could gather, she crushed the apprehension beneath the heel of her will and resolved to talk to Gage about the note … in the morning. Receiving such news this late at night would only mean disturbing the whole household.

The sun rose in a clear sky with only an occasional wisp of clouds softening the vivid blue. Shanna had not yet seen Gage and she wondered about it. It was his habit to rise early, usually before anyone else even thought to stir.

She began the coffee-making process, glancing out the kitchen window occasionally to admire the bare limbs of the trees all washed in morning gold. She would start breakfast and keep her hands and her mind busy seeing after her house guests.

Sensing a presence behind her Shanna turned, then halted in surprise as she saw Gage, leaning against the door frame in a white shirt and faded jeans. A spicy whiff of aftershave drifted on the air, mixing with the scent of coffee. "Good morning."

"About time you got up. I was seriously thinking of driving to Jackson to find a Starbucks," he teased.

"I'll try to be more prompt in the future," Shanna apologized, sweetly contrite.

"Well, I'll overlook it—this time."

Gage was in a lighthearted mood. One Shanna had rarely seen. Her eyes flickered downward briefly as she thought about a conversation she would soon have with him.

Noticing a quick look of remorse, Gage studied Shanna's face as if he were sighting a weapon at her. "Something bothering you?"

Her heart pounded as she retrieved the note from the counter and handed it to him. She watched as he read the message, his brow furrowing in confusion.

"Where did you get this?"

"Sky Norris." She leaned back against the counter and folded her arms.

Gage's mind raced down several paths. "Can you trust—Trooper Norris? Where did he get this information?"

"I trust him. We met in Natchez when I was, uh...along the bluff, visiting the site where my parents had died. He pulled up. I was upset and he thought I was...well, I don't know what he thought, but he stayed and we talked. He asked me to get a coffee with him. We went out to dinner a few times after that, shared a few stories. That's when he told me he had arrested a truck driver earlier that day, said he was hauling logs from the lumberyard."

"Arrested him for what?"

"Speeding. It wasn't until yesterday that he found out that the guy had a previous criminal record and wanted to make a deal to keep out of jail. He told Sky that there was a plan in place to burn you out on Christmas Day. It wasn't until I talked to Sky this morning that I learned that the man had been stealing lumber. Enough to put the company out of business, which it did, forcing the previous owner to sell."

"But it doesn't make sense. Why threaten to burn down the company?" He tapped the note. "The threat is pretty clear."

"Apparently you broke up their little game when you fired Gunner. Maybe whoever is behind it just wants revenge."

Gage shook his head. "No, there's more to the story — there has to be."

Shanna knew Gage would do what needed to be done. Like a bolt tightened into place, he snapped his neck and made a quick decision. "I have a few people to see. Do you mind looking after my family until I get back?"

"Of course not. What are you going to do?"

"I'm going to make a stand."

It was Christmas Eve and a week had flown past since she'd last seen Gage Barrington. Shanna sat in her chair, looking through the window toward the river. It was wet outside; the sky was gray and dismal. Nothing stirred. For a fleeting moment the shape of a barge appeared, and then it melted back into the mist like a ghost disappearing into the depth of the netherworld.

Earlier in the week, by sheer force of will, she'd determined to put up a Christmas tree. Now as she looked at it, the glow from the lights made her feel even more alone. Her throat tightened and she swallowed hard to choke back the tears, wanting to avoid the image completely.

Is this, Shanna wondered, *what's in store for me?* It had been easier to do nothing, to simply shrug and accept her circumstances. She was a widow at twenty-three. Although technically she didn't qualify as an orphan, her heart felt every inch a motherless child.

What now? she asked herself. *Sit here in this big house and wallow in self-pity?* Dropping her head into her hands, she remembered Gage's words. "Pity is noble — self-pity, despicable" or, something like that. A sinking feeling came over her on that dreary Christmas Eve. The whole world seemed so full of joy and there she sat in all of her misery.

Sky had phoned earlier and asked if she wanted to stay at his place for Christmas, but Shanna had declined. He pretended to understand, though she knew he hadn't. *James would've understood,* she thought. But James was gone. That thought used to feel like a stab of cold steel in her gut, but time had worked its balm on Shanna, changing her grief into something sweeter: memory.

It was the memory of James Muir on that Christmas Eve night that prompted Shanna to pick up the phone and change the direction of her life, forever.

CHAPTER 24

The month of January was nearing the end with Christmas and New Year's Day a memory. Myra and Quinn had made it safely back home to Terrapin Island, relieving Gage of the worry of their safety. There had been only one incident at Barrington Lumber since the threat. A small grass fire had been detected and, thanks to the watchful eye of the workforce, only a minimal amount of damage ha d taken place.

Gage drove his truck down to the loading dock and got out, scanning the area as he flipped the collar up on his jacket to block the icy wind. He noticed the charred sticks in the burned-over ground, thankful that the nearby lumber had not been ignited.

Among the stacks of lumber, he spotted Roy, a loose-jointed man at the edge of a row. He was long with huge hands that held firm a long-barreled rifle. The hollow-cheeked face of the man bore a look of determination. The handles of his mustache thrust out on either side of his face like the horns of a steer. "No one is getting past me, Boss. I guarantee," Roy said, before spitting to the ground.

Those were the first words Gage had ever heard the man utter. "Good." He reached into the cab of the truck and pulled out a thermos. "Thought you might like some hot coffee. Probably need to light that kerosene heater in the river shed, too. They're predicting snow and ice once the sun goes down."

Roy took the thermos and gestured with his hand. "Will do."

As Gage drove back up to the office, the snowflakes began falling through the last light of the day. It was a sight so rare in the Deep South that he had to take a second look. It amazed him how the smallest threat of snow could change the atmosphere of an entire town. In fact, Port St. Joe seemed to come alive under the threat of severe weather. The markets were packed with shoppers stocking up on milk and bread. Kerosene heaters with several years' worth of collected dust were flying off the shelves.

He stomped and scraped his boots on the porch steps, knocking off bits of caked mud before pushing through the office door. Shoving a chair back with his foot, he sat down with his coffee and stared out the window, taking a slow pull of the steamy brew. His mind wandered. Something just as peculiar as the snow had taken place at the lumberyard since Gage had hired the six women from Bon Secour: the men had become protective and territorial.

He was still thinking about the change he'd seen in his men when the door pushed open and the cold-snapping air blew across his face.

"Shanna! What are you doing out in this weather?"

"I tried to call but you didn't answer, so I thought I better come down here and warn you. The roads are beginning to freeze over. It's worse further west. Reports are saying that Sugar Land sounds like it's under siege with frozen limbs snapping power lines right and left. I wouldn't try driving back to Briarleigh Inn tonight. I came to tell you that you're all welcome to stay at my place."

The chair scraped the floor as Gage got up, went to the counter, and poured another cup of coffee. He looked over his shoulder. "How do you take it?"

"Black. And yes I know — it'll put hair on my chest."

Gage quirked a brow as he handed her the coffee. "If it does that, I'm filing a grievance against the coffee industry."

She gave him a tight smile, taking the cup from his hand. "Funny." Just then she noticed a small mound of gray-brown fur curled up on a blanket in the corner. "Is that the island dog?" she asked, surprised.

"One and the same." He set the pot back on the burner. "Quinn talked *Mimi*," he stressed the name, "into shipping the mutt to me so I wouldn't get lonely." He shook his head. "Can you believe that?"

"Of course I believe it," she said, taking a sip of the coffee. "Quinn has a kind heart."

His eyes lightly but politely skimmed her. "I don't know what you've done to that boy, but whatever it is, he has a bad case of it. Mother said that he'd called her from school the other day, told her to go to the store and buy some clothes and shoes for a girl in his class. The only instructions were to make sure they were colorful. Apparently the little girl was being laughed at for coming to class in a nightgown, flip flops, and a ratty coat."

Her face twisted with sympathy. "What did Myra do?"

"She went to town and bought a variety of clothes and shoes and brought them to the school." He drew his head back as if in amazement. "And everything fit!"

A surge of excitement raced through Shanna and she had to swallow the coffee down hard before she could speak. "That's my boy!" she said, proudly. "I'll make a preacher out of him yet."

The windows were getting steamed up as the temperature continued to drop. Sprays of ice pellets hit the glass panes, bouncing off and collecting on the boardwalks. Shanna stepped to the window, rubbed a circle on the glass, and peered out. "You better round up everyone. It's getting bad out there."

"Everyone is gone."

She glanced at him through the reflection of the glass, trying to sound relaxed and casual. "Oh?"

"Mack Blackwell called a few minutes ago; they made it to Briarleigh safe and sound. The power is out but they have everyone in the main house where they have an emergency generator. Said they have four inches of snow on the ground already and it's still coming down."

"So, you're here by yourself?"

"Yeah, except for Roy and Jack Dog. They're warm and dry down at the river shed. It's their night on guard."

Gage knew in his gut that if there was an attempt at sabotage, it would happen at night. He'd realized early on how crucial it was to have the right men in the right places, everyone on guard. He felt like a military strategist planning a defensive. The men of Barrington Lumber Company had been put to the test, and they had, up to this point, prevailed.

It seemed to Gage a test they'd always wanted, waited for, even. Now, with the presence of women in the company, he had noticed a difference in them. Like they all shared something new, the feeling that there was more to protect than lumber or even their jobs. It was the heart of these men that had changed.

"Well, what about you?" She thought she saw him smile as he dipped his head to take a sip from his coffee. Meeting his amused eyes, she felt a blush deepen—starting at her neck, it moved all the way up to heat her ears.

"I can't leave. And I'd prefer it if you wouldn't either." The quirk in his lips expanded into a one-sided grin as he noticed her eyes widening. "With all those trees around your house, the power may go out and if the roads are closed, I'll have a hard time getting to you."

Shanna visibly relaxed for the first time that day. She took a deep releasing breath, letting go of the stress. "I'm relieved," she said, then worried that she had spoken with too much enthusiasm. "I mean, I'm out of firewood and…," she cringed inwardly, "Not that I would expect you to chop wood for me or anything."

He grinned. "I'd do it whether you'd expected me to or not."

She turned back to the window, staring out to hide her flushed face and wanting nothing more than to press her flaming cheeks to the cold windowpanes. The ground was covered. Snow in Port St. Joe was not only an event, it seemed supernatural. She watched with childlike fascination as a gust of wind blew and whirled the snowflakes. They swept along the roof like a whirlwind before taking up the chase along the ground.

"What about Trooper Norris?" Gage said, curious about the man's whereabouts. "Can't he chop wood?"

She turned from the window, rubbing her arms. "I'm sure he can."

He took a seat again. His long fingers picked up a pen and he tapped it on the desk. "I suppose he's working a lot of overtime in weather like this."

She turned aside to avoid his eyes. "He is."

Picking up on her evasiveness, he questioned further. "Are you two still seeing each other? Not that it's any of my business."

"He offered me a ring," she said, rubbing her hands over her arms, not bothering to look up.

Gage froze at her words. He felt like a fish pulled quick from a stream and slapped hard to the ground. He glanced at her hand and saw that it was bare.

She smoothed her hair behind her ears, thinking it was probably best to be completely honest with him. "He…um…wanted me to move in with him. I think the ring was meant as a kind of…symbolic gesture."

He rose from his chair and stepped toward the coffee pot for a warm up, anxious to get the blood flowing to his head again. "I see. And you weren't interested in that kind of arrangement?" he asked, topping off his coffee with the piping hot liquid. He set the pot down with a clank.

She drew back from the window and shot him a look full of fire. "No. I'm not interested in being 'engaged.'" The word tasted bitter on her tongue. Once a symbol of a promise, lately it had become more of a synonym for stupidity. "I don't expect you to understand."

"Oh, I understand," he said. "He wants all of the benefits of marriage without the commitment. He wants a trial marriage. He's saying, 'I vow to stay together with you as long as you make me happy and we get along'. That's not a marriage, that's a deal. In a marriage, a couple should focus on getting through the good and bad of life together. Sounds to me like he wants to keep his options open in case he has doubts down the road."

"I guess you would know. Most men seem to feel that way." Her pert nose rose to a regal angle.

Gage's jaw tensed. Without a long story he went straight to the point. "And some women." He let his eyes drift toward hers. "When I ask a woman to marry me, I won't have any doubts. No long engagement either. I don't believe in all that ridiculous nonsense." He lifted his coat from the hook on the wall and yanked it on. "I'm going to clear the road." He pointed to the back. "There are a few blankets in the back room. I'm not sure what it looks like back there—may need...."

"I believe I can handle that. It'll be like old times." She pointed to the mutt. "The dog adds a nice touch of home."

"Keep a check on the kerosene level in the heater if you don't mind. Let me know if it gets low. If it runs out, it'll smoke up the place."

"Will do."

Tight-lipped, Gage took a final glance at Shanna before closing the door behind him.

After spending nearly an hour cleaning the back rooms, Shanna made a circuit of the interior, sweeping out every corner and tossing away the trash before she plopped down in front of the kerosene heater.

The wind was rising, howling in the pines that grew along the hillside near the entrance. The building began to pop and creak around the rafters. From where she sat she could look out the window and watch Gage as he took cautious steps, walking slowly on the icy road scattering something. Now and then he would pause and lean on the shovel as if tired. Then, working again, the shuck and the scrape of the shovel would begin once more.

The door opened and the north wind blew its cold breath inside the room. Gage stepped inside, stomping his boots near the door, rubbing his hands together to warm them. He looked around at the now clean room and marveled at the transformation. It even smelled good, like fresh pine.

"I see you haven't lost your touch," he said, admiring the tidiness of the space.

"It's a gift," she said, shrugging her shoulders. It seemed as if they had both lost a lot of the steam they had worked up earlier. Neither one of them were as edgy.

"I can't believe I'm so tired. I usually have a hard time going to sleep, but I don't think I'll have trouble tonight. You?" she asked.

"Are you kidding me? I sleep like the drowned."

"The floor is clean, so I think I'll make a pallet near the heater. I got you a few blankets. They're on your desk." She lifted her sweater over her head; her hair snapped with static and the scent of lavender diffused into the room. Adjusting her undershirt, she crawled under the blankets.

Gage snatched up the stack of blankets and tossed them near the door.

Their situation, though not under the best conditions, proved to be comfortable … cozy, even. The winter storm beat its fury over them, and the small lumberyard office with its wood-paneled walls and beamed ceilings became a protected hideaway.

The power had gone out, but the red glow from the heater cast a radiance over the room. Their source of heat was the only thing separating them. She rested her head on a pillow, blinking slowly as her body relaxed. Gage was braced with his back against the door, staring at the light. His gaze drifted over to Shanna's face, all amber in the glow from the heater.

"Do you have a favorite number?" she asked. "Mine is three."

"What's so special about it?" He reached over and turned the knob on the heater, adjusting the temperature so the light dimmed slightly.

"I don't know, but God used it a lot. There's the Trinity … Jesus rose on the third day … Jonah was in the—"

"Okay, I get your point," he interrupted.

"What about weather? Snow?" she asked, teasingly.

"Rain."

"Rain? Why?"

"It usually comes with a storm," he said. There was a long pause. "I know yours already — wind. And your favorite drink is hot cocoa."

She rose up on her elbow and looked at him. "How did you know that?"

"Because I actually listen when you ramble on and on. Now, try to go to sleep before you completely exhaust me from all of your talking."

Shanna smiled. "You remind me of Father Cleo sometimes."

"I'm sure we have a lot in common…especially lately," he added under his breath.

Between them that night was something vague and floating. Gage remembered another time being so relaxed and that was one other night he'd spent with Shanna. Even the mutt seemed to sense the comfort Shanna brought with her presence. He found a soft place on the blanket near her feet and, after circling several times, settled down with a heavy plop.

Sometime later in the night Gage's eyes came open with a start, and he was suddenly alert. The dog was positioned at the crack of the door, sniffing, and then he yanked his head back with a snarl.

Shanna awakened at the sound of the snarl and without moving, watched as Gage pulled on his jacket and stepped to the desk drawer, carefully sliding it open. He lifted a pistol from the drawer, turning it in his hand as if checking it before quietly stepping to the door.

Glancing over his shoulder he noticed Shanna's eyes open, staring at him. He signaled for her to stay put before turning the door handle and slipping out into the night. The dog pushed the crack in the door wide with his nose and shot past Gage, flushing a gray shape from the area near the warehouse. A clang was heard as the shadow fled, disappearing into the trees.

Gage ran after the figure, slowing slightly as he came upon the empty gas can, tossed in the snow. He hesitated only a moment, then continued at breakneck speed, tracking the fleeing man. Judging from the size of the footprint in the snow, this was no kid. He fired a couple of warning shots as he caught sight of the man.

Seconds later, Gage lunged toward the fleeing man, tackling him to the ground. A hoarse screech twisted the stranger's face as he leapt forward. Gage ducked beneath his aimed blow and then came back with his fist, catching the attacker squarely on the jaw. With a raging bellow, the intruder launched himself in a soaring leap and came down hard upon Gage, his fists flailing wildly. In a quick reflex, Gage pulled the pistol from his coat pocket and drew it on the man, jabbing the steel in his gut.

Feeling the pistol, the man froze instantly, his attention solely on the gun and the hand that held it. Gage pushed him and he staggered backward.

Swiping at the blood oozing from the corner of his mouth, Gage said, "Who hired you?"

"I'll tell you, I'll tell you—just don't shoot."

There was a shout from behind as Roy and Jack Dog ran toward them. Gage's eyes narrowed dangerously. "Then you better start talking."

There was quite a commotion at the lumberyard later that night as the sheriff, fire chief, two fire trucks, and three Port St. Joe police cars arrived along with nearly everybody else in town that followed a police scanner.

Once the suspect had been turned over to the authorities, the clamor grew around the gasoline-doused warehouses. As they were inspecting the buildings, Gage ducked between the warehouses and sank his hands into the slush before bringing them to his face. The snow was numbing, exactly what he wanted. His face felt as if it had been burned with a branding iron. The gasoline guy had fought a lot harder than he'd expected. But Gage knew the man had been scared and an adrenaline rush could make a superhero out of anybody.

He let the bloodstained ice pack drop to the ground. Turning, he spotted Shanna on the far side of the office, her back facing him as she walked oddly backward. *Probably talking on her cell phone to her State Trooper*, he thought. "Might as well invite him to the party. Have all the civil servants represented here tonight," he mumbled under his breath.

Shanna backed out into the open, bracing her feet wide apart as she squared her sights on a thick wide chest with both hands clutching a pistol.

Taking in the scene, Gage rushed forward. He took the gun from Shanna's hand as she surrendered it to him.

"The dog caught this one," Shanna said. "He must've been hiding and saw his chance to make a break for it while everyone else was distracted. I heard him yell when the dog took a bite out of him." Despite herself, Shanna smiled as she watched the dog thump his tail. "I'd say the mutt has earned a name."

"Where did you get this gun?" Gage asked impatiently.

"My purse. You don't think I'd live alone at Noble Hill without a gun, do you?"

Gage opened his mouth to comment, but Shanna moved past him. He called to her back. "Go get the sheriff."

She glanced over her shoulder. "Where do you think I'm going—to get hot cocoa!"

He grinned in spite of himself, then waved the man around and motioned for him to sit on the walkway. "Your buddy did a lot of talking. Unless you want to spend the rest of your life wearing an orange jumpsuit, I'd do the same."

As the sheriff walked up, Gage caught a glimpse of Shanna over the man's shoulder. She was leaning back on a Highway Patrol vehicle, talking to a trooper. "You call in the Calvary?" Gage asked, nodding toward the trooper.

The Sheriff looked back. "Naw, that's just Norris … seeing about all the commotion." The sheriff scratched his head. "Somebody ought to tell that guy that he's facing the wrong way for all the action." He turned back around with a grin and winked at Gage. "Or, maybe not."

Painfully Gage averted his eyes from the scene and turned his attention back to the sheriff. "This guy was in on the dousing … he threw his gas can in the weeds over there." He pointed toward a wooded area. "If you need anything from me, numbers, anything, I'll be in the office. I plan to head back to Charleston in the morning."

The sheriff glanced up sharply. "Charleston? Why?"

"I'm going for the head of the snake."

CHAPTER 25

At day break, Gage was on the highway. The winter storm had finally moved north, leaving behind an icy slush on the roads that were somehow passable. As he settled behind the wheel of the truck, he thought about the difficult job that lay ahead of him. He thought of his son and of the ways he planned to make up for his long absence. His mind wandered to Shanna and the astounded look on her face when he told her he was leaving.

It seemed to Gage like Shanna's whole life had been taken from the pages of a Faulkner novel. She had a calmness about her, like the deep bottom of the sea, which remained stable no matter what storm churned overhead. Even when she was aiming the barrel of a gun at a man's chest, her honey- smooth drawl sounded warm enough to melt wax. Throughout all of the trouble in the young girl's life, one thing had remained — her faith in her Creator. Gage marveled at that. He wanted that.

He cast a glance toward the backseat where the dog slept, curled up on his coat. A wheezing snore came from the mutt Shanna had said earned the right to a name. "Okay, boy, since you went after gasoline man with both guns blazing, I guess we'll call you Big Duke."

He lifted his cell phone from the console, then hesitated. *No ... not this time.*

He'd expected the trip home to be long and uneventful, and wasn't disappointed. The snow and ice had vanished from the landscape as soon as he'd crossed over the Alabama, Georgia, line. After a quick night's sleep at an inn somewhere east of Atlanta, Gage and Big Duke struck out bright and early.

The road conditions had improved considerably, making the last leg of the journey much easier. He smiled to himself remembering the face of the desk clerk as he walked in the lobby with a satchel in one hand and a scruffy dog in the other.

When he placed the bag on the floor and registered, the young desk clerk touched Gage's hand in a kind of silent acknowledgment, then rubbed the dog behind the ear. An obvious dog lover, she was willing to overlook the hotel's policy of no pets allowed. "You two have a restful night," she said in a sweet tone to the dog. Lynch had always said that dogs were chick bait. Guess his old friend was right about that ... too.

Traveling the slender road in the center of Terrapin Island was like crossing an ocean of golden sweet grass. Gage passed men selling "head-on" shrimp from the backs of their trucks and early crabbers with dip nets navigating the waterways. Water, mudflats, and marshes for as far as the eye could see. A scattering of clapboard houses peeked out from maritime forests along the road and at the first whiff of pluff mud, Gage felt at home.

Slamming the truck door, he stood in front of his home, Summer's Keep. He had to order himself to move, knowing in his gut that things would be revealed in the next few hours that would change everything.

After their long meal and tucking in of Quinn, Gage joined Myra on the porch. As he leaned back in the chair, he decided it was good to be home. Even with the gnawing uneasiness in the pit of his stomach, he was glad to be in the presence of his mother.

"How's Quinn doing in school?" Gage asked.

She waved a hand in the air. "He takes after me and struggles with math." She gathered her hair behind her neck and relaxed against the cushion of the chair. "I think he's interested in animals."

"Yeah, I noticed. He seemed as happy to see Big Duke as he was to see me."

Myra laughed. "Well, that was quite a story you told about how Big Duke captured that … that … what was it — barn burner?"

Gage looked straight into his mother's eyes. "That was no made-up story, Mother. Someone hired two men to burn down Barrington Lumber. I caught one and the dog and Shanna caught the other. They'd doused the entire place in gasoline. Thankfully, Big Duke heard them and growled at the door. It woke us up and we were able to catch them."

Myra raised an eyebrow. "Us?"

Gage shot his mother an incredulous look. "I just told you that two men tried to burn down my lumberyard and all you care about is whether Shanna and I spent the night together?"

"Well?" She looked at him intently and hadn't released her breath.

"Yes! We spent the night together — with a kerosene heater between us! We were in the middle of a winter storm, for heaven's sake!" He tossed the last swallow of coffee over the porch rail.

"Sounds romantic … except for the part about the arsonists." Myra brushed away a moth.

Gage's face was without emotion. An observant person might have noticed a slight hardening of his jaw and the flintlike quality to his stare and taken the warning. "I don't have the luxury of a flippant attitude where my investments are concerned and you really don't, either. If I hadn't caused … if your husband was still alive, things would be different for you."

Myra's head snapped up. "You didn't kill your father—I did." She saw the shock of her words in his clear blue eyes, but before he could find his voice, she burst forth in a rush of words. "All your father cared about was his standing in the community, his charities, his precious name, and his holdings. We had a terrible argument the night he died."

He pressed his lips together and his face looked pained. "You and Dad always argued, Mother. He loved nothing better than to get your good Irish blood up."

"This was different. He knew I spoke the truth. I told him that he was driving you away with his constant push to make you into something he wanted you to be. Something you were not. I told Breck that if we lost you, I'd never forgive him for it. I told him that I despised what the name Barrington had come to mean, how the Barrington Empire was first and foremost over everything, even his family."

Gage swiped his hand across his chin, clinging to that line of control that kept him silent. Myra Barrington needed to speak—for her own good.

"If you want the truth of the matter, I'll tell you. Your grandfather, Locke, chose me for your father. Breck went along with whatever Locke Barrington wanted, like most all of Charleston in those days. 'Whatever's best for the family' Breck would always say."

Gage's face went rigid. "Are you trying to say that Dad didn't love you?" Gage's tone was low and skeptical.

"I mean Locke told Breck to marry me. He liked my spirit because I stood up to him. He used to come into the store and ask me a lot of personal questions. I told him to mind his own business back in Charleston."

"What store?" There was a moment of silence in which Gage realized how very little he knew of his mother's life before Breck Barrington.

"Doo Lottie's. I worked there. Locke would cruise in, slide his yacht into a slip, throw his weight around, and expect everyone to step and fetch for him, which they did. Everyone except me. I gave it back to the old man."

"I remember Granddad liked that about you. He told me once that you were one of only two women he'd ever respected."

She met her son's gaze and held it. "Your father went on an all-out campaign to win me — for the family bloodstock! Even lied to my boyfriend at the time. I only found out about that a few weeks ago."

"I can't buy that; Dad loved you."

"You find it hard to believe that your father manipulated and controlled people? He moved people around like pieces on a chessboard." Myra puckered her lips thoughtfully. "Oh, I know your father grew to love me. What's not to love? I'm just saying that Locke was the reason your father married me."

He silently recalled the time his father had gotten rid of Tinsley. *Would Tinsley have been different today if Breck Barrington had not interfered with her life. Would he? More importantly — would Quinn?*

"Why do I get the sense that none of what I've told you about the attempted burning of Barrington Lumber surprises you?"

"Because Evan-Cerise came to see me this morning."

"Evan-Cerise?" He paused. "What does she have to do with anything?"

A ravine of quiet opened between them before she spoke. "May I be blunt?"

"When are you never?"

Myra glanced down at her ring, twisting it on her finger. "She overheard Renault tell his wife about the botched arson attempt on Barrington Lumber. They thought they were alone. Evan-Cerise had forgotten her cell phone and went back inside to get it. She managed to sneak out without being detected. When she told Lynch about it, he persuaded her to take him to the office that night. They spent hours digging through all the files."

"And?" Gage said, shifting his position on the seat. "What did they find?"

"They saved copies on a flash drive of all of the documents they could find pertaining to the lumberyard and ... other things you may find interesting. Records of when they paid some of the workers at the lumberyard who stole loads. They wanted to force you out of business, like they had the previous owner. Renault must've been afraid you'd stumble onto something, or someone would tell you what had been going on there. Once you look at the evidence, you'll realize just *how* Renault and your father made their millions. The lumberyard is the tip of the iceberg."

It was too much to take in. "I came here to confront Renault. His hired help pointed the finger at him. But now you're telling me that my father was in on this, too?"

"Yes. That's exactly what I'm telling you. They were in on this together. While Renault was the rainmaker for Barrington and Porcher, nothing happened without Breck's seal of approval. They were serial acquirers — never friendly, always hostile when it came to acquisitions. Somewhere along the way, your father lost his moral compass." She tapped on the glass of the side table with her fingernail, making a clicking sound. "This is a time of action! Now, what are you going to do about it."

Gage was a man who was used to taking control of his circumstances, but his venture into the Delta had changed him. It seemed a series of lessons in trust and submission. Submitting the control of his life to the Creator of it.

"I've changed," he said, bluntly.

Myra looked at her son more deeply. He seemed to hold a circle of calm within the clamor of evil. The long, shaded stare made her squirm. "Tell me what has happened to you."

"I've heard from … One … I never guessed would speak to me — here," he tapped his chest. "I've spent most of my life with the influential, the money-minded, playing their games and talking their talk. As a consequence, I've had an empty, self-absorbed, joyless life. But not anymore. And, I'm going to do my best to see to it that Quinn doesn't go down that same path of a wasted life. That boy needs direction more than anything … so do I, before our lives dribble off to nothing."

"I get that, son. I think that's what happened to your father. Growing up in that kind of life can change a person. Right and wrong doesn't look too different after a while. Small wrongs you allow get attached to you like moss growing on the north side of a rock. Pretty soon it begins to take over. But in this situation, what are you planning to do?"

The shadowy face held a wolf gleam in his eyes. "Scrape off the moss."

CHAPTER 26

A gray mist hovered undecidedly over Charleston Harbor, and aside from the occasional sound of a distant ship's horn, all was quiet as Gage Barrington sat motionless on a bench in Battery Park.

He thought it fitting how in addition to the wartime history of the Battery, the shaded spot where he sat under a giant oak was thought to be where dozens of pirates were hanged in the early 1700s. They had been left dangling from their nooses for days on end as a warning to prevent other pirates from entering the waters of Charleston Harbor.

It turned out that *his* father had been every bit as much a pirate. He wondered how he could go back out there—to all the greed and consumption. The Barrington empire had collapsed—he'd read it in the papers just that morning—and it hadn't even fazed him. He had to return to that world, to right the wrongs and pick up the pieces of the lives shattered and ruined by the men at the helm. The dread of it all weighted his body to the spot.

Through the haze he glimpsed a few scudding clouds in the distance and a cerulean blue sky, and it made him think of the island. Of Summer's Keep. He pulled himself up from the bench and with a heavy heart, slid his cell phone into his pocket. The deed was done. A detective would soon arrive and the investigation into the crimes committed by his father and his father's partner would begin.

He thought about all of the events that had led up to this point in his life, wondering what his life and the lives of those he loved would look like after this day. At thirty-one he was hardly old; still, he felt a deep weariness down to the marrow of his bones. But intertwined with the uncertainty of the future was a light sense of freedom he could not explain, a peace he'd never experienced.

A boat passed by, heading for the open sea. And as he watched the gentle lap of the water touch the bleached oyster shells of the shore, he felt a longing. While he stood there, another more powerful thought pushed to the forefront of his mind. *I miss your presence, Shanna Muir.*

A car door slammed somewhere and broke the spell; he was mad at himself for listening for the sound of bracelets jangling. He caught sight of his mother and Gabriel walking toward him.

"We came to take you to dinner," Myra said as she offered her hand to her son. "LuBelle is watching Quinn. We left them playing some game on her iPad. They didn't even look up when we said goodbye."

"I think your mother is jealous of LuBelle," Gabriel said, squeezing Myra's hand. "Tell me, how's Shanna doing in Noble?"

Gage believed he understood the man enough to know that he wouldn't have brought up the subject of Shanna unless he was genuinely concerned about her. Shanna and Gabriel were a lot alike. Both had lost nearly every member of their immediate family; both had a deep and abiding faith in God.

"She's fine. I'll fill you in over dinner. I need to be back here in an hour. The detective is meeting me," Gage said, grabbing his jacket from the back of the bench.

Ten minutes later they were walking through the front door of Cane Break's, only to be met by Lynch and Evan-Cerise.

Reprieve broke across Gage's features. It was good to see his friends. "I can't thank you two enough for risking so much for me. Without all that documentation, I wouldn't have a case."

Lynch slapped Gage's back then grabbed him into a bear hug. "After all is said and done, you're gonna need a few friends."

"Hey, you two—our hostess is waiting and you're creating a spectacle," Evan-Cerise said, pretending to be annoyed. She threw a smile over her shoulder as she followed the hostess to the table.

As their plates arrived, Gabriel asked, "May I pray over the meal?"

Gage removed his cap and bowed his head with the others at the table. Lynch grabbed his shoulder and squeezed it.

"Father, we are all family here and our family is strong with love because of You. The troubles and the joys we share will only make us closer as our circle widens. And, whatever time we're allowed by You before we pass over, let us use it to deepen our love. Then our years will be powerful because love never dies, it goes on and on. Now, if there is any prayer to be answered, let it be this, that You would have our descendants grow up together and walk in the light and learn the ways of our Lord. And bless the food to the nourishment of our bodies, in Jesus' name, amen."

Returning to the island later that night, Myra became restless. Leaving her room, she passed the open study door and could only guess that Gage had finished his business and gone on to his room. Feeling the need to escape from the house, she slipped out the front door and let her eyes wander over the natural beauty of the land.

The bracing breeze had only a slight chill, and she filled her lungs with it. She walked the length of the yard, casting her eyes into the distance where Sassabee Creek drifted toward the sea. Myra paused, convinced that something was calling her. On that final thought, she followed the path worn in the dirt to the fence where it ended near the garden house. Ducking under the rail, she moved with fluid grace, and for no good reason at all, began to run toward The Prayer House.

The moon crept higher in the sky as Myra tried the door on The Prayer House, finding it unlocked. She slipped inside and felt along the wall, seeking the light switch. With a single flip the light at the front of the sanctuary above the baptistery came on. Satisfied with the soft glow she moved, little by little, toward the front of the church.

The pulpit stood in front of her like a silent witness. Unconsciously she took a step backward, but with a slow deliberation, she slipped into a pew. Her feelings at the moment were as foreign to her as anything she'd ever experienced. She tried to explain it away, saying it was so long ago, or thinking so many things have happened since; whatever excuse she wanted to use to try and water it down—one thing remained, and that one thing wasn't dead. It still pulsed with life. The thought that she still loved Gabriel Muir struck her so clearly that it might as well have been shouted from the pulpit. But that wasn't the relationship she sought to reconcile … not this night. No, this reunion was more intimate … this reunion was between a prodigal daughter and her Father.

The feelings were powerful, like being carried away by a swiftly moving current. The explosion that would soon rock her family to their roots would carry with it aftereffects, falling on them all and sticking like ash. *Can I handle it? Will I be strong enough to bear the rejection, shame, hardship?* From the depths of her being, she knew that in her own strength she could not. In fact, she recognized that she would need God's strength, his direction, and his wise counsel, now and in the difficult days to come. "I've come home, Father … if you'll have me."

The long, brutal summer could be a test of endurance for those not used to the scorching heat of Noble, Mississippi. But the warm lulling breezes of spring that now filled the air were enough to stir most creatures from their winter hideouts.

The late afternoon sun seemed bent on toasting Shanna until she passed under the cooler, dappled shade of the lofty trees flanking the road to the river.

Much had happened since that fateful Christmas Eve night when she determined in her heart to change direction in her life. Noble Hill was now an active and thriving boarding house for unwed mothers and their babies. It seemed unthinkable that she had become a proprietor of sorts to eight young mothers and their babies. Toward that end, she strongly suspected a few of the girls might be leaving soon. There had been talk of marriage from at least two of the women to men from Barrington Lumber.

Earlier, Shanna had passed Mrs. Lynn and Yancey seated on the porch with a baby, little Carrie, in a nearby playpen. At the moment, the aging widow seemed far more robust than her years might normally have indicated. Shanna was sure the reason to be her love interest of late. Rarely could you open a door at Noble Hill without bumping into Yancey Bain.

Father Cleo had been thrilled with the news of the home and quickly sent Father Dominic to access the situation for a possible outreach to support. As Shanna walked toward the pier at the river, she smiled and shook her head. The priest liked to travel by boat when he could, and not just any boat, but a custom-made cruiser with a teak wood interior. It was alleged to have been given to him by a repentant gambler who had taken the boat in a bet. The rumor stated that the gambler gave the boat to Father Dominic in order to soothe his conscience.

As the boat neared shore, the captain came out and directed a deckhand until the boat carefully nudged against the pier.

"Tie her down!" the captain bellowed. And it was then that she caught her first glimpse of the priest as the deckhand turned to escort him from the boat.

Father Dominic, even now in his advanced years, seemed to wear piety like some trophy of well-deserved honor. There was no show of warmth or greeting and he gave no sign of recognition as he walked down the pier toward her. He stopped in front of her. When he looked down his long, thin nose at her, she had the same impression she used to have as a little girl at Holy Trinity, one that he had judged her and found her seriously flawed.

"Thank you for coming, Father Dominic. What would you care to see first?" she asked, kindly.

His dark eyes narrowed significantly. "I care to see if there are any men present at this... so-called boarding house."

Shanna nodded, turned her back to him, and started walking toward the house, rolling her eyes upward and feeling like a petulant teenager. The fact that these girls had already suffered enough because a man had either abandoned them or they had abandoned the man apparently hadn't even entered into the priest's thinking. "Since most of the men who have been involved with these women have either been cowards or no counts, I doubt you'll find what you're looking for. Unless you happen to find one chained up in the basement being tortured."

Her mild sarcasm seemed to go unnoticed as they continued walking along the plain stretch of road. Vivid green grass and violets covered the center section between the ruts and colored their way to the house.

"Before I left Holy Trinity, I heard rumors that a man was known to frequent Noble Hill. My concerns are not unfounded." He cocked an eye toward her.

Her brow furrowed, then she widened her eyes. "Oh, you must mean Yancey Bain! He's here now... I'll introduce you."

As they approached the front porch, Yancey stood to his feet immediately, as if some Head of State had just arrived.

Father Dominic lifted his chin in pompous arrogance, a brief look of flattery playing across his features before he caught it.

Yancey softly harrumphed and then graciously greeted the priest. "Father Dominic, it is our great pleasure to welcome you to Noble Hill. My name is Yancey Bain and this," he turned to present Mrs. Lynn, "is Mrs. Abigail Lynn."

Quite taken with Yancey Bain's manner, Father Dominic nodded to the woman. He then asked if Yancey would be so kind as to give him a tour of the property.

As the men walked out of earshot from the women, Father Dominic asked, "Is it your intention to marry Mrs. Lynn? Or, do you consider yourselves just friends?"

"Oh, no, sir. I consider her more than a friend. If she'll have me, I intend to marry her."

"Is there some doubt?" he asked, glancing up to admire a purple clematis growing over a trellis.

"In her mind, yes. But I don't plan on giving up anytime soon."

"What is her concern?"

He pressed his teeth into his bottom lip, considering the question before he spoke. "Her age, mostly. You see, Father, I'm a few years younger, that's all. It doesn't matter to me one bit. In fact, I love her — and her age doesn't change any of that."

When Yancey made his decision to ask Abigail for her hand in marriage, he had never thought to have a priest authorize the deal, but the more he thought about it, the better he liked it. Knowing Abigail was a practicing Catholic, he was not above seeking out a little pressure from the church to seal the deal.

"If I can convince Abigail to marry me," Yancey said, "I'd consider it an honor to have you counsel us before marriage. We've both lost our spouses … and I'm sure you can instruct us on how best to prepare for the challenges ahead."

The priest's mouth twisted with pleasure. "Of course. It would be an honor. I'm a servant to all."

Mrs. Lynn patted Shanna's hand. "Don't worry yourself none over those two, dear. They're just old men, set in their ways. Why, everyone knows this is your place and you're running it good." She tossed her head toward the men. "Let them play their games. It makes them feel important."

Shanna sank into a chair beside her. "You're right. This is *my* home and I can do what I want with it. With or without the help of Holy Trinity. God will make a way."

"Why don't you mention that to the priest, dear? Tell him that your father-in-law is a pastor and you'll approach him about the ministry opportunity."

A dawning occurred in her eyes. "Mrs. Lynn, you're a genius!" She reached over and clasped Mrs. Lynn's face with her hands. "A pure genius!"

Shanna knew one thing about Father Dominic — he was competitive. There was no way in hades the man would allow some protestant pastor from some spit of an island to beat him out of an outreach opportunity.

Shanna's knowledge of the priest proved true. They had secured the funding for Noble Hill, and, after escorting Father Dominic back to his awaiting boat, she practically ran up the darkened lane to share the news.

CHAPTER 27

The months traveled on and May, with all her color and warmth, was upon them. Overhead, the sky was milk-white and it hid the sun and the blue of the day behind a moist heat. Sweet morning air smelled like a thousand fruit trees had released their breath all at once. The scent seeped into Quinn's bedroom through a half-opened window as he stirred, hearing the faint sound of tires rolling over gravel. His head came up. Squinting through sleep swollen eyes, he scratched his snarled hair as he watched a silver Pontiac Grand Prix make its way down the lane and toward the house. It rolled to a stop under the spreading oak near the walk.

Quinn sat up, panic-stricken as he fixed his eyes on his mother as she got out of the car. She sidestepped the dog, Big Duke, in her three-inch heels and continued on to the door, intent in her purpose. She looked overstuffed. Her too-tight clothing strained against the fabric like it might erupt at any moment, releasing the pent-up pressure.

The screen door slapped behind Tinsley and the sound filled Quinn with a sickening dread. The fear his mother might return for him one day had always swirled around in the back of his head like a toxic fume. Then a thought struck him and he turned to look at the car. She'd left the car running with the driver's side door ajar. He'd seen her do that many times before and it always meant the same thing—she wasn't staying very long.

Gage flipped his pillow and smiled as he felt a fresh breeze caress his face. For a brief moment, his mind was free, then darker thoughts intruded, disturbing his peace as a familiar voice filled his head.

"Is it true?"

Hesitantly he cocked one eye half open. There she stood, Tinsley, arms crossed, glaring down at him. With a groan he clamped his eyes shut again, wishing for her to disappear. She was like a bad rash, showing up at the worst time to annoy and bother him.

"Well, is it?" she demanded, her voice rising to the level of a shout.

"Yes. It's true!" He forced himself in an upright position, snatched his shirt from the foot of the bed, and yanked it on.

Tinsley stared at him, and all her hatred made itself known in the sneer of pure rage that twisted her face. "How can you be so thoughtless—look at the lives that depend on you! What about your son!"

He stood and tugged on his jeans. "I don't normally dress in front of a woman, but you're not like most women." He buttoned then zipped his pants. "Most women wouldn't barge into a man's room—uninvited."

A long string of oaths spewed from her lips. "Save the altar boy routine for someone who didn't get knocked up by you."

"What is it you want, Tinsley? Money? I'm fresh out at the moment. Believe me when I say if I had it I would gladly give it to you just to get rid of you."

"You're not getting off that easy. Why should I be left raising the kid—he's your responsibility. I've had him for eight years; you're stuck with him now."

Gage's head snapped around so fast that Tinsley took a step backward. "Just one condition: from now on you stay clear of me. Do you understand me, Tinsley?"

She pointed a finger in his face. "You are worth nothing to me now. Your good Charleston name is mud, ruined, and gone—just like your money." She laughed. "You're worthless to me. In fact, you're an embarrassment." She dug a paper out of her purse and slapped it on the dresser as she walked out the door.

After hearing the slam of the front door, Gage reached for the paper, his hand shaking. He scanned the document, closed his eyes and mumbled a silent prayer of thanks. Quinn was now officially his.

The drowsy beauty of late spring on Terrapin Island held a strange contentment for Shanna. Mornings on the island usually whispered a fine mist over the inlets, hovering around the marshes and reeds until midday when it would gradually dissipate into the moist air.

Driving across the bridge with the windows down, the familiar scent of sun-warmed creosote from the nearby docks and decaying marine life mingled on the briny breeze. In many ways Terrapin Island was entirely different from Noble, Mississippi. Hundreds of miles away and hundreds of years it often seemed. Seeking refuge, Shanna had returned to the little island in hopes of escaping the sad stares and pitying looks. The final decision to return to the island came after a well-meaning neighbor cornered her at the market. "Such a tragic life you've led," he'd said to her with a pained expression. "Our Sunday School class has been discussing how best to help you. We're told in scripture to care for widows and orphans… you, actually, may qualify as both."

It was the word "qualify" that finally got Shanna's attention. One thing was certain: she would not live the rest of her life as the town of Noble's Sunday school charity project! Besides, she thought, the island offered more solace and opportunity than anything else at the time. She'd been promised a job at the marina if she ever returned, and the position with Molly was always on the table.

Shanna pulled in front of Three Course Catering and hurried up the walk. As she neared the steps, she was struck by a feeling of being watched. She slowed her pace, half turned, and peered down the main street of town. She could see no one. Scanning the area again, she noticed the door of a pickup truck slam shut before pulling away slowly. Mildly curious, she watched as the truck disappeared around the corner.

"Molly? Are you here?" Shanna called, pushing her way through the front door.

An answer came from the kitchen. "Back here."

She became aware of another voice, a man's voice that said, "I'm too fat and mean. I'd hurt feelings all over the place. Get yourself a girl." She heard the back door slam as she pushed through the swinging door into the kitchen.

Molly jumped with surprise, wiping her hands on her apron as she jostled toward Shanna. "Goodness gracious, girl, but you have good timing! Quick, grab an apron and help me. We have a party to get together for this afternoon!"

Like most of the low-lying Sea Islands the light at times could seem diffused, blurring the line of the horizon in the brutal heat. But the intimate little garden nook where Molly and Shanna worked was cool and inviting. Backdropped by a vine-covered wall, they busily arranged white dishes on a panel of soft green toile fabric draped across the table. Well protected under the shade of a live oak, a slight breeze ruffled their pressed cotton aprons as they moved about, setting the buffet in order.

Shanna's eyes, as gray as the stucco, glanced over the structure in admiration of the old Southern home. The stucco was known as "tabby" and told of the house's age at a glance. But the old Georgian dowager held her age well, glowing subtly in the shifting light. It was the perfect venue for gatherings, and Shanna was pleased to see yet another antebellum home that survived Grant's march to the sea.

People were beginning to wander outside and gather near the tables set up under the trees. The little soirée seemed made up of young business men and women, fresh from the office. A few of the guys began shucking their suit jackets and yanking off ties as they mingled around, talking and gesturing with their cocktail glasses as they loosened up.

Gage was seated at a table, his collar open and his tie flung over his chair. He glanced up, noticing Shanna over the top of his drink, and froze. Lately the filter seemed to have been removed from Gage Barrington's eyes, allowing him to see the world with all of its scars and ugliness. But, just as a vivid sunset at the end of a long and grueling day could be like an unexpected gift, the lovely sight of Shanna developed right before his eyes. He felt suddenly young. A feeling he'd not felt in years.

Gage appeared beside Shanna as she was busy stacking plates at the end of the table. Arming himself with a fork, he reached in front of her to slide a plate from the stack as he scanned the buffet.

"If it's all the same to you, I'll wait on the pecan pie," he said, the corners of his lips barely lifting.

Surprised, she began to busily smooth the toile around the dishes as a slow grin spread across her lips. "That may be awhile. You better go for the turtle brownies." When she turned to leave, he caught her hand, stopping her.

Something flashed in his eyes that she could not interpret. "I don't mind waiting for what I really want." He half-smiled then slid the plate back on the stack.

She smiled before she could stop herself. "Well, I hate to disappoint you. I'll see what I can do about that later."

At her words, he lifted his gaze and settled it on her with such intensity that her face felt a rush of heat. "You do that," he said.

Gage saw what everyone saw when they looked at Shanna Muir: a long graceful form, burnished mahogany hair pulled back into a twist, random strands falling around her face, and expressive gray eyes. But it was her puritan conscience that intrigued him most. She was someone who didn't care about money — whether a person came from wealth or from some backwoods shanty, it was all the same to her. She valued people, as only God working through her could.

"So, what are you doing back on the island? Somebody sent up an SOS?" he asked.

"Something like that." Anxious to get the conversation back on comfortable terms, she asked, "So, is this a business meeting of yours?"

He nodded once. "My attorney and I have been working on placement for the former employees of Barrington & Porcher. Most are with local companies, but we've worked a deal for some of them with a company that manages 300,000 acres of timberland along 700 miles of the Mississippi River Corridor. I've gotten to know them through Barrington Lumber. Most of these people will oversee the management of forest and harvesting operations, conservation, regrowth, things like that. This is a mingle for all of them to get to know each other." He grinned. "I was able to find a place in this same company for the former owner of my lumber business. He now makes twice the money without the headache. I still have the headache."

She caught herself leaning toward his voice, then blinked and reoriented herself, placing a silver spoon in a deep bowl of butterscotch sauce. "We have espresso... interested?"

He shifted his attention from her eyes to her lips. "Always."

She was having a difficult time getting her thoughts together. The look in his eyes was doing strange things to her, and she was somewhat relieved when a pretty young blond came up and took his arm, pulling him away.

"The party's over here, Gage," the woman said, flashing a bright smile. "They want to hear more about this Godforsaken place you're sending the exiles."

Walking backward, Gage caught Shanna's eye and winked. "Oh, it's an uncultured place, Nikki. Savage, really. Sure, they have Faulkner, and Williams—but they don't have anyone like Earnest T. Bass."

Whatever it was that Shanna was going to say died on her lips. The way he was looking at her, with those sparkling blue eyes, sent a shiver straight through her. He had pulled her, in some deep chamber of her heart. The feeling caught her off guard and left her cheeks heated.

"Hey, where are you staying?" he called back to Shanna.

"With Molly."

"My door is always open … you know that, right?"

She nodded, smiling.

Molly had turned down the bed covers in the guest room of the old Victorian home, making Shanna smile as she entered the room. Looking around, she could easily imagine herself in another century. She noticed the faded rose wallpaper covering the walls and a tiffany lamp on the bedside table. Long, sheer curtains hung from the tall six-paneled bay window in a turret that faced the ocean. From that vantage point, Shanna supposed, you could observe rolling fog banks, thunderheads, and brilliant skies in vivid blue.

Several long minutes passed before she finally popped open her suitcase at the end of the four poster bed and slipped out her pajamas. She loosed her hair from the twist as she crossed the room, moving in and out of the moonlight that streamed in from the windows.

Parting the sheers, she glanced out the window and stopped so quickly she nearly fell over. Someone was standing in the middle of the yard, in the darkness, looking up at her window.

Her heart was in her throat. Swallowing down the fear, she eased to the side of the window and peered out. It was a girl. *What could she want?*

After retracing her steps back down the staircase to the front door, Shanna cautiously pulled it open. "May I help you?" she asked, keeping one foot in the door.

The girl shook her head. "No."

Shanna hesitated then stepped back into the house. But before she could close the door, the girl held up a hand as if to stop her.

"Yes. I mean … I have something for you," the girl said.

Suddenly, being alone outside with a stranger didn't seem like such a good idea. She thought about waking Molly but changed her mind. "Come up here," Shanna said, not trusting the dark surroundings.

The girl cautiously approached the porch, taking the steps slowly until she was standing in front of Shanna. Her hair was light brown and straight as the rain. Almond-shaped dark eyes shifted to the porch floor. She turned her hand and opened her fist. A small wooden cross hung from a leather cord.

"I found this on the beach and thought of you … wanted to give it to you if I ever saw you again."

Shanna took the cross necklace from the girl's hand. "It's beautiful. Thank you, but … why?"

The girl crossed her arms over her chest and tightened them, looking over her shoulder as if reluctant to speak. Several long minutes passed as they stood in the darkness, the girl rubbing her hands nervously over her arms.

"What's your name?" Shanna asked.

"Jade. I was … one of Gypsy's girls."

She nodded.

Jade bowed her head for several moments before she spoke. Then, in a rush of words she said, "I ran away. They hunted me down; kicked me and stomped me like a dog. They put me in a black hole, the cellar of some old house. Buried me like a corpse. I sat there in pain, wanting to die — to feel my life drain away. But I couldn't die."

It was difficult for Shanna to move — she stood frozen, fearing that any sudden movement might cause the girl to flee.

"At first they would open the cellar door and throw things down—scraps of food, a bottle of water. And then one day that stopped. When the swelling of my eyes went down, I started looking around, trying to find a way out. That's when I found the Bible. It was splayed open like it had been tossed down with the rest of the trash. I saw your name and the quote you wrote on the front page. 'May it be a light to you in dark places, when all other lights go out.'"

"J. R. R. Tolkien—" Shanna whispered, remembering the day she had scrolled the message. At the time it had seemed almost a sacrilege not to quote a scripture, so she added beneath the words, Psalm 27:1.

"It spoke to me. I didn't read anything from it right away. I sat in the dark and remembered my life before … before things fell apart. There was no one to miss me, no one who cared what had happened to me. Sometime in all of that misery, I cried out to God. 'You're my last chance! My only hope in this life!.'"

"And … he answered you?" Shanna whispered.

Jade nodded. "I found a small dirty window and knocked it out. It gave me fresh air and enough light to read by. All through the storm I read. It wasn't until later that I realized a hurricane had hit the island. I'd heard and felt a crash or two, but nothing disturbed me, I was strangely at peace. One morning I heard voices and chainsaws outside the window. Emergency crews were working to remove a tree that had fallen on the house. I screamed and they found me and rescued me."

Gripping the cross tightly in her hand, Shanna was overcome with emotion. "If there had not been a storm, you would not have been found."

"And if you hadn't given that bible to Gypsy…," she let her words drop, wiping her cheeks with the back of her hand. "I remembered seeing you a couple of times, when you came down to the bridge. I saw you earlier today. I had to see you again, tell you thank you. I'm not where I need to be—yet. But, I'm working on that."

"Where are you staying?"

"Dr. Mooreland got me a job with a veterinarian. I live in a room on site so I can look in on the animals after hours. One of the members of The Prayer House gave me an old truck. It's not much to look at, but it runs." She shrugged, "I'm alive for a reason. God has a purpose for me. That's what Pastor Gabriel says. He says that we're called to be faithful—and not necessarily successful, as the world defines success. He said that a simple and meaningful job is sometimes the best we can do on a broken earth."

This time Shanna couldn't keep herself from shuddering when the words of truth came to her with full force. "You're going to The Prayer House?"

"I am."

"Good. I'll see you in the morning, then."

CHAPTER 28

Lately Gage had begun to realize that life was short. If he wasn't careful, time would rush by and the opportunity to provide guidance to his son would be gone forever. For five long minutes he argued with himself about whether or not to attend The Prayer House. Whether it might be best to go a more traditional route with a church in town. He was partial to stained-glass … but did that really matter?

As the warm breeze stroked the tops of the sage grasses, Gage relaxed back in his chair. From his position on the porch he could see the ocean glistening in the distance under the bright morning sun. He drew a deep breath, stretched his arms above his head, then clasped his hands behind his neck. His mind wandered to Shanna. Until he'd met her, family name and accomplishments were all he'd known about life. He wondered, *Why has she returned to the island?*

It wasn't until after he'd taken a seat that Gage realized he had been holding his breath. He glanced down the pew at his mother and son who were sitting wide-eyed and erect, and a certain feeling of satisfaction came over him. It had not been as difficult as he had imagined convincing his mother to attend church.

The service had begun and prayers were being offered. Looking around, he spotted Molly seated next to an older woman. Dr. Mooreland and his wife were sitting near the front. The old fisherman, Butrous, and several families he'd seen around town filled in the seats. His eyes fell on Shanna. She was seated beside a young girl who was leaning over, whispering to her. Shanna smiled, patted the girl's hand and lifted her head.

Her eyes passed Gage twice before locking on him. So much was said in the brief exchange that a smile started in her lips and then crimped the lines beneath her eyes.

He lifted an eyebrow, as if seeing him in church was the most natural of occurrences. Turning his attention back to the service, Gage fumbled with a hymnal as he fought a grin.

By the end of the message, Gage felt a sense of rightness, hope, and was beginning to imagine that he could carry that buoyant feeling with him right out the door and along with him the entire week. He stood waiting for his family to file out of the pew when Pastor Gabriel approached him from behind and dropped a hand on his shoulder.

"Enjoyed having you and your family with us today," Gabriel said. "We'd love to have you stay and join us for a picnic—we have plenty. I've always wanted to have an old-fashioned Dinner on the Ground…seemed like a good time for it."

Gage glanced at Myra, seeing the expectation on her face, and nodded his head. "Sounds like a good idea." The man had come too far down the road of new life to be put off by a church gathering. In fact, he thought, as he watched Shanna's graceful hands lift a pie carrier from the seat, this could be a real pleasure.

It took an effort of sheer will for Shanna to draw her eyes away from the Barrington family. She had watched discreetly as Pastor Gabriel spoke with Gage, hoping that an invitation to the picnic had been extended to them. A second later she had her answer as two thin arms wrapped around her waist. She winced slightly, and shifted her weight to the other foot.

"We're going to the picnic!" Quinn said, grinning ear to ear.

She brushed the top of the boy's head with her hand. "Good. Now we'll all have some fun."

A light breeze caressed Shanna's face, bringing her awareness of her surroundings. She had wandered off from the others, after helping set the tables for the meal, and retraced a familiar path to the creek.

As she passed the cemetery gate she saw a leaf, yellow and dangling as it hung from a thin line of gossamer web. *And there am I,* Shanna thought, *suspended in midair, neither touching the earth nor belonging to heaven. Just hanging there, caught between two worlds.*

Finding a mossy patch, she sat down and picked up a stick, snapping off tiny pieces and tossing them into the creek. A shadow fell across her lap.

"Mind a little company?" Gage said.

She stared in mute surprise as he sat down beside her. "Not at all." She brushed a few twigs from her lap. "Where are the others?"

"Playing games — tug-of-war. Quinn's side is winning … he has Butrous and Molly on his team."

"Smart boy."

"Just like his father."

He let his thoughts wander without restraint, resting his eyes against the water as the wind gave chase over the surface of the creek. A long, lean finger pointed toward the opposite bank. "You miss the garden house?"

Conscious of the man's stare, she looked down and fidgeted with her shirt. "Why would you ask that?"

White teeth gleamed in a reckless smile. "Because it's like a home for a woodland Sprite…you know, someone who communes with nature and God, picks flowers and reads poetry."

Her face shot up. "Is that how you see me?"

"No…." His voice was subdued and peace hung on the air along with the buzzing sound of the cicadas. "That's not how I see you."

"It doesn't matter." She spoke so softly Gage had to strain to hear her voice. Turning her face away from him, she ran a hand idly over her skirt.

Realizing his mistake, he looked for some path to state the obvious. "I see you as a woman with Godly courage. Courage that trembles and fears, but still trusts and loves. You are not without fear, but you, like your husband was, are noble in your trembling."

She opened her mouth to reply, but a breeze blew across her face, sweeping the words from her. Brushing the hair from her eyes, she felt her throat tighten.

"Until I met you, I just hadn't seen a love for God so passionate. Not in a long time. Not since Lilly Rose. At times you're so like my grandmother that you could be her ghost."

"It's not so rare," she said, shoving up the sleeves to her butter cream blouse. She swallowed hard against her raw emotions.

"Maybe in your circles, but not in mine." He turned to her and smirked. "Lilly Rose used to say to me, 'Don't lay your pipe too short Kof the fountain, son, or you'll never touch the eternal spring. You've got to stay connected to the source of life-giving water.'" His tone was scoffing. "I didn't have a clue what she was talking about. In fact, not until recently."

She was having trouble forming a coherent thought; like a person swept into a swift current, she grasped at any branch to keep from drowning, "I've heard my husband say that before."

He cleared his throat, his words gravelly with emotion. "I'm sure he heard it from Lilly Rose." Gage knew what plagued him, what bore on his mind more than anything. "My father refused to let me see my grandmother after I reached a certain age. Said she was unstable and would fill my head with nonsense." He picked up a stone and hurled it into the creek. "Breck Barrington handled his business and personal affairs with the steadiness of a business transaction. Controlling his world meant shutting off feelings. I think I've inherited some of that. I don't want it—but, it's there." *Is this how Catholics feel in the confessional?* he thought to himself.

She tensed, listening over the wild thumping of her heart.

He looked at Shanna, his eyes full of regret. "Your husband was a better grandson to Lilly Rose than I ever was. I'm glad she had him in her life. At least he was there for her."

She faced him, a dark scowl knitting her brow. "It wasn't your fault—you were just a boy obeying your father!"

"I could have fought him on it. I should've. He was so proficient at blotting people out. If you crossed him or didn't measure up, he was finished with you. Whether that meant whipping out a quick check or questioning your sanity, whatever it took, he could write you off all nice and clean and tidy."

"How could you bear it?" she said, fingering her wooden cross necklace, unaware she was doing it.

"Most things become bearable over time. We get caught up in the day-to-day struggle of life where there is no place for painful memories. But … some memories we can never fling away from us. They're always there, haunting us."

She rubbed her slim nose with the back of her knuckle as her face grimaced and her body began to hitch with suppressed sobs. And then the tears flowed freely, trailing paths down her cheeks.

Gage hadn't had a lot of experience with crying women. So, he got to his feet and pulled her up; taking a deep breath, he held on to her. "It's alright, shhh." He lifted his shirt corner and dabbed at her face as he spoke. "I'm sorry I upset you with my — my.…"

"No!" she interrupted, looking up into his troubled face. "It's — not — you — it's me." She took a deep juddered breath. "I'm just as haunted as you are. I've held on to James, not relaxing my fist for a long time now! It's time I loosened my fingers and let him go. I know in my heart that everything is going according to God's plan, whether I understand it or not. All I need to know is this: God is good and he allowed it for a reason. It's the same with you and your grandmother, don't you see? They gave us the example of what happens when a person of faith goes about the business of following God on this earth. We're meant to learn from that."

A stiff breeze blew up the creek and swirled around them, catching them in the whirlwind before dissipating over the church grounds.

"What a strange effect you have on me, Shanna Muir. You … and," he stared at the twisting wind for several long moments before he turned back to her, as if awakening from a trance, "this place."

The relationship between The Prayer House and Sassabee Creek seemed to be an intimate one. The church was tied to its creek by the hopes and prayers that connected them, binding them together as if the very life force of the Almighty flowed between them.

Gage sensed in her words a wisdom beyond her years. He had recognized early on that behind that pretty young face was a brain—and an active one at that! And, at the moment, he was exactly where he wanted to be—holding Shanna close to his heart.

Neither moved until a cough gained their attention.

"Pardon the interruption," Gabriel said in scarcely concealed amusement. "But everyone is waiting for you two to join us before we say the blessing."

It took an effort of sheer will for Gage to let go of Shanna. Even then, it was not until they had neared the church that his reasoning ability began to function again.

The old South Carolina island church, with its clouds of wisteria falling from the corner eaves, looked out across the gathering. A magnificent spreading tree sat behind the church and shaded a wide swath of yard.

Long tables laid for the outdoor meal looked inviting as billowing white sheets rose and fell with the stiff breeze. Standing under the oak, the Pastor pronounced a blessing over the dinner and everyone moved toward their seats.

"Sit here by me," Myra said to Shanna, patting the seat next to her. "I want to hear all about my brother and that woman from Noble who's put a spell on him." She winked across the table at her son. "I warned him, of course, but Yancey has a mind of his own."

"Mrs. Lynn?" Gage asked, making himself part of the conversation. He reached for a piece of chicken as the basket passed in front of him.

"Mrs. Abigail Lynn," Myra answered. "Oh, what money I'd give to see my brother fall all over himself for a woman. Jedidiah told me he has it bad."

Gage gave a lopsided grin and considered his mother more closely. It seemed she was enjoying the excitement of her brother's newfound love. "Mrs. Lynn is quite a lovely woman, Mother. She'll make a fine sister-in-law."

"That's where it's headed—and soon, if you ask me," Shanna said. "They're going to be running Noble Hill."

"Noble Hill?" Gage questioned. "Doing what?"

"It's now a home for single mothers—Holy Trinity supports it. It's the next step up from Bon Secour. Women can live there with their children while they get on their feet. As a matter of fact, most of the women you hired at Barrington Lumber now live there. Yancey and Abigail are going to be overseers. Once they're married, of course." Shanna's smile faded to be replaced by a sad introspection.

Myra smirked, placing her napkin down on the table. "Yancey, for all of his gruffness, has always had a tenderness toward children. He's the perfect man for the job."

Gage studied Shanna, unable to defeat the concern that showed on his face. "What about you? Your home?"

"I have … complex feelings about my home. I feel, or I did feel once, at home there. But I'm not sure anymore." She looked down at her plate, imagining the intense blue eyes directed at her. "I've given up the thought of living there again. It's too full of ghosts, I guess."

Stroking his jaw, Gage leaned back in his seat. "There's a difference between giving up and strategic disengagement. Seems to me like you've found a good ministry for your home and you've found good people to run it for you. Now you're free to live wherever you choose."

Myra quietly slipped from her seat and feigned interest in the ham on Quinn's plate.

Dr. Mooreland rose from his chair and came to sit in Myra's vacant seat. Troubled, he looked down at Shanna's foot, rubbed his fingers through his thick, gray thatch of hair, and spoke of what had been troubling him.

"Shanna, I've noticed you limping slightly." The old doctor shrugged. "Gage mentioned it to me this morning," he confessed. "Seems you've got an infection. Mind if I take a look?"

She folded her arms and her voice was barely heard. "Not here while people are trying to eat."

"Then we'll go to the church," Gage said, getting up from his chair. He didn't pause for a reply.

Seeing the situation, she slipped from the chair graciously held by the doctor. As they walked toward the church, she gave a brief recounting of the injury and when it had taken place.

"I was down at the bridge and my sandal caught on a board. My foot came out of my shoe and something stuck it. I thought it was getting better, but it has never completely healed."

"And you've never felt the need to have it looked at by a doctor?" Gage looked at her sternly over the tops of his sunglasses before snatching them off and pulling on the church door. "After you," he said, struggling to contain his annoyance.

Dr. Mooreland motioned for her to take a seat in a pew. "Prop that foot up and let's have a look." He examined the foot closely, prodded the leg. He tapped his knuckles lightly on her toes and caught her eyes with his own. "I recommend that you soak your foot in hot water with Epsom salt four times a day for up to 20 minutes at each soaking. Get it as hot as you can stand it."

Shanna's eyes widened as she watched the older man closely.

"Stay off of it for at least a week. I'll see how things look after that."

"But why—"

The doctor raised a hand to halt her questions. "I'm ordering an antibiotic. You could lose your foot, Shanna, if you continue to ignore it. You'll do as I say?"

She sat as one stunned, staring up at the man. The doctor held his tongue, letting the full impact of his words sink in.

Taking the decision from her, Gage took charge of the situation. "She'll be at the garden house. I'll see that she has all she needs and follows your orders to the letter."

Shanna wanted so badly to find some problem with Gage's plan, some flaw in his reasoning, but she couldn't. It wouldn't be fair to ask for Molly's help. She'll already be short-handed while Shanna recovers. Besides, Shanna knew the garden house would be much easier to maneuver around in than the old two-story Victorian of Molly's.

"You've had a puncture wound," Dr. Mooreland explained, offering his wisdom freely. "An object pierced your skin, creating a small hole. Could've been a fish hook, anything."

She shook her head. "I don't understand. How can such a small wound cause all this?"

"A puncture wound causes infection because it forces bacteria deep into the tissue. The wound closes quickly, forming an ideal place for infections. Now," the doctor turned to Gage, "start the treatment immediately."

Slowly Shanna meandered out of the church and into the yard. She turned back to see Gage and the doctor talking in the doorway. Gage pointed her to his truck with a wave of his finger, then continued on with his conversation. She swallowed down the feeling of being directed like a child and waited, somewhat petulantly, for them to finish up their discussion of her life.

Chapter 29

By the time they arrived at the garden house, the sun was dipping over the tops of the willow oaks as a cool, languid breeze gently swayed their branches.

Stepping into the house, Shanna glanced around, surprised at the tidiness.

"Molly's bringing your things over later," Gage said, placing a drink down on the side table as he dropped a book next to it. He paused before clearing his throat. "Ahem."

She turned with a questioning look and found Gage standing, his arms crossed in front of him. Though the shadow of his cap hid his eyes, she detected a note of disapproval in his stance.

"The sooner you sit down and elevate your foot, the quicker you'll heal. You heard what the doctor said."

Hobbling across the room to a small cushioned chair, she sat down rigid, her chin rising a few degrees.

"Are you going to be difficult?" he asked, taking note of the stubborn set of her jaw.

She could see a shadow of a smile play across his lips. "I think I was doing much better before I was diagnosed. I mean, I wasn't even limping too much. Now I'm hobbling around like a cripple."

"You can only receive help once you recognize your need for it. Didn't I hear you say something like that once in a sermon?" His eyes gleamed devilishly as he stepped to the kitchen and started rummaging in the cabinets. He placed a box of Epsom salt on the counter, pulled out a tub, and began filling it with hot water.

She watched from her chair as he tested the water with his fingers, stirring the salt into the liquid with his hand. Carefully he walked toward her, placing the tub in front of her foot. He turned back to pick up a drink and two Advils.

"I guess you're right. You do actually listen when I ramble on and on," she said, scooting back in the seat. She raised her eyebrow in a question as she accepted the drink.

"You could use a couple of fingers of bourbon in this if you ask me, but Cherry Coke is all I could find."

Ignoring his comment, she didn't glance up but swallowed the pills down in one easy gulp.

"*Ease* your foot into it," he said, watching with a pained expression as he mirrored her reaction to the hot water. "Go slow...."

Sinking her foot into the steamy liquid, she caught her breath and closed her eyes, waiting for the sensation of heat to subside.

Nearing the chair opposite her, he picked up his drink and slid a thick volume of Lansing's *The Endurance* from the table and sat down, letting out a deep breath. He felt uneasy, plagued by a new kind of stress, one that brought with it a strange sense of powerlessness and a greater weight in the region of the heart.

"So... tell me what's going on with you?" Shanna commented offhandedly as she gathered her hair away from her neck. There was no way she was going to let him sit in the same room with her and read a novel. Not in *this* lifetime.

He looked up from his book and for the first time he let his guard down all at once. "Barrington and Porcher is no more. It remains to be seen how much jail time Renault is facing. Our house in Charleston has been sold, along with most of our landholdings."

"Myra?" Shanna questioned gently. She saw his eyes shift to the book in his lap.

"Piece by piece my mother watched as our furniture was bought by neighbors, strangers, and a few antique dealers. A man from Wilmington bought the house and pointed out all the changes he would make so it would be 'livable' again."

Shanna lowered her gaze, remembering the awful feeling of displacement.

"I had to get Mother to the island … put it all behind us." He let out a long sigh. "Tomorrow we see the attorney to find out what's to become of Summer's Keep. I haven't looked into that matter … never saw a need to until recently."

"What about your lumber business? The marina?"

"Barrington Lumber is still in my possession, as well as the marina, but … it's doubtful that the marina will continue to thrive. I'm not the most popular man in Charleston these days."

Shanna lifted her foot out of the water, looked at it, and then submerged it again. "What about your men? Are they staying in Port St. Joe?"

"Jedidiah is on his way back now." Gage grew quiet. "If I allow myself to think too much about the possibility of…."

"You're doing the right thing," Shanna interrupted, "and it's going to work out."

"That's easy for you to say. You've never lost—" he stopped abruptly, remembering who he was speaking to.

She raised an eyebrow, a smirk on her lips. "You're in a hard spot, I'll grant you that, but, whatever happens, you'll make it through."

"What am I crying about...." He snapped the book closed and tossed it on the table. "I have more than most. It will kill me to lose Summer's Keep, but I certainly don't deserve it." Leaning forward, he looked her squarely in the eyes. "I abandoned my own grandmother ... for my father's empire." Halting abruptly, his eyes went over Shanna's head and took in the sight of a small yellow note floating down from the ceiling beam. It lighted softly on the kitchen table. Standing to his feet, he walked over and lifted the note, slowly straightening himself as he recognized the familiar script.

The astonished look on his face caused Shanna some concern. "Gage?" Her voice was small, even in the dead silence of the room. "What is it?"

Tight-lipped, he handed her the note and answered the unspoken question he saw in her eyes. "Lilly Rose." Shanna widened her eyes as Gage gestured toward the paper. "Please ... read it."

Rather guardedly she began. "Love never gives up. Love cares more for others than for self. Love doesn't want what it doesn't have. Love doesn't force itself on others. Doesn't keep score of the sins of others. Takes pleasure in the truth. Put's up with anything. Trusts God always. Always looks for the best. Never looks back, but keeps going to the end. Love never fails." Shanna carefully kept her gaze on the paper in her hand, worried that if she looked up she would not be able to handle what she would find in his eyes.

"Is that a scripture?" he asked, his voice low and husky.

"Lilly Rose's version of 1 Corinthian 13, I think."

Gage's jaw tensed. He reached over and flipped the knob on the small window air conditioner, anxious to remove the heat from the room.

Listening to the hiss of the air conditioner, he watched as wisps of Shanna's hair blew freely around her face. The smell of the cool musty air transported him back in time. "Would you care for something to eat?" Gage asked. "I could go get something."

"I've troubled you enough." She pointed to her foot. "I really appreciate what you've done for me."

"Thanks, but back to your dinner. What would you eat if you were back at Noble Hill? Tamales?"

She thought for a moment. "Chicken. No one does fried chicken better than a Mississippi gas station."

He smiled in bemusement. "Okay, I'll head down to the Chevron and see what's cooking."

"I doubt it's the same … not just anybody can fry chicken to perfection. It takes generations to cultivate a skill like that."

"There's a place I know on the island that makes a mean chicken sandwich. It comes loaded with a house-made Texas Pete spiked mayo, shredded lettuce, and dill pickles on a homemade roll. You interested?"

"I could be persuaded," she said, sitting up on the couch and propping her foot on the coffee table.

Gage Barrington's presence in the garden house brought with it a certain orderliness. Clearly the man had a system for getting things done. Nothing had been mentioned again about Lilly Rose's note. But Shanna noticed it was gone. She sensed a change in Gage and watched as he snatched his cap and his truck keys off the table and headed out the door.

The truck negotiated a sharp turn as it approached the front of a duplex on the outskirts of Charleston. Gage rolled to a stop under a palmetto tree.

It seemed the door to the truck opened too quickly, though in reality the driver had waited long enough for the neighbors to grow suspicious. He stared at the sidewalk that led to Nikki Bailey's front door for several long moments before he stepped to the ground. With a reluctant breath, he approached the door.

Gage had begun casually seeing Nikki a few months after his return to the island from Mississippi. After her first invitation to join her at her apartment, under the pretense of business, one thing had led to another and before he knew it, they were involved with each other.

He raised his knuckles to rap on the door and then froze as an image of Shanna came to his mind. Shaking his head as if to clear it, he was suddenly more sure of what needed to be done. A quick second later, the door opened and he faced Nikki Bailey, wearing a breezy little dress that draped over her well-tanned form.

"Gage!" she said in surprise. "I expected you an hour ago. Where've you been?" She caught his hand, pulling him into the apartment. "Let's have a drink, then you can take me to dinner." She smiled mischievously before snatching his cap off and sailing it across the room.

"I ... can't stay, Nikki." For lack of something better to say, he looked around grasping for words. "I uh ... just came by to tell you ... goodbye."

A scowl creased her brow. "What? What do you mean?" In an attempt to persuade him, she rose on tiptoes and slid her hands behind his neck, pulling his lips down to meet hers. She was somewhat surprised by his lack of response. "Gage? Is this about Jeremy? I told you we're just friends."

Looking down into her confused face, he realized now that he had made a mistake in coming here. In some strange way, he felt like he was cheating. Uncomfortable with the situation, he wanted out fast. "I'm sorry … I'm going now, Nikki."

"Are you coming back?"

He met her gaze directly. "No. I haven't worked all of this out for myself yet, but I know this isn't right."

"Who says?"

"I do," he tapped his chest. He was just as baffled about the sudden attack of fidelity as Nikki, considering he didn't have anyone in his life right now to be faithful to.

As he left the apartment, and one very confused girl, he wondered about it. The warmth of his decision began to work its way through his whole being. He walked a few more steps and then paused. He felt good.

Glistening in the afternoon sun, a dusty pink rose swayed in the breath of an approaching storm as Gage's long strides took him to the garden house door. He turned the knob until the catch clicked free. Rather than give the impression that he was in a hurry to eat, he paused beside the door, placing the sack of sandwiches on a side table.

A wave of mahogany hair partially masked Shanna's face until she blew it out of her eyes and looked up at him.

"What did your husband die from?" he asked, sitting down abruptly beside her on the couch.

"Autonomic hyperreflexia — a life-threatening rise in blood pressure. It's caused from circulatory problems," she said, sitting up. She looked at him curiously.

Gage glanced down at the floor. "What caused it?"

"The short answer—a roadside bomb. It left him paralyzed from the waist down." She swallowed hard to soothe her suddenly dry throat, wondering about his sudden interest.

His eyes swept her, realizing the depth of loyalty and love she had for her husband. He caught himself instantly before the curse escaped. He tried again, this time more gently. "I can't imagine what that must've been like."

"I knew we'd face our challenges, but I always thought we'd face them together. I never expected...," she broke off, clearing her throat. "God seems to gather his children according to his own calendar, not mine."

"It's been my experience that life seldom takes us where we think we're going." He got up and grabbed the bag of sandwiches off the table. "I'll get some plates."

Shanna spoke over her shoulder. "I guess you've had a little experience with that yourself, haven't you?"

"Yeah, I never thought my father's partner would hijack our family business and collapse our financial world, yet here we are." Ice cracked in the glasses as Gage began to fill them. "But that's not the worst thing that can happen to a person. The *worst* thing is to live without meaning, without love, purpose, hope— without God. A wise woman once told me that." He placed a tray with their meal on it on the coffee table. "I believe I was meant to meet you, Shanna. In fact, I'm almost certain of it."

Eyes the color of storm clouds flicked up to him. "Oh? What makes you say that?"

Something he didn't completely understand compelled him forward. He knew he loved her. In fact, he had for some time now. But how could he possibly compete with the man who owned her heart. Her mind still talked to him, her heart still looked for him? James is what her soul seemed to want.

"When I first met you, I felt sorry for you. At times you've made me angry, confused, comforted, happy, annoyed, and just about every other emotion you can think of. Now, you've become a great source of joy in my life. When that happened I haven't a clue."

Once Gage was committed to a course of action, you could write it in ink — she knew that much about the man. But what could he possibly be saying to her? "That's a sweet thing to say, but why are you saying that to me?"

"Because you're that one book I've found in a vast library that I want to get lost in … I want to get to know you better, Shanna."

She felt relief, however odd the emotion of such a time. It was as if she had slipped into the cool shadows from the harsh sun. "I think I'd like that."

They ate their dinner quietly, an awkward silence filling the room. Gage swallowed down a bite and said, "Once I began listening, it seems to me that God is speaking to us. He's saying things about healing after death and rebuilding after disaster. He's saying that hope is greater than despair."

"I believe that," she said, in almost a whisper.

There are things in life without explanation, moments when your past and present become arranged in such a way as to collide with the life of another. As if that had been the plan all along. The moment felt like that to Shanna.

"Yes," Shanna said, "hope…." A little burst of green seemed to shoot right up in her heart. It was the first time she'd given voice to those particular feelings — in fact, it was the first time she'd felt them in a long time. She swallowed hard against the tightness in her throat.

He snatched his keys from the table. "Good word to leave on. Stay off the foot and call me if you need me."

Chapter 30

Gage sat motionless staring out the window half listening to the rereading of the terms of Breck Barrington's last will and testament. He didn't care about the stocks, corporate holdings, bonds; none of that mattered now. At the mention of Summer's Keep, he pulled his attention away from the window and back to Attorney Tuck Davis.

"I thought that might get your attention," Tuck said, pushing a sheaf of paper across the desk.

"I'm sorry, Tuck. You were saying?" Gage said, noticing his mother had straightened in her chair.

Tuck smiled, nodding toward the paper. "This concerns your grandfather Locke's estate."

Gage picked up the paper and began scanning it. It was mostly about a trust fund stipulation. All of it confused him. "Can you please tell me what this is all about?" he asked, growing more annoyed by the second.

Tuck coughed lightly to clear his throat. "You might not be aware of what I'm about to tell you, but please hear me out. Your grandfather, Locke, and your maternal grandmother, Lilly Rose, were connected by the piece of property known as Summer's Keep."

Myra opened her mouth as if to interrupt, but Gage beat her to the question. "I'm not sure I'm following you. What does Summer's Keep have to do with my grandfather?"

"I'd feel better if someone besides me tells that story. Someone a little closer to the situation. That's why I called Wes Mooreland." He leaned forward and buzzed the secretary. "Dorothy, please send in Dr. Mooreland."

When Dr. Mooreland entered the office, Tuck rose from his desk and moved past him to close the door. He grabbed a chair from the corner and placed it beside his desk. "Sit, please."

Dr. Mooreland smiled and nodded his head in greeting toward Myra and shook Gage's hand before he took a seat. He began to tap his fingers on the side of his leg, as if unsure how to proceed. The doctor and Tuck exchanged the briefest of glances, then he began. "Years ago Sassabee Creek was little known outside of the area except to a few of us. And, like most teenage boys, we found the stories of the creek a little fascinating. All that talk of mystical powers in the water and such. Anyway, one day Locke and I ventured up the creek in a canoe to do some fishing. When we got near The Prayer House, we became a little frightened."

"Frightened? Why's that?" Gage asked, adjusting himself forward in his seat.

"Because of the stillness. No wind, no sound, not even a bird could be heard. The hair began to stand up on the back of my head. Just as we were about to hightail it out of there, Locke caught sight of Lilly Rose standing beside a tree on the opposite bank from the church. Well, after he laid eyes on her, he had little desire to leave or dabble with fishing. Lilly Rose was a beauty back in the day and I believe Locke was smitten from that very moment. Something grew between them that summer. They had one of those rare connections the rest of us only dream about."

"What are you saying?" Myra had held her silence long enough. "That my mother and Locke Barrington were involved with each other?"

Gage's chin came up a notch. "If you're implying that—that...."

Dr. Mooreland held up a hand. "Now just simmer down. I'm saying nothing of the kind. They had a summer romance that would have—maybe even should have—developed into something more if—if your grandmother Dresden hadn't interfered." The doctor rubbed the back of his stiff neck. "You see, it had always been understood by the family that one day Locke and Dresden would marry. Their fathers were friends and their fortunes would have combined nicely, but Locke never paid attention to that sort of thing. You can trust me when I say that Lilly Rose was Locke Barrington's first true love."

"What do you mean by 'interfered'?" Gage stated more firmly than he intended. At the moment, he couldn't make sense of the drama between his grandparents.

"Of course I can't begin to tell the whole sweep of the story; only Locke and Lilly Rose could have spoken to that. All I'm expressing is what I believe to be true. Dresden enlisted the help of Locke's family to get their son away from Lilly Rose by whatever means necessary. Whatever they did worked. Before long, Locke agreed to marry Dresden, but he insisted on the means to purchase the land known as Summer's Keep. His father met the terms. Locke was very clear about Lilly Rose living on the land. Even arranged to have the garden house built for her. My friend carried an enormous sense of responsibility where his family was concerned, but where Lilly Rose was concerned? Well, that was nothing short of love."

Myra was startled to see that the color had all but drained from her son's face. She faced the doctor. "Locke Barrington owned Summer's Keep? Is that what you're telling us? Do you expect me to believe that my father would have lived on a piece of land—raised his family on a piece of land—that another man owned?" Her voice had an overtone of skepticism. "Broder Bain was no man's charity case!"

Dr. Mooreland carefully tapped his fingers on the armrest. "It appears, Myra, that in this case Broder Bain believed what he'd been told: that Summer's Keep belonged to your mother. And, in a sense, it did. Locke wanted to protect Lilly Rose by keeping the estate in his name. He trusted only himself with her welfare. Now, whether that was right or wrong is not for us to decide. We all knew Broder to be a proud, likable, and hardworking man; fond of the sea, confident, and with good sense most of the time … except when he was drinking."

Her voice was hard and crisp. "My father was not a careless drunk, as you're implying."

He looked at her doubtingly. "Forgive me. I stand corrected."

A hot blush of color burned Myra's cheeks as she remembered her father's tendency to drown his troubles for days on end if the fishing went poorly.

Tuck Davis interjected without a trace of apology. "Locke owned the property and Lilly Rose acquired it— that is, Locke Barrington—bequeathed it to her upon his death. And now, as you know, Lilly Rose bequeathed it to Gage. Whatever transpired between them, it is clear that Locke Barrington had a purpose in mind with the setting up of the trust, and Lilly Rose was in agreement with it."

Gage leaned back and let out a deep breath. "Why would he consider using a trust fund?"

The doctor shrugged. "Protection—to protect assets, such as Summer's Keep, from creditors. Also to make sure his wishes were followed to the letter after his passing. Grandparents do it all the time, though not usually to children yet to be born, as in this case. But, thankfully, Summer's Keep remains safe."

The truth of the matter had impaled then imbedded in Gage's heart. Certain vague remembrances began to find solid ground. It was all beginning to make sense. He felt the sensation of a chilly breath on the back of his neck and he rubbed it, fighting off the shiver. He remembered his grandmother Dresden's hatred of the island and her cool demeanor toward his mother. There had never been any display of love or warmth between Dresden and Myra. Had Dresden been the one to poison the thinking of her son, Breck? Was she the one responsible for Gage's banishment from the island *and* Lilly Rose?

Lifting a brow, Dr. Mooreland regarded the mother and son seated in front of him, suppressed humor dancing in his bright eyes. "It seems my friend, Locke, got his wish after all."

Confused, Gage met his gaze, sensing his approval. "What wish would that be?"

"To have a family with Lilly Rose. Your life, Gage, has joined them together."

Shanna Muir sat in the small church on the island of Terrapin and listened to Gabriel Muir's voice rise to the rafters. Her mind was not on the sermon but wandered back to the previous day.

The island had seemed lonely since her return to work after her weeklong confinement with a foot injury.

There was something missing. After resuming her job at the marina, life moved on as usual, slowing in the heat of the day as boats docked for lunch, getting a break from the scorching sun. Business at Bainbridge Marina had picked up and not fallen off as most people had speculated. They busied themselves in the rush and took orders from Lynch when Gage was in Port St. Joe. It was exciting, but now the joy seemed gone from the accomplishment with Gage away so often.

She thought of the look on Gage's face last week when Nikki surprised him by showing up at the marina in a streamline cruiser wearing a streamline bikini. His eyes had widened as she stood on the prow of the vessel and sailed his Cooper River Marina cap through the air. He'd caught it and positioned it on his head, throwing a two-fingered salute to her with a barely detectible grin. Nikki had smiled back with a playful grin.

It was at that very moment that something she couldn't explain came over her. It felt like she had been sucker punched in the gut and the breath shot out of her. She turned this over in her mind, as if looking for a hidden meaning. Jealousy seemed the only answer.

She glanced at the pew where Gage and his family usually sat, her imagination running away with her when her attention fell on his empty seat. Her eyes went again to Gabriel, then to the vacant place Gage's form usually filled.

Was I too forward? she wondered, thinking about the times in recent days when she and Gage had shared so much of themselves with each other. She kept visualizing Nikki sailing Gage's cap through the air and the look they'd exchanged. Did the long walks on the beach mean nothing? The intimate moments when they'd shared kisses, was it all just a distraction for him?

Shaking her head as if to clear it, she looked up at the rough-hewn cross behind the pulpit, watching as a shaft of soft light illuminated the beams. Shanna's Catholic training made her cross herself, caught in the awe of the moment. *What am I to do, Lord?*

Gabriel had finished his sermon and was calling for all to stand to their feet for the final song when he paused and a slow grin began to take over his face as he stared toward the rear of the church.

Before Shanna could turn, a masculine hand, gripping the stem of a delicate pink rose, appeared in front of her. She glanced up to see the familiar face of Gage Barrington smiling down at her.

Gage saw the surprise in Shanna's eyes as she stared at him. He bent low to whisper to her over the notes of the closing song. "This is a Summer's Keep rose," he said. "This rose holds a promise." A breath of wind from the open church door caused the rose to sway on the stem as if nodding in agreement.

Shanna studied Gage's face: it held a mixture of hopefulness and uncertainty. It was then that she realized the importance of the rose. With a trembling hand she took the flower from his hand, accepting it, *and* the one who had so completely captured her heart.

In the slowed down pace of the mellow afternoon, Shanna shifted in the canoe seat and turned her face to the sky, soaking in the last rays of the day's sun.

Gage paused, resting on his paddles, aware of the deep silence of the creek. He felt as if he'd intruded, trespassed into a sacred place. The sound of water dripping from his paddle into Sassabee Creek caused his throat to tighten as he reflected on his life.

Certain truths lost to him before were now becoming understood. The truth that God doesn't care about your last name, your money, or your social standing. The solid truth that God wants a *relationship* with *us* had landed Gage Barrington in an altogether unexpected place.

His eyes fell on Shanna and he smiled. There were certainly worse places to find oneself marooned than Terrapin Island. He slid the paddles back into the water and directed it toward the bank where he spotted a patch of green moss under a shady tree. There he planned to get better acquainted with the woman who had just agreed to marry him.

The creek will flow on and the winds will rustle through the trees on the same sandy banks as they've done for centuries. The men and women of that earlier time are on earth no more, but hardly forgotten. Their legacy of faith will live on after them throughout the generations. And while most are deaf to the echoes of faith in times gone by, that is not true for all. No, the new inhabitants of Summer's Keep will bring up their children in this strange and enchanted place, where the past mingles with the present and the waters of the creek will never forget a prayer of hope.

~